# GIFTED
# &
# TALENTED

## TOR BOOKS BY OLIVIE BLAKE

THE ATLAS SERIES
*The Atlas Six*
*The Atlas Paradox*
*The Atlas Complex*

*Alone with You in the Ether*

*One for My Enemy*

*Masters of Death*

*Januaries: Stories of Love, Magic & Betrayal*

## TOR TEEN BOOKS BY
## ALEXENE FAROL FOLLMUTH

*Twelfth Knight*

# GIFTED
# &
# TALENTED

## Olivie Blake

**TOR**

TOR PUBLISHING GROUP

NEW YORK

GIFTED & TALENTED

Interior illustrations by Paula Toriacio (polarts)
Endpaper design by Jamie Stafford-Hill
Endpaper illustration by H.C. Richter,
courtesy of The New York Public Library

A Tor Book
Published by Tom Doherty Associates / Tor Publishing Group
120 Broadway
New York, NY 10271

Tor® is a registered trademark of Macmillan Publishing Group, LLC.

ISBN 978-1-250-88340-7

Printed in the United States of America

For my family
(lol)

## Meredith Honora Liang Wren

The Ainsworth Academy

HONORS: Class Valedictorian, 2007 National Women's Class A Singles
    Tennis Champion, Most Likely to Succeed

"What lies behind us and what lies before us are tiny matters compared to
    what lies within us."


## Arthur Everett Liang Wren

Canongate Hall

HONORS: First-team All-American, Scholar Athlete with Distinction,
    Most Likely to Be in Movies

"Be the change you wish to see in the world."


## Eilidh Olympia Liang Wren

Manhattan Academy of Ballet

HONORS: youngest first soloist, youngest principal dancer, Manhattan
    Academy Prima Ballerina Assoluta two consecutive years

"Oh, the places you'll go!"

# MONDAY

(Before).

# 1

Meredith Wren, a fucking asshole, not that it matters at this stage of the narrative but it's worth pointing out, sat blinded by the overhead lights from the stage, squinting unflatteringly into the brand-new, state-of-the-art auditorium that had just been completed on Tyche's unethically verdant campus. Too large a venue for an event of this nature, which would reasonably be attended by only the most ardent of nerds. Well, them, and anyone who stood to gain from her success financially. A forum for dorks and despots.

As her eyes adjusted to the masses bearing witness to her greatness, Meredith saw nothing but the pockets of empty seats. Jesus Christ, she thought, and wondered if the squinting was worsening her burgeoning crow's feet. Blinking, she made a concerted effort to simply go blind. She became aware of something, a stye most likely, oh god, a stye, she hadn't had one of those since her early college days, back when she'd still had the balls to fall into bed with makeup on, recklessly. She was meticulous now with her skincare ritual, how was it possible she could accumulate grime at this stage of her life? At this *great age*, how could she succumb to something so pedestrian as a stye? She blinked and wanted desperately to lie down, to eat a whole sleeve of pistachio macarons. To gorge herself from bed and never rise again. Just kidding. Ha ha.

From the crowd she became aware of notable faces. Ward, obviously. He was her business partner, like it or not. Cass, too, that was nice. Expected to some extent, as he was something-something operations at Tyche (she and Cass had had to disclose their personal relationship when Tyche's partnership with Birdsong first went public, a relationship that was then only hazy at best—she'd been surprised Cass had managed to come up with a term that wasn't "fucking sometimes"), but still, nice. Foster was smiling benevolently at her, the cunt. She'd taken the money, what did that make her? A traitor, fine, shut up. (She always heard unwelcome commentary in

Lou's voice.) Don't bite the hand that feeds, Meredith thought for the eight millionth time. One of her father's pet wisdoms—you can have money or you can have pride, and guess which one changes the world? Then there was a row of normal-looking people, suitably showered, probably journalists. Press badges, yep, journalists. Someone from *Wired*, a few from *Magitek*, someone who looked a lot like the boy she'd nearly cut and run for, but that was par for the course—she saw Jamie Ammar at least five times a week, usually in line at the grocery store. At Demeter, specifically. It was always some other absurdly handsome man in the ill-fitting jeans of the aughts.

God, but this one really looked like Jamie.

"Please welcome to the Tyche stage Meredith Wren, the CEO of Birdsong!" called the disembodied voice overhead as Meredith froze a smile on her face, bracing for the unbearable cringe of listening to her own insufferable bio. "Once the most highly sought-after biomancy prodigy of her age, Meredith began her career by dropping out of Harvard and hightailing it to sunny SoCal to pursue an interest in treating mental illness that would become one of the most significant, world-altering technomantic advances in the growing science of neuromancy—"

Meredith's phone buzzed in her pocket. She ignored it. A missed call popped up on the face of her watch: ugh, her father's personal assistant, what was her name. Jenny something. Or had that been the last one? Meredith so rarely bothered to check in, and certainly nobody from her father's office had reached out to her in the last nine months, maybe longer. It was never anything beyond the ceremonial—invitations to the annual company party, or the usual scheduling song and dance for meals or calls that would never take place.

Meredith blinked, a sudden blur to her vision—it was definitely a stye, god damn it. The stage lights remained arduously bright, but the journalist sitting in the second row really looked like Jamie. Which—there was no way it *was* Jamie, obviously. Although Jamie was indeed a journalist. Not that Meredith was keeping tabs. (In her head, Lou gave an unsolicited laugh.) The journalist who was definitely, absolutely not Jamie slid his phone out of his jacket pocket, typing something into it. Rude.

"—more than ten billion dollars, one of the largest biomantic valuations in history, larger even than the initial investment into Wrenfare Magitech. After extensive hype, Chirp was finally made available to the public last year, with hundreds of thousands of people—and growing by the day!—

now able to find the one thing we all so desperately want: *happiness.* Yes, that's right, we said it: This woman will make you happy. Please give a warm welcome to the incomparable Meredith Wren!"

Her phone buzzed in her pocket. Another call from Jenny or something. She glanced at her watch screen, which showed a message from—

Holy fuck. Holy fuck. Holy fuck.

Jamie Ammar.

Some producer on stage gestured wildly from Meredith's periphery and she jumped. Her mic was now hot. Her talk was now live. It was time to get up and give a rousing speech about saving the world, which she could do. Which she had done.

What could the message say? Not that it mattered! She did not need to know what a man receding invisibly into the previous decade of her life could possibly have to say to her. They'd both said as much as they'd needed to when she left Boston twelve years ago, which on his end had been "fuck you" or something lightly of that equivalent. They'd spoken three, maybe four times since then? Once when she'd called him drunk to say things she wished she couldn't remember, another time to say that the previous night had been a mistake, a third time when she'd been in Manhattan for work, a call that went unanswered. A fourth to congratulate him on his engagement, five years ago, to a very nice girl. A really, really nice girl.

Meredith Wren, CEO of Birdsong, daughter of Thayer Wren and Persephone Liang, erstwhile cover star of Forbes 30 Under 30, rose to her feet and glanced surreptitiously at the message from her ex, because of course she did. I think we all knew she was going to. Then she looked into the crowd and felt her heart cascade into her vagina.

I know what you did.

And I'm going to publish it.

# 2

The ads blinking along Tottenham Court Road all read the same thing, like a deranged echo or a Greek chorus. THIS APP WILL MAKE YOU HAPPY! :)

By now, Arthur Wren paid no attention to the hallmarks of his family's success, having come to regard them as a sort of monotony, almost a drudgery. Like watching the trailer of a film too many times or hearing an overplayed song on the radio. He took no notice of Wrenfare's towering London offices as he sped past them, just as he had done five years ago when walking past the perennial billboards of his younger sister, Eilidh—all things that faded unremarkably to the background, like the constancy of white noise.

The first time Arthur had seen a Chirp ad on the subway in DC—THIS APP WILL MAKE YOU HAPPY! :) —he'd snapped an ironic selfie with it for Meredith, throwing up an infantile peace sign and praying he wouldn't be caught by the *Post*. (Imagine the headline! Arthur could and often did; too often, if you ask me. This one would go something like CONGRESSMAN WREN TOO BUSY TAKING SELFIES, BUYING AVOCADO TOAST TO VIRTUE SIGNAL OPPRESSIVE TERRORISM FUNDED BY ACTIONS OF OWN GOVERNMENT. Or, you know, something translatable to that effect, which Arthur usually heard in Lou's melodic drawl.)

In the accompanying message, Arthur had typed: Sister Insufferable, savior of the people!

Brother Unbearable, Meredith had replied, shut, and I can't emphasize this enough, up.

At the moment, Meredith was giving some sort of tech talk about the future of neuromancy, going on about the state of collective human ennui as if it were something from which to bravely opt out. Arthur, meanwhile, was very busy transporting himself among the fray, relishing some spare hours of hard-fought anonymity despite the infinite scroll of ledes about his failures as a politician and a man. He had forgone the usual navy suit for the occasion (Gillian said black was too harsh on him and Gillian was always right) and instead dressed casually, itself a sort of disguise. From his pocket his phone buzzed, and he pulled it out to check the screen. His father's office line.

Interesting.

Unusual.

Nearly unusual enough to compel him back to the real world, what with its enigmatic authority figures and unguessable personal matters. Of course, there was no chance Thayer had picked up the phone himself—Arthur was an Important Person, too, mind you, but never so important that his own team of underlings became relevant to Thayer Wren's fleeting whims—so it was likely Thayer's personal assistant, Julie. In all likelihood serving an underwhelming reveal such as hello Arthur, can you hold the first weekend in December open for the holiday party or do you intend to throw your career away before then?

Hm. Failing Arthur, Gillian would be the next best point of contact. Whatever it was, Gillian would handle it painlessly, in a mere thirty seconds or less.

Under the circumstances, it could wait.

Arthur felt a renewed thrill of excitement at the thought of the evening and swept away the missed call from his screen, choosing instead a more secure messaging app and a contact labeled with the image of a mouse. **Can't wait to see you**, he typed.

No reply, but that was fine. Give or take some city traffic, he'd be there soon enough.

He meant to tuck his phone back into his pocket but paused, checking the more public-facing messaging app to see if there was anything from Gillian. Nothing, aside from his text that he had landed, to which she had given a demure thumbs-up. He supposed she was enjoying her time off as well, presumably with military tactics and rugby, or some alternate hobby du jour that Gillian found appropriate for that evening's relaxation, usually strategy games and bloodshed.

Just then, Arthur's relentless news app pinged with a headline: CON-GRESSMAN ARTHUR WREN (D-CA) TO ADDRESS THE WAYS AND MEA . . .

It trailed off and Arthur successfully ignored it, as he often did. (This is a lie. Arthur has something of a chronic nosiness as to the nature of his public perception. Call it a vocational hazard or casual narcissism; either will apply.) There was no purpose to wading into the obvious, though Arthur anticipated the usual comments. Something-something nepo baby—*that* never got old, never mind that nearly every sitting congressman came from some sort of wealth, and for fuck's sake, where would they prefer he got the money? Big Tobacco? The NRA? Wasn't it sort of *relaxing* to know that Arthur Wren's campaign funding came from somewhere banally ambivalent—in fact, so uninterested in his political agenda that it could not be persuaded to call him personally, only reaching out by virtue of an assistant whose name Arthur wasn't entirely sure he'd gotten right?

Not that this was the time to think about his father, a surefire erection killer if ever a thing existed. The point is, voters were more likely to connect Arthur to his father or sisters than to his grandparents, who weren't railway tycoons anyway, so contextually, "nepo baby" felt a bit unfair. Arthur's theoretical value was mostly unrealized—generational via his father, i.e., not strictly Arthur's—and even with the inheritance from his mother, he was normal rich, not blood-money rich. Not *Philippa* rich, which was presumably his appeal to her.

Ah, there it was again, the thrill he so unfailingly associated with Philippa. Arthur caught on to it and shivered in the sensation, familiarly electric. His normal life, outside of this one escape, had become increasingly untenable. He was on the campaign trail again, facing down a hung Congress and a looming presidential election whose end results he doubted he could bear. The bills he proposed, which came from a place of forward-leaning—nay, radical!—progressivism were functionally toothless by the time they came before committee, rendering him a sort of new-age jester who'd accomplished nothing but the turntable warp of a sitcom laugh track. Social media itself, the thing that had first positioned Arthur for greatness like the rise of a cutting-edge trend, had brutally turned on him. What, the echo chamber hive mind demanded to know, had come of Arthur's promises to end American-sponsored colonialism? To replenish the resources of the planet? To do away with his generation's mounting debts? To revitalize critical social programs and increase the availability of affordable housing, for which money had been redirected over the course of their lifetimes to warmongering, genocide, and lining the very congressional pockets that he, Arthur Wren, now counted among?

What he could *not* say aloud (because it was undignified and whiny) was the obvious: that it wasn't as if he wasn't trying! Arthur's rosy-eyed attempt at a straightforward bill to increase environmental jobs wound up with an unintended rider cutting educational budgets for nutritional resources to low-income schools. And *that* fiasco, horrifically enough, was all he had to claim as an accomplishment! His impassioned speech on the congressional floor calling for intervention in the Congo had been a mere afterthought in media coverage, mentioned only *after* Arthur and a mining-sponsored congressman had been photographed walking together—a result of poor timing, the enmity of the fates, and the limited radius of good coffee spots open past three around the Capitol. (Arthur could have just sent an aide like all his contemporaries did, but *nooooooo*, he had to believe in fetching his own coffee, inviting the ire of public opinion like Odysseus taunting the Cyclops.)

Serious question—what was the appropriate alternative? It was this that left Arthur's mind reeling, his thumb scrolling until it went numb. Should he have instead shoved the other congressman into traffic and screamed, *Death to the industrial complex, literally*? Maybe so! That seemed to be the consensus online, but instead Arthur had simply walked and smiled tersely and committed the violence of silence, and for his crimes, he had been featured being handsomely duplicitous on the landing page of every liberal digital imprint, read to filth by the very demographic from whence he'd progressively come.

In sum: To everyone actually *in* Congress, Arthur was far too liberal to be taken seriously. To everyone who had put him there, Arthur wasn't liberal enough. The constancy of his failures—the mythology of his individualized, sinister hypocrisy rather than the darker institutional truth, which was that sociopolitical compromise meant the lesser of two evils was often not letting things get immeasurably worse—was enough to make Arthur want to get swallowed up by quicksand.

Or, better yet, disappear into an orgy, never to emerge.

Finally! The car slowed to a stop and it was all Arthur could do not to jump out and perform an outsized musical number about the street where Philippa . . . well, not lived, but where she had a house, and where she and Yves occasionally spent their time when they were not otherwise absconding to a country estate or touring Europe or generously debauching Arthur on his home turf.

Lady Philippa Villiers-DeMagnon (Pippa, Lady Philippa, or PVDM to the press; Pipsqueak or Mouse to Yves and, when appropriate, to Arthur) was of course fashionably unemployed, being an heiress and an aristocrat who generally made her living by flitting from one charitable cause to the next. Her current project was the publication of a cookbook by a refugee shelter in central London. Philippa didn't cook herself, obviously, not because of luxury (partially because of luxury) but because it was utterly domestic, though she considered herself to have a particularly interesting palate due to her childhood in Barbados.

Whether this allegedly cosmopolitan taste of hers was real or not was of no pressing concern to Arthur, whose attraction to Philippa granted him a certain blessed blindness. Her generosity, her fundamental strangeness, her almost pathological contrariness, her enthusiastic embrace of his . . . occasional technical malfunctions—these were the things he loved about her, the oddities, the sort of howling-at-the-moon quality she seemed to preternaturally possess, so as a rule he did not ask himself too many questions about the nature of her class. Arthur chose to focus on Philippa's well-meaning attempts to empower women and devote her brilliant mind to such universally worthy causes.

If Arthur did *not* focus on this aspect of Philippa, then of course his mind would wander elsewhere: to the frothing symbiosis of Philippa's tabloid coverage; to what her fondness for Barbados (and, at times, a suspiciously unspecific adoration for "Africa") might actually suggest; to whether Arthur's own mantle of hypocrisy was dismally fitting, however itchy it happened to be. But it was easy not to ponder such things while being *near* Philippa, who was one of those wealthy people whose wealth seems to make them effortlessly generous, not only with money but with time, and whose disposition was occasionally so sweet it wounded Arthur's heart—just properly *melted* it, soldering parts of it to his rib cage and leaving a sticky-toffee residue of unfading, unfaltering affection.

Arthur had first met Philippa at a charity exhibition of her family's private collection in the National Gallery, where he was drawn to her because she spoke so lovingly and animatedly about each of the pieces. So invested was she in their style and history and the inherently sexual nature of the baroque that Arthur initially mistook her for a scholar of art history. That was the thing with Philippa, who was so dazzlingly bright and quick-witted and cultured and refined that at times it nearly hurt to look at her. She was very beautiful, but more importantly she was incredibly weird, a buffet of idiosyncrasies. It created this mystique about her, this sense that she was not exactly for everyone. Arthur stayed up the whole night with her, never imagining her to take any interest in him, already aware that she was famously dating Yves Reza, a Formula Magitech racecar driver who was not a musician and yet was, somehow, the only man of their generation whom Arthur felt could properly be called a rock star. But Philippa must have sniffed out the weird in Arthur, too, and so now, well, here they were.

The door was open even before Arthur reached for the knocker, his hand still typing something in his phone. "Finally, you're here!" proclaimed a voice that Arthur recognized as Yves's, though he wasn't entirely sure at first it *was* Yves, because the latter was wearing an ornate golden mask and the entryway was so packed with slick, squirming bodies in elaborate masquerade that Arthur was instantly overwhelmed.

"Arthur, open your mouth," said Yves, who was definitely Yves, because other people did not usually say things like that to Arthur.

"What is it this time?" asked Arthur gaily, or as gaily as it was possible to be after a seven-hour flight. Which was surprisingly gay indeed, because Congressman Arthur Wren of the twelfth district of California was about to be (for once) the good kind of fucked.

"Just something to liven you up, you know, for the jet lag!" added Yves, lifting his mask and leaning in to greet Arthur with a kiss that was at once very wet and very dry. Arthur coughed, choking on the chalkiness of whatever had just been passed to him by Yves's tongue.

"Darling, go easy on him, he's only just arrived." From the undulating crowd came Philippa in a heady swirl of orchids, effulgent purplish-black robes swelling out from around her hips like a bruise-colored Georgia O'Keeffe. She adjusted her matching Venetian mask with one hand, pressing a still-sizzling flute of champagne into Arthur's with the other as he leaned in to brush his lips to her cheek.

"Beloved." Present company made Arthur hopelessly pretentious, more so than usual. (That's my take on the matter, not his.) In any case, Arthur downed the pill, swishing the drink around in his mouth until it fizzed, happily domesticated, on his tongue, and Yves shifted to sling an arm around his waist. "Can't thank you enough for your hospitality, as ever," said Arthur.

"Well, I'm sure you'll get the opportunity to try," Philippa purred fondly, reaching out to cup Arthur's cheek with her palm. "Now stand up straight and let me look at you."

Standing there in the doorway of a party—where, for once, Arthur could feel properly accepted, not an underachieving product of nepotism (for who here wasn't that?) but simply a man with a very fine cock and the heartily won know-how to back it up—Arthur felt his heart flood with elation. It reached him like a heady onslaught of tears, a sudden pent-up release that caused the foyer's chandelier to flicker, individual bulbs ebbing and flaring as if to fanatically perform the wave.

It was an oddity that hadn't gone unnoticed, particularly where it had occurred right above Arthur's head. "Who's this?" asked another masked member of the crowd, materializing to squint accusingly at Arthur, the only person in the foyer not concealing his face. Belatedly, Arthur reached into the inner pocket of his jacket, producing a simple black leather mask in a wordless gesture of apology.

"He's our boyfriend," said Yves, "so fuck off, Felix."

"Yes," agreed Philippa, "fuck off, Felix!"

There was a near-instantaneous booing akin to a medieval mob, and Felix made a gesture that was meant to either wash his hands of them or vigorously masturbate, and then he disappeared again into the maelstrom of the crowd.

"Felix?" echoed Arthur, recalling vaguely that Felix was the name of a foreign prince Philippa sort of knew, but by then she was pulling his hand. The chandelier flickered again, then began to spark dangerously, releasing a meteor shower in miniature as the room dimmed to black. This time, the juxtaposition of Arthur with his backdrop of fiber-optic electrical failure attracted the undivided attention of the madding crowd, who pressed in around their trio to catch a closer glimpse of apparent pyrotechnics.

"Christ," said Arthur, looking over the backs of his hands. Every hair stood on end, and the malfunctioning chandelier that reached for him with greedy tendrils suddenly exploded in a frantic spray of dissipating fairy lights, a final flare of power outage like a ray of dying sun. "What did you give me?"

Unbeknownst to the various partygoers, all oohing and ahhing in unison as the very stoned were wont to do, what they were currently witnessing was the confidential source of Arthur's ongoing . . . not *hiatus,* exactly, but the careful, anxiety-inducing, borderline-obsessive concealment of an adolescent glitch he'd thought he'd outgrown, like wet dreams and voice cracks; the lovely reminder that Arthur Wren, supposed harbinger of a new era, was basically just an almost-thirty teenage boy.

Given Arthur's string of political disappointments, his recent withdrawal from the public eye had seemed more than coincidental—optically, it amounted to laziness, cuckoldry, or insidious ambivalence, such that Arthur had always been a traitor after all. Oh, so the poor little rich boy turned out to have thin skin? PRIVILEGE! screeched user @FuckThePatriarchy420. It could really weigh a person down!

Of course, Arthur would have liked to believe the sudden cancellation of his last four public appearances could be understandably forgiven had They (the ominous, media-dwelling They) only known the truth, which was the spontaneous release of tiny rockets in flight from any overeager technical system Arthur encountered whenever he was—as he nearly always was—at work. Wi-Fi routinely went out. Cameras always failed. Apps consistently crashed. Most recently, broadcast signals had malfunctioned via an electrical surge so infernal that a terrified journalist had been concussed by a boom and fallen briefly into a coma. It was as if Arthur was some kind of still-living (arguably half-alive) poltergeist, haunting every highbrow political venue with the occult situationship between himself and every electrical current.

Surely the uptick in mishaps wouldn't last—it simply *couldn't* last; that was an unimaginable scenario involving all sorts of horrors—so his decision to withdraw, deal with the problem, and heal in private was actually quite a reasonable one—if, that is, such a thing as accidental electrokinesis could reasonably be (1) said, (2) believed, or (3) understood.

To be clear, it couldn't. Which was why the rumors went uncorrected; the lesser of two evils being, in this case, to lose a little more shine in lieu of revealing an uncontrollable, witchcraft-adjacent mutation, for which no Notes app apology could possibly suit. Arthur didn't know how to stop what he couldn't explain, and even Gillian, brilliant tactician though she was, agreed there was nothing for it—that the best they could do for now was to simply let it pass, as it had done once before.

Luckily, there was nothing notable about revealing it here, given that internet use was banned for social safety, and besides, no self-respecting aristocrat actually believed there was anything beyond their personal control.

Provided everybody stayed a safe distance from any electrical outlets, all would be well—or in the alternative, all would be forgotten by the morning.

"Just something to elevate your natural talents," Yves offered in explanation as Philippa laughed, leaning over for a kiss. "You are always magical to *us*, Arthur, but consider the possibility of being . . . erotically godlike?"

Arthur looked down at his palm, the subcutaneous crackle of static, test-ing the fluidity of whatever you might call this; "power" being too com-plimentary a word. Normally it was little more than personal hazard, no different from an unsolicited spark or intrusive thought (like the memory of Lou's laugh or a caustic line of criticism). A flicker of light shot out from the chandelier to Arthur's palm, dancing across his fingertips. The buzz of electricity in the room, briefly dormant, shot to attention the moment Arthur called it forth, dazzling before his eyes like the glitter of tropical lightning, rendering the corridor a veritable marching band of Georgian sconces. This Arthur hadn't done in ages—over a decade, at least, since he'd managed anything remarkable on purpose. It had been longer than years since Arthur had last felt in control.

Which meant it was the profound opposite of the depressing month Ar-thur had spent cloistered in his office, appearing only for mandatory congres-sional votes before hurrying away with his chin locked partway to his chest, mumbling demurrals and skirting cameras, effectively choosing headlines that read "irresponsible louche" over "magical circus freak" because what, pray tell, was the reasonable, progressive-but-not-too-radical, voter-swaying, public-approving, laws-of-physics-ly plausible explanation for any of this?

Or so Arthur asked himself, perhaps more often than a less egotistical person would. Not that we are here to judge. Although we're here, so why not have at it.

Suddenly, Arthur became aware that he was starving, that he had come all this way just to strip down and be devoured, that his father would never forgive him for the man he'd turned out to be. God, what fun it was to be such a profound disappointment! Arthur drained his glass of champagne and reached for his phone, noticing before he tucked it away for the evening that Gillian had sent him a message.

Ah, well, it wasn't allowed, and anyway, it could wait. The chandelier sparked again, the world thrumming in unison, illicit and sinful, wanton and free. He felt connected, he felt profound, he felt *online*!

The lights dimmed and roared, then flickered to the soundless synth-pop bass that was Arthur's racing heart.

"Who wants to see a magic trick?"

# 3

At the moment Arthur Wren crossed the threshold of an orgy and Meredith Wren nearly pissed her lady-pantsuit on stage, Eilidh Wren—slightly less of an asshole, but only by virtue of personal misfortune so extreme it derailed all potential assholery she might have otherwise blossomed into like a peony in June—was plummeting to her death on a last-minute flight back to San Francisco aboard a budget airline, her tailbone practically rattling against the skeletal economy seat (an aisle seat, 16D), while an ad winked sadistically up at her from the in-flight magazine (THIS APP WILL MAKE YOU HAPPY! :), a particularly insidious taunt).

The plane had been undulating wildly for several minutes, such that the oxygen masks had already dropped into the cabin and Eilidh was, ultimately, impressed they did not require an additional fee to use. This was what she got for coming home early, bypassing the ample preparation she'd so recklessly elected to ignore. This plane was almost certainly going down, something that Eilidh had not previously believed was possible. True, she was not a person of any mechanical know-how, but she was familiar enough with the family business to be comfortably sure that even *this* cabin had been equipped with the industry-standard technomantic computing her father had developed over the last four decades with Wrenfare. Assuming the airline had kept up with the latest system updates, the plane ought to be borderline sentient. Shouldn't it practically land itself?

Someone in the pipeline of airline safety had fucked up monumentally—which, Eilidh was displeased to reflect, was an uncharitable thought on her part. She had been doing so well. She hadn't had a bitchy thought for nearly two entire days. (She, unlike the other two Wren siblings, did not have Lou living in her head, which was better or worse for Eilidh depending on whether you find it more oppressive to be insulted by the ghost of childhoods past or your own insipid thoughts.)

Eilidh's impressive departure from misanthropy was new, and far from the usual. She had just returned from a silent retreat in Vermont that she was fully prepared to lie about. Of course she had loved it. Of course she was refreshed. No, she had not missed her phone. No, she wasn't *at all* devastated that three days of total silence was something for which she had not had to bargain for or fight about with a partner because she had no partner, not even a roommate or a cat (she felt it would be rude to The Cat, the one she might one day adopt but wasn't currently ready for, as she was not yet her ideal person). Yes, she was terribly glad she'd done it! Well, that part was true, sort of. She wasn't *not* glad she'd done it, except for the fact that she was maybe about to die on her way home.

The plane dropped again in the sky, like a toy clutched in the hand of a giant. The lights flickered almost hysterically—almost *more* hysterically than the woman beside Eilidh, who was presently hyperventilating into a paper bag. Earlier, Eilidh had tried to reach for the woman's hand in an effort at solidarity, but the woman had only been more terrified, as if the well-meaning touch of a stranger was proof this was very bad, very bad indeed.

Eilidh's hand tightened on the armrest of her seat as she considered the prospect of dying, a thought she entertained somewhat routinely, about three times a week (tops). She once again had the counterproductive thought that her body was useless, then corrected herself firmly, compulsively consulting the mental sticky note that read YOUR BODY WORKS BETTER THAN MOST AND YOU SHOULD BE GRATEFUL :) before another roil of turbulence knocked her mindfulness somewhere into her colon.

God, but maybe it wouldn't be so bad, would it? What did she really have to bind her to this world, to keep her even remotely interested in her life? It had been five years since the injury. Five entire years since the surgery. And in that time, what had she done?

(Here's what she had *not* done: played the Sugar Plum Fairy, or Juliet, or Odette, or woken up unaware of her back, though the last time Eilidh had mentioned that to Meredith she'd been briskly told to stop complaining, they were all getting older, gravity wasn't specifically invested in ruining Eilidh's life, even though Meredith had once sprained her ankle and missed a round of the USTA Junior National Championship finals when she was ten years old and had never, ever let anyone forget about it, which wasn't technically the same thing because Meredith had moved on from tennis and Eilidh had never fallen out of love with ballet. But it was a similar flavor, and anyway this was all in Eilidh's head, and she did not have to defend herself to anyone outside of it.)

Eilidh was, at present, a marketing executive at Wrenfare. Well, "executive" was maybe too lofty a term. (Her amendment, not mine—"executive" is technically accurate, if spiritually controversial.) She worked in marketing at Wrenfare, though because her last name was obviously Wren and her father, the founder and CEO, had a photo of her on his desk, people assumed that Eilidh was slightly more important than she actually was. She was routinely asked to sign off on things that she considered quite frankly none of her business, and people often specifically requested to work with her, thinking that her presence on a project might ensure that it favorably crossed the boss's desk.

Which wasn't wholly false. Her father *did* like to keep tabs on what she was up to, and they had a standing lunch date near the offices on Tuesdays. At these lunches, familial and casual though they purported to be, Eilidh might mention a person who would later be promoted, or she might reference a project that would later be green-lit, so it didn't really matter what her title was. Still, she was primarily just an ordinary person who worked in marketing, because it was the only thing for which she was even remotely qualified. (She had worked on the annual gala for her ballet academy, an extracurricular she'd taken up as a bit of quid pro quo because she'd overslept after a particularly grueling rehearsal for which she held the principal role—okay, she hadn't meant to brag, but since you're so obviously curious, it was Princess Aurora from *Sleeping Beauty*—and missed an exam.)

Eilidh was good at her job. Eilidh was not, generally speaking, an idiot. And—this part is the Big Secret—Eilidh did not technically have to die in this plane crash if she didn't want to.

As if to belabor the point, Eilidh felt a stirring up her spine, something sprouting like an emergency hatch, a panic button presented from inside herself. It was a different sensation every time, but its presence was always noticeable. Often the feeling lived dormantly, alive but inactive from somewhere within Eilidh's chest cavity, but this particular flourish of motion was both muted and undeniable, like the crook of a lover's finger. A quiet but unmissable unfurling where a set of wings would be. It was rare that she and the thing were of similar minds, but even so, the message was unmistakable. All she would have to do to save everyone on this plane was give in.

Provided she could stand the cost.

The plane was going down, that was for certain. Inclement weather, poor planning, technical malfunction, maybe some unholy combination of all three. The pilot had somehow left his microphone on and was crying audibly, which was not very beneficial for the vibes. Some rows ahead of Eilidh, a woman was clutching her screaming baby, unable to keep from sobbing into the child's head despite her ardent rocking, her desperate attempts to make these final moments good, to make them sweet. Who boarded a plane with a baby unless they absolutely had to? Eilidh felt a pang of something horrible then, almost criminal, as if this were single-handedly her fault. She looked away and spotted an older woman who was praying a rosary; a man who was weeping openly, his thumb gently stroking a picture of three young children on his phone.

If circumstances were left to the parasite's whims, it was narrowly possible Eilidh might survive the impending crash against her will—against the laws of physics, against all conceivable odds. The parasite—the thing that seemed to have taken residency like a squatter in her chest—had already intervened for her in the past, unless there was some other reason she'd survived carbon monoxide poisoning (the doctors had insisted there was, but then again they'd had no subsequent explanation for the frogs).

Of course, the consequences might be worse if she accepted its help rather than simply leaving her demise up for grabs. Terrible things always happened where the parasite was involved. Though, was there really a worse, given the scale of things? How did one assign a measurable degree of disaster to a pestilence of livestock, or to the seas turning red? The death of firstborn sons was understandably catastrophic, but did stars falling from heaven to earth outrank the leveling of mountains to plains? If Eilidh said help me and the thing said yes but turned all potable water to blood in exchange, how was that equitable preservation of life? Certainly the government would be no help whatsoever.

And even with all apocalypses being equal, at what point would they stop being warning shots? How much calamity could strike at the parasite's hands before the world was *actually* ending, and therefore Eilidh was, too? Because at some point surely there'd be no more posturing. Eventually the earth would stop fucking around and call it quits.

But these weren't the real questions. Eilidh's mortality, her intellectualizing of life itself, these thoughts were trivial, extraneous at best. The real concern was, what of the others on the plane, the bystanders, all presumably parasite-free, with only one outcome written on their fates unless Eilidh so charitably intervened, risking only the continuity of life on earth over a bargain with an eldritch thing for which she had no rational explanation . . . ?

Oh, it was all so fucked, thought Eilidh tiredly, with all her young, young, youngyoungyoungyoung twenty-six years of exhaustion in her bones. All these people for other people to miss. Might the plausible horrors be worth it? Philanthropically speaking, if nothing else? Maybe the world wouldn't end today. Maybe, theoretically, it would just be one tiny, survivable plague. Mere roulette, with suboptimal (but dismissable) nonzero odds of complete annihilation! Just another thing she'd simply have to suck it up and live through, like all the rest.

In any case, her father would miss her, a quiet voice reminded her. Eilidh imagined him sitting at the restaurant alone, looking at the door, checking his phone. Waiting, as he always did, for her to walk in and meet him at their usual table, in their usual place. Could she really bear to disappoint him? She had never been able to before.

In the wake of Eilidh's indecision, the situation irreversibly worsened. Nothing could help Budget Airline Flight 2276 now except a miracle, or whatever you might call a miracle that did its job but in the worst imaginable way. Still, the choice was a simple one, somewhere between carnage or ugliness. Either a combustible mass grave somewhere in the Rockies, or . . .

Truthfully, Eilidh hated to find out. But the sensation in her body, the monstrous creature she housed, it was both guardian and jailer—it would do her bidding, yes, but only if she wished for life at every other living thing's expense. She could feel it now, the power that was really more like capitulation. The red button she only had to press for temporary salvation, which would feel like destruction right up until it passed.

The flight attendants screamed for everyone to assume the brace position when Eilidh, lacking persuasive alternatives, finally gave in. She compromised with the universe, making her peace, taking a deep breath and hoping for something mild. Something not too . . . destructive. (Surely there'd be fallout, but then again, a compromise means neither party truly wins.)

The irony, really, was how hard Eilidh had to fight on a daily basis to keep it at bay, barely contained, versus the ease of letting it loose, which was only metaphysically difficult. What would happen now that she'd set it loose on purpose? A flood? A plague? A fire?

The end of the world?

Abruptly, the plane's cabin went dark. The parasite living in her chest unfurled, a greedy, gleeful rattling at the bars of its perilous cage. *Just enough to live*, Eilidh thought desperately. *Please, just rein it in.*

*Nah*, she practically heard in answer.

Then, as if with a gentlemanly shake upon contracted offer and acceptance, Eilidh felt the wings burst free.

# 4

A stye! A fucking stye! Meredith kept folding her eyelid over in front of the mirror, compulsively checking it. She nudged it with the corner of her nail, wondering if she could just . . . pop it. Like a zit. The internet plainly stated that under no circumstances was she to touch it. She should do a warm compress ten times an hour or something for a zillion intervals a day, as if she had that sort of time. Alternatively, suggested the internet, she could see a doctor. Right, a doctor! Meredith wanted to laugh hysterically. Yes, she could do an online visit—if she pushed a button on her phone right now, she'd be placed into a queue for three to four hours just for someone to tell her she'd be fine in three to fourteen days.

She nudged the stye again. It wasn't visible from the outside—she didn't *think* it was visible, anyway, and even if it was, it wasn't contagious—but still, it was a damned inconvenience. She couldn't focus on anything else, and to make matters worse, her phone was ringing again.

She glanced down at her watch screen and silenced the call from her father's assistant. The third one that day. Certainly this persistence was heightening to unusual, but it wasn't as if Meredith could speak to her father (or any representative of her father) in this agitated state of mind. She'd only pick a fight or do something stupid, like acknowledge he'd been right.

Meredith glared at her reflection.

*I know what you did,* Jamie's message taunted in her head. She heard it in Jamie's voice now, like he stood languid beside her at the bathroom counter, fingertips brushing the line of her neck. She saw him tucking her hair behind one ear, that little crease of fondness in his brow. An old incarnation of Jamie, dead and buried in a girlhood tomb.

*I know what you did, and I'm going to publish it.*

Ghosts begot ghosts. Lou appeared then beside Meredith's reflection, like clockwork. Despite the years of teenage malaise they'd intimately shared until they hadn't, the Lou in Meredith's memory was always ten years old, round-cheeked and scowling.

"Hey, dumbass," said the Lou-shaped specter. "You can't honestly be surprised if he's on to you. I mean, you knew it was inevitable. You've always been a fraud and this whole thing is idiotically transparent."

"Shut up," muttered Meredith, maturely.

"And if Jamie knows, I *definitely* know," Lou reminded her, a smug look on her nonexistent face. "I'm the one who taught you how to get away with it, you ungrateful bitch."

Meredith shook herself, recalling that this was psychologically unproductive.

"Fuck you," she whispered to imaginary Lou, turning to imaginary Jamie, who gave her a breezy smile because he, too, didn't exist. "You don't know shit," she informed him, and watched him disappear astride the high horse he'd intrusively ridden in on.

Bolstered, and determined not to think about her stye (her mother had always said thinking about a zit made it worse, which was presumably also true for styes), Meredith fucking Wren shoved open the door to the women's restroom and took off down the corridor, grudgingly returning the call from her father's office only to brutally collide with someone who'd just turned the corner.

"Fucking *Christ*," Meredith nearly screamed, dropping her phone.

Then she registered her assailant.

"Meredith," said Jamie Ammar. The real one, who bent down to retrieve the ringing phone, placing it carefully back in her palm.

Her pulse was in double time, maybe worse. A feminine voice in her hand sounding tinny and far away as Meredith hastily ended the call. "You nearly killed me, Jamie. Oh my god." She stared, taking advantage of their collision to have a long look at him. She tried to fashion it as a glare, which she achieved, because Meredith did not have resting bitch face. She had active bitch face, because everything she did was with purpose. (But in moments of rest it was extraordinarily bitchy, too.)

Jamie was what, thirty-two now? She tried desperately to be repulsed by him, but alas, it was not to be. He was even better looking than he'd been in his early twenties, because of course he was. He was now approaching the sweet spot, the tipping point where the truly, extravagantly handsome

men began to lap their more generic contemporaries—those pretty, polished, peaked-in-high-school chumps who were slowly losing their hair and
putting on weight and all sorts of normal things that happened to human
men as they aged.

Alas, not Jamie. Jamie had flecks of gray now streaking the temples of his
coal-black curls and dusting the fashionably libertine stubble that filled the
pages of GQ, but the tiny, expected unsightliness of age only made Jamie look
better, somehow, more valuable. Leave it to society to create a term like silver
fox for the men, Meredith had always thought, and save haggard old crone for
the ladies. Jamie! For fuck's sake. He had always been angular, sharp, lanky,
his skin tone warmer than her bisque-y shade by some scant handful of degrees, glowing in brazen defiance of Bostonian winters. Now he was fine-
edged and gilded, a man, lean and battle-worn, fit to unironically wield a
sword. He belonged on the cover of some ethnically progressive Arthurian
romance—the hero in a lusty, bodice-ripping tale of old. Christ, the fucking
injustice.

She realized Jamie was looking at her expectantly. What did he want? A
sonnet? "What?"

He rolled his eyes, as if the last time they'd spoken had been Thursday
rather than years ago, from prior lives. "I know you saw my message."

"Excuse me?" She had read receipts turned off, because she was no dilet-
tante in avoidance.

"Pretty sure the whole auditorium saw you get my message, Meredith,"
Jamie said.

A herd of Tyche software employees ("Kip Hughes's army of goddamn
sheep," as Meredith's father typically called them) rounded the corner as
Meredith took hold of Jamie's arm, shoving him into the confines of a vacant conference room. It was dark as they entered, the contents of the room
visible only by the light from the corridor through the door's small window
by the time the latch clicked shut.

Meredith had assumed the conference room lights would come on automatically. They did not, but it seemed too late to grope the walls looking
for a switch.

"We've barely spoken for almost a *decade*," she seethed at Jamie, or the
half of his face she could see from the sliver of corridor light. "And now
you've resorted to blackmail?"

"Meredith, I'm not blackmailing you." It was difficult to tell, given the way the shadows bled into the dark room, but he looked borderline amused by her, which was sinfully annoying.

"So that was your idea of a joke? Unbelievable." She made to storm out when Jamie caught her by the elbow, pulling her back.

"No, Meredith—" He shook his head, folding his arms over his chest. "I know what Tyche is doing. I know what you did," he repeated, and it was difficult, in the moment, to ascertain whether this, too, was an episode from Meredith's rich fantasy life or an actual, concrete accusation. "This isn't blackmail. I don't require any leverage. I'm saying that I know what you did because I've spent the last six months tracking down every clinical patient Birdsong ever worked with, and now I'm going to publish my findings."

"Which are?" (The word "arrhythmia" sprang to mind.)

"That your product doesn't work," said Jamie conclusively, "and Tyche knows it. That Chirp is a scam that was never actually *meant* to work." He leaned closer, a hair's breadth. "And that it only got this far because of you."

Briefly, a buzzing sound filled Meredith's ears, to the point where she could only scarcely hear him.

"—only here to give you fair warning," Jamie was saying, the traitor, as if he hadn't placed their history into the empty space between them. As if he hadn't brandished it at her like a weapon. "I figured I owed you at least that much. I didn't want you to see it for the first time on your desk Monday morning. I wanted you to hear it from me."

Meredith looked at him for a long time. A variety of thoughts raced through her head. All of them were panic. The vast majority were guilty panic, and rightly so. Without really doing the math, I'd ballpark Meredith's wrongdoing at somewhere around a dozen counts of felony corporate fraud. But obviously I digress.

Meredith had some thoughts about being dangerously perceived; about losing the gamble over the knife she'd proverbially stuck in her father's chest; about watching her life's work go down the drain; about giving up the dream of Wrenfare; about watching herself dim in Jamie's eyes in real time.

*It does work,* she nearly said. It was on the tip of her tongue. *Sure, everyone hyperbolizes a little, but that's what this industry is! "Value" is subjective— capital is self-fulfilling prophecy—all money comes with strings—the point is, I know what I made. It does work. It does work.*

*It does, technically, work.*

Then, thankfully, a modicum of reason returned to her. The buzzing sound faded away as she forced a disinterested smile.

An old trick of Meredith's, which I can confirm took her further than it should have: deny, deny, deny.

"Jamie, this is absurd. I'm sure you're aware that our results were incredibly conclusive. Extraordinary, even."

"Yes," Jamie agreed. Even in the dark, his eyes found hers. "And I think you and I both know why that is."

This time, the word in her head was: *Caught.*

Meredith felt intensely aware of his position in the room. The distance from his mouth to hers. The motion of her own breasts. Christ, even fighting for her livelihood was erotic with him. Survival demanded a change of subject.

"I'm seeing someone," she said.

"Congratulations," said Jamie, his eyes not leaving hers.

Her phone buzzed again in her hand. Exhaling sharply, Meredith silenced it with a swipe across the screen, grateful for the temporary break in concentration.

"How's Sarah?" she said, in a tone of marked indifference delivered so successfully she almost wanted to cheer until she heard his answer.

"Fine," said Jamie. "She just gave birth a few weeks ago."

Something in Meredith's chest withered and died, though her voice came out harsher, meaner. So much for indifference. "That's how you announce that you have a baby? 'She gave birth,' no mention of your *child,* or I don't know, your utter fucking joy? God, domesticity clearly suits you," Meredith snarled.

Jamie looked at her for a long, long time.

Then he gave the tiniest shake of his head. "As far as I know, it suits Sarah and her husband just fine."

"You—" Meredith blinked and her fucking stye distracted her for a second. She blinked several times, trying to clear her vision. "You didn't marry Sarah?" she managed, which even under these circumstances was obviously lame as hell.

But Jamie seemed to know there was no point traveling any further down that particular path.

"You and I both know what you can do, Meredith." He'd collected himself, which was a shame. She would have liked to hear something, whatever there was to hear about why he hadn't married the woman he'd decided all those years ago he couldn't live without. "No other journalist had any reason to investigate why your clinical results and the results of your paid users don't match up. But I do." He gave her a significant look, summoning before the court a wordless exhibition of their years together.

Well. *Year,* with some spare change for irresponsible behavior.

Meredith felt her mouth tighten. "What is it you think I did?" She wondered if he'd say it aloud. He'd never been able to before. Not even when they were fighting. Not even when his doubt in her had been heaviest, and most profound.

"I know you're lying," said Jamie, which was such blatant hedging that Meredith felt rickety, unsteady. "Early product testing for Chirp was through the roof. Every clinical patient is changed, substantially, as if their entire personality has been rewritten. But no results since have shown any evidence of *happiness,* Meredith."

"There's no way you could prove that." Her mind raced with rationalities. The identities of those trial patients weren't public. Even so, all of this was anecdotal.

"I'm an investigative journalist, Meredith. This is literally what I do."

"How could you even know who was a patient in the trials?"

"Investigative journalism," Jamie coolly repeated, which Meredith hotly ignored.

"Unless you broke into our facilities or—"

She stopped. Something occurred to her belatedly. Somewhere in the cogs of the tireless, calculating machine that Meredith Wren called a deductive process, a red flag quietly rose, no less unavoidable than the strike of a match.

She lunged.

It was unclear what Jamie had expected. It was less appropriate to call his reaction a dodge than it was a flinch, and whether there was to be any sort of reciprocal reaction or pendulum defense was initially unreadable. Meredith, for her part, scrabbled unsuccessfully to pry apart his shirt, an undercooked course of action that did not play out as planned.

"Jesus, Meredith, *what*—"

"I'm checking for a wire," she said calmly, struggling to free the second button after the first, then the third, and so on sequentially, with Jamie too stunned to physically remove her, despite the difficulty she was having with his clothing. "Since I clearly can't trust you anymore."

By the time Jamie regained the presence of mind to lift her hands from his garment, Meredith had gotten all the way to the top of his trousers, at that point unable to say with certainty that the dark trail of hair leading to his zipper was unchanged from what lived on in her imagination. In the shadows of the fractionally lit conference room, it was unclear if there were hints of silver there or any other indicators of the passage of time. Only that he had remained diligent with his core.

There was, however, no wire. They both seemed to realize in the same instance the strangeness of the moment and briefly locked eyes, until Meredith, clinging to the reserves of her dignity, opted to say aloud, "I'm just now realizing that I don't know how wires work. You could have planted a mic anywhere."

Her eyes narrowed before dropping to his trousers.

"Are you insane?" Jamie asked her seriously, with no attempts to resolve his current state of half dress. "I know this is a touchy subject, but sincerely, and with all due respect, are you in your right mind?"

"That," Meredith snapped, "is a ridiculous thing to say."

Jamie glanced crossly down at her. "Now that we both agree I'm not some kind of gumshoe narc, maybe I should be the one determining what is or isn't ridiculous."

"*You're* the one who's threatening me," she reminded him with a sudden, blistering recollection of the stakes. "How am I supposed to know how low you're willing to go?"

"You think what *I'm* doing is low?" Jamie stared at her, seemingly astounded in a way he had not been moments before. "Meredith, I owe you nothing. The fact that I'm warning you at all is purely a matter of personal ethics. I know what you're doing," he said with another meaningful glance, or a sliver of one she knew to be unavoidably puncturing, "and I know what Tyche is monetizing, and if you think I'm going to stand by and let you defraud not only your investors but *every single human alive*—"

"I'm not a fraud." Her breathing had suddenly become very labored. She realized that over the course of his rant, Jamie had stepped closer to her in the shadows of the darkened room. "It's not all a lie."

"No, it's never all a lie, is it? But it's a lie nonetheless." She could see the motion of Jamie's chest rising and falling, or maybe she could just chart it like stars, like navigating there from memory.

She was aware of everything. His closeness. The way it was punitive, wrathful in some way, an intimacy meant for suffering. (From my point of view: deserved.)

"You know, you've always had a tell," remarked Jamie, after a moment.

"Do I?"

She'd meant it to be mocking. Maybe it was, maybe it wasn't. Either way, she felt her eyes drop briefly to his mouth.

His smile took on a blatant lilt of arrogance.

"Told you," he said.

Just then the door beside them opened, followed by the flickering buzz of the conference room lights being switched on. Meredith, who was temporarily blinded, took a moment to register exactly who it was.

Then it became gradually, karmically clear. The casual brown-black swoop for which she knew precisely which pomade he used. The Tom Ford tortoiseshell frames paired with the effortlessly tactile, preppy oxford. The towering height—which exceeded Jamie's, for the record. Not that it mattered, or that anyone asked.

"Meredith," said her boyfriend, Cass, spotting her first before his eyes traveled slowly to Jamie. Cass's brow twitched with apparent calculation as he registered their positions in the room, followed by the disheveled way Jamie's shirt had been left undone. "I thought I heard your voice. Is everything . . ." Cass flicked a glance from Meredith to Jamie again, and then lingered there overlong as Jamie began to quickly and efficiently button his shirt, only a faint tightness in his mouth to reveal any evidence of shame or embarrassment. ". . . all right?"

"Cass Mizuno," said Meredith with an air of forced elegance, "Jamie Ammar. Jamie is a reporter for—" She broke off, realizing she hadn't the faintest idea who he was a reporter for. "Jamie's a journalist. And Cass is—"

"VP Operations for Tyche. I know." Jamie's mouth was still unreadably stiff. "Congratulations on your recent promotion."

"Congratulations on being alone in a dark room with Meredith Wren," replied Cass.

"Oh, grow up," said Meredith with a sudden wave of exasperation. "He's just threatening to destroy my life and career, Cass, we're not fucking. It's apparently deeply impersonal."

"I wouldn't say deeply impersonal," said Jamie under his breath, with the light, playful tone of insouciance that made her remember the man he had been at twenty-one, when that particular tone was reserved for dealing with customer service representatives and/or diffusing her temper.

"Well then mazel tov to me," snapped Meredith, glaring at him before realizing that Cass was still in the room. "What? Cass, I swear to god, if you're going to make a scene—"

"I wasn't, actually," said Cass with a neutrality that was—fucking Christ—nearly the same tone Jamie had just weaponized against her moments before. "Your father's assistant just called me. Apparently she's struggling to reach you."

"I'm busy," said Meredith. "Whatever it is, it can wait until—"

"It's your father," said Cass. "He's dead."

# 5

As far as orgies went, it was a success, or maybe a failure. Largely because Arthur had only had eyes for his lovers, and though he had twice as many of those as the average person, it still seemed antithetical to the principles of an orgy to limit himself to the usual fare.

"Darling, you've been away from us for ages," said Philippa, tutting a little in the matronly way she seemed to affect only when she was feeling sexiest. "I hate it when you're gone so long."

She had her hands on his chest, Yves's hands traveling Arthur's hips, guiding him gradually up the stairs. They seemed to be shedding what few garments remained as they went, or at least Yves seemed to be. He'd long since done away with his mask, which made sense, as Yves became very sensual when he was aroused. Every moment called for a slow, pliant kiss, which Arthur quite liked, as it felt unhurried and primordially luxurious, as if true wealth could only be meaningfully defined by this kind of excess of time.

Arthur's shirt had already been unbuttoned, but now he felt his arms lock behind his back, Philippa's attempts to fully disrobe him providing a not-unwelcome service of restraint. "I've been very foolish indeed," he said, adopting the British musicality of diction that was so temptingly in reach whenever he was cross-faded and two orgasms in. "I suddenly can't think what could have possibly been more important."

Philippa smiled radiantly at him then, or a smile that was not very radiant on a normal woman—it was a little too smug, something Arthur only noticed when Philippa was around the many others who did not understand her—but on Philippa was as good as spraying him with molten gold. "You should give up your silly little game of politics. Don't you ever get bored with it, all the infighting and do-gooding?"

Arguably there was very little do-gooding. Ask the internet. "Where else would I keep up with the latest trends in dinner conversation?"

Philippa laughed, tossing her arms around his neck and clinging to him like a sexy little koala. Yves, too, laughed, his tongue busying itself somewhere below the waistband of Arthur's trousers.

Arthur realized belatedly that he had forgotten to take off the tiny American flag pin that Gillian had bought him when he'd won his first election. "All the important ones have one," she'd said matter-of-factly, "and now you do, too." It had felt to him as solemn as a proposal, like sliding a ring onto the finger of his beloved, but he knew Gillian lacked that kind of sentimentality. To her, all of it—symbolic jewelry, patriotism itself—was a tactic. He himself was a tactic of sorts, though for what he had never actually understood.

The pin tumbled to the floor, lost in the floorboards, in the shuffle to the bedroom. It was abandoned in the God-given pursuit of happiness, among other things.

Occasionally when Arthur Wren had been very small and very sad, he had heard a voice calling to him, speaking as what seemed to Arthur (who was admittedly very imaginative and had not actually read the book) to be a ghost of Christmas future, a message from someone important whom he had yet to meet. He couldn't have said whether the voice was masculine or feminine, only that it seemed to him very kind and very intimate, gentle in a way but also steadfast and unfailing, and most often what the voice said to him was *I love you,* as if he were confusingly reliving the memory of a quiet moment between paramours that had not yet occurred. It had faded into the recesses of his memory as he got older, but not really. He no longer heard the voice anymore, not actively, and he couldn't have described the tone or timbre, but he retained the memory of hearing it, and the way it made him feel to know he was destined for something that lovely. That kind.

He looked for it in his lovers from time to time in moments of desperation, but life has a way of minimizing the efficacy of imaginary voices that make loneliness gentler to bear. (All conditions are ultimately survivable, which is to say that despite grief, despite loss, Arthur did eventually grow up.) How could Arthur still be so riddled with holes, like a colander of a person? As a man, or whatever he was, Arthur collected all the affection he could hold and was still somehow left with nothing, only the imaginary weight of three overused words.

But then again there were moments, glimmers even, when the voice and its implications seemed not only very real, but powerfully, presciently his, as if he had always had it in him to see the future. It made him a believer in a blueprint, which was in its way a form of relaxation, stress relief. Because it meant that no matter how badly he fucked up, there was a cosmic path he could never actually stray from, and therefore this moment was meant to be his, and so was this, and so was this. He'd felt it long ago with Lou, and again when he'd first run for office, and he felt it with painful severity now.

"I love you," said Arthur to Yves, one hand on the structured cheekbones for which so many would gladly shed their knickers. "I love you," Arthur said also to Philippa, imagining himself a handfasting ceremony wherein he bound his life to theirs. He pictured this moment as one of matrimony, almost. As if the voice was somewhere in this room with him now, and maybe if he thought about it hard enough, it had always been his voice. Maybe this was the moment he'd so long remembered as a child—only he hadn't known it would happen this way, falling into the king-sized bed while reaching for the halos around both his lovers' heads.

By then the drugs were coursing fully through his system, alive in his veins, the bedroom's recessed lighting twinkling in and out like the sultriness of candle flame. His magic, or whatever it was (it seemed very silly to call it magic, grown men did not have magic, just as grown men did not imagine bodiless voices professing love to them, sometimes in the anthropomorphized form of the company his father had built, as if Wrenfare were a sexy cartoon fox), was skitteringly potent. Arthur himself was just a series of sparks by then, cascading onto the linen sheets below like stardust. He felt the faintest tug of reality, the buzz of his phone with all the loathing its apps and their denizens had for him, and was surprised to find he still had arms and legs, a pocket. He ignored it, felt Yves digging it out, wonderful Yves, clever Yves, excising the tumor like a surgeon, saving Arthur's life with his wonderful, clever, lifesaving hands. Arthur could have kissed him. I love you, I love you! It was never meant to be a quiet moment, then. It had always been this moment, this Arthur, reassuring his child-self not with the high of drugs or the lure of sex but with something else, the feeling of existing wholly in the *right* moment, the opportune place at the opportune time, which Arthur never seemed to find.

Why had he not chased *this* feeling, chosen *this* life? The monotony of municipal chambers, snippy headlines, angry tags. The lives Arthur wanted devotedly to fix but never could, probably never would. The irony of it! Of loving this deeply and yet being this powerless; nothing but stars and emptiness after all.

His vision was hazy, filled with the deep purple of Philippa's robes. Philippa, darling Philippa. He twirled a finger in her curls, imagining a world where he woke up to her each morning, alive as she was now with unfiltered love. Not just the little slivers he was allowed to have, but every morning. Oh god, the luxuries of such a life! The downstairs television ran the gamut of Arthur's emotions, skimming through every channel of barking dogs and tears of joy.

Imagine it: Philippa fresh out of the shower, Philippa's perfume on the dresser, brewing a fresh pot of herbal tea for Philippa, because cheesecake gave Philippa the shits. And Yves! Darling Yves, like the silver lining to Philippa's cloud. Imagine the nights spent with Yves's long toes in his lap, stroking Yves's silken mahogany waves, Yves as some sort of symbol of luxury, always reclined like a cat on a velvet chaise lounge even in Arthur's most domestic fantasies. Arthur kissed him, then kissed Philippa. Oh, he loved them. He loved them, he wanted them, he longed for a life like this!

He leaned over to bury his lips in Yves's neck. "I want all of it," he murmured, his mouth muffled by skin slicked with salt and the particular flavor of Arthur's magic, which was a bit like grape Tylenol, and had technically been used under these conditions as a sort of advanced vibrator, that proverbial electric touch.

"I want all of it," Arthur said again when Philippa's breathy moan sounded in his ear, like the call of a siren from afar. Her hands were elsewhere, on Yves. "I want all of it, everything, the baby—"

"Is that your phone?" said Philippa, and Arthur didn't know, his trousers were gone, everything was euphoria, would only be euphoria from now until forever, it was euphoria eternal, euphoria evermore. He turned to kiss Yves, who was no longer within reach, and Arthur felt confusingly marooned. Everything seemed to shrink a little. The bed, which had seemed so large and uncontainable just breaths ago now seemed too small, his fingertips and toes already bursting from its edges.

He didn't quite realize what was happening until Gillian's voice was already in his ear, tinny and far away, like an astronaut in deep and distant space.

"Arthur," said his wife's voice. Yes, you heard me correctly. "Art, are you there?"

"Yes." He struggled to sit up, holding the phone to his ear and squinting at Philippa, who was tracing delicate filigrees of nothing on his thigh.

"I'm very sorry to have to spoil your trip, but your father is dead." Arthur heard the faint sound of static in his head, like the connection was bad, the blueprint was failing. "I've emailed you your flight itinerary; it leaves in three hours. I'll take care of everything at the office and send a car to SFO if I can't be there myself. Do give Yves and Philippa my love."

*I love you,* said the voice in Arthur's head, which in reality could have been any voice but was always supposed to be his father's. *I love you.* Like the tumble of the flag pin to the floor, the neatness of an ending, gone as it had never been before.

And with it, the phone fell from Arthur's hand.

# 6

The transaction between Eilidh and her demonic parasite completed, the plane righted itself. Not gradually, as if the pilot had somehow regained control through his own volition. Instead, the lights simply stopped flickering, the turbulence fell instantly away, and the world—the portion of it that had nearly ended on a commercial flight from Vermont to San Francisco—suddenly stabilized, the woman with the rosary looking heavenward, awestruck, as if a wordless god had seen fit to answer her prayers. The baby's cries began to fade away, slowing to a whine, then a series of hiccups. There was a collective intake of breath, a gripping of hands between passengers. The man who'd been weeping looked as if he had righted the plane himself, as a product of masculine resilience.

Eilidh Wren exhaled her own relief in private, quietly glancing at the image on the lock screen of her phone, still uselessly in airplane mode. Her father's smiling face—no teeth, but that was his way—was a momentary balm, temporarily reassuring. He would not have to wait alone for her in a restaurant now. And she would tell all of this to her company-provided therapist—not the details, obviously, but the important bit, in which she had chosen life, which was not always a guarantee in the way you'd sort of hope it would be—and everything would be fine, and she would oversee some kind of social media campaign and do nothing really of consequence, but maybe the baby in 22A would grow up to cure cancer.

And wasn't it kind of a gift, in its way, that Eilidh would never know?

Passengers had begun opening their window shades, emboldened now, hoping to see the universal gift of blue sky, searching for the evidence of their communal miracle. Thirstily, light slaked in from both sides of the plane, intoxicating, garish, bright.

Eilidh, meanwhile, braced herself. Alongside the benedictions of life lived its unavoidable horrors. Not a metaphor, or at least not solely one. Survival was only half the bargain, and she understood the way the others couldn't that nothing came for free.

So Eilidh sat white-knuckled in her aisle seat, waiting for the jump scare. For the unavoidable drop. She closed her eyes. Her heart thudded in her chest, uncontrollable.

There. She could feel it—feel it before she could place it. Thud-thud in her chest, a wild ricochet.

And then, like clockwork, there it was.

At first it was a light—the kind you're cautioned not to follow. The kind that leads to the end of a tunnel, to the ultimate swallowing up. The light pouring in from outside the plane grew gradually overwhelming, a heady jolt to their collective senses. Passenger by passenger, seat by seat, aisle by aisle, every occupant of the plane began to squint.

The light—was it sun?—was offensive, infernal, like staring into the grainy screen after *The Exorcist* on VHS. It was . . . *bright,* but not sunlight bright— the brightness of realizing the dark room had never been empty. The brightness of revelation that despite what you believed, you were never in there alone.

Eilidh looked into the window, blinking back corneal damage. The saturation of the brightness was white and somehow viscous—the shade of pus draining from an open wound. From the windows, the ensorceling blindness expanded, becoming increasingly offensive, insidious. Some people hastily slammed their window shades shut; her seatmate didn't. To her right, Eilidh could sense the suggestion of movement, a ubiquity of thickness that now seemed to breathe. Each pane of light that remained open was crammed with the blurring, indecipherable presence of something solid. Something festering, fidgeting.

Alive.

"What's that?" came a newly panicked voice some rows ahead of Eilidh. "Look outside, what *are* those?"

The horde, such as it was, became identifiable, visible suddenly as if to finally find the subject in a Magic Eye painting with your eyes half-closed. First the suggestion of an image, then the actual presence. Individual, first, then in groups. Each one taking shape like a pearl of water dropped perilously into an empty metal bowl.

Not quite a drip—more like sharp stabs of parental disapproval.

Tsk.

Tsk.

Tsk.

"Oh my god," came the voice of a teenage girl. "Oh my god, Mom, are those *bugs*?"

Disapproval became rage, became the heightening sense of violence. No longer a tsk, now a smack. Smack. How dare you? Smack. Look what horrors you've wrought! Smack. The smack of an open hand for now, but how much longer? How soon before it was a closed fist, a shattered glass bottle, the schlick of a disabled safety? Such was the growing sensation, the tremulent dread, the pulsating fear.

Faster and faster, smacksmacksmacksmack—

Tiny bodies thwapped against the windows of the plane like skyward stones, like countless writhing opals. Their bellies wriggled fleshily; like a billion exposed, swallowing throats. They crushed against the glass—so thick was the swarm that each one seemed to be suffocating, undulating with a mix of hunger for entry and desperation for release.

The woman with the rosary let out a shriek, shout-whispering prayers with her head over her beads.

"It's a *plague of locusts*," gasped the weeping man to the mother of the baby.

Inside an eternity that must have been moments—Eilidh had counted eighty-eight pounding heartbeats; eighty-nine, ninety, ninety-one—the purulent brightness had become disfigured by the presence of the plague, a different sort of darkness now enshrouding the unlucky plane. The hum of wings was unavoidable, deafening. Ninety-eight. Ninety-nine. One hundred.

Some bugs had been pulverized into the panes by the force of their own swarm, carcasses oozing thickly across the glass. A hundred and four. A hundred and five. Splintered wings and contorted hairline legs punctuated slathered softshell underbellies. A hundred and ten. A hundred eleven. Inside the plane, the dim sterility of emergency lighting flashed soullessly, a quiet signal for the end of days.

Abruptly, Eilidh lost count of her own pulse, succumbing to the wilds of arrhythmia. Her seatmate had finally closed the window, not that it mattered anymore. They could still hear the scratch and the crawl, the buzz of wings and the pelting of bodies, like the sound of the word infestation. The way the word pestilence felt on the tongue. Someday, assuming they survived this particular plague, it would hail and they would all say *Huh, sounds like locusts,* all of them now one step closer to knowing how it ends.

"Fuck," Eilidh whispered to nobody.

The thing in her chest seemed to chuckle, licking its lips, sated for the time being. Promises, promises. In Eilidh's head she heard Wagner, Beethoven, the beauty of notes played by hate. Darkness you could taste, a chord you're meant to suffer. Like if a miracle were ugly, or fate could only sing a grisly song.

# A Brief Note from God

Here's what you need to know about the Wren family: Aside from being assholes, they're also fucking frauds.

And I don't say that from a place of bias. I'm what the experts call a voice of God narration (God for short—who has the time for honorifics?) and I'm mostly here to observe and make the occasional comment as related to your understanding of the plot. So, like I said, the first thing to know about the Almighty House of Wren is that it's a crumbling mess of conflict and lies, with the general obfuscation of reality as a treat.

Take, for example, the name Wren, which suggests an Anglo-Saxon origin, perhaps even a veritable and renowned one. False. Both sides of the family involve a wide variety of helter-skelter refuge-seeking immigrants concealed behind more dignified origins—Singaporean and Malaysian success stories emphasized on one side, conveniently making no public reference to the hodgepodge of Filipino and Cambodian mixed in, and on the other, a sprinkle of Old New York Dutch to narratively overshadow the Russian Jewish roots; altogether, a genetic smoothing tool that was not so much a lie as it was a contour light for a prettier, more dignified picture. (True, some might argue that it's better to be a thirsty charlatan bitch than an actual blue-blooded colonizer, to which I say—yeah, sure, whatever. I am not an interventionist voice of God.)

The things you should know about the world, assuming you don't already know them, mostly have to do with the magitech industry, the basis of which is Magic—the elegant architectural system of transporting electromagnetic waves as trademarked by one Upland M. Carmichael as of approximately 1890, shortly after Nikola Tesla bounced from Edison Machine Works. (I know you don't care about any of this, but what can I say? One hobbyist to another, I get a little overexcited when it comes to the subject of creation.) Anyway, the long and short of it is that Magic™ is essentially the channeling of unusually potent electromagnetic waves en masse—a primitive form of supercomputing, essentially, and not unlike the work of Tesla's induction motor—allowing open communication where there would otherwise be one-way traffic.

Normal electromagnetic waves send energy from one place to another, but thanks to the infrastructure of Magic, information can be sent, received, *and* interpreted, and at extraordinary speed, too. You can see why someone would call it magic, though despite all its eventual applications, its patent simply sat dormant for multiple decades, waiting for someone more enterprising and less dorky to put it to meaningful use.

Which leads us, with some hops, skips, and jumps, to Wrenfare Magitech, the brainchild of the late Thayer Wren—may he rest in, you know, peace.

From my position of sublime omniscience, Thayer was both myth and man, almost interchangeably. Impressive in his quest for innovation, visionary in his sense of progress, but also, fortunate by circumstance, as all billionaires ultimately are. Had he never met his late cofounder, Marike Fransson, or the financier Merritt Foster, who would ultimately prove Thayer's most lethal betrayer until his daughter Meredith took the crown—had Thayer simply been born to a village with no computer or literacy—he would not have been the Thayer Wren who was both adored and despised, nor the Thayer Wren who drove all three of his children to varying extremes of success and, unavoidably, madness. (More on that later. I promised you enlightenment on the House of Wren, and I'm nothing if not divinely reliable.)

While the telecommunications systems underpinning today's technomancy began in the early twentieth century, and the development of Magic as a harnessable source of electromagnetic waves even earlier than that, it was actually war that produced the necessary conditions for the Wren children. Firstly, in that the need for instant, encrypted, far-reaching intelligence systems around the Second World War led to an unprecedented outpouring of military spending into the formerly dormant use of Magic as a power source for a new, rapid communications network—such that by the time Thayer Wren was of an age to reasonably connect two dots and implement the first viable deep neural network, the infrastructure for a Magic-based tech company was already in place. More efficient superconductors were already in development, quantum computing was already ideologically in play, and all that remained was an ability to produce parallel, complete internets running on individual devices—all sharing and informing each other to adapt by the billions every nanosecond—at an appreciable scale.

Genius, right? But also, importantly, inevitable.

The second war-related condition leading to a generation of tiny geniuses involved Persephone Liang, the mother of Meredith, Arthur, and Eilidh Wren, and the daughter of two luxury hoteliers who technically made the early part of their wealth in pharmaceuticals. It was Persephone's father's father who invented an alternative to penicillin, an extremely lucrative product that launched one of the most prominent pharmaceutical chains throughout emerging Asian markets. After sending Persephone to the finest Western boarding schools and impressing upon her the significance of an Oxbridge degree and general upper crust acceptance, the Liangs' wonderfully clever and breathtakingly attractive daughter (and the trust fund she had newly aged into) eventually found her way to a college dropout with long hair and a cloying tendency to wax poetic about the qubit, prompting both her parents to die spontaneously of shame.

But Persephone was cleverer than she seemed, depending on whether it is clever to throw your own fortune and accomplishments into the support of a man whose ambitions bordered on zealotry. Because yes, knowing what you now know, perhaps it doesn't look so problematic to choose the future CEO of Wrenfare over a life of predictable sameness (even if that sameness looks very suspiciously like creature comforts in other, more flattering lights). At the time Persephone Liang met Thayer Wren, she was in dire need of inspiration; of something Persephone called motion that other people might call spontaneity, or perhaps a hypomanic episode.

As for Thayer, he had been dragged to London, having been told by various industry mentors—most notably Merritt Foster, then a young Harvard graduate whose spare $250,000 would provide the first angel investment for Wrenfare and eventually yield the fortune to cofound rival magitech giant Tyche Inc. after Foster and Thayer publicly cut ties—that he might find investors there. Thayer, the father of both magitech and the three assholes in this book, was three years Persephone's junior, and had recently dropped out of Stanford University with an idea so consuming he could no longer focus on the drudgery of his studies, particularly not his calculus prerequisite or the asinine general education requirements (both of which he'd failed). Thayer had a mind that needed to work quickly, to be constantly engaged with a single complex, ever-changing, Sisyphean-seeming but ultimately conquerable toy.

Relatedly, this insistence on change for the sake of change was why the version of Wrenfare that Thayer would ultimately die with bore few similarities to the Wrenfare he had started with. Absent his technical cofounder, his charismatic wife, and his savvy financier, there was no one left to convince Thayer that wheels do not require reinventing, even if reinventing wheels is your dearest, most precious wish.

But that is, obviously, getting ahead of myself. The story of Persephone Liang Wren's demise is better left to one of her children, namely Meredith, whose own life story would follow the trajectory of her father's so closely it would seem at first to be the actions of a lunatic, or an idiot, when in fact it's just one of those silly ironies, like the self-fulfilling prophecy of Oedipus finding his own mother hot. What's important to know is that Wrenfare Magitech—the company that Thayer Wren, at nineteen years old, already knew would revolutionize the way human beings communicated with each other—had developed so successfully and quickly that it seemed unstoppable, even inimitable, and yet had begun, by the middle of the 2010s, to falter. Profit margins dipped; competitors swarmed the magitech market like Visigoths sacking Rome. Think pieces began to emerge, first about whether Wrenfare's hegemony was reaching its end, then about whether its doom could be prevented. At the time of Thayer Wren's death, public reception to Wrenfare's longtime CEO had transitioned from idolatry boasting the kind of black-and-white portraiture usually reserved for military generals to reductive clickbait about his failures as a leader and a man. Wrenfare the company was besmirched by flagging leadership; thanks to Thayer, Wrenfare the product now lived in the shadow of public doubt.

But what would become of Wrenfare the idea, Wrenfare the system, Wrenfare the *revolution,* which had launched an industry and rewritten the course of modern life?

To many, the answer lay somewhere beyond Thayer—to his successors, whoever they might be. Which was why, on the Monday that news broke of his death, the *New York Times* would be forced to narrowly pull a feature called "The Rise and Fall of the House of Wren," a deep dive into the lives of Thayer's three children that revolved around a single, arresting question: Which of the Wrens now deserved the Wrenfare throne?

First there was Meredith Wren, the oldest and most obvious candidate, at least until you dug a little deeper into her past. Now CEO of her own magitech company, Birdsong, Meredith had not only been selected as a U.S. Presidential Scholar but had also graduated valedictorian of her renowned private high school, and was singularly recognized as one of the most disliked people ever to walk its hallowed halls. Despite a promising start in the burgeoning academy of biomantic research (itself built in large part on the quantum computing pioneered by her father's CTO, Marike Fransson, who would pass away during the early 2000s and coincidentally go unmentioned in all but the most technical accounts of magitech's rise), Meredith would drop out of Harvard at age nineteen. It was a choice that seemed at first to be completely mysterious—the actions of a spoiled child who did not believe the rules were meant to apply to her.

Meredith disappeared from public view, and when she and her life's work, Chirp, made their resurgence five years later with the full support of venture capital behind her, public opinion soon turned. Never mind the thing they said before—she was, like her father, an innovator! The decision to publicly partner with Tyche, the company cofounded by her own father's former financier, Merritt Foster, sent shock waves through Silicon Beach—a power move, many ruled, that revealed an impressive, almost horrific professional ruthlessness. Immediately, Meredith Wren was listed fourth on the Forbes 30 Under 30 list, the only woman in what was widely considered the top five and the only woman of color of any real significance in tech.

But was the betrayal merely professional, or was Meredith actually a calculating snake? Despite her unprecedented success—or perhaps because of it—there soon came some noise about Meredith's personal unpopularity. Her colleagues did not like her. Her contemporaries, the other CEOs vying for unicorn valuations, believed her to be not only an unbearable, arrogant, class-sympathizing snob, but also, quite frankly, a bitch. According to a widely publicized rumor—nonetheless published due to the reliability of its male source—Meredith did not really seem capable of the accomplishments to her name. One year after Chirp's release, the clinical trials that were always too good to be true—the app that so zealously proposed it could *make you happy*—became a topic of intensifying speculation. Was such idolatry really owed to Meredith and Birdsong, or was some other dystopian capitalist fuckery afoot?

As of the month of her father's demise, the tide was turning on Meredith Wren. Was she as competent as she seemed, or was it all a smoke screen mired in excessive wealth? Was it even possible to do the things she claimed Chirp could do? Or as Jamie Ammar would later put it in his pitch to *Magitek* magazine, were the biomantic functions of the world's first neuromancy transmitter legitimately improving the brain chemistry of its users, or did people simply feel better while they were shopping at the grocery store Tyche happened to own?

Another rumor, one suspiciously similar in tone to the first rumor, was that Thayer had always believed his eldest daughter flawed. He had denied her a position in Wrenfare's technical leadership—said to be her dearest ambition, and even her younger sister had qualified for a director position in-house—and then had snubbed her a second time by deliberately passing on the chance to invest in her product despite Wrenfare's known entry to the biomantic sphere (apparent from their latest product, a watch connected to the Wrenfare network that, curiously, also sought to offer subcutaneous delivery). Initially the snub had seemed in the interest of fairness, but now that the effectiveness of Meredith's leadership had come under fire, Thayer's choice to disregard his eldest child's company seemed much more telling. What had Thayer Wren known about his traitorous daughter that the rest of the world had overlooked until, well, now?

Then there was Congressman Arthur Wren, the second-youngest congressman in history, elected at the age of twenty-eight to a progressive eastern district in the larger San Francisco Bay Area. Arthur had married young by neoliberal standards, at the age of just twenty-six, and despite a lukewarm performance in NCAA baseball—he had been an All-American top recruit out of high school, but flagged in investment quality as he revealed himself to be prone to the yips—Arthur had, like his sister, disappeared for a time in his early twenties, appearing to find the pressure to succeed to be too much too soon.

But then he was suddenly out in the world campaigning, his social media feeds bright and overflowing with progressive ideas and the unique virality of the young and hip, his private life open for what seemed to be perfectly willing consumption. Arthur Wren did not beg for privacy. His public image was curated so neatly, in such buttery, sycophantic shades of sorbet (successors to the destitution of millennial pink) that it seemed impossible to certain prolific armchair experts that it could not be a ruse, and yet seemingly the entire internet—his father's own internet—crowned him their boyfriend without a second thought.

By the end of two years, now running for reelection in the lead-up to his thirtieth birthday, Arthur had not accomplished much of anything. News outlets covering his campaign routinely speculated that he was actually quite useless. As Arthur accomplished less and less, he grew more visibly distracted, photographed not only out of his district but out of the country, often rubbing elbows with the hoity-toity set. His pictures with his wife, Gillian, looked increasingly staged and stiff, and his social media feeds offered little in the realm of meaningful engagement. At one point, Arthur was seen to frantically abscond from a closed congressional hearing, hair and eyes wild with uncontrolled static as he screeched "no comment" at nearby cameras and fled. To many, Arthur seemed to be shrinking, disappearing. By the time local polls revealed that he was losing ground to his more conservative challenger—in the *Bay Area,* no less!—it seemed likely that Arthur Wren had gotten the yips yet again.

Still, constant punditry as to Arthur Wren's political uselessness aside, his tragedy in this particular story is private—unless you consider the fact that Thayer, despite a longstanding invitation to Arthur's fundraising events, ultimately contributed nothing to his campaign.

Finally, there was Eilidh Wren, the perpetual ingenue, whose public face would never age beyond her teens thanks to the miserly cruelty of the media. Eilidh, known among the Wren family's inner circles to be her father's favorite, was at one point primed to be the world's most recognizable ballerina—one of a scant twenty individuals and the only dancer to be sponsored by a primary athletic company at the age of eighteen, when she made her debut with the New York Ballet. It was Eilidh's elegant, ambiguously mixed-race face, placid and poised, that graced the city's billboards like a supermodel; it was her lithe, sculpted, second-gen-American musculature that was celebrated in advertisements about the virtues of talent and hard work. Eilidh was the token poster child for the rituals of mind over matter, and for the gracious acceptance—nay, the divine necessity!—of pain.

Then, later, coverage of her injury created a hollow mausoleum of a life, complete with the vast, prolonged funeral held publicly for her career. Pictures of little Asian girls setting flowers outside the New York ballet graced the cover of every magazine. Eilidh Wren, who had once been everything to her community, was gone! What a waste, a life cut short, the It Girl who would eventually succumb to her own personal tragedy, as though the goddess Athena had struck Eilidh Wren down for the crime of being too beautiful, too talented, too young.

Of course, Eilidh wasn't *actually* dead. She was a respected employee at her father's company, clocking in her nine-to-five like everyone else, which was incalculably worse. If only she'd died! The only thing more virtuous than an ingenue was a dead ingenue, which was something like a saint. Rest in peace.

The reality of the House of Wren, as the *Times* article would have concluded had it actually made it to press, was that despite boasting a family of prodigies, Thayer Wren had raised a trio of sad, underperforming adults who'd peaked too soon. Thayer Wren himself was no different—a difficult, curmudgeonly man who personified toxic work environments and had, in recent times, fallen prey to the trap of his own invention. Toward the end of his life, Thayer's legacy was compromised by the trials of his own desire to be seen, a cautionary tale about the narcissism of a man self-consciously bereft of equals; who simply believed it when his yes-men told him he was singular, unmatched. There was a lawsuit currently being compiled against him, rumors of employee abuse, whispers of sexual misconduct. It was said that his own board was soon to turn against him; that the future of Wrenfare Magitech was unclear. The most valuable thing Thayer owned—not technical expertise, which had been Marike Fransson's, or financial brilliance, which had been Merritt Foster's, or the right connections, which had been his wife Persephone's, but Thayer's own singular innovation, his once clear-eyed drive to create—was being widely and publicly questioned. Perhaps he had only gotten this far by taking advantage of the genius of others? His rise came on the backs of laxer labor laws; of early business partners and smarter collaborators who'd been quietly passed over; of a monied wife who'd died before anyone could openly question what she'd contributed to her husband's success; of a public led to believe that eccentricity could only mean genius; of an era less scrutinizing of men who looked and spoke like Thayer Wren.

What would it mean, then, for his children, for his progeny and his creations, for the consumer-driven world that he himself had helped create? What would happen to Wrenfare, and to the very society Wrenfare had built—and which of the Wren children, if any, could be left with the task of seeing it through?

Moments before his last unassisted breath—while sitting alone in his ceremonial office, burning the midnight oil as he had not been accustomed to doing for decades by then—Thayer Wren typed into his favorite microblogging site a single sentence and hit post: *I've learned to expect the least out of the people I thought the highest of.* A fitting end, thought the *Times* reporter, to a story about the falseness of perfection and the disappointment inherent in its pursuit. About what happens when a bright star—and the promise of the stars his own light produced—invariably burns out.

But then, of course, Thayer Wren fucking died—he had a stroke later that night and was declared dead by Monday morning, not that his children could be bothered to pick up the phone—and there was no way the *Times* could publish something so incisive. It would seem insensitive, and journalism had enough problems as it was. The article was pulled, and in its place ran a simpler, less abrasive headline:

FOUNDER OF MODERN MAGITECH THAYER WREN HAS DIED.

Anyway, back to the subject of magic. Does it exist, you ask? Of course it does, or how else to explain Wrenfare's operational system, which is otherwise unfathomable at this scale?

Okay, but does it *exist,* you may reasonably press me, and that answer is—perhaps this is a surprise to you?—an additional, unequivocal yes. Magic, as in the stuff of fairy tales—the stuff that individual people can access, which is both the same as and different from the stuff keeping Wrenfare's neural network alive—isn't *not* real. The majority of the world may believe so, but there are lots of things in which the world believes (the American dream, the efficacy of dieting, the concept of fairness) that aren't necessarily the whole truth.

You do understand that magic can be much more than just a technical network of communication and energy, right? The line between magic and science is fuzzy to begin with—ask any physicist—but even so, instinctively you know that something out there is far more lawless; you feel it in your bones. Take it from your lola who's at least half-psychic, for example, or your abuela who dabbles in curses. Magic, real magic, is much more fluid than capital or industry, and it's also bound by far fewer rules.

Just because the majority of the world doesn't produce magic doesn't mean it doesn't exist. And just because magic *can* sit still and listen doesn't mean it always chooses to. Truthfully, there are so many different, equally plausible pathways to magic's effects that it would be impossible to sit here and list the myriad ways an individual could conceivably bend it to their will. Can magic securely deliver a document in less than the time it takes to lose your train of thought? Of course. Can magic be used to pick a lock in someone's mind, reshaping the train of *their* thoughts? With the right set of talents, absolutely. Can magic spontaneously create an electrical charge that resembles a miniaturized bolt of lightning? If you've got a weird form of the yips, why not.

Can magic belong to something larger than ourselves, a network of something bigger than this earth, more vast and more ineffable than energy, something called upon as if it were, say, a demon, or nature herself? Yes, yes, and yes. Technically, magic is unbounded, and if we cannot name every creature in the sea, then we cannot determine with certainty who was individually responsible for the ten plagues of Egypt we all learned about in Sunday school (or from a beautifully scored work of animation, pending the devoutness of your parents). Nor do we technically know for sure that there were only ten, because things do get lost in translation.

So, to sum up, magic—as Magic—can be monetized, militarized, and/or mass-produced electromagnetic energy. As far as the world knows, it can end there, as something to drive capital and disrupt the system within which we've learned to coexist. But to those fashionably in the know, magic can also be called upon in variable forms by any knowledgeable practitioner (and quite possibly also a secret third thing, known only to Moses, King Ramses II, and Eilidh Wren).

The point is: Magic has existed in various shades throughout history, alternately called by names like technology or witchcraft or shamanism, depending on who authors the story—but I, of course, am the God writing this one, and I choose to call it what it is.

As to the question of which Wren deserves to reign, magic is not and has never cared about the answer. It has loftier goals, bigger problems. For the purposes of the story, though, let's say hypothetically that it matters; that within every discussion of magic there is an inherent question of worthiness, and of worth itself. If Wrenfare is glory and glory is Eden, it's hardly my place to decide which asshole stays. I'm but a mere voice of God—I neither play favorites nor offer condemnation.

Nor do I need to. By the time their father's death irreversibly changes the trajectory of all three lives, it's pretty clear they've all equally fucked themselves.

# Meredith, Five Years Ago

A quiet conference room, gray walls, the thrum of a solemn air conditioner. An interviewer with a clipboard, a patient with an appointment.

The scrawl of notes taken in the margin of a standard introductory question. "How would you describe your moods prior to using Chirp?"

The anxious shuffle of a tepid response. "Um. Well. I'm pretty, you know, anxious. And I have panic attacks sometimes and stuff. And, like, problems with depression sometimes. Not like, you know, suicidal or anything." Quickly, defensively: "I just get depressed and stuff."

"Understood," said the interviewer—reassuringly, pacifyingly. Clinical ambivalence. "And how have you been feeling since you started using Chirp?"

"Um . . . better, I guess?" The patient, 76A—Colette Bothe to someone looking at her confidential file, though more importantly, Patient 76A—bit her lip. "Sort of? I mean . . . is it supposed to work right away? I don't totally understand. Like, to be honest, I really did this for the money." A sheepish, humorless laugh.

The interviewer's eyes cut briefly up from his file before he answered with a carefully rehearsed, "Chirp is a biomantic monitor, comparable to an insulin monitor for diabetics. Not to get too technical, but when your brain chemistry shifts, Chirp administers the appropriate counteracting chemicals, not unlike selective serotonin reuptake inhibitors, or SSRIs. But pharmaceuticals of the past are no more effective than trial and error. Now, instead of taking antidepressants or antipsychotics that only serve as Band-Aids for your neurological condition, Chirp administers exactly what you need to manage your brain chemistry, as well as learning your tendencies over time and adjusting its reactivity to make you feel better."

"Oh. Well, yeah, I do feel—" Patient 76A shifted in her chair. "Better, I guess."

The interviewer's eyes shot up from the clipboard again, his pen pausing above the file. "Can you explain that further?"

Patient 76A shrugged. "I was on antidepressants before, and I guess it feels the same. Ish."

"Fuck," announced Meredith from the small observation room behind the one-way mirror. "*Ish?* What the fuck is *ish?*"

"Well, I have your chart here," said the interviewer. "Thank you for filling it out, by the way. So, before we began your trial with Chirp, during the weeks you spent unmedicated, your average mood score was about a five, with dips here and there and some better days as well. And for the month since you began using Chirp, your mood score is an average of six."

"Yeah, I mean, it's . . . better." Patient 76A began pulling the loose skin at her elbow. "But I thought I was supposed to be happy?"

"You're damn right you're supposed to be happy," snapped Meredith.

"Relax," said Ward, who stood beside her scrolling his Wrenfare phone. Meredith felt a surge of unspecific loathing.

"Fuck you," she said, glancing at the clock before cutting another scowl at Ward Varela, her chief technology officer. "Why aren't you freaking out? This is the twenty-fifth patient we've seen today showing no sign of significant improvement."

Ward shrugged without looking up. "It takes time, that's all. And anyway, it's working, isn't it?"

"Barely. That increase could be purely circumstantial. What if she got a better job or just bought a new vibrator? *Fuck,*" was Meredith's economical summation. "We need a wow factor. We need *life-changing.* We need *can't live without it.* Tyche isn't going to be impressed that they threw us ten billion dollars and we responded with 'better-*ish,*'" she concluded with venom.

"Haters gon' hate," said Ward louchely. He was over ten years Meredith's senior and yet occasionally, talking to him was like ministering to the teenager in the back of the classroom, begging them fruitlessly to care about the quadratic formula or their own civil rights.

"This should have been an easy one," said Meredith, more to herself than to him. "It's just clinical depression, for fuck's sake. It's not like it's bipolar or schizophrenia. This should be like pushing a goddamn button."

"So should the female orgasm," said Ward, "and yet."

To that, Meredith spared him a glare.

"Meredith, this is just the first round of product testing." Ward gave her a meaningful arch of his brow. "You can't actually expect to heal the human condition overnight."

"That is *literally* what Foster expects me to do," Meredith hissed. "Our whole valuation is riding on this." She started to pace the small room, feeling the walls gaining ground on the breadth of her panic. "If Tyche doesn't get the numbers they want, they'll bail. They'll *bail.*"

"Sure, and that sucks," acknowledged Ward with the air of an incoming lecture. "If Tyche bails, then your dad leaves another annoying I-told-you-so voicemail, some tech bloggers nobody's ever heard of do some think pieces ravaging your reputation, and in a few years, you try again with a better product, something that actually works—"

"*This* product works!" snapped Meredith. "This is my fucking *life's work*, Ward—"

"Mer, come on. Those are two different things—"

"I dropped out of Harvard for this. I signed with *Kip Hughes* for this." She shuddered and rounded on him. "Don't you get it? I gambled *everything* on this—"

"Harvard is a dinosaur," Ward interjected with a shrug. "Their biomancy program is nothing compared to the one at Xiamen."

Briefly, the image of Ward choking to death in a pool of his own blood floated uncharitably across the forefront of Meredith's mind. Followed by the possibility of strangling him.

Then, finally, something useful appeared. An idea, half-formed. The holy glow of revelation. Epiphany! Something no less criminal than killing her business partner, but certainly more useful. Something that wouldn't cost her a billion—*ten* billion—dollars. Something that would make all of this worthwhile.

Empowered, desperate, and doomed from the moment the light turned on, Meredith turned to the observation room's door.

"Mer," said Ward, leaping to block her first step the moment he caught the glint of mania on her face. "No. Mer."

"Move," said Meredith.

"Meredith, listen to me, *look me in the eyes.* Whatever you're thinking of doing—"

"Edward," Meredith coolly replied, "if you don't get out of the way, I'm going through you."

"Meredith. Please." Ward's voice reached a rare edge of panic. "What are you going to do? You can't interfere with the clinical process. It's unethical. It's . . . it's fucking *illegal*," he spluttered, "and it's the first step to felony fraud."

"I can fix it," she said simply. He wouldn't understand, but why should he? For better or worse, she was the one branded for life by the letters CEO.

"How?" demanded Ward. "What are you going to do, falsify the results? Threaten the patient? Either way, you'd go to prison, we'd lose everything—"

"Why? Are you planning to turn me in?" she asked him.

"I—" He balked at her, then seemed to switch tack, appealing desperately to her logic. "Meredith. You know you can't interfere."

"The whole point was always to interfere, Ward. It was always the plan to intervene, specifically to make things *better*. Which I can't do," she gritted out, "if these tests aren't *meaningfully* conclusive."

"Meredith—"

"Do you want to move out of your parents' basement, Ward?"

"Just *think* about what you're doing—"

"My father founded Wrenfare on a hunch, with no concrete proof that he could bring any of it to market, with everyone in the industry claiming that kind of deep learning was impossible. You really think he was worried about ethics?"

"A human being is not an *operational system*—"

"They sure aren't, Ward, and that's the goddamn point. The whole world changed because some guy said 'Fuck the rules, I have faith in this,' and now I'm saying it. I'm saying it because I know I can make this woman's life better. I *know* it." She felt her expression sour. "Do you not have faith in me? In what we built?"

"Of course I do, *obviously* I do—"

"Then get out of the way, Ward."

He gave her a pained look. But there was a reason she'd plucked him from obscurity. There was a reason he'd failed and failed and failed before, and only Meredith had gotten him here. He knew his role, and he knew hers.

"Don't be stupid, that's all I'm saying," Ward managed eventually, proving her right.

"Move," replied Meredith.

Ward stared at her a moment.

Then he let out a breath and took one step to his left.

By then, Meredith's heart was pounding in her chest. She took a step, then another, heading straight for the door.

"Cut the camera," she said as she passed, leaving Ward to suppress a grimace.

"Meredith, I am not your fucking *henchman*—"

"No, but you're an accomplice now, Edward, so wise up," she called over her shoulder, just before the door slammed shut. Her heels clipped into the linoleum hallway, echoing down the corridor until she reached the conference room.

She took a deep breath, then shoved open the door.

"Hi," she said to the interviewer, who looked up with a startled glance. "Sorry, there's just been a call for you from the front desk. Something about a family emergency."

"Oh god, is my wife in labor?" asked the interviewer.

"Yes," said Meredith Wren, without hesitation.

"Oh Jesus, okay, I just have t—" He glanced apologetically at Patient 76A, who looked confused. "We'll have to reschedule and continue this later, I'm so sorry—"

"I'll take over," said Meredith, placing a reassuring hand on the interviewer's shoulder. "They sent me in to finish your interview."

"Right, okay, great—sorry, your name?" asked the interviewer. "Just, you know, in case they ask—"

"It's Eilidh," said Meredith.

"Haley?"

"Just get going, would you?" suggested Meredith, forcing a casual colleague's unbothered laugh. "I doubt your wife intends to hold it in until you arrive."

"Right, right, sorry—"

"Just leave the files, it's fine—"

"Right, yes, thank you!" The interviewer hurried out the door.

Meredith took a seat in his place, looking up to scrutinize the face of Patient 76A. Colette Bothe. She had lovely, dead eyes.

"Listen to me," said Meredith, in her most quiet, calming voice. The one she had once used to soothe her mother, and occasionally her brother, and in times of real fuckery, herself. "Everything is about to change, okay? All that emptiness you feel, all the worthlessness . . . it's a lie," said Meredith softly. "It's a lie your brain is telling you. You don't have to take it anymore. You don't have to feel this way anymore."

Patient 76A looked at her with skittish uncertainty. She didn't believe

Meredith, but she didn't have to, not yet. All she had to do was sustain eye contact for several seconds. Five more, maybe. Maybe ten, just to be sure.

All the training. Boarding school from the age of twelve so Meredith could compete with the very best. The exclusive summer camps, the private tutoring, the people she'd been forced to gut from her life, the perfection she was made to chase. All those years of fucking tennis, day in and day out, just so that she could hold it longer, endure it worse, survive it more. She hadn't suffered just for fear of obsolescence or the goddamn economy.

It was always, always for this.

Meredith reached for Patient 76A's hands, grasping them tightly. The patient was too startled to pull away. Overhead, the red light blinked out. Somewhere on the other side of the glass, Ward had figured out the security monitor.

All those years of being a prodigy. A baby genius. The future of magitech personified had spent most of her twenties proverbially on her knees. If this didn't work, she wouldn't be anything anymore, nothing worth looking at. She'd just be another girl who grew up, who got old. A college dropout. She'd been working on the same project so long her hair had started turning gray, lines were starting to show on her face, she was constantly aware of a knot in her back. Her father had let her down and she had betrayed him. Her best friend was gone, excised for life. When Meredith fell in love it had to be forever, so now what? Where did it end?

A drop of sweat snaked down Meredith's spine.

"You're going to be happy," whispered Meredith, locking eyes with Patient 76A and speaking as deliberately, as persuasively, as unbendingly as she knew how. "I promise."

A vision of Jamie standing in the doorway swam briefly before her eyes. She was out of practice. Normally she could keep him at bay for longer.

A little longer. Just a little longer. *All you have to do,* the young, eternal version of Lou whispered in Meredith's mind, *is really, actually want it.*

There. There it was, just a little fix, like flipping a switch. Like pushing a button.

When Patient 76A finally blinked, there were tears in her eyes.

"Is this what I've been waiting for?" she whispered.

Ten minutes later, Patient 76A had gathered her things, broken up with her boyfriend, enrolled in a calligraphy class, ordered Chipotle from her phone, and decided to finally paint her bedroom yellow. Colette Bothe was happy.

And Meredith Wren sat back in her chair, the drop of sweat on her spine seeping into the silk of her shirt.

"Send in the next one," she said to the empty room.

And from somewhere on the other side of the glass, Ward did.

# MONDAY

(After).

# 7

"Oh please," said Meredith Wren upon hearing the news that her father had passed. "That son of a bitch will outlive us all."

"Meredith," Cass said with a barely audible sigh, adjusting his glasses on the bridge of his nose. "I'm sorry. Your father had a stroke. I'm sorry," he said again.

It was a touch robotic, as Cass sometimes had the tendency to be. He wasn't emotionally unintelligent, per se; he just occasionally lacked the energy to reach whatever octave of compassion he was being asked to deliver. It had evidently been a problem for his first wife, who was a more emotional person—excessively emotional, to Meredith's mind—in that she wanted Cass to not only predict her moods but also offer comfort for them preemptively, without being asked. Which was an expectation that Cass did not consider unreasonable in retrospect, mature grown adult that he was, although Meredith was not like that at all.

The erstwhile Mrs. Mizuno was now an executive somewhere. Meredith had looked her up extensively on every platform she could find, reassuring herself that her transition to dating divorced men was not, as people liked to think, akin to picking through damaged merchandise but rather more like determining whether secondhand vintage might fit her better than the sale bin, with its overstocked, mass-produced garbage she was otherwise expected to buy, and thus she had discovered that Tatiana Shea-Mizuno was actually brilliant and beautiful and there had been no infidelity, just the gradual growing apart of two people who had met when they were both in their teens, which made all of this not only fine but honestly kind of admirable.

Of course, Meredith's father did not care for Cass, nor even the idea of Cass, but now he was dead, which meant he would never walk Meredith down the aisle whether she sorted through the bins or not, and therefore his opinion either no longer mattered or it never had. Or, more favorably, both.

"Meredith." It was only when Jamie said her name that Meredith realized she had been silent for several minutes, which was too long for something like this. She was meant to have responded immediately, with tears or shock or grief or howling or some other thing she was never going to produce, not ever, because her mother had been dead for years and now her father was dead and he had never taught her how to react appropriately to death in general. And now, probably, nobody ever would, because she was thirty years old and expected to already understand how to respond to normal social situations, such as being told one's parents were dead. Dead dead dead. She kept saying it in her head; measuring it, almost. She wondered if Thayer Wren was somewhere in the underworld right now, his heart on a scale beside an ostrich feather. Where was he bound for, heaven or hell? Or maybe death was just nothing, a quiet sigh before returning to the earth. She wondered what would become of her father. She wondered what would become of her father's money. His board of investors. His legacy. His company.

"I'm fine," she said to Jamie, whose expression bore traces of concern. Then she turned to Cass. "When did it happen?" Ridiculous question. What would knowing that change. "Never mi—"

"This morning," said Cass. "He was taken to the hospital after a stroke late last night."

"Oh." She thought fleetingly of the calls she'd missed. "Does my brother know?"

"I didn't ask," Cass replied.

"Okay. I'll have to call Arthur." And Eilidh, although Meredith felt certain she already knew. Eilidh was probably at Thayer's bedside right now, performing the rituals of grief that Meredith was once again failing to produce on account of her profound lack of fucks. God! Thayer had probably already promised the whole company to Eilidh, his entire fortune, the beloved fucking house, the ratty shearling Birkenstocks. Because unlike Meredith—to whom Thayer Wren had always said there were no such things as setbacks, only ill preparation, and the only excuse for mediocrity was laziness, and that Meredith was a cold-hearted person who was not actually capable of love—Eilidh had only ever heard from their father that love and happiness were the important things in life, that success was purely a state of mind, and that ultimately, loyalty was everything. As if Meredith had ever been anything but loyal to him! You know, until she wasn't. But Thayer's disappointment in her had begun somewhere else, somewhere long before Foster had asked to talk and she'd said yes. It began somewhere inside her, in something she already was and had always been. As if by choosing to be ruled by some velocity inside herself she was somehow a worse daughter, *less virtuous* than her younger sister. As if it were inherently disloyal to want precisely what Thayer would have demanded for himself. As if Meredith—as a person with ambitions and plans and all the things Thayer had wanted his son to have, only to overlook those same similarities in his eldest daughter—had *betrayed* him by not remaining devotedly at his side, practically his personal maidservant, and had instead done what children are supposed to do and grown up.

"I'm fine," Meredith said again to Jamie, who was still looking at her with that strange expression on his face. It wasn't pity, thank god. Jamie out of everyone would understand this moment was not one for pity. He knew how she felt about her father, or had known it once, intimately enough to be aware that Thayer's death was not something for Meredith to uncomplicatedly mourn. Not that it was something to celebrate, but the loss of Thayer Wren would not, for Meredith, be cause for any normal, comprehensible sadness. It would not have been inaccurate to use the word "estranged." Not that Jamie would know that, but he would know she'd sold out to the man she had once considered the world's most conscienceless traitor. Jamie would know that Meredith was not now, where she stood, next in line for the Wrenfare throne. Jamie would know what it meant that her path had diverged so spectacularly from everything she'd once confided in him about her wildest dreams and her most precious future, and therefore he would know something. She felt sure he knew something, and the look on his face said just that, I know.

"I know," said Jamie in a tone that matched the expression on his face, at the same time Cass said, "Dzhuliya booked us plane tickets for this afternoon. Our flight leaves in three hours."

"I'm still talking to Jamie," said Meredith, before realizing what Cass had just said. "Wait, who's Julia? Why are you coming?"

"Dzhuliya," Cass enunciated, scrawling the silent letters out in the air, "is your father's assistant, whom we have both met several times in the past. And I'm coming because your father just died," he added matter-of-factly.

Meredith frowned. "But you have a board meeting this week."

"I can work remotely."

"But it's just my father."

"Yes," Cass agreed. "And to my knowledge you only have one of those."

For a moment Meredith stared at him, aware in some objective way that she was meant to find this commendable. That in periods of difficulty, people who were boyfriend-girlfriend supported each other with physical touch and words of affirmation and quality time. She just couldn't bring herself to understand that the people in this scenario were her and Cass, two people who did not engage the performative social tendency to fuss. They got on with their lives. Meredith had lost her mother at nine years old and gotten on with it. Cass had lost his wife at thirty and gotten on with it. Meredith could not imagine a world where she was expected to need comfort in this moment, although she recalled that there would be lots to do, logistically speaking, and therefore maybe Cass would be useful. He was very good at logistics. He had lovely mahogany hair that had, for the most part, bravely withstood the test of time. He was extremely handsome and, to her knowledge, faithful. He was a steady, reliable, attractive partner who could make incredibly decent dinner conversation. She enjoyed him. Sexually he was no slouch. It wasn't as if his wife had left because he was in any way inept at foreplay. Meredith loved him. She loved him.

She just didn't really want to be close to him right now.

"I'm going to drive," said Meredith suddenly. The thought overtook her like a vise.

"Are you sure?" said Cass mildly. It was at least a six-hour drive to her father's house in Marin. Maybe five with the way she drove.

"Yes. I need the time to be with my thoughts." She noticed that Jamie wasn't saying anything. "You take the flight, though," she added to Cass. "If I leave now, I should arrive at around the same time."

"I've got to run home and pack if I'm going to make it to the airport on time." Cass's eyes slid to Jamie and back to Meredith. "Would you like me to bring a few things for you?"

"Whatever's in my drawer at yours," she said, thinking it was a little light at present. But there would be pajamas, a pair of sweats, her toothbrush in the sink, most of her necessary cosmetics and skincare, carefully partitioned in travel-sized jars. She would have to buy a new dress for the funeral anyway. Everything she needed she could buy. That had always been the way of things, and what was the point of pretending otherwise now?

"Okay. I'll go, then." Cass cut a glance at Jamie, who was standing very still, as if not to startle a predator among the high savanna grass. "Let me know if you need anything," Cass said finally to Meredith, who nodded.

Then Cass pulled open the conference room door and stepped outside, his footsteps echoing down the hallway until the door fell shut once again.

"Meredith," said Jamie, with what seemed to be the intention to say something soothing. "Do you want to talk about it?"

"What's to talk about?" she replied in a clipped voice, resolving the expression that had previously been on her face—she wasn't entirely sure what it was, only that it would not be effective in remedying the situation—and proceeding to withdraw from her wardrobe of identities one that was slightly softer, or at very least more persuasive. "I assume you're going to pull that article, Jamie, considering the news. It would be in extremely poor taste."

Jamie blinked at her for a moment.

Then, very upsettingly, he laughed.

"Meredith," he said with a roll of his eyes, "I'm not pulling the article."

Instantly, she felt her more placating expression fall away. "What?"

"I'm sorry you lost your father," Jamie said with a shrug, "but even I can see the gears turning in your head. You think this will buy you time, but it won't. I told you, I'm going to press with the story, full stop. My telling you about it was only a matter of fair warning, as an ethical matter."

"Ethical matter? I can't decide if you're aware how stupid you sound. What if I'd hired someone to get rid of you, Jamie, hm? What if I decided to blackmail your publisher? Which is something I could absolutely do," Meredith realized abruptly. "I could hire someone right now," she announced as her phone buzzed again in her hand, her watch screen now lighting up with the name of her sister-in-law, Arthur's wife, Gillian. "You wouldn't even make it outside the building if I decided that would be less of a mess. Hello?" she said into the phone.

"Are you threatening to put out a hit on me?" asked Jamie. "To my actual face?"

"Meredith, have you heard? I'm just checking that someone was able to reach you," said Gillian.

"I'm not threatening you," Meredith said to Jamie. "I just think you obviously wanted to tell me for some reason other than 'fair warning,' because Tyche has way too much money for you to believe I can't physically stop you from going to print. And yes, Gill, I just heard, Cass told me."

"Arthur's on his way back now," said Gillian.

"What else would I want from you, Meredith?" sighed Jamie.

"Where's he coming back from?" Meredith asked Gillian before looking plainly at Jamie and replying, "How should I know? Maybe you want me to stop you. Maybe you want me to forgive you. Maybe you want sex, I don't know, how am I supposed to guess? It could be literally anything, Jamie, I just think nobility is too weak an excuse."

"I believe Arthur was at a sex party in London," said Gillian.

"Another one?" said Meredith.

"I'm not trying to have *sex with you*, Meredith," scoffed Jamie, with an uncharitable note of repulsion. "I've been working on this story for six months. And even if this was some kind of diabolical seductory ploy, how would threatening your livelihood have worked?"

"It's actually a lot more than my livelihood, and you know it," snapped Meredith as Gillian explained that yes, it was Lady Philippa again, Arthur seemed very taken with her (Meredith, for her part, was largely unimpressed with aristocracy, as she had always lacked her father's burning desire for knighthood or whatever Thayer had expected to receive from the hoity-toity set) and Yves Reza the racer as well, a combination that to Gillian seemed apt.

"I have frankly always had my suspicions that the best kind of lover for Arthur was multiple lovers," explained Gillian. "His ideal form of intimacy is lots of it, simultaneously."

"God, I'm going to have a panic attack just thinking about it," said Meredith, shuddering.

"Look, at least this way you'll get the chance to put your affairs in order," said Jamie. "You won't be caught by surprise. You can engage a lawyer and prepare a public statement. You can do what you can to soften the blow."

"How do you even know I'm guilty?" demanded Meredith.

"Aside from the fact that you just threatened to have me assassinated?" countered Jamie.

"Oh please, this hardly rises to the level of assassination," said Meredith.

"I think it was just a stroke," commented Gillian, then added tangentially, "I don't suppose you have a theory about who gets Wrenfare, do you?"

"Yes, but I'm trying not to think about it," muttered Meredith, by then exceedingly capable of envisioning Eilidh's inevitable facade of virtuous shock at discovering, as if for the first time, that she had always been their father's first choice. Almost without noticing, Meredith had curled a fist. "Hard to tell where favoritism ends and narcissism begins, though. Arthur looks the most like him physically. And contingency plans for a ceramic bust will almost certainly be involved."

"In any case—" Gillian diplomatically sidestepped Meredith's sardonicism, as she often did, with, "You'll need to be here soon. Be careful—everything you do over the next few hours is going to be scrutinized by the press," she pointed out, and sighed, half to herself. "I wish Art didn't have such catastrophic timing. He'll be papped for sure, if not at Heathrow then definitely at SFO. Though maybe it's not such a bad thing? Grief and hangover might look similar on Art."

"You're right," said Meredith, realizing belatedly that optics were becoming more critical with each moment that passed. Gillian was much better about this sort of thing, but of course Meredith would be watched from the moment she left this conference room. People still lingered in the building from her talk, which meant a high probability she could be photographed. Had the news already gone to the press? Probably, since the first call she'd ignored from Dzhuliya (was that really her name?) had been hours ago now. "I'm going to have to get a car—fuck, I should have asked Cass for his." Tyche's campus was in the heart of Silicon Beach, lushly centered in Playa Vista, and Cass's commute from the Marina was minimal—he could have easily taken one of Tyche's employee shuttles. "Can I have one delivered?"

"Oh, I don't know," said Gillian, "we really try to avoid cars. The environment, you know."

Meredith rolled her eyes. "Arthur's on a plane, Gill, he's already a climate criminal—"

"Meredith," said Jamie with an expression of exasperation on his face. "You live in LA and you don't have a car?"

"I'm hardly ever home, Jamie," she told him impatiently. "In case you've failed to notice, I'm very busy and important."

"Then why did you decide to—? Never mind." Jamie seemed to find her impossible to reason with at the moment. "No, you cannot order a rental car. You'll have to go to a facility like all the other plebs."

Meredith squinted at him. "I don't believe you," she said finally, "since I'm almost certain that's got to be false. But also, you're right, it would probably be better if I handled this more relatably."

"Good thinking," confirmed Gillian.

"There's not a chance that anything you've done thus far could be considered relatable," said Jamie.

"I've got to go, Gill," said Meredith. "I'll see you soon."

"Kisses," said Gillian before promptly hanging up. She was extremely efficient. Despite Meredith's grand plans to dislike any woman who chose to devote herself to her brother, Meredith had always quietly been a fan.

Jamie, meanwhile, was messing around on his phone.

"Look, here's the closest place you could get a car," he said, showing her Playa Vista's finest backwoods outpost. "You can probably still catch your boyfriend for a ride, or get a car to drop you off there now—"

"Oh, you're coming with me," said Meredith on a whim, pulling the conference room door open and letting it fall shut again without bothering to check if Jamie was following. "We're not done discussing this."

"Meredith." She heard the telltale sound of him chasing after her and suppressed the urge to smile. Vengeful joy would really not be ideal if captured on film, given the number of times she'd already been referred to as a traitor. "Meredith, there's nothing left to say."

"Don't you want my side of the story?" she asked Jamie, glancing sideways at him. "Seems like your article will have a much better shot at national acclaim if you actually consult the source."

For a moment—a breath—he faltered, and she won herself another point.

"Meredith," Jamie managed impressively, with a scoff, "I really don't think your side of the story is relevant unless you're planning to confess to—"

"Jamie." Meredith fell to a halt, turning to look at him. He paused, too, seemingly caught off guard. She realized in the light of the corridor that he wasn't exactly the same, though the difference was in the little details, the small things. She had previously been the one to shave the hair on the back of his neck to keep it from looking overgrown, which it had a tendency to be, considering they'd been libertine university students at the time. Now, it seemed quite noticeable to Meredith that it had been a long while since his last proper haircut. "Why did you come to see me tonight?"

She caught a moment's hesitation, a glimpse of truth that danced across Jamie's thoughts. Despite his insistence that she had a tell, he was no different. She'd always liked that she could read him so plainly, while everyone else was such a chore to interpret. She was constantly behaving like a person who didn't actually speak English—listening, translating, thinking, then translating again to try to say something back in a language the other person understood. Exhausting. More often than not she disregarded the effort altogether, just as she did now.

Beside her in the corridor, a neat row of digital screens chased a loop of company advertisements, sunset scenes of Playa Vista, popular mantras by

Kip Hughes. A brief, neon flash promised THIS APP WILL MAKE YOU HAPPY! :), and Meredith didn't flinch.

"I'll save you the trouble of telling me the truth," she told him, with something she considered gentleness, although it probably sounded like the normal resoluteness of her voice. "Instead, I'll put it to you this way. Come with me to my father's house or I might kill you." She shrugged. "Might just wipe your devices and cancel the storage payments to your preferred avenue in the cloud. The point is," she concluded, "you'll never know for sure what I am or am not capable of doing to you until you're already too late to stop me."

His eyes flickered with something. Flatteringly it could have been respect. Less flatteringly, an eye roll. "Is that how much this means to you?"

"Did you ever have any doubt that it did?" she said without hesitation.

They stared at each other a moment longer.

"I know there's a reason," said Jamie, a little side shuffle to a previous unanswered question, proffered candor in exchange for something she wasn't yet confident she wouldn't give. "I want to know what it is. But you're not going to be able to stop me from publishing the truth, Meredith."

"I know." Lies, she was lying. She could stop him. She knew it, and he knew it, too, but it was a double-edged sword, that, because once she used it, she proved him right. The look on his face seemed a challenge, a gauntlet thrown, and a more sympathetic part of her thought it might be a form of self-harm, in its way. Like anyone who texted an ex or investigated them for fraud, apparently to the point of hyperfixation.

But surely there was another way. She felt sure she could convince him otherwise, via the preferable route of rational thought, if she could just get him alone for a while. There was no way she was letting the article go to print. She had no idea what it contained, only that if anyone else ever saw its contents, then Chirp would be nothing. The last decade of her life would be wasted. Even if Jamie knew enough about Tyche to bring them down—which she already doubted, or she wouldn't be in this deep; for better or worse, she was the daughter of Thayer Wren, and she knew what a man like Kip Hughes could cover up—*her* hands were by far the dirtiest. She was an accomplice—worse, a weapon—and would almost certainly go to prison for her crimes.

Meredith Wren, most likely to succeed—what would they say about her then? If anyone knew what she'd done to get here, they'd burn her for a witch, metaphorically if not actually. She was halfway to obscurity already.

What came after 30 Under 30? What happened when she was no longer a prodigy, just a liar? A traitor? A fraud? Time would not be kind to her, and neither would anyone else.

"No," Thayer had said to Meredith once, unequivocally. "No, you can't have Wrenfare. I told you to stay in school. I told you that if you got your degree, there would be space for you here—eventually."

"But *you* dropped out," protested Meredith. "*You* had an idea, and so do I—"

"I dropped out because the timing was right for me to move forward on something I already knew to be profitable. Your 'idea' is insubstantial at best," said Thayer. "And if you want people to follow you, you have to build a team. You have to earn respect. You can't just have things handed to you."

Lou hadn't been there—Lou was long gone by then—but Meredith already knew what she would say. *Just get over it, Meredith. Grow up.*

So Meredith had done it. She grew up. She built the team. She earned the respect. No one had handed her anything. She'd made all the choices, climbed every step of the way by herself. She had built all of this with her own two hands, her own blood and sweat. It was hers, and she had lost Jamie Ammar once already. She could do it again if that's what it took.

"Look, my dad just died," she said. "I want some company, that's all. And I want to know what you're publishing, because of course I do. Because I want a chance to tell my own story. Is that so unreasonable?"

Jamie was, had always been, a good person. She was banking on it, his goodness, because goodness was predictable. It was its own kind of trap.

"Okay," he said, which to Meredith Wren was like saying fuck me up, darling. And to that she thought yes, that sounds nice, I think I will.

# 8

There was a collective breath of relief when Eilidh's plane finally touched down. Everyone applauded, which was a silly ritual at the best of times that now seemed underwhelming.

"We'll be taxiing to the nearest gate," said the flight attendant calmly over the speakers, "as we will require some . . . immediate maintenance."

She was referring, most likely, to the carcasses of locusts that were now plastered to the full exterior of the plane, having been sucked into the engines and spat back out again, or whatever happened when a machine flew into a visibility-obscuring swarm of insects. As far as plagues went, it could have been worse. There were no crops to destroy at forty thousand feet, though Eilidh shuddered to think what might have happened below them. In any case, the world was still standing.

Inside her chest, the thing that lived there slumped down in woozy contentedness, as if unzipping its pants after a meal.

Eilidh toggled airplane mode off on her phone, resuming the use of communication and waiting for anything new. A seizure-inducing flurry of notifications on her social apps, nothing immediately pertinent to her, mostly just an attempt to persuade her to interact with the world in a way that could be successfully monetized. An ad blinked across her screen for Chirp. THIS APP WILL MAKE YOU HAPPY! :)

Eilidh suppressed a grimace. Having recently traded her life for whatever came of the locusts, it seemed undignified to consider punching her sister's smug face, however briefly.

"I can't understate that this flight was an actual circle of hell," the weeping man (who was no longer weeping) was saying on the phone. "Like, literally, hell. I'm not sure what the signs of the apocalypse are but I'm very confident we witnessed at least three of them."

No, thought Eilidh, one was a normal traumatic event and the other was a plague. That was different from a full apocalypse foretelling. Thanks to the parasite, they did occasionally happen—Eilidh had been the source of an earthquake at least once over the course of her vesselhood for demon kind, though the extent of "apocalypse" versus the natural hazards of California residency remained largely indeterminate—but there had been no leveling of plains, no stars falling to earth, no sudden loss of language. She had obviously researched these things, for vocational reasons, after the first time she turned the sea red.

Although, again, Eilidh did not feel that she, personally, was making these things happen. That was the worst part, actually, and the thing she tried hardest to fight—the sense that she was not in control of these things at all. She couldn't make sense of sequence (none that she could determine, having reread the childhood Bible story of Moses and the Pharaoh quite literally hundreds of times) or escalation (arbitrary at best), or why certain internal sensations resulted in variable atmospheric ends. All she could do was submit or reject, and sometimes even rejection did not seem to matter. Whatever was causing this, it clearly had a mind of its own, and what seemed occasionally to be a morbid sense of humor.

Eilidh's phone did not process voicemails until after the bedraggled passengers began making their way off the plane, leaving nothing but distress in their wake. Twice Eilidh felt certain she'd heard a life-altering conversation, someone leaving his boyfriend and another promising her life to her ex. Eilidh imagined making a call to someone then herself, saying either that they belonged together or that, actually, what she really needed was freedom, she knew that now. But no, nothing life-changing came to mind.

There was, however, a missed call from Dzhuliya Aguilar, Eilidh's father's personal assistant—"Julia" to Thayer, who despite naming his own daughter Eilidh was unable to summon the energy for phonetic deadweight—and eventually the voicemail showed up. It didn't count as a call from an ex-lover, though it wasn't technically not.

"Call me back" was the extent of the message. Eilidh hit erase and dragged herself off the plane, breathing in the refreshing crispness of the evening San Francisco air.

It seemed utterly inconceivable now that she had done something as stupidly unnecessary as attend a silent retreat on the East Coast. She still maintained every intention to lie about how wonderful it had been—that much had not changed even in the face of her fragile mortality—but the temporary peace she'd been granted for her hours of wordless reflection had fizzled out and disappeared somewhere into the fullness of her bladder, her desperation for caffeine. She wished she had not checked a bag. Carousel five, the informative bulletin board told her. God, what if she actually *had* died? Then there would be no need to traverse the baggage claim. There would be no need to stand there and perform the usual rituals, holding her breath (proverbially) until her baggage finally appeared. What drudgery. She collected her bag, she was a bag lady now, her worldly possessions back within the radius of her control. For this she had chanced a doomsday. It made everything seem bleak, an unwelcome change from dire. How quickly the miracle of life could become stale.

"Eilidh!"

Eilidh blinked, startled to hear the sound of her name, and realized it was Dzhuliya standing expectantly in arrivals. Dzhuliya's dark hair, typically down and shoulder-grazing, was currently swept up in a high ponytail, her face its usual gloss of healthy, sun-kissed perfection, minus the stray instances of hormonal acne that occasionally cropped up around her chin—a reminder that perfection was largely implausible, albeit never out of the question. Dzhuliya was wearing an oversized sweatshirt, looking like the hot girl from the soccer movie Eilidh had watched twenty thousand times as a teen. No coincidence there, surely.

Eilidh had planned to order a car, but apparently her father had sent Dzhuliya to collect her. That was sweet.

"Oh, hi," said Eilidh, suddenly feeling a bit breathless, certainly no result of Dzhuliya's proximity—she was, if anything, a mere amicable colleague. New forms of drudgery manifested: conscientious avoidance of shop talk (everyone at Wrenfare was on edge these days, the whole office an ecosystem of excessive frequency and chattering teeth), awkward power differentials (Eilidh was, however impostorly, ranked above Dzhuliya in Wrenfare's corporate structure despite their similarity in age), the song and dance of small talk, the quiet tension between two people who had previously fooled around, the inevitable shifting of Dzhuliya's things from the passenger seat to the back seat so that Eilidh could find a place for her long useless legs. The cans of energy drinks likely littering the floor, protein bar wrappers that seemed to exist solely as evidence of how hard Dzhuliya Aguilar worked and how infrequently she had time to eat or rest, which naturally Eilidh would try to ignore, because to acknowledge it would be like admitting that capitalism was among the nightmares for which Eilidh was personally responsible. Well, maybe not responsible, but culpable, certainly. Without a doubt.

"You don't have to run errands for my dad off the clock," said Eilidh, ideally from a place of benevolent upper management (we're all family here!). "I could have easily gotten a car."

"Yes, um. I just thought you might want some company." Dzhuliya took a deep breath, preparing to deliver some piece of news, and then apparently changed her mind. "So, how was the flight?" she said in a tone of excessive warmth, like impersonating an older, matronly relative.

"Oh, I'm dead now," said Eilidh. "This is actually an unlikely paranormal event."

"Ha!" said Dzhuliya. "Ha! Ha!"

Weird, thought Eilidh. They weren't exactly friends, but neither were they usually this awkward. With the occasional—brief—highly singular—exceptions, amicability cut both ways.

"Have you heard from your sister?" Dzhuliya asked, a lingering sense of oddness to her voice. "Or your brother?"

"What, you mean since Christmas?" said Eilidh. "No. I'm pretty sure Meredith had one of her Tyche talks today." If only she could know that so casually, as if she'd been personally informed via sisterly check-in, and not because she was subscribed to media alerts for both her siblings. "And Arthur is on the campaign trail again." Campaign trail, ha. Given one guess, Eilidh felt sure Arthur was with Lady Philippa, the socialite Eilidh had clocked repeatedly in the background of Arthur's grid who seemed dangerously close to aging out of It Girl–hood. Philippa must know it, too, even if Arthur didn't (and everything about Arthur, good and bad, suggested he wouldn't). There was a raw desperation to the @LadyPVDM content these days, something approximating thirst, which was a hefty crime on the socials. One did not want to be a Try-Hard. It was worse than supporting terrorism, a bare step above hawking MLMs. Either Philippa's vault of blood diamonds had run dry or she could sense the looming shadow of replacement, chased down by some faceless new ingenue stepping in to play her role.

Eilidh disliked Philippa greatly, for reasons she tried not to understand.

"Ah. I see." Dzhuliya was uncharacteristically fidgety, and kept adjusting her posture, as if something was bothering her. Every motion shifted the sweatshirt over, revealing a glimpse of shoulder, smooth and kissed by summer sun.

Eilidh looked away, gripping the handle of her suitcase harder. In lieu of pursuing less amicable trains of thought, she wondered why they weren't doing something much more normal, like progressing to the short-term parking lot, though she felt saying so would be to assert some unearned form of dominance, throwing her weight around like the worst kind of person. OK boomer, Eilidh self-flagellatingly thought.

"Why didn't you just send a car, by the way?" she asked again, perhaps in the hopes that Dzhuliya would tell her she simply *loved* driving, that actually she had *begged* to come to the airport, it had been on her way home. (It wasn't. Dzhuliya lived somewhere in downtown San Francisco, one of the top ten most difficult places to get to in the world, in Eilidh's opinion. Dislike of city traffic was one of the rare arenas where she and Meredith agreed, because when they had both briefly lived in LA, Meredith had not crossed the 405 for anything less than a billion dollars. Eilidh herself had then lived on the wrong side of the 405, in the arts district of Culver City, which despite having some of the city's best restaurants and the entertainment headquarters for at least four tech companies was still a nightmare according to Meredith, who never once stopped by.) "I'm sure my dad didn't mean for you to *literally* collect me—"

"Eilidh." Dzhuliya's voice became slightly stern, and Eilidh compiled the mounting evidence to conclude that Dzhuliya was not as put together as she usually was. A certain level of dishevelment was characteristic to magitech—even at the best of times, everyone in tech occupied a shared wavelength of anxiety, never knowing until too late that the tide of benevolence had turned and a project's funding had been cut—but perhaps due to Dzhuliya's residency in Thayer's inner circle, where Eilidh also lived, Eilidh had always associated Dzhuliya with an inherent calmness, a degree of rationality typically suited to an older person, someone thirty or beyond. It was a quality that bordered on competency porn, assuming a person was not on their guard for amicability at all times.

In any case, Dzhuliya seemed very tired, and uncharacteristically stressed, albeit in the way people often did when the company they worked for had been rippling with rumors of layoffs for several months. She also seemed like her bra was causing her discomfort, which was a very specific thing to notice, meaning that Eilidh should clearly now look away.

"I have . . . some news," Dzhuliya said. "Some bad news."

Just then, Eilidh's phone rang with a call from Meredith, which seemed another apocalyptic sign. As if, by speaking the name of the devil, they had summoned her. The thing in Eilidh's chest lifted its head and Eilidh clamped it hastily back down. "Sorry, one second," said Eilidh, before hitting answer. "Hello?"

"Can you believe this motherfucker had the gall to just up and die?" said Meredith, speaking with such unexpected vigor that Eilidh wasn't confident she was catching every word. "God, I'm so annoyed I can hardly see. I don't mean it literally, Jamie, for fuck's sake," she added, ostensibly to someone else. "You act like you've never been in a car before. We were supposed to have had a final blowout, you know?" This was directed at Eilidh again, maybe. "You're supposed to achieve closure with your parents before they die."

"I . . . did you say Jamie?" asked Eilidh, who felt more puzzled by Meredith than usual, although Meredith was always impenetrable to some degree. "Jamie? *Your* Jamie?"

"Eilidh, for fuck's sake, you're on speaker. Try to conserve your idiocy for at least the next five minutes. Stop looking at me like that." Presumably that last bit was not intended for Eilidh, who gestured apologetically for Dzhuliya to commence the walk to the parking structure. Dzhuliya, looking relieved, nodded and hastily took off, charging forward as if recently revived.

Her leggings were very nice, Eilidh thought. In a textile way. She should ask where Dzhuliya had gotten them.

"I don't even know why I'm calling," Meredith continued. "I assume you're there already."

"What, home? I just landed," said Eilidh. There was a gasp of warm September air from the opening doors as she and Dzhuliya traversed the terminal, followed by the sounds of a thousand assholes honking.

"I can't hear you," said Meredith impatiently. "Where are you?"

"I told you, the airport—"

"Which airport?"

Eilidh hurried after Dzhuliya as she mounted the elevator, lugging her bag behind her with the sort of gracelessness that made Eilidh feel that her past as a dancer must have been entirely imagined. It could not have been real, or else wouldn't it have carried over into this moment? Imagine Odette from *Swan Lake* pulling along a suitcase. Imagine it. "SFO. I just got back."

"From where?" Now Meredith seemed bewildered as well as annoyed.

"I went on a silent retreat."

"A what?"

"A silent retreat."

"What?"

The elevator dinged with their floor. "Are you not hearing me?"

"I'm not *understanding* you," said Meredith with brutal, weaponized annoyance. "Don't tell me you actually paid money for someone to take your phone away and force you to be quiet."

"Well, not technically," said Eilidh weakly. For fuck's sake, she had been a prodigy once. The word artist used to be casually thrown around alongside her name, with nobody ever once questioning whether it was a mantle that was earned. She was supposed to be someone!

"Oh, of course, Daddy Dearest paid for it." Eilidh could hear Meredith's eyes rolling into the back of her head. "What are you going to do with yourself now that he's not there to gift you with such precious wastes of time? Well, you'll be able to afford it," she muttered. "I assume you're the only one he's put in the will. Christ. If you're next in line for CEO, I swear to god, I'll leap headfirst into the Grand Canyon."

"I always saw you as more of a Miss Havisham," said a distant masculine voice from Meredith's end that must have been Jamie. "You know, pacing the attic in a tattered old pantsuit, crowing over your lost executive power while teaching some younger version of you to destroy men for sport."

"Arguably I am already doing that, so compliment taken," said Meredith. "Also, shut up."

"Wait," said Eilidh, who was still having trouble understanding why Meredith had called her, firstly; secondly what Meredith was talking about; thirdly why Meredith was in a car casually bantering with the ex-boyfriend whose name she had refused for a decade to even speak aloud due to unsurvivable heart-crush. "Why would I be CEO? CEO of what?"

"Has Jenny not called you?" asked Meredith, whose tone had shifted from annoyance to something much darker, which was usually a sign that a genuine emotion was involved. Meredith did not like to feel things. (On more than one occasion while watching romantic movies over the course of their adolescence, Eilidh had seen Meredith blink with apparent lack of understanding as to the concept of sadness and/or affection.)

"Jenny . . . you mean Dzhuliya?" That's right, Meredith could not—more likely would not—remember the names of their father's staff, as Meredith chose to believe their father slept with all of his employees instead of simply accepting that actually, sometimes young, obscenely pretty women needed jobs, too. "She's right here. I'm getting into the car with her right now."

Technically, Eilidh was lugging her suitcase with some effort into Dzhuliya's trunk right now. Not that Dzhuliya was meant to do any more than she had already done, having chosen to pick Eilidh up from the airport, an act akin to helping someone move or declaring everlasting love, but Eilidh did have a bad back and a tendency to overpack. It seemed a bit rude not to at least *offer,* but Dzhuliya was already settling herself in the driver's seat of her actually very cute SUV.

Eilidh knew with certainty and a small, ignorable degree of arousal that the last time she'd been in a car with Dzhuliya, it had been in a tiny, aging coupe. They'd been forced to wrestle erotically in the back seat until—well, until it had hurt Eilidh's back, severing their tryst, and so now she was back where she started.

"Mer, what on earth are you talking about?"

"Oh, Christ," said Meredith. "No, no. You can't hear this from me."

"What?" Suitcase finally settled in the trunk, Eilidh made her way to the passenger side of Dzhuliya's astonishingly clean vehicle. Was it . . . new? Was that an appropriate thing to ask? Had there ever been an appropriate version of their relationship? Not that it was ever a *relationship*—

"Call Arthur," suggested Meredith. "Or, well, Arthur's incommunicado at the moment, I assume. Not that I've been to an orgy, but I have my guesses."

"What?" said Eilidh, for what seemed to be the hundredth time. Meredith was chatting away as if this was something they always did rather than something Meredith would only do under extremely limited circumstances, like deciding what to buy Aunt Fern for Christmas or grapevining news of a horrific accident. "Meredith, just tell me why you're calling. Did someone die?" asked Eilidh, wrenching open the door to the passenger seat of Dzhuliya's car.

"Oh, for fuck's sake, I'm assuming we're done now with Jenny—"

"Dzhuliya." Eilidh glanced askance at Dzhuliya then, who did not meet her eye.

"—but if we're not, she's so fired for this. Jamie, you tell her."

The tinny, masculine voice was back. "What? Meredith—"

"Come on, you'll be better at it than me, you'll be doing her a favor—"

"It has to come from *you,* Meredith, not me—"

"Jamie." Eilidh felt a mix of irritation and dread. She had always had a tendency to remember everything Meredith said to her, in detail, verbatim. Every little nit Meredith had to pick. Every throwaway comment Meredith seemed to sprinkle like pixie dust, sometimes meaningless and sometimes not, but it was impossible to tell in the moment which it was, and so Eilidh would replay the conversation in her head for hours and hours and hours until she felt certain which things Meredith meant and which things Meredith, who was at least forty percent machine, thought were simply facts or quips or even witticisms. *Can you believe this motherfucker had the gall to up and die? I'm assuming we're done with Jenny—If you're next in line for CEO—What are you going to do yourself now that he's not there—*

"Jamie, I've had a very difficult day, and you know what my sister is like. Please tell me," Eilidh felt herself say in a small voice. "Please just tell me."

"Oh, Eilidh." They had only spoken a handful of times over the course of his courtship with Meredith; they'd never actually met. It seemed unfair to put this on him, but such was life. "I'm so sorry," Jamie sighed, closer now, as if he'd leaned toward the speaker. "It's your father."

"I told you, right? The gall," said Meredith irritably, but Eilidh couldn't hear her.

She couldn't hear anything. Everything seemed to be drowned out by a low buzz, the faint sound of her heart beating in her ears, the agonized flutter of a locust wing. She felt as if everything around her had suddenly gone white, and there was a slow, gentle curl around her ribs from the thing in her chest, as if it was now snaking around her comfortingly, holding her like an embrace.

Not now, thought Eilidh impatiently, no disasters now, please, but it did feel nice, and she realized why Dzhuliya was here, and that amicable or not Dzhuliya had not wanted to be the one to have to comfort her, and neither would Meredith, and unless Eilidh wanted to wait for Arthur, nobody would give her a hug.

So Eilidh swallowed hard and sat alone with it, the sadness, the monster inside her chest that seemed to vibrate consolingly, its own bitterness and wrath entwining gently with hers.

"But seriously, if you're Wrenfare's next CEO, I'm going to lose my fucking mind," her sister said.

# Eilidh, Five Years Ago

The light flickered directly above Eilidh's head. A small but unavoidable glitch.

"Sorry," said the nurse, whose name was Angelica, an ordinary, not uncommon name that Eilidh would come to irrationally despise. "I put in a work request for that last week, but you know how these things go."

Eilidh said nothing. She was aware, distantly, that her silence was rude and probably abrasive, but she had given herself permission, just for twenty-four hours, to not concern herself with what was or wasn't rude.

Angelica, a remarkably decent person upon whom Eilidh should really not have wished such ill, didn't seem to mind her silence. "Weather's great today," she said, and seemed to hesitate, unsure whether continuing to chat was better or worse as a tactic. "If you're feeling up for it, I can take you outside for a bit."

The good news was that Eilidh was going to be able to walk. She was going to regain mobility very soon—or soon enough, anyway, compared to the course of human existence. The good news was the taxi driver was fine. The good news was the other driver was, also, fine. The good news was her understudy was well prepared, she'd sold nearly as many tickets as the much-hyped Eilidh Wren, and the season was already almost over. The good news was that the understudy had learned *so much* from Eilidh—it really was an honor just to dance with her. (*Was.*) The good news was that Eilidh had lived. The good news was the weather was great today, and if Eilidh was feeling up for it, she could maybe be wheeled outside.

Meredith had done ballet, too, up until her studies got too rigorous for her to keep up with so many extracurriculars. Ballet, tennis, piano, her volunteer work at the summer camp for holy vagrants (that's what Arthur jokingly called it, more of a reflection on Meredith herself than on the . . . fuck, suddenly Eilidh couldn't think of a term that wasn't "vagrants"), plus a full load of honors and AP classes. So Meredith bailed out of ballet, crediting her perfect posture and the unmistakable whiff of rigorous discipline you got just from being near her to something that had been formative but fleeting, merely a thing she'd once done. For Meredith, ballet was an aesthetic, a reason to keep her hair neatly tied in a bun at all times from the ages of six to sixteen.

For Eilidh, it was different.

It engulfed her. It made her feel the way love was supposed to make her feel, the way other people talked about sex. She couldn't talk about ballet without a noticeable degree of horniness, as if desire and dance were inseverable, as if she couldn't feel passion any other way but on her toes, with the tips of her fingers so far outstretched as if to graze the cheek of God. She only ever slept with other dancers, never understanding how to explain to the normies the way she ate, her early bedtime, her early rising, the way that one mistake over the course of a near-perfect performance would paralyze her for hours afterward, ultimately driving her right back to the barre. How did you tell someone—man, woman, anyone—that you would rather achieve perfection than eat a slice of pizza? And in New York! Not a single person could understand her, not even the lovers she did take, who were all—put frankly—artistically inferior. Even the ones who claimed her same level of devotion still concerned themselves to some degree with rest, with sex, which Eilidh didn't. She partook in it. She dabbled in it. But even in bed she was dancing. It was all she had ever wanted to do.

"The doctor says everything is progressing really well post-surgery," added Angelica, who was looking over Eilidh's chart. "You should be able to go home soon."

Home! Eilidh didn't even know where home was. She barely did anything in her apartment aside from sleep. Home was the New York Ballet, it was the stage, it was somewhere coming from the crowd, the lifeblood of public adoration. She had always been an anxious person, a stammerer as a child. She spoke only one language that other people could understand. What logic was that, to rob her of her voice?

Though she could, technically, talk. "Could I just sit here a minute?" asked Eilidh, her voice rougher than she intended, though again, she was not concerning herself with politeness just then. Her siblings would argue that she concerned herself too much with politeness, even now, though that was to be expected from them, as they almost never spared her any measure of compassion. They were too wrapped up in each other and themselves, and Eilidh was always an external part of the equation, some third party who could neither understand nor keep up with the other two.

Granted, Meredith and Arthur weren't *the same,* nor were they even similar, arguably, except in their senses of humor, which were exacting to the point of near meanness. Or at least that was how they seemed to Eilidh, who, it can't be understated, had never understood a single word that passed between them, as if they spoke another language entirely, one in which every word they used meant something different but they'd already agreed not to tell Eilidh, and so she typically sat there wordless and puzzled, nodding along just so they wouldn't think she was fucking comatose.

"Oh, sure." Angelica gave Eilidh a look of pity that Eilidh would see again many times over the course of her life from that moment, or technically from some hours prior, when she might have just died and been spared all the nonsense that came with feeling badly, followed by feeling worse when other people *also* felt badly but in too obvious a way. It was a look that meant *I'm glad I'm not in your position,* which was not the look that Eilidh was accustomed to.

Maybe other women disliked the threatening state of being envied, but not Eilidh. Someone had warned her once—a bitter old dancer, who had been a principal ballerina five or six cycles before, who now worked for the ballet and always wore battered shoes, her perennial French manicure slightly chipped—that Eilidh would always be looking over her shoulder, always looking for the next pretty little ingenue who would come to take her place.

*Maybe* you *had to look over your shoulder,* thought Eilidh, who never bothered with her own, because nobody else could come close. They never had.

Angelica left, and Eilidh closed her eyes, thinking morbid things. She thought about the rest of her life. A wife or a husband or children, god, what drudgery. The idea of buying curtains or picking out silverware, she wanted to die. She'd always thought of herself as destined for a short life anyway, since a dancer's career was truncated as it was. She'd thought she would never need to worry about the future, because for her, life was only as long as she could reasonably stay in the corps. It would end where, forty if she was really lucky? Thirty if she was not? She could not then, at twenty-one, even imagine being thirty. There was something dull to it, like picking up a glimmer on the sidewalk that turned out to be trash.

Things darkened in her thoughts. The morbidity got weirder, more twisted. She had been told once by one of those old women on the Venice boardwalk that she was carrying around a latent curse. *Everyone has an inevitability,* Eilidh thought. *I thought mine would be my knees, maybe my ankles.* She'd gotten tendinitis everywhere a person reasonably could, including the tops of her feet. *My end is written in me somewhere, and I'm going to dance until it implodes.*

She supposed she had done it, then.

Just then, when she thought nothing could possibly mean anything to her ever again, her phone screen lit up with a call. She raised it numbly to her ear.

"Sweetheart," said her father gently, with so much kindness in his voice that she could not answer, instead beginning to cry, eventually sobbing so hard for so long she thought she'd never run out of tears. That her lungs would empty and she'd still be soaked in this, in misery, in agony, in heartbreak. The actual, physical tearing of her heart.

She felt something like a tap inside her rib cage, the quiet knocking of a ghost. Something that wanted space from inside her, like filling an unseen puncture up with hope. She didn't make room for it. No vacancy, bitch. She shoved it out, hard, because she understood that was something she would do now. Push and push and push so she could be alone with her grief, mourning it like Orpheus. Following it until it led her out of hell.

She didn't notice at first when the hospital sprinklers went off, liquid pouring down a rapid shower of unlikely rain. The light was still flickering overhead, and her hands were already wet, her cheeks already slick, parts of her hair and bedding soaked, nothing really out of place so much as everything. It wasn't until a stain of rust had flecked her knuckles, then her fingers. Then, as she began to register the saturation of her hospital gown and the panicked screams from the orderlies outside her room, she tasted it on her tongue. Not tears.

She smeared her thumb across her lips and then looked down, her fingers salty with it. She understood somehow that the thing inside her chest had done it. That *she* had been the vessel for it, like becoming the red button that called down an annihilating flood.

"Eilidh," her father was saying on the phone. "Eilidh, are you all right?"

Not tears. She clocked it belatedly, salted rain turning copper in her mouth.

Blood.

# 9

Arthur opened his eyes to a dismal, splitting headache. There was a roar in his ears, thick dryness in his throat. He felt like death itself, or so he imagined death to feel. It wasn't nearly as merciful as he'd hoped. Resurrection had also strongly resembled the feeling of being slapped awake by his seatmate, which he realized some seconds later was an event that was actually taking place.

"Good, you're up," said Yves chirpily, seeming altogether too refreshed for someone currently occupying the middle seat. "I've never flown in this part of the plane before. My arse is very uncomfortable. I think it's very cute, very communal, like we are all here together in a village." There was no gradation in tone between these sentiments.

"Hello," called Yves, waving at one of the people across the aisle. The passenger, a middle-aged woman who seemed probably British rather than American, appeared slightly dumbstruck, as if uncertain whether Yves could possibly be who he was. Then, perhaps reasoning a famous racecar driver would not fly coach on a red-eye, the other passenger shrugged him off in apparent irritation. (True, Yves did not seem to know the rule among coach passengers, which was not to make eye contact or move or breathe or acknowledge each other or make small talk or hog the armrests. Such were the laws and customs of the land, to be punishable by cold shoulder and the occasional outright glare—something Arthur understood from a politically motivated thirst for relatability.)

Arthur lifted his head groggily from where it had been shoved into the side of the plane and squinted at Yves, seeing two or three of him floating before his vision. He waited for the sense that he could pick the right one out before asking, "You came with me?"

He did not remember boarding the plane, or anything really beyond his conversation with his wife Gillian. Arthur supposed Yves must have given him something, or maybe Philippa had. Combined, they were a walking medicine cabinet, and tranquilizers were among Philippa's favorites, her most precious tools. Had she come along as well?

Arthur glanced at the aisle seat, which was occupied by an elderly man currently snoring with his head on Yves's shoulder (and was not, therefore, Philippa).

"Arthur, your father has died," said Yves solemnly. "This is the time you need your family around you for support. Mouse will be coming along as well," he said, seeming to have noticed Arthur's scan of the row for her. "She's just taking care of some things before she joins us. You know how she hates to be rushed." Yves began playing with the tray table, lowering it down and lifting it back up. "You look dreadful," Yves added with some fondness to Arthur. "Would you like a little something?"

"Oh god, yes." Arthur had no idea what sorts of things Yves could get away with bringing on a commercial flight, but blindly accepted a piece of what seemed to be chocolate in his palm before tossing it into his mouth. The result was near-instantaneous—a Pavlovian pseudo-serenity like the lifting of an existential burden. "Should Philippa be flying?" Arthur asked as an afterthought.

"Oh, Arthur, it is only in the final months when a woman cannot fly." Yves shrugged, then also proceeded to take a bite of chocolate himself.

"Sure," said Arthur, who couldn't help worrying regardless. He could practically hear his father's voice in his head, insulting his manhood. Which part, specifically? Unclear, but somewhere, Arthur felt certain his manhood was at risk. "But what about, I don't know, morning sickness? Or just, like, general discomfort—"

"Don't worry about it," Yves reassured him, somewhat distractedly. "She knows what she's doing. And anyway, we both just want to be there for you, that's all," he added, this time with a tangible degree of doting.

"Right." And Arthur did feel relieved, in a way. Yves could have very easily sent him off alone, but he hadn't. Arthur wished Philippa had joined him as well, but he could at least admit to himself that being seen so near his home district with a woman who wasn't his wife was much more problematic than exiting the plane alongside Yves, whose entire mystique was characterized by the many spontaneous things he could get up to in a twenty-four-hour period. The unspecifically artistic quality belonging to the coupling of Philippa and Yves was something that did not apply to Arthur and the myriad ways his political reputation hung by a thread, and he had always appreciated the care they took to preserve his public image on his behalf.

Though, with increasing frequency, Arthur felt the reckless urge to do less. "Yves, do you know, has Philippa thought any more about—"

"Ladies and gentlemen, the pilot has advised that we will be landing soon," came the calm, tonally orienting voice of the flight attendant from somewhere overhead. "Please return your seat-back trays to the upright and locked position—"

"Arthur, this is a very difficult time for you," Yves said solemnly, turning as far toward Arthur as he could without disturbing the slumber of the aisle-seat passenger, who simply snorted and snuggled deeper into the recess of Yves's shoulder. "I remember that when my father passed, I was a wreck, an absolute wreck. And you know, my father was not a perfect man," Yves said with a shake of his head. "He was often very violent with us, especially me, because I was the only boy and he did not think of me as a serious person. But in the end he was my father, and it is like losing a piece of yourself, don't you think? To lose something so formative to you, good or bad."

It was very Yves to say something so profound while having just taken an unknown confectionary intoxicant. Yves had many moments where he became very vintage-ly wise, to the point where Arthur remained permanently confused about how smart Yves actually was and whether Yves might be some kind of bog-dwelling immortal. For example, at present Yves was continuing to toy with the seat-back tray despite having been expressly told not to, up until Arthur reached forward and locked it in place.

"My father was never violent," said Arthur, who was considering it now, all the things he had not yet had time to think about as related to his father's loss. "He never laid a hand on us." That would have been more intimacy than Thayer was capable of. Meredith and Arthur both went to boarding school in New England, ostensibly for their education despite the definite existence of fancy private schools in Los Angeles, and Eilidh had gone to ballet academy in New York. "But I do think he also wanted me to be a more serious person."

"You're weak" had been Thayer's pronouncement of Arthur after the first time he was pulled from the pitcher's mound during the second inning of his first NCAA championship. "You could never live with the kind of pressure I'm under from day to day, moment to moment. I thought you had something in you, some spark, but I suppose it's not enough. Your mother spoiled you when you were a child and now even the slightest pressure is too much for you. When things get challenging, when people are looking to you for steadiness, you fall apart."

Arthur felt something lodge in his throat just then, at the words he wanted to forget but couldn't, much like the pop songs of his youth or the way Lou's fabric softener had smelled. The all-natural stuff he and Gillian bought now was almost oppressively mature, a fashionable spray of dead botanicals. Arthur reached for Yves's bottle of flavored water, which Yves always carried. He was famous for it, strawberry lemon water. For a moment, it was almost sickly sweet. But the moment passed, as moments did, and thoughts of Arthur's father became thoughts of himself, and of the father Arthur himself planned to be.

There was, of course, no definite proof that the child was or wasn't his, given the machinations of their varying forms of sexual congress, though in Arthur's opinion it didn't really matter. What difference did it make whose microscopic sperm had won the race? The important thing was that he loved Philippa, he loved Yves, and he loved the possibility of a family, which had receded further and further as his marriage to Gillian proved to be more partnership than anything else.

Which was not to say that Arthur did not care for Gillian, who was still the smartest person he had ever met besides his sister. But love with Philippa and Yves felt like the kind you were *supposed* to feel when you welcomed a baby into the world, and while Arthur suspected that his career had to do with Philippa's reticence on the subject—perhaps she did not think he was serious when he told her of his intentions to live as a family, to give everything up for love if necessary, as all the good poets had done?—and he intended to prove his commitment to her, whatever it took. The whole thing might hurt Gillian's image a bit, but Arthur felt certain she'd be happier without him. After all, what had he turned her life into? She was practically his manager, his publicist, and his political adviser all rolled into one, none of which had been her aspiration. She would be happier, more able to focus on herself, her freedom an inevitable reward for her years of loyal, browbeaten service. She had her dissertation to worry about, and as for the rest, Arthur would make sure she was taken care of..

Come to think of it, at least Arthur was about to receive a sizable inheritance, which would come in handy in the event of a very public, very tawdry divorce. Assuming Thayer hadn't actually hated him enough to disinherit him. As far as Arthur understood his father, it really could go either way.

The plane began its descent, the man in the aisle seat snorting himself awake just in time for Yves to lean excitedly over Arthur's lap, gazing out the window with all the enthusiasm of a young child. Yes, thought Arthur, they would be perfect together, the three of them. It would be unconventional—of course it would be!—but wouldn't it also be *admirable,* in some way? What Arthur had with Yves and Philippa was the very definition of love beyond social constructs, love beyond obligation. Love beyond the silliness of convention. For everyone who still believed he was just another rich centrist (i.e., the *Chronicle* and that heinous new video platform launched by Tyche), wouldn't this be, at least, proof of concept? That the world Arthur Wren actually believed in was ruled not by the faceless *they* but by the convictions of his own earnest heart?

"Personally, myself, I would very much like to teach a child to fly a plane," said Yves, ostensibly to Arthur, though Yves was still looking greedily out the window.

"You're a pilot?" asked Arthur. It was very possible. Yves had a soaring variety of talents, and anyway he was a very good driver, so long as he was going in a circle.

"No, not yet, but certainly in five or so years when it comes time for a baby to learn such things. I hope to have a boy," added Yves tangentially, appearing to disregard his estimate for child development. "There is something terrifying about a girl, particularly if she would be anything like Mouse."

Arthur chuckled in agreement, which immediately felt disloyal. Because while a smaller version of Philippa was equally terrifying to him, he felt that terror as someone might feel a blind leap into the unknown; the thrill of skydiving for fun and not from a sense of danger. Philippa was obstinate, she was capricious, she changed her mind from moment to moment and seemed very intent on shock value, destabilizing people either to charm them or get her way.

But what Arthur wanted to say was how lovely it would be to have a daughter like Philippa, who would be brave and unconforming. It was the chance to create some actual hope in the world, a thing he could not seem to do via politics, which were swallowing him avariciously up. Wouldn't it be wonderful to know that he could make a very *dangerous* woman, someone so headstrong and visionary that she would become a problem money couldn't solve? A little feminist, a tiny riot.

Riot, Arthur realized fondly, the sound of it coming to him like an epiphany, like the relief of Yves's medicinal chocolate or a glow of godly light. Riot Wren, or even Riot Reza—he wasn't particularly interested in possessing his daughter, just in raising her, and either way it would be alliterative and symbolic. Unlike Arthur, Riot would not be assigned some stuffy old name, her future chosen for her out of some neoliberal sensibility. Arthur saw himself five years from now, ten or twenty, with his arm around Yves, his hand in Philippa's. "Why shouldn't we call her Riot? That's what she is," Arthur heard himself say proudly. Wouldn't that be sweet?

Rather than voice his disagreement with Yves, though, Arthur indulged the rare opportunity to speak openly about their collective future. He was even willing to believe in Yves's version of it; to believe, absolutely, that his daughter Riot would pilot a commercial jet at the tender age of five.

"I'd like a girl, I think," Arthur admitted. "It's hard to raise a boy. Well, hard to raise a man," he corrected himself, before being swallowed up once again by overtrodden memories of his father. Specifically, by memories of being told what a man ought to be, like notches on a growth chart that Arthur had yet to reach.

He supposed he could give all of that up now, laugh in his father's face, take the money and run. Rob the bank and live for every moment. Who could judge him now? Aside from Meredith, who was going to regardless.

"I suppose. I am very hungry," announced Yves, apparently having lost interest in the subject of their daughter, though Arthur could not imagine doing so himself. He felt a nostalgia, an aching, pulsating *missing* of her despite the fact that he'd only had her for a moment, for a breath of imaginary time. The distance Arthur traveled from the Riot in his mind's eye back to any comparable matter of tedium was a long beat of wordless melancholy.

"We can order some food for when we get home," Arthur said eventually to Yves, after they had deplaned. Neither of them had baggage, thank god (Philippa never traveled without a veritable fleet), so they made their way out of the terminal in the direction of the arrivals bank. Gillian had texted Arthur that she would meet him at the airport, though she hadn't specified whether they would be staying in his childhood house in Marin or their own cozier but oft unlived-in house, where they stayed when Congress wasn't in session. Unlikely, Arthur realized, as it was a trek that involved a bridge however you went about it. Which meant almost certainly that they were headed for the gloomy, architecturally significant (to the point of sterility) old house in the Mill Valley foothills, where Arthur had lost his virginity and written bad poetry and desperately missed his mom.

In shaking himself of the thought, Arthur realized abruptly that if Yves had been a surprise to him, then Yves would also very likely be a surprise to Gillian. Arthur texted her quickly that by the way, Yves was here and they were outside, naming the terminal door they stood beside. "Or we can—"

"I am craving pancakes," said Yves, in something of a formal pronouncement.

Gillian texted back via voice message that she was circling and would be right there. "Well, that's easy," said Arthur distractedly, typing back that that was fine. "We can get those anywhere—"

"I would like to visit the International House of Pancakes. Have you been?"

"I . . . yes," said Arthur, unsure at first whether Yves had actually meant IHOP or if he was referring to some other, hipper place in San Francisco. It had been a while since Arthur had been in the city proper, rather than his district in Oakland, and when he was, he didn't usually have time to explore the culinary fare. "And sure, but first I'll have to—"

"Oh, don't worry about me, I will find you," said Yves, peeling off from Arthur's side so suddenly that Arthur didn't notice until he'd looked up from his screen, realizing that he was alone and that Gillian had pulled neatly to the curb in front of him.

"Oh," said Arthur at the sight of her. She hopped out of the driver's seat, greeting him with a kiss on the cheek. "You drove? Yourself?"

"Don't make it sound so remarkable, Art, I'll hate to think I've lost touch with my proletarian roots," she said in something that was possibly a joke, possibly deadly serious. "Where is Yves?"

"IHOP, I think?" Arthur looked around for him but he had vanished. "I didn't even get a chance to give him the address of where we're going. Where *are* we going, by the way?" he asked, hoping she'd say almost anything else aside from what she'd inevitably say.

Just then, Arthur caught a glimpse of a phone camera flashing from his periphery and realized why Gillian had driven herself, and why she had disembarked from the driver's seat to greet him. He had forgotten for a moment that he was still a widely recognizable politician; that someone would

almost certainly write derogatorily about him; that if he was trending anywhere it was never good news; that he was not yet Riot's father. Well, he was
that, but not to anyone else's knowledge. That was a warm little secret he
carried around in the center of his chest, a little bubble of molten gold for
only him.

*I love you,* whispered the old ghost. Was it Arthur himself, speaking to
Riot? Was that the love he'd been meant for all along?

"Darling?" Gillian prompted him. She had opened the trunk of the rental
car, or what Arthur assumed was a rental car, though it was possible she had
already gone to his father's house and picked out a vehicle of his. Thayer had
liked Gillian, actually. *She has bigger balls than you* had been one of Thayer's favorite jokes. "We've got to get back. Meredith should be arriving any
minute, and Eilidh's on her way."

"Where?" But he knew, of course. Where else did you go when your parents died but backward? Back to childhood. Back to the place he hadn't
called home for a decade, and arguably had not considered home before
that.

Briefly, he felt a set of thin, uncertain arms wrapping around his waist
and realized he'd been staring blankly into nothing. "I *am* sorry," said Gillian softly. "I know it's not as simple a sadness as you'd like it to be, but it is
sad, and I am sad with you."

Arthur looked down at the top of his wife's braided head with a little
sense of shock before recalling her expertise in curating moments like this.
He was grateful to her, could not do his job without her, would miss her
to massive, constitution-riddling extent when the dust was finally settled.
Maybe she wouldn't mind staying in his life, being someone of importance
to Riot? Maybe when you built your own family the titles were rendered
unimportant, the traditional roles null and void.

Arthur leaned down to bury his nose in the familiar scent of her sensitive
skin shampoo, the coconut oil that was essentially Gillian-scented. Elsewhere, the phone camera flashed again.

"Thank you," Arthur managed roughly, and it was dignified, at least.

"You're welcome," replied Gillian, exhaling with visible relief once he
disentangled himself and slid into the passenger side.

# Arthur, Five Years Ago

Not a church wedding for them, they said at first. They were hip, cool, out-doorsy! Not a priest, but an old friend of Gillian's! Not a stodgy old cake that no one would eat, but something unconventional and different! Do-nuts, a sign of the times!

But in the end, of course, they caved to expectations.

"I now pronounce you husband and wife. You may kiss the bride!"

Light streamed in overhead through the stained glass, temporarily blinding Arthur as he leaned forward, one hand carefully angled alongside Gillian's slender hip. They had practiced this several times—Gillian was meticulous about camera angles—but still, he caught a flicker of revulsion in the mahogany of her eyes, registering that not even frequent rehearsal or a nine-month engagement had done anything to make the moment more palatable for her.

Her lips were cool and soft, a little of the sacramental wine on her breath. Arthur closed his eyes and tried to be present in the moment, to live *inside* the moment, to curl up in it, to take up all its space, to force it into a differ-ent shape, to beg the moment to transform, to be something different. They parted and Arthur saw his father's unsmiling face out of the corner of his eye.

"She's a good choice, you know." The conversation between Thayer and Arthur on the evening of his and Gillian's engagement had been almost laughably civilized, although it carried with it the usual undertone of cru-elty, detectable only when Arthur's father spoke to him in private. "Possibly too good a choice," Thayer added, with a sense of impending bomb. "It's—" The elder Wren waved an unflappable hand. "Transparent."

He meant that Gillian was well educated but without the whiff of excess that Arthur couldn't escape. She was, like Arthur, a first generation Ameri-can on one side with some family lineage dating back to the traders of New

Amsterdam on the other. Unlike Arthur, though, Gillian was a bootstrap person—as in, *she* had pulled herself up. Thayer, too, had been a bootstrap person. Arthur was not. Arthur was soft and spoiled. Arthur got the yips. Gillian was beautiful, but not *too* beautiful—more like architecturally well-made in an understated way. A feminist, whose politics were politely left-leaning but mostly unknown, because she did not say anything on social media. It was Arthur who was the radical, or who could afford to be one, anyway, because rich people recognized him as one of their own and trusted him to cave at some point, to be a capitalist in woke clothing the way people were so fashionably capable of being these days. Arthur was, of course, more sincere in his politics than that, and people knew it. Or so he believed at the time.

"Maybe we're just exceptionally well matched," suggested Arthur, in a tone that had won over the stricter teachers at boarding school and also, notably, Lou, but had never once worked on his father. As predicted, Arthur again struck out.

"What is she, Egyptian?" asked his father, who was not racist, or wasn't racist in the way white men were usually not racist, which was that they did not *see color.* They simply did not care for the person *individually*—nothing that could be reasonably attributed to race, because they were frankly too evolved!

"French-Moroccan," corrected Arthur. Gillian was technically multiracial—as was Arthur himself—but he knew which part specifically his father was asking about. "And Indian."

"Not fully, though," commented his father, presumably reflecting on Gillian's father's surname, which was Hayes. (Gillian's was Yadav.)

"No, her father is from the far more exotic Kansas City."

"She's what, a lawyer?"

"She is." Though she didn't want to be. That was the appeal, she'd said on the first date. Gillian had always wanted to be a singer, actually. But she'd never make it, she wasn't actually good enough, just mediocre, really. She loved it but wasn't especially talented at it, which was the usual kind of personal tragedy befalling constituents of the world. She needed health insurance but hated the culture at her firm, wanted out of the rat race altogether. She was fairly confident they'd fire her in favor of some fresh, eager, newly ripened (the word "succulent" came to mind, or "luscious," "sumptuous," "*young*") law school graduate over the option of promoting her to partner and, thus, paying her what she was worth. She'd gone to law school only because her father had insisted that she do something, quote, sustainable. Her father was in manufacturing, her mother was a retired catalog model, neither career path was exceptionally fitting. She could have been a doctor, that was technically on the table, and with Gillian's disarming directness and blazing, otherworldly competence, she did have a ring of neurosurgeon to her. She was never very good at science—she felt she could have been better at it had she really applied herself, but she just loved Shakespeare too much and there was really only so much time in the day—so then law school it was. But god, wasn't it awful doing something just because your father wants you to?

(At which point Arthur said, "I think, at this moment, that if you came out of the ladies' room with some sort of Sermon on the Mount, I'd seriously consider devoting myself to you body and soul," to which Gillian correctly replied, "Arthur, my goodness, rein it in.")

Anyway, Gillian had ambitions of pursuing a PhD, though she felt she could make time for a congressional campaign if it didn't interfere with her studies.

"Well, she looks nice on your arm, if you can get past the fact that she seems thoroughly uninterested in fucking you," commented the ever-paternal Thayer Wren. "Though I suppose what politician actually fucks his wife?"

"I'm going to," said Arthur heatedly, before checking himself. "I mean, it's none of your business," he muttered, "and the point is I like her."

"You like her. Wow." Thayer mimicked an explosion beside his head. "Groundbreaking."

"I love her. Of course I love her." And Arthur did love her. Though, how meaningful was that love, exactly? Seeing as Arthur could love almost anything if he thought about it long enough. Whether Arthur was actually aware of this remains critically unstudied, despite it being pointed out to him many times. Candidly, between you and me, that was just Arthur's way, in some ways his fundamental flaw, and the reason he was actually quite fond of his sister Meredith. Arthur was just one of those people who could feel something for anyone, which many people in his life would mistake for a sort of saintly quality, but of course wasn't. Because in his own way, Arthur was an asshole, too, and worse, he was an idiot. But obviously we'll get to that.

Three years from the date of their marriage, Gillian Wren would be well on her way to a doctorate in Napoleonic military tactics with an emphasis on the flexible use of artillery (which at one point during her initial dissertation proposal Gillian had compared quite brilliantly to the triangle offense of Phil Jackson's Chicago Bulls, before Wrenfare's experimental technomantic program made human coaching largely irrelevant) and Arthur would perform multiple congressional duties with his boxers on inside out due to the ministrations of Yves Reza from the bathroom of Philippa's hotel.

But before any of that happened, there was just one moment of significance, of utter, ringing clarity, which would define all the days of Arthur's life right up until the moment he learned of his father's passing.

"I'm sorry," Arthur said to Gillian as they parted from their first official kiss as husband and wife, though he wasn't quite sure why he'd said it, as he hadn't technically done anything wrong. He'd performed just as they'd rehearsed, and at the time, pre–Philippa and Yves, he'd been perfectly behaved. Gillian had wanted to wait for any physical intimacy until their wedding day, and Arthur had been delighted to oblige. It seemed romantic to him, and pleasantly—almost cozily—old-fashioned, and he'd assumed that his attraction to her mind would ultimately reveal itself insatiably in the bedroom.

At the moment of avowal, though, Arthur understood the truth, which was that he was a lifeline of some sort for Gillian, and now that the rings were exchanged, she could relax, set down the weight she'd been carrying around— presumably that of any woman in her late twenties—and stop worrying about the whole thing, because everything would be fine. Because Arthur would never leave her—a divorce would be ugly for his political ambitions, and anyway, he had obvious attachment issues—and they would almost certainly receive a pastel stand mixer that would look lovely in her dream kitchen, and she would never want for anything again, and there was only one small catch, which was that she did not, at all, want him to touch her.

Which was how Arthur Wren came to understand that he had tied himself to a woman who did not love him, which was an almost unbearable irony, because as we have already established, Arthur Wren wanted nothing so much as he wanted to be loved.

"Don't cry," whispered Gillian kindly, and Arthur was grateful to her for that, because he understood that she would keep it secret. Him, that is. His heart and his heartbreak, everything he would one day do, everything he could *already* do—that is, Arthur's magic, which was then an eccentricity too ridiculous to be worth sharing, something he thought was buried deeply in the past, like Lou—and Gillian would keep all of that a secret on his behalf. She had bound her life to his and so their marriage was a vault, a fact driven by either genuine fondness or the artillery-driven tactic at which Gillian was already so adept. *In the end,* asked a voice that Arthur felt morbidly certain was his sister Meredith's, *does it really matter which?*

And it was at that very moment that Arthur Wren started to die.

# 10

"So you've kidnapped me, is what you're saying," commented Jamie ruefully from the passenger side of Meredith's rented vehicle. It was a gas model, of all things—urgency had left little room for choosiness, despite the fact that she had the money for a magitech model, or even a normal electric car that was just as good and cheaper to manufacture than the M-batteries her father had developed—though this one had come equipped with external Wrenfare GPS, so if Meredith got lost, she would know precisely which dead man to blame. "You never intended to tell me anything at all, did you?"

It was then hour three of Meredith's . . . "abduction" was a strong word. Indeed, it had not felt like abduction at the moment she'd had the idea. (We know; we were all there.) Instead, Meredith had sagely thought, *Well, can't let Jamie run free with his silly little story about my massive corporate fraud*—and had not, at the time, considered what preventing him from doing so might mean.

Within the first hour, though, it became very obvious that the lie she'd always intended to tell—something about how Jamie hadn't understood what he'd seen her do back when he'd seen her do it, or that he was letting his personal feelings get the better of him, or that the problem was in Chirp's popularity leading to it being distributed so indiscriminately, creating a mythos of negativity and the general sense that it was not, per se, good, as with paranormal romances of the aughts—was actually a very short conversation. She said all three things in the span of about five minutes and then realized there were five hours left of the drive, possibly more with traffic (and there would be traffic, heaven help them, because no amount of magitech could get the political support for an at-grade train line built across a landscape intended in obscure but unignorable ways for military defense).

Which was when Meredith had called her sister, forced Jamie to tell Eilidh the news of their father's death, and then put on an audiobook that was actually fairly engaging until Jamie abruptly turned it off, having realized the predicament he'd put himself in.

"What am I supposed to do when we get to Marin?" he asked her. "What did you foresee happening from there?"

"I could ask you the same question," Meredith pointed out. "You're the one who got in the car with me. By the way, do you need to use the restroom?"

"A bit, yeah, now that you mention it," said Jamie. "But aren't you concerned I'll run?"

"Run where? You live three hours in the opposite direction. Want to switch when we get to the rest stop?"

"Switch? Switch?" Jamie's voice sounded maniacal with indignation. "You think I'm going to drive?"

"I'm just *asking*, for heaven's sake, James—"

"And for the record, I don't even live in Venice anymore," Jamie muttered. "I was only in town to cover your tech talk for *Magitek*."

"What do you mean you don't live in Venice *anymore*? You were living in Venice ever? At all?" asked Meredith, stunned enough to look at him then. "But I live in Venice."

"I know." Jamie was looking resolutely out the window. "I didn't live there long."

"How long did you live there?" Her voice sounded very strange to her, with a porous element, like there were holes in it.

Jamie shrugged, or gave the indication of having been trying to shrug. "Just a couple of years."

"*A couple of*—" They missed the exit for the rest stop. "You've just *been* there? Skulking in the shadows? This whole time?"

"I told you, I don't live there anymore, I've been on the road for the past six months. And I was never skulking in the shadows. I was writing out of the coworking place on Rose and shopping at the grocery store and surfing on Thursday mornings. None of those things are considered skulking."

"What grocery store?" demanded Meredith, and this time it sounded a little like a shriek.

"Not Demeter, if that's what you're asking." Jamie's tone of judgment was audibly insulting. "I'm a freelance writer, Meredith. I shop at places that don't slice their own kiwis or get milk from the happiest cows. And anyway, you're in cahoots with Demeter. And in bed with Tyche." He gave her a meaningful look then. "What made you agree to it?"

"Agree to what?" Meredith drummed the steering wheel innocently and missed the exit for the next potential place to stop, which meant at least fifty more miles.

"Your product does work," Jamie pointed out, and Meredith had to physically stop herself from adding "to an extent," realizing that despite Jamie's careful return to the subject of his article, this was not a casual chat. She ought to have been counting those words as a win.

"Oh, so *now* you admit I'm not actually a fraud? Maybe *you're* a fraud," Meredith huffed at him. "You're the one threatening my livelihood over something you freely admit is a lie."

"Your product works—as a tool for Tyche," Jamie corrected, seemingly gleeful over his semantic trap. "It does something very effectively, for sure. But it doesn't do what you said it would do." They both heard the words like the unmistakable bleat of a tiny passenger in the back seat: THIS APP WILL MAKE YOU HAPPY! :)

Jamie paused, then added, "Aren't you going to ask me what I was doing for the last six months?"

"No," snapped Meredith.

"I was tracking down as many Chirp users as I could find, including the trial patients. Do you remember Colette Bothe?" he asked in a tone that loomed with disaster. "Because she remembers someone who looked an awful lot like you."

Colette's dead eyes bore into Meredith's skull from the inside. Patient 76A. "Everyone looks like me, Jamie. I'm generic."

"You don't believe that."

"I'm biracial Asian, it happens!" she said, overzealously.

"Colette's doing well," Jamie commented. "Very well. Much better than anyone else I've spoken to who bought Chirp on the market. Far better than any Chirp customer who hasn't spent time with an abrasive biracial Asian woman who couldn't *possibly* be you—"

"Happiness is a high bar, Jamie," snapped Meredith. "It takes longer than six months."

To that, Jamie scoffed. "Please. You wouldn't know happiness if it tapped you on the shoulder and asked you to dance."

"You didn't ask me to dance. You asked me to talk." She could see him there briefly in his crimson prelaw association T-shirt, his hair in long, wild curls as he disrupted her Tuesday and nearly every Tuesday she'd lived through since.

From the corner of her eye, Meredith saw the edges of Jamie's mouth flicker threateningly with a smile. "I wasn't talking about me, Meredith."

"Chirp works." Meredith realized her knuckles were tight around the steering wheel and made a concerted effort to relax them. "It does exactly what I said it would do. It monitors brain chemistry. It delivers the appropriate SSRI subcutaneously in response to whatever your brain chemistry is doing. It takes the guesswork out of treating mental illness." If she sounded robotic, that was just a natural byproduct of her voice.

"And what happens when a person wearing a product funded by Tyche walks into a store funded by Tyche?" asked Jamie, with a tone of innocence that did nothing to mask the journalistic expression on his face.

Meredith again became aware of the presence of eggshells. "Advanced third-party research shows that—"

"Oh come on, Meredith, don't." Jamie gave her a withering look. "You and I both know what really happens. When someone wearing Chirp walks into Demeter and the GPS location of their device shows them at the register, Chirp pushes serotonin regardless of their actual mood."

Meredith said nothing.

"Chirp is nothing more than a glorified version of the bell Pavlov rang for his dogs. It's not solving mental health. It's just—" Jamie looked disgusted. "It's just another tool of late-stage capitalism. It's making people *buy things*. How long before other companies like Tyche do the same thing? How long before a market disruption becomes just another high-capital valuation with no actual contribution to wellness, or goodness, or anything of meaningful humanitarian change? How long before this thing you made renders every human being incapable of separating real, actual joy from retail therapy, until 'happiness' means nothing at all?"

Meredith's mouth felt dry, her lips chapped. THIS APP, exclaimed their imaginary passenger, WILL MAKE YOU HAPPY!, only this time with the undertone of a threat. :)

"You sold your soul to Tyche," Jamie concluded, this time sounding sad or angry or—no, just disappointed. "And you're profiting off that choice. You're profiting off the vulnerability and desperation of others despite the fact that you are a *Wren*." Ah, and there it was, the repulsion was back. "Meredith,"

Jamie gritted out, "you couldn't die in poverty even if you never worked another day in your life, so what is the point of any of this?"

He was silent then, and Meredith realized he was waiting for an answer. She cleared her throat, considering her response.

"Well," she eventually began. "These allegations are obviously—"

Instantly, Jamie groaned. "Seriously? Forget it." He practically spat the words at her before letting his head fall back against the seat. He closed his eyes, shaking his head, like she was a bad dream he could wake from if he simply tried hard enough.

She drove in silence, wondering if she could get away with putting the audiobook back on.

Then, some minutes later, Jamie leaned over and hit play, filling the car once again with the soothing sound of performatively British narration.

Meredith shut it off.

"Why didn't you tell me you were living in Venice?" she asked without looking at him. "You could have called. Or sent me a message."

"Would you have answered?" asked Jamie in a tired voice.

"Yes." She did look at him that time, though only briefly. "Yes, Jamie, I have always answered your calls. I will always answer them." She turned to look at the road again. "I thought you understood that."

He said nothing.

Then he shook his head.

"There's an exit," he said, pointing. "Can you stop?"

"Yes." She flicked her turn signal.

"I can drive if you're tired."

"It's fine, don't worry about it. I'm okay."

"You sure?"

"Yeah, it's kind of relaxing, actually. I don't mind."

"Okay." He fidgeted, picking at his cuticles as she took the curved exit toward the nearest gas station. She pulled into a parking spot and cut the ignition, catching his eye by accident.

"Please," said Jamie. "Just tell me you didn't do it for the money."

*Deny it,* said the gremlin who lived in Meredith's brain. *Use the word "allegedly" again. Make it conditional. Do not say something quotable. He is not your friend. He is not your lover. He is a journalist. He is a member of the faceless public. He will not hesitate to put you in jail.*

*But,* a smaller voice said, *if you lie to him, he won't get back in this car.*

And for probably sane and normal reasons, that was an unacceptable condition.

"I can't honestly tell you that," said Meredith. "I wish I could. But it's . . ." She looked away, then back at him. "It's not what I wanted."

Her hands were still on the wheel. The moment felt heavy and unfinished.

"Can you believe that?" she asked him.

Jamie exhaled swiftly, like he'd just been given bad news. Like the tumor was malignant. Like the symptoms had already suggested the disease.

I probably don't need to tell you that Jamie Ammar is very firmly not an asshole. He is, however, an idiot, and while there is definitely some truth to what Meredith is currently saying to him, we can't actually point to it and name it honesty. And because Meredith is spectacularly absent self-reflection, we can only speculate as to whether she was telling Jamie the truth or just telling him the acceptable *degree* of truth she knew would still allow her to hold him in her web.

We haven't discussed Meredith's past with Jamie Ammar, but surely you've grasped some idea of it by now. It was powerful and lifelong, and Meredith, like a spider, consumes her mates. Whether by biological, survival-driven instinct or on purpose, just for fun, is really the question, though, isn't it?

Or maybe it isn't. Maybe there is no question, and Meredith is just a dick.

"Meredith," Jamie said, "if I didn't already believe the woman I loved still existed in there somewhere, I wouldn't have gotten in the car."

See? What did I tell you? An idiot. As if Meredith couldn't be worth loving and a fucking liar at the same time. Even *she* knows he's allowing her a small but significant sliver of falsity, a place to exist between guilt and innocence without necessarily confessing to one or the other or both. He is practically handing her the means to get away with it, to change his mind.

And Meredith is a lot of things, including a so-called genius. So she said nothing. She reached out and tapped Jamie's knuckle with one unpolished but carefully manicured finger. In response, he gave her something of a grimace that was as good as a promise. They split up temporarily to empty their respective bladders and Meredith thought melancholically about the grammatical use of past tense.

Then she got back in the car and so did he. He put a bag of her favorite gummy candy in the cup holder, presumably as some sort of peace offering. She put the car in reverse, then drive.

"What if I tell you part of the story?" she said.

"Okay," said Jamie with palpable relief, despite the fact that Meredith had rehearsed this line and everything to follow in the mirror of the gas station bathroom. Despite the fact that over the course of their technically very brief courtship, Meredith had lied to him as often as she had told the truth. Despite the fact that he knew this, and had loved her anyway—despite the fact that Meredith Wren had never technically learned that love was a tacit agreement not to grievously injure the other person—despite the many people Meredith Wren had already fucked over and left behind, because her tolerance for pain was high—despite the fact that just because she loved someone did not mean she couldn't also stand to hurt them—

Despite *all of this,* Jamie Ammar, who had once been a very promising prelaw student at Harvard until Meredith Wren broke his heart—Jamie Ammar, a very talented investigative journalist who coincidentally did not have health insurance or a life partner or anything really beyond a ratty futon in storage and a set of lifestyle choices that didn't really fit and whose job was currently being threatened by the use of content-deriving machines that spat out listicles and grammatically accurate drivel that was, to be fair, indistinguishable from what an overworked, underpaid human being could probably write—which happened to be developed by *the very same father Meredith was going home to mourn—*

Despite all this, Jamie simply said to her okay, I'm listening, go ahead.

# 11

Dzhuliya pulled into the open-air carport of the Wren family home in the foothills of Mount Tamalpais, nestled at the base of a circle of redwoods very near the Cascade Falls trailhead, which was incredibly far from her apartment in downtown San Francisco. That was all Eilidh could think about, how inconvenient this was, probably because the inconvenience she was subjecting Dzhuliya to was more of a straightforward anxiety than any of the other horrors filling her mind, including but not limited to the demon-thing in her chest.

Eilidh had just finished crying about her father's death ten minutes ago, but the drive was long enough that there was an awkward period of bonus time post–initial bout of grief. Now, Eilidh resisted the urge to shove a gratuitous handful of bills in Dzhuliya's face. Amicable payment for services rendered! Not that she carried cash. What if she sent Dzhuliya something from her bank app? Would that make it better or worse?

"Can I ask you something?" said Dzhuliya, and Eilidh jumped.

"What? Yes, oh gosh, of course." She should have felt relieved, probably, that Dzhuliya was lost in thought herself, and not just sitting there wishing Eilidh would stop crying or at very least do something useful, like assure her that industry turnover was normal and she'd probably still have a job.

"I don't really know how to say this. Your siblings," began Dzhuliya, and then stopped with a wince. "Sorry if this is still fresh."

"No, they've always been like that," said Eilidh in a half-hearted attempt at levity. Ladies and gentlemen, behold a chronic people pleaser in the wild!

"Ha, right," said Dzhuliya, in a second rendition of vocal laughter. "I just . . . do you know where your father stood with them? You know, in terms of . . . their relationship, before he—" She paused, and then added hastily, "I'm just curious. You know—professionally speaking."

Right, of course, professional, as all things between them were. It was impossible for Eilidh not to think of Wrenfare in the context of her father's loss; more accurately, it was impossible not to think of her father without also thinking of Wrenfare. Eilidh supposed it was normal for Dzhuliya to wonder where the other Wren children stood, because Meredith had always been secretly desperate to run Wrenfare and because Dzhuliya currently worked for Wrenfare, which meant the question of her livelihood was inherently involved. Really, the vibes at Wrenfare had been indeterminate for months. It wasn't all that surprising that it would be the first thing to cross Dzhuliya's mind.

Would Dzhuliya be passed along as assistant to the next CEO? Not if it was Meredith, who didn't like having a personal assistant—not because she was too noble for it or something, but because she really believed that nobody on earth could match her efficiency. Give Meredith's precious calendar to someone else, a probable incompetent? Meredith had a business partner, Ward Varela, and while Meredith respected his technical knowledge to some degree, Eilidh knew their dynamic had never actually been equal. Meredith treated Ward like a storage container for the thoughts she didn't want cluttering up her own head. He did the product research while Meredith was the face of the company, the one who identified their goals, steered the ship. As far as Eilidh knew, Meredith did not accept help from anyone else, much less a paid employee.

Eilidh supposed there was a chance their father might have left the company to Arthur, who did have a job, but could easily step down in favor of running Wrenfare if that's what Thayer asked of him. It seemed highly unlikely and probably was. Still, there was no ruling it out, and there was also the possibility that Thayer, who had been in excellent health right up until he apparently wasn't, had never actually determined who should succeed him. His money, his assets, his legacy, his life's work . . . to whom could it realistically belong? Meredith worked in the industry, Arthur had national name recognition, but only one of Thayer's children actually worked for Wrenfare, and it was Eilidh herself.

Eilidh felt a temporary shiver of prophecy. Not that she was fit to run a company, much less a company of Wrenfare's size and scope, but if there was a chance that she and her siblings had inherited equal shares—meaning that they and/or the company's board would decide among themselves who would take over—then there was also a chance that Thayer's focus on Eilidh in recent years (the standing Tuesday lunch, the many questions about her projects) had been intentional. It wasn't as if it had never crossed her mind that Thayer had been trying to teach her something, to show her something, to give her some exposure that the other two would never get.

Suddenly, Eilidh couldn't shake the image of her father's furrowed brow; his tacit urgency to impart something unto her, the apprentice to his bearded archetypal sage. It was the same fleeting image she hadn't been able to shake during her aborted tryst with Dzhuliya. The sense that there was a level of worthiness to reach, an obligation of venerability to fulfill, and perhaps dry-humping the administrative underling wasn't a stop on the noble path.

But back to the subject of Thayer's guidance, Eilidh hoped she had been paying enough attention. She had never been an expert before, as such a thing implied maturity and age; instead, she'd been only an ingenue, a protégée, a possibility of a person. A break on the horizon. It occurred to her that the chance to grow up was an appealing one, if terrifying.

The reminder of a life without her father hit her square in the chest. The heartache kept coming back, like maybe she dreamed it. Like maybe if she walked inside the house right now, he'd still be sitting there, scrolling his tablet in his slippers and mentioning to Eilidh that a new restaurant had just opened in San Rafael and they should go.

The thing in her chest bit down on something, an artery that burst. A flood of grief and fluid. Over the drive they'd passed a blur of bus benches. THIS APP WILL MAKE YOU HAPPY! :), over and over, like a sadistic tiger's patterned stripes.

"I really wouldn't know how Dad left things with the others. Not with any certainty," Eilidh equivocated slowly in answer to Dzhuliya's question, the contusion of loss again crowding out the space for more logical thought. "You'd probably know better than I would how he felt about Meredith and Arthur in a professional context. We weren't together all that often when I was younger." Eilidh had gone to the ballet academy at thirteen, and Meredith and Arthur had already been away at boarding school for years before that. Her siblings had made the time to befriend each other, but never her. "Did he give you any idea that he'd pass it along to them? Or to all of us?"

Dzhuliya seemed to consider her words very carefully. "I really couldn't say," she managed politically. "That wasn't the sort of thing he usually discussed with me."

"Well, whatever happens, we'll make sure you're taken care of," said Eilidh, reaching out to rest her hand on Dzhuliya's.

It was too intimate. Eilidh knew it was a mistake the moment they touched, and it was immediately obvious to her that Dzhuliya was straining not to react.

"Sorry," said Eilidh, pulling her hand away, and Dzhuliya exhaled with a hint of loss, or maybe Eilidh was imagining that.

Thayer had always said that Eilidh needed to have more confidence, some surety beyond her athletic prowess or her performance on the stage. But actually, Eilidh had always been sort of an anxious person, and being able to wear a character had been her only confidence, so maybe it was never technically real. It was inseverable, the feeling of being the best at something and the ideation of confidence as a quality one could possess. Eilidh wasn't Meredith, who was lethally smart and seemed to make things happen for herself by sheer force of will, nor was Eilidh Arthur, who was funny and impossible not to like once he'd decided that he wanted you to like him. Theirs were very separate powers, but equal in magnitude. Since being injured—since seeing her value decrease in real time—Eilidh had been forced to reconsider the way she saw the world, which no longer seemed a thing designed for her to conquer.

"If it were up to me, I'd pick you," Dzhuliya said in a quiet voice, and it was reassuring to Eilidh, albeit sad. Nobody at work spoke to her directly about their concerns—whatever the position on her resume, she was still one of Them, the upper-floor Them, not one of the comrade proletariat who needed the work, so how would they look at her now? As a savior, a promise, a beacon? She doubted it. The thing in her chest felt weighty, unmissable. Imagine having to put your faith in someone who wore eau de apocalypse like it was perfume. Eilidh always wondered if other people could feel it—if the reason she was so universally alien now was because other people could sniff out the doom on her, could no longer be their natural selves in her presence.

But Dzhuliya wanted it to be her, and her father had loved her enough to spend time with her, and wasn't that something neither Meredith nor Arthur could say?

Pettily, Eilidh stroked her win, the thing in her chest stretching out, catlike, with a pulse of satisfaction. Which was somewhere adjacent to the spectrum of happiness, if nowhere near the thing itself. "Thanks, Dzhuliya."

Then she heard a car pull up behind them in the carport, the silhouette of her brother stepping out from the passenger side.

# 12

"Where's Death?" asked Arthur, not even thinking about the oddity of the phrasing until Eilidh looked like she might cry. In fairness, Eilidh often looked like she might cry, and had been that way ever since her accident. Arthur tried not to think of Eilidh as a sad person, but it was very hard not to. He himself had been injured many times, and it wasn't as if he still waited around for a miracle to land him the professional baseball career he'd lost. The past was the past, and Arthur felt it was part of his job as a human being to move on.

But he could see that mentioning death—well, Death, which was his nickname for Meredith, something she outwardly claimed to hate but that Arthur felt sure she secretly loved because it was, in some highly Meredithian way, distinguished—set Eilidh off on an alarming course of emotion. Certainly alarming to Arthur, who was for this very reason on drugs.

Beside him, having climbed out of the driver's side, Gillian let out an audible sigh at the sight of the stairway leading the sixty-some feet up to the house, which was all but carved into the side of a cliff. The staircase, a sort of reverse inferno, took seven sharp turns as it clawed its way up, limiting any visibility from the darkness of the hillside floor. The house itself was austere, Californian late modernist, with a massive A-frame design—the better to see the sunrise from deep among the redwoods.

Not that anyone would know that from where they presently stood. Thayer Wren's lovely fortress took the high ground—part divinity, part defense. Though it remained unclear to Arthur who Thayer had been so fearful might attack.

Gillian's voice awakened him from his momentary distraction. "I ordered matzo ball soup," she announced in her most soothing tones of administrative competency. Her love language, assuming Arthur could claim any knowledge of such a thing.

"Can I have a hug?" Eilidh asked Arthur then, who jumped at her sudden nearness. Eilidh was still very graceful from her years as a ballerina, which had rendered her somewhat stealthy, in Arthur's mind. She moved like a fucking snake.

"What? Why?" Oh yes, their dead father. "Right, sorry, come here." Arthur held open one arm and Eilidh plastered herself into it like she hoped to be absorbed into his skin. "Is that Dzhuliya in the car?"

Their father's assistant, a pretty woman in her midtwenties who normally seemed very posh and restrained, like a former child pop star now promoting her lifestyle blog, hastily waved from behind the closed window of the driver's side. She had just completed some sort of awkward fifteen-point turn in the carport, followed by a careful reverse behind Gillian's car, apparently desiring to flee the scene without having to ask Gillian to clear some space for her to do so.

"Well, bye," offered Arthur uncertainly, finding it strange that Dzhuliya had not done the polite thing and lowered the window down. However, the effect of the chocolate Yves had given him was fully coursing through him at this point, and he did not have the energy to dwell on it.

"Did you say matzo ball soup?" he asked Gillian belatedly.

"I tried to get some pho but it's quite late," Gillian explained with a shrug. "Only the deli was still open."

"Is there a reason you were specifically drawn to soup?" asked Arthur, who realized in the precise moment he said it, "Come to think of it, soup does sound nice."

"Soup felt like a bereavement food," Gillian agreed. "Eilidh, would you like a hug from me as well, or is this more of an Arthur thing?"

"Oh, um." Eilidh sniffled. "I'd love a hug, Gillian. It's been a tough day." She disentangled from Arthur and the two women embraced awkwardly, with as little physical contact as possible. "How was it getting in from DC?"

"Well, I do appreciate that airplanes have phone chargers now," said Gillian, tactically obscuring the need for Arthur to comment on his actual whereabouts. "The food will be here in fifteen minutes. Also there's a photographer in those bushes."

Eilidh and Arthur both turned to see that Gillian was indeed correct. The photographer snapped another picture, at which point Gillian stalked over with an air of removal and Arthur exchanged a glance with Eilidh. He could sense himself being looked to for guidance in the moment, much in the way an injured toddler looks to their parent to determine whether they should cry. Being the elder of the two, Arthur tried to reassure his sister visually. *Everything is fine,* his posture attempted to convey, *insofar as I understand the plausible definition of fineness, though it bears acknowledging that entering our father's house without glacial procrastination will simply not be feasible at this time.*

On perhaps a related subject, the drugs were doing something counterproductive to Arthur's reaction times. Thankfully, Gillian had had the presence of mind to position herself at Arthur's side in something of a comforting manner after threatening the photographer's livelihood and sanity or whatever Gillian customarily did to make things go away. Though really, why shouldn't they all be acting a bit strange, considering the news? (Press surveillance did not technically matter to Arthur, who lived with a permanent audience in his head at all times: an amphitheater of faceless content creators. Nothing new or even different here.)

"It's very shocking," said Arthur. It felt accurate, and helpfully not inappropriate for a potential quote, should he happen to be surveilled.

"Yes," said Eilidh.

He pressed himself for more. "It just happened so suddenly."

"I know."

"Was he sick? Or something?" There, that was a cogent interrogative.

"No," said Eilidh. "He'd been to a physical just a few weeks ago, on his birthday. Perfectly clean bill of health."

"So sad," said Arthur.

"Yes," said Eilidh. "It really is."

They were silent another long moment.

"Well," prompted Gillian, perhaps recognizing the ongoing reticence of her audience, "should we go inside? The food will be here in thirteen minutes."

Right. Yes. Inside. Arthur looked up at his family home where it towered above them, nestled into the side of the hill. The sheer volume of steps to the front door was such that physical fitness was not only implied, it was a prerequisite for entry. (How, exactly, would Thayer have traversed sixty flights of stairs with a bad hip, or even the slightest loss of mobility? But, then, never mind. Thayer would never have to come to terms with the unmanliness of reasonable accessibility, because he no longer existed. Like a bill that died on the Senate floor. Crash, boom, gone.)

Arthur took in the familiar falseness of the carport's decorative Italianate facade, the vines that had been specifically planted around it. There was a small garden to his left, beside a burbling creek, that was the product of substantial landscaping rather than any labor of love. The flowers were almost obscenely bright, like lipstick; like a painted clown's mouth parting to laugh at him, to mime despair at his expense.

This wasn't the house Arthur was born in—the family had lived in suburban Palo Alto until the magitech boom had launched Wrenfare to such heights that city-averse Thayer Wren no longer needed to commute to the office on a daily basis—and Persephone had lived here only a year, before most of the renovations to the house's kitchen, home office, and bedrooms had even been finished. But Arthur had returned here from boarding school every year since the sixth grade, and had lost his virginity here, which made it close enough to home. Arguably it was worse, since there was no evidence of his mother here, nothing to feel fondly over—not even the sex, which had ended badly. All that remained was the prepubescent angst of someone discovering his penis amid the dulcet sympathies of malaising pop-punk.

"I hate this house," Arthur murmured in answer to Gillian's dutiful nudge for progress; a tacit *thank you, but no*. She gave his elbow a tap with hers, a rare contact she performed only in moments of direst sympathy, and proceeded to make her way up the stairs alone, mountaineering up to the front door.

Arthur remained behind at the carport, beside the burbling creek, with Eilidh lingering uncertainly at his side. "Are you staying here as well?" he asked her.

He looked at her for the first time, really looked, and realized she was taller than he remembered. Not a new development—they just didn't see each other often enough for Arthur to properly envision her as a living, space-occupying thing beyond a message on his screen every now and then.

Then he noticed the suitcase in her hand. "I guess you did pack," he commented, pointing at it.

"Oh, I just got home from a silent retreat in Vermont." Eilidh, too, was staring at the house like she worried something monstrous might lurk inside it.

"I've been to one of those. Did you like it?"

"Oh yes, very refreshing." She shifted a little, like she was in pain.

"I thought it sucked," murmured Arthur. "But I told Meredith I had a fabulous time because I thought it would be funny to watch someone pry her phone away."

Eilidh cracked a smile then. "It would be."

"She never went, though. I think it was the year she went into production on the Chirp."

"It's Chirp."

"What?"

"It's Chirp," repeated Eilidh, louder. "Not 'the' Chirp."

"Oh." He looked at his younger sister again, realizing that she had come to resemble a full-grown woman. He supposed that had happened some years ago, though it felt impossible that such a thing could ever be true. Whenever Arthur thought of Eilidh, he thought of a small girl in the back seat clutching a teddy bear that appeared to have no ears.

"Have you tried it?" Eilidh asked.

"Tried what? The Chirp?"

"Chirp," she said again. "It's Chirp."

"Why?" said Arthur. "Don't LA people put 'the' in front of the freeway numbers? Why isn't it 'the' Chirp?"

"You sound absolutely geriatric," she said. "Why would it need an article?"

"Formality. Also because it is an object."

"I used it for about six months." Eilidh looked embarrassed. "I still use it sometimes."

Arthur contemplated saying nothing, or asking a question to be polite.

"I stopped a couple of weeks ago," he admitted.

They were both still staring at the house. At the front door above—the one that Gillian had just windedly entered through—that would lead to a house that contained all their father's things, but not their father.

How strange, Arthur thought. The ease with which a person could vanish was really quite terrifying. He felt a little twitch in his hand then, like someone small reaching for his fingers. *Don't worry, Riot,* he told the little girl who did not yet exist. *You'll be so much better than me, but I'll be at least a little bit better than him.*

"It doesn't work, does it?" Eilidh turned to him, and for a moment Arthur hadn't the faintest idea what she was talking about.

Then he remembered, and felt an instant pang of guilt that his intestines read as disloyalty. He also managed (impressively!) to recall that if *one* photographer had been in the bushes, then who knew how many others there were. He simply assumed Gillian would take care of that somehow—though perhaps he ought to unlearn that reflex.

"No, of course the Chirp works," he performatively emphasized in lieu of doing the obvious and going inside. (Even if today was the day he learned to dispatch his own photographers, what could be worse than a shot of him lunging across the *Times* landing page? Well, but he knew what would be worse, and it was going inside.) "I felt much better when I was using it," Arthur continued, well-versed by then in the meaningless rhythms of spon-con. "I just don't like wearing too many gadgets, you know. Plus it's still a bit of a luxury item, and since my district has been struggling with inflation and unemployment and, well, there's been sort of a mass exodus thanks to skyrocketing high street land value—"

"Totally," said Eilidh. Her voice sounded deflated, half-cooked. Perhaps she recognized that he'd spontaneously transformed into an ad. "Yeah, that makes sense."

"There's just . . . a certain degree of approachability I have to emulate. And the Chirp's price point isn't terrible, but it's, you know, still a bit out of reach. For now."

"Meredith's doing great, though," said Eilidh.

"She's doing great!" Arthur agreed. Look at him, mayor of quote city!

"I see ads for it all the time—"

"Oh yes, absolutely—"

"And people are wearing it, you know, out and stuff. I actually saw that some party girls in Manhattan were wearing it, so it's, like, sexy, I think."

"Do you see it out in the clubs?" asked Arthur, forgetting for a moment that he'd been trying to accomplish something. What it was, he couldn't recall.

"The clubs?" echoed Eilidh, bewildered.

"The clubs. The bars. You know, wherever young people go to meet people."

"How old *are* you?" asked Eilidh.

"I just mean, you know, nightlife—"

"I don't have 'nightlife,'" said Eilidh with apparent disgust, having put the phrase in air quotes. "I'm twenty-six, not twenty-one. I occasionally go on dates, but mostly I go to work and I go to yoga and I go to my physical therapist and I go to lunch with—"

Eilidh stopped abruptly. "I mean, I have friends," she said, or rather mumbled. "But I'm not, like, up in the club."

"Well, it's nice to have friends," said Arthur, who didn't technically have any. Briefly, Lou hovered in the periphery of his mind's eye.

The silence between the two younger Wrens was suddenly very uncomfortable.

Then there was an onslaught of blinding headlights from behind them on the road, startling both Eilidh and Arthur as another vehicle pulled into the carport beside Gillian's rental car.

"Is that Death?" asked Arthur, blinking away the headlight flash, and Eilidh shook her head with a frown, opening her mouth to answer when a man, maybe mid- or late thirties, stepped out from the car's driver's side.

Before Arthur could place him, though, he was distracted by the passenger door, which opened and shut to reveal Yves disembarking with a Styrofoam container in hand.

"Yves?" asked Arthur in disbelief. Not that he had ever really doubted that Yves would be able to find him. Yves had a way of doing that, a sort of power of magical thinking that Arthur had considered easily put down to luck until he realized just how routine it was for Yves to "hope for the best" and wind up wherever he needed to go, whenever he wanted to be there.

"Arthur!" exclaimed Yves happily, as if they had been parted for weeks instead of hours. "I have pancakes!" he added, before wandering into the patch of garden to smell the roses.

Oh yes, Arthur realized belatedly, he was *also* on drugs.

"Oh good, you're here," announced Gillian, who had breezed back down the stairwell from the door, first waving to Yves—who, it seemed, had found a ladybug—before offering the older man a smile as if they knew each other.

The older man was the person she looked happier to see, which was interesting. Maybe, Arthur mused in his head, this was Gillian's boyfriend? It was reasonable that she would have one, and if she did, it would likely be someone like this, who was slight in an elegant way (unlike Arthur, who—with some effort—was still built like a person who'd played baseball from the tender age of four). The man had a silver tinge to his hair, making him seem like someone who enjoyed quiet evenings playing chess and drinking scotch—both of which were among Gillian's favorite things, alongside the blood sports and gin.

Good god, Arthur thought with a discombobulating tilt from his inner ear, a mix of preexisting intoxication and a sharp, acid-based revulsion. This was Gillian's boyfriend.

So many things struck him at once. Relief was present somewhere. Good! So then when Arthur finally managed the balls to tell her about Riot, at least Gillian would not be alone. She had found someone obviously good and stable, and adult. Yes, this was a man, Arthur thought with a heavy sadness, suddenly feeble and shrunken, like a child who could not yet reach the shelf. This was the sort of man his father had wanted him to be. This man looked like a politician, actually—unlike Arthur, who by comparison looked like the overgrown frat boy the *New York Post* had accused him of being some days ago, leading to a trending cartoon of a beer-helmeted Arthur wolfishly greeting some fellow kids.

This man looked like a father! By god, *that was it*, thought Arthur, who was really in it now. Gillian would marry this man and have an entire fleet of tactical children. She would start an empire. She would go forth and take France.

Well, at least Arthur would have Riot, not to mention Philippa and Yves, and surely some fraction of the internet still found him handsome, if disastrously ineffective. He'd once reached the final round of a March Madness–style bracket before losing to the Canadian prime minister, which counted for something, he was pretty sure. He managed to relax a bit as Gillian said obligingly, "Cass, you remember Arthur."

"Wrenfare Christmas party, wasn't it?" asked the man, who was apparently called Cass, before stepping forward to shake Arthur's hand. Arthur took a bit of pride in the fact that at least Arthur was a man's name. An elderly man, infirm, but still.

"Right, yes," lied Arthur, fighting the urge to check his social feeds and hungering vaguely for more drugs. "Wonderful to see you again."

"We were hoping you were the deli guy," said Eilidh when it was her turn to be greeted. She, unlike Arthur, appeared to be familiar with Cass, which Arthur found somewhat less comforting. Couldn't Gillian have chosen someone who was not an apparent household face for his entire family? At least *he'd* had the decency to choose lovers outside their immediate circle.

"Oh, sincerest apologies for showing up empty-handed. There is no bereavement to my knowledge that a matzo ball soup cannot ease," said Cass, and Arthur's heart sank even deeper into his kidneys at the thought that yes, Gillian had clearly found her perfect match. Had Arthur been left in charge of food, he would have gotten one of those giant, cheese-smothered wet burritos to share and they'd all sit around moaning in varying states of digestive unease (Arthur was sensitive to dairy). Now they would have antioxidants. Whatever the fuck those were!

"I'm terribly sorry for your loss," Cass continued, a sentiment he expressed to both Eilidh and Arthur. It was a perfunctory offering that Arthur could take or leave, but that Eilidh seemed to appreciate. She tilted her chin gratefully in the way she had always done as a child. At the age of three or four, it had been a party trick, Eilidh's head tilt. *Cute baby!* people would coo. They loved it, Arthur recalled, the way she could look so demure and doll-like. Her earliest performance art.

"There's a photographer in those roses," said Yves, tromping back through the garden to join their strange little circle of cordial small talk.

"Oh, for heaven's sake," said Gillian, who vigorously repeated the ascent up to the house, leaving Cass to turn his mechanized look of apparent sympathy back to Eilidh and Arthur.

"Is Meredith not here yet?" he asked them.

"She should be here soon," Eilidh said, glancing at her watch. It was a new Wrenfare model, Arthur noticed. He did not wear one himself, but he did listen to his father's keynote speeches. He realized with a sudden jolt that perhaps Eilidh would be giving those speeches now—or Meredith, who was the better choice for running the company, albeit not as talented as Eilidh at garnering public adoration—which was another confusing rush of emotions. Not that Arthur envied the speeches, per se, but this was *Wrenfare Magitech*. It was more than just a company. It was the touchstone of an industry, as ubiquitous to modern society as indoor plumbing and personal computing. It was worth at least tens of billions, conservatively speaking, and more importantly, Wrenfare was their birthright, their collective legacy, and their meaningful claim to history, which was far more than Arthur could say after two dismal years in Congress.

Given that Arthur would almost certainly be out of a job come November—this thought he suffered with an emoticon grimace, followed by the caving in of his own chest—wouldn't it be a neat little sidestep for him to fill the role of Wrenfare CEO? Politics were tiresome anyway, he looked pretty on a stage, and he could devote a significant portion of the Wrenfare budget to philanthropic efforts. Hell, he'd probably get more done as an anonymous donor than he would as an elected official. Money did have a very particular magic when it came to accomplishing things quickly, and everything Arthur knew about the world suggested that wealth, at Wrenfare's scale, was the one thing that didn't have any rules.

It occurred to him belatedly that Eilidh seemed to know where Meredith was, and that he had not gotten an answer to that question earlier, and that in the moments since realizing this, Yves had sat on the ground, opening his doggie bag of pancakes and beginning to eat them like tiny, rolled taquitos, dipping them euphorically in syrup. "You've spoken to Meredith?" Arthur asked Eilidh, beginning to wonder where drugs began and Yves ended. Arthur was suddenly in the mood for pancakes as well, which was another of Yves's talents. It was like he could predict the perfect thing before anyone else could identify a craving.

Soup wasn't always the perfect food for bereavement, Arthur realized, weaponizing the thought at Cass with a flush of loathing. Suddenly he felt deeply in love with Yves all over again.

"Oh yes, sorry, I forgot to tell you. She called me from the car," said Eilidh just as Gillian returned from the house's stairwell, this time bearing the antique rifle that hung in their father's study as she waded into the greenery. The rifle had never been loaded, having been gifted by one of the conservative presidents at some point during Arthur's childhood, though of course any paparazzo hiding in the bushes would not have any reason to know that. There was a brief scuttle, some yelps, and a few fleeing figures before Gillian returned to Arthur's side, tucking a handful of SIM cards into her pocket with only the faintest indication of sweat.

Not for the first time, Arthur thought fleetingly of kissing her in gratitude, though he had other things on the mind, and anyway, it wouldn't work.

"Wait, Meredith called *you*?" Arthur asked Eilidh, bewildered. He realized he hadn't checked his phone very carefully, short of looking for Gillian's arrival message. He dug it out of his pocket and realized that yes, he had several notifications he had apparently missed in the haze of deplaning, including multiple calls from Meredith and countless alerts for himself from every major publication (these he consulted with routine dread, waiting to be canceled; so far so good, but there was always, inevitably, tomorrow).

"Actually, Meredith's the one who told me the news." Eilidh's expression became very stiff, forcefully pleasant, which was how it looked when she was experiencing any strong emotion. "Well, I suppose technically Jamie was."

"Who's Jamie?" asked Gillian at the same time that Cass said, "She's still with Jamie?"

"Oh, is that—? I mean, I wasn't . . . ? I don't think," Eilidh began, and then ran out of steam. She looked at Cass, then at Arthur, as if she assumed Arthur could fix whatever she'd just done, which was very unclear to him.

"Jamie is Meredith's ex-boyfriend," Arthur explained to Gillian, deciding to start there, and then thought about it for another millisecond. "Wait, she's with Jamie?"

"Who is Meredith?" asked Yves, who was smiling. He bit into a pancake taquito, still smiling.

"Well, that explains a lot," said Cass, looking a bit surlier, the way older men tended to do. It was an expression that Arthur associated with paying taxes and telling people they'd inevitably become more conservative as they aged, which was of course to disregard the reality that social services were not what they once were, meaning that almost nobody would have the same resources their parents had (Arthur excepted—he'd have *more,* he realized, the reality of his father's death dawning on him once again. Although that was neither here nor there).

"Oh, it's nothing," Gillian said reassuringly to Cass, inspecting Arthur's father's gun. (It was actually Napoleonic in origin, and Gillian took great pains to keep it clean. It occurred to Arthur to hope his father had left it to her, because it would make her really happy. Something Arthur did technically know how to do, so suck on that, Cass.) "I spoke to her earlier. It's really more blackmail related than romantic."

"What?" said Eilidh and Arthur simultaneously.

"Oh good, the food's here," said Gillian as another set of headlights appeared in the driveway, marching toward it with the rifle held in the crook of her arm like a newborn baby.

Oh, thought Arthur with another pang. Oh, Riot, what a shame it will be if you can't have Gillian in your life, though at least your mother will be plenty of entertainment.

He missed Philippa feverishly then. What would Philippa be doing right this moment, had she been there? Probably trying to get them to write a play about their feelings, not that Arthur had any. But for Philippa, he would make some up.

Arthur jumped at the sudden clap of a hand on his shoulder. "This will be a difficult few days for you, Arthur," said Yves soberly. "There is much to be done when a loved one passes."

"Yes," said Gillian, her arms now laden down with enormous containers of soup. "I called the funeral home and explained our need to protect the family's privacy, what with all of you being such public figures"—and one of us, Arthur thought, being an electrokinetic menace—"and I gave him the go-ahead to start arranging the funeral for Friday, but beyond that, I don't know what Thayer's estate plan entails. The executor will have to see to the details. Do you know who it is?"

"Me," said Eilidh with another forced look of pleasantness, which likely meant she was dying inside.

"You'll all have to speak with the attorneys, probably tomorrow," said Cass, and Arthur thought briefly of challenging him to a fight. Not over Gillian's honor, necessarily, but Cass was meddling in Arthur's family affairs, which was a step too far. It was Gillian's family, too, but only insofar as she remained married to Arthur, which made Cass tertiary to the situation at best. At best!

"Once Meredith gets here," Cass continued, unperturbed by Arthur's growing agitation, "you should get in touch with any remaining family members and friends. When you have the will, you can start sorting through the assets and clearing out the house. Unless one of you plans to live here?"

He looked between Arthur and Eilidh, who looked at each other, and then back at Cass.

"Well, like I said, that can wait," said Cass with apparent indifference.

"I meant that there was much to do with your soul," said Yves, who was resting nearly his entire weight on Arthur's shoulder. "Grief can be a heavy thing, and only when tended to properly can new things begin to grow. Do I smell chicken soup?" he added with a sudden look of ecstasy.

"Matzo ball," said Gillian.

"Oh, yummy," exclaimed Yves, taking a bag from her and leaving her with a free hand to hoist the rifle against her shoulder as she followed him up the stairs.

"I'd better go help them," said Cass, gesturing, before putting his hands in his pockets to begin the ascent. He was carrying a leather overnight bag, very stylish. He was a stylish person, Arthur realized glumly, and reached out just before Cass passed him for the stairs.

"Hey," said Arthur quietly. "Be good to her, all right?"

Cass seemed surprised at first, but then nodded as if tasked with something holy. He strode forward then, looking contemplatively at the canopy of trees that beheld patches of moonlit sky before taking hold of the stairwell banister and beginning to climb.

"That was sweet," said Eilidh, and Arthur glanced back at her with surprise. "Not really helping your case that you're not, you know, completely geriatric at the age of twenty-nine," she said. "Though now that Dad's gone, I hope you'll be like that for me if I ever bring someone home."

She seemed genuinely sad, though Arthur supposed that wasn't much of a surprise. Their father had always been sweet to Eilidh in a way that didn't otherwise exist, like he'd made it up specifically for her enjoyment. Thayer had always looked at Meredith with a sense of caution, as if keeping his distance was something he did in the interest of public safety. He looked at Arthur with something closer to effort, like if he simply looked hard enough for long enough then eventually Arthur would transform, miraculously becoming something else.

"The headlights on Cass's car are sparking," said Eilidh, the way she might have told him his fly was down. Arthur jumped a little, realizing he'd rounded a fist, and shook out his hands. They were almost arthritically tense, so cramped he struggled to uncurl them.

"Yeah, weird," he said, pretending to frown bemusedly at the car. "That's . . . wow, he really ought to have that looked at—"

But Eilidh was looking unmistakably at his hands.

"Still?" she asked him. Entirely the worst question, because asking if Arthur still suffered from the fiasco they should have long ago forgotten was like asking if he still wet the bed. He had not, after all, caused any damage to himself or others via near-fatal electrical fire for decades, not since Lou. (Unless you counted all the damage he'd caused over the last few months, which was, again, a temporary condition Arthur was hoping to be rid of at the universe's earliest convenience.)

"It's nothing," he assured her. "I've got it under control."

"I'm not judging you," Eilidh said quickly. "I'm just curious. Because—" She broke off, hesitating. "Well, I hadn't planned to . . . to talk about this. But I guess, you know, since you're here, and honestly, I'd rather talk about this right now than Dad—"

Arthur stopped listening, realizing that dear god, he'd have to talk about his father *a lot* over the coming days. It wasn't just Yves who would want him to wrestle with grief, but everyone. The press! Oh god, the press. Imagine what the *Los Angeles Times* would say about him as a man, as a son, if he couldn't conjure up something more meaningful than "fuck you" to say to an urn. Because surely the man would want a secret extravagance—the quiet luxury of an *organic* urn, undecorated but designed by Frank Gehry, a fact known only to those *in the know.*

The possibility existed that Thayer Wren had given so little thought to his mortality that he had not specified any funereal eccentricities, but then it would be even worse, because Arthur, Meredith, and Eilidh would be responsible for *inventing* the pomp and circumstance that would be suitable to their father, which was unimaginable at this moment in time, an era in which anything Arthur thought was right or even acceptable would surely be met with revilement en masse. And to think he would have to say words, publicly, on the nature of his relationship with his father! Full sentences, even! And what of the circus that was surely coming on social media, assuming it wasn't already here? The comments, which would no doubt alternate wildly between adulation and vitriol, the unavoidable polarity of in memoriams and memes?

The sudden, world-upending feeling Arthur had given in to when he'd first heard the news was back, and for a moment, he felt as though the ground had slipped out from under him.

Then yet another set of blinding white headlights struck him between the eyes like a godless curse.

"You know what, Jamie? Have the car! Write your little article! Have a fantastic life subsisting on the grief of other people like some kind of scumsucking bristle worm and see where it gets you!" shouted Arthur's sister Meredith, slamming the door shut on a still-running car before suddenly materializing by Arthur's side, so impressively unchanged from when he'd last seen her that he wanted temporarily to drop to the ground and kiss her feet.

"What?" Meredith demanded, apparently of Eilidh, who wasn't doing anything particularly, aside from being Eilidh, as the car's headlights receded in reverse.

"Bristle worm?" asked Eilidh.

"They're scavengers," snapped Meredith. "They keep aquarium ecosystems clean."

"No, makes sense," said Eilidh in the haughty way that Meredith hated, which was really Eilidh mirroring Meredith in a way she subconsciously put on, like a costume.

"Do shut up," said Meredith in the Meredith way that Eilidh hated, or perhaps "hated" was too strong a word. It was unclear what Eilidh felt, since she was perpetually a child to Arthur despite having very clearly grown up. "Art, you look shit."

He didn't feel well, come to think of it. Cass's headlights were sparking again; the taillights now, too. They'd been going like that for several seconds, he realized, lighting up like the Fourth of July. He saw them streaming with starlight, a haze of bright white rising up like a banner in the sky. He felt . . . suddenly painless, as if he'd swallowed a ball of light whole.

*Oh wow,* he thought, which probably should have been *oh no,* under the circumstances.

Because although Arthur Wren had started to die some decades ago, depending on how closely one was keeping track—and really, aren't we all dying from birth, in some sense?—this was actually the first time death had ever happened in a tangible, recognizable way, such that he wouldn't even feel it by the time he hit the ground.

# 13

When Meredith was nine years old, her mother died of heart complications from an eating disorder that had been killing her slowly over the course of several decades, having taken root in her teens. Persephone Liang had been deemed anemic and malnourished several times over the course of her youth—and you'll recall she had the money *not* to starve—before she eventually became Persephone Wren and began committing fashionably to juice cleanses and intermittent fasting and exercising to the point of collapse, usually saying things like "I just feel so much *better* when I'm active and don't eat carbs" while simultaneously lacking the energy to remain upright for the entire day.

Throughout her childhood, Meredith watched it happen, and although she did not then know how to fix it, she did understand that her mother had a disease, and the disease was hatred. Persephone hated herself, which was absurd to Meredith, who loved her mother more than she had ever loved anybody—more than she thought she would ever love anyone again. She confided all this in Lou, who tried to help in the silly ways that girlhood friends do, by making potions out of twigs and burning sage in small, ineffective piles. But it didn't work, and eventually Meredith went through school and learned about mental disorders, and specifically about one that caused you to sometimes be extremely active and sometimes very sedentary and depressed, and that sometimes, if the wires got crossed badly enough, you did things like stop taking care of yourself. And occasionally stop eating and go for such a long, dangerous hike on so few nutrients that a heart attack was a woefully inaccurate way to describe the suicide that would ultimately go unwritten across the death certificate bearing your name.

It was in high school, when Meredith was sixteen and finally realizing in retrospect which *specific* disease her mother had had, that she understood why the girlhood witchcraft hadn't worked to bring her back. Maybe it would have if Meredith had come into her whole power in time, she thought. Maybe if she'd caught it quickly enough and understood it in a way that a nine-year-old would never have the world-wise maturity to do. Lou was still with her then, having set off for the same illustrious boarding school Meredith attended, and together they spent their summers in Marin obsessing over the possibility that a mind could be changed, that a brain could be fixed.

Unfortunately, Lou had mistakenly considered Meredith to be the normal sort of motivated instead of fucking pathological, and thus, upon realizing what Meredith wanted to be able to do—and the way she wanted to practice it—Lou realized it would necessarily imply small violations here and there to a person's mental and physical autonomy. Whether for the greater good or not, it still seemed kind of fucked. So Lou said some variation of "Uh, I think you're going too far," which put a damper on their collective exploration of witchcraft. ("BIOMANCY," screamed Meredith at the time, a convenient shorthand for *I'm out here doing* science, *you fucking cunt!*)

Shortly after, for probably unrelated reasons—said the Lord God, sarcastically—Meredith would have Lou expelled by revealing a minor history of plagiarism, which the school did not tolerate. But the point is that Meredith had an obsession, and that obsession was rewriting the past into a version where she had the power to save her dead mother's life, which would ultimately become a tool that could make you happy—an invention that Meredith called Chirp.

This was not the speech that Meredith had given earlier that day on the Tyche stage. That one was more about having a research idea you then guided in a methodical, meticulous way to fruition, with the assistance of venture capital so phenomenally massive it gave you a near-magical ability to overlook your father's failure to invest or your own nauseating transgressions. She mostly talked about how difficult it was to be a woman of color in magitech, which was true. Most of Meredith's poor reputation in the industry came from a place of personal dislike, because in order to become as successful as she was, she had had to tell a lot of men to suck her dick in various ways, largely for the crime of having been smarter than they were to begin with.

The truth, oh, the truth—again from a place of divine narrative impartiality, bordering on indifference—is that Meredith Wren was absolutely, without question smarter than any man she'd ever worked with or for. Meredith Wren was smarter than her peers, smarter than her rivals, smarter than her siblings, smarter than her father. But this isn't a world that actually *embraces* genius, not when it doesn't come with the right packaging, and anyway she was also an asshole, and actively unethical, and so powerfully single-minded that to call Meredith Wren a danger to herself and others was not only warranted by the metrics of professional psychiatry, but also completely, profoundly true.

So this was not the story that Meredith told Jamie over the course of their six-hour drive, either. But I'll leave that story for a later time, because right now Meredith's brother has just dropped dead in the carport of their father's house, so in terms of priorities the current moment has just reached a whole new scale of urgency.

"Oh my god," said Eilidh, leaping back from the place Arthur had fallen between them on the floor of the carport. "Oh my god. Oh my god. Oh my god!"

"Would you get ahold of yourself," hissed Meredith, bending to check Arthur's pulse. "Call 911," she added, as Eilidh fumbled gracelessly for her phone.

Oh, another thing about Meredith—she's actually fantastic in a crisis. She's definitely the person you want around if you ever accidentally stab yourself too close to an artery. If you would like a display of human emotion, however, you're what the French call shit out of luck.

Case in point: "Well, fuck," said Meredith, after determining Arthur's pulse to be nonexistent.

"Oh my god," said Eilidh again. (Eilidh, who has not yet acknowledged nor dealt with ninety-nine percent of her personal problems, is less helpful under conditions of catastrophe, and the thing living in her chest even less so.) "Oh my god—my brother just collapsed and he isn't moving," she shouted into the screen of her phone, so ostensibly someone had answered. In a moment of what seemed to be utter helplessness, she added tangentially, "And my father just died!"

Meredith was bent over Arthur, methodically performing the CPR she had learned around the age of ten, just in case. *C is for chest compressions,* she recited quietly to herself as she adjusted Arthur's head, *A is for opening the airway, B is for rescue breaths*—

"Yes, my sister is doing that now—no, he's only twenty-nine, he's in completely perfect health except for—" She broke off, hesitating around the issue of uncanny electrical malfunction. "I mean, yes, he's in perfect health—"

Meredith kept one eye on her watch, wrestling with the seconds as she pushed two inches down onto Arthur's chest. Every twenty seconds, two rescue breaths. One, two, and back to compressions.

One, two, and back to compressions.

One, two, and back to compressions.

"—no, no history that I know of—is he breathing? Meredith—MEREDITH," Eilidh shouted, "they want to know if he's breathing—"

One, two, and back to compressions.

One, two, and back to compressions.

One, two—

"MEREDITH, DOES HE HAVE A PULSE?" Eilidh said. A wave of dark hair fell across Arthur's forehead, otherworldly and serene.

Meredith straightened then with an almost eerie calmness, as if part of her brain had just shut down. "Eilidh." She looked down over the long stretch of sightless foothill road. "I don't think they'll get here in time."

Eilidh's eyes widened, the phone all but forgotten in her hand. "Meredith, don't fuck with me. Does Arthur have a goddamn pulse?"

She already knew the answer. Still, Meredith pressed her fingers harder into the side of Arthur's jugular. She skewered an unpolished nail into the underside of his chin. "No. No pulse."

*Is he dead?*" Eilidh shrieked. (Unbeknownst to Meredith, the thing in Eilidh's chest was doing kick-flips, soaring ollies off her ribs.)

"Is that 911 asking?" Meredith said.

"It's me," Eilidh screeched. *"I'm* asking—*they're* sending someone—"

"Then yes," said Meredith calmly. "'Dead' is my current diagnosis, yes."

"Oh my god," said Eilidh, somewhat redundantly. She didn't seem aware that she'd already been hyperventilating for multiple minutes.

"There's nothing we can do." Meredith sat back wearily from Arthur's body, pulling her knees into her chest. "Though I do hope someone checked the bushes for photographers," she exhaled with a frown.

"How can you think about photographers right now?" Eilidh flung accusingly at her. "Our brother just died!"

"Oh, I know," Meredith agreed from a fugue-like stupor. "I'm furious. I honestly can't feel my face."

If it wasn't already clear, the seam between the Wren sisters was easily damaged, frayed as it was to a near-irreparable degree by an almost psychotic divergence in coping mechanisms. Take, for example, this conversation.

Eilidh was frantic in her distress, hysterical to the point of incoherence. "Is this—? I mean, is this . . . ? Is it even possible for two people to die *on the same day*?"

"Statistically it's very unlikely," Meredith said. "So, you know, maybe we're wrong."

"What do you mean wrong?" Eilidh dropped to the ground, wincing a little from the contortion of pressing her cheek to Arthur's chest. "I don't hear anything," she said helplessly, her voice off by at least a major fourth. "Should I hear anything?"

"No, I believe silence is very normal," said Meredith, "from a dead body."

Probably for the best, Eilidh hadn't heard her. "He's still so warm," Eilidh whispered instead, looking very much as she had done the day she performed as Juliet. Meredith had ditched school to go see her during a matinee performance, and had sat in the balcony so Eilidh would not see it when the tears began to slip down her face.

"Stirring," that was the word the critic had used. *Eilidh Wren is more than gifted—she is blessed. Her performance upon discovering the body of Romeo was so stirring I found that, despite having witnessed dozens of versions of Juliet—all of which professed many merits of their own—for the first time in my career, I truly could not breathe.*

The sobering reality of death struck Meredith like a weight. The doneness of it, the finality. The way Arthur would not call her some silly nickname; he would not whisper to her in the corner while they buried their father, each mimicking in their own diabolical way some approximation of grown adults who were sad but unharmed. Arthur, the only other person who remembered their mother as Meredith herself remembered her . . . that wasn't absence. It was loss.

"Oh my god." A sudden, thundering look of epiphany manifested on Meredith's face that, to the uninformed, would look like mania. "This is fucking unacceptable."

"He can't be *dead*," Eilidh argued with herself, sounding vaguely as if she wanted to speak to customer service about it.

"No, you're right, he absolutely cannot." A rare but portentous moment of sisterly concurrence. "Wake up," Meredith commanded, crouching beside

Arthur's body with a sudden flame of ire. "Arthur," she said to the veritable carcass she had failed to revive, "wake up this instant or I swear to god, I'll bring you back myself just to kill you again."

"How is that helpful?" demanded Eilidh in a wail. A somewhat less elegant performance.

"Arthur," said Meredith again, the rage igniting to something darker, or perhaps sadder. "Arthur. This isn't funny." Meredith had not yet realized she was crying.

Eilidh, meanwhile, seemed to have shocked herself out of tears and into hiccups. "Should we . . . Should I go inside? Should I get Gillian?"

"Oh, for fuck's sake." The realization thundered in Meredith's head, a single-handed tension headache. Gillian. Gillian would find this even less convenient than Meredith! "Arthur, do you really want to have to explain this to your wife?" Meredith posed threateningly. Although Gillian was very practical, and would surely see this as a convenient excuse for losing a congressional election. Not that Meredith really believed Arthur was losing (though the *San Francisco Chronicle* made some compelling points).

Then, with a strike of fractal clarity, Meredith asked herself: Was this a situation resolvable by magic? An old, desperate portion of Meredith longed to ask Lou—Lou, who was already long gone, who would have been no help even if she'd been there, because she was prone to unhelpfulness in a very specific, annoying way. Because Lou would have only told Meredith what Meredith already knew: that her powers had limits that fell far short of her ambitions. That what Meredith wanted, and had always wanted, exceeded anything Meredith could plausibly control.

Whatever extraordinariness Meredith was capable of, her life was more closely defined by what she couldn't do—which was, and had always been, to bring back the dead.

That final fight with Lou returned to Meredith then, the sneering glare that shallowly masked old envy. Because Meredith had always been capable of many things Lou wasn't, but also, dealing rationally with grief had never been one of those things.

Not this again. Not *again*.

Not Arthur.

"Arthur, you *shitbag*!" screamed Meredith in a quicksilver fit of desperation and impatience, right before she slapped his unmoving corpse.

The moment she did it, she understood from a place of distant observation that she'd exceeded the limits of humane behavior. Still, being aware of these things doesn't always help the situation, because instant regret over the casual defilement of your brother's dead body does not mitigate your sister's horror at having to watch.

"Meredith!" barked Eilidh, lunging across Arthur's ossifying body to tackle Meredith to the ground. "Are—you—serious?" Eilidh managed to force the words out between efforts of pinning Meredith's wrists. Which was difficult to do, because Meredith boxed four times a week and Eilidh had a bad back, a weakness that Meredith took no shame in leveraging. They grappled with each other on the ground, equally ineffective in technique but well matched as far as emotional propulsion.

After a few more increasingly inept attempts at wrestling holds beside Arthur's departed soul, Eilidh forced Meredith's face at arm's length while Meredith held Eilidh's braid like the tightened expanse of a set of reins.

"Meredith," Eilidh panted, "you—look—*deranged*—"

"Why is it never you?" sobbed Meredith, suddenly explosive with heartache. She released Eilidh with a sense of something sharper than catharsis. Hatred, that's what it was. "Why is it always me, and never you?"

Stunned, Eilidh reared back from Meredith as if she'd been struck.

Then, like a bullet from the dark, Arthur's chest inflated with a gasp, the taillights of an abutting sedan releasing a shower of sparks that set the canvas exterior of Eilidh's suitcase on fire.

# TUESDAY.

# 14

When Arthur Wren awoke the next morning, he remembered that his father was dead and that he was alive. He'd regained consciousness the evening prior with both his sisters lying beside him on the floor of the carport, jagged pieces of Eilidh's braid pulled free from its elastic hold while Meredith bore a redness around her neck in the shape of Eilidh's hand. Eilidh's suitcase was on fire, and Arthur himself was lying on his back on the ground, suddenly ravenous.

"I'm starving," he said, and sat up. Meredith, who seemed worked up about something, reached out with one hand and slapped him hard across the face.

"Excuse me, Sister Violent," said Arthur, realizing it was the second time that day that someone had found it appropriate to slap him (the third, actually, but not to Arthur's knowledge). "What the fuck was that about?"

For a moment, Meredith moved as if to slap him again. Eilidh made no motion to intervene, though she was looking at him like he was a ghost, her own face bloodless with shock.

"Brother Idiot," Meredith finally managed in lieu of contact, as Arthur belatedly registered the two pale hollows on her cheeks that seemed to be fresh tracks of tears. "How dearly I intend to make you wish you'd died instead."

Despite his sisters relaying a surprisingly cohesive recap—Meredith and Eilidh were almost never in agreement, even about things that were objectively proven facts—Arthur felt sure they were somehow mistaken about the circumstances of his "death." Not to overuse the phrase, but it did seem greatly exaggerated. Then Gillian had come outside double-fisting two halves of a Reuben to ask what all the commotion was about. Out of some childhood impulse to tell lies at their father's house, the Wren siblings had replied—without prior discussion and in perfect unison—that nothing had happened. Then they proceeded to go inside for soup.

But Arthur, for all his insistence that no death had transpired, did feel that something was amiss. In an instinctual, quiet way, living symbiotically inside the marrow of his bones or in reflexes better known to some prior version of his life, Arthur vaguely recalled a period of nothingness that had felt . . . not *peaceful,* exactly, because emptiness was not the same as peace. It wasn't something to crave or long for or fear so much as something to be aware of, like spotting a blemish that could not then be unseen. A patch of amnesia, a blackout as if from a wild night, was probably the best way to describe it—or no, maybe the opposite, like an unexplained memory. Déjà vu, the amorphous sense that he had been in a particular moment before but without the means to describe when or how.

He felt different in some unnameable way, like something had gone wrong from the inside. The start of a malignant growth, only Arthur felt quite certain that an actual biological problem would eventually begin to pain him and this would not. It didn't take up space inside him; didn't put pressure on anything else. A hospitable occupant, something lying in wait. Like living with a small pool of quicksand in the bathroom, something to step over carefully but otherwise not disturb.

None of which made any sense, of course, which was why Arthur told Meredith she must have been wrong (Meredith was never wrong according to Meredith, so this was not technically different from any other disagreements between them) and then he simply went about his life, attending to matters of hospitality and dental floss.

Nobody even spoke of Thayer, really, not beyond the necessity of schedule. Gillian made some logistical suggestions and the others nodded where appropriate, but Eilidh seemed unwilling to mention their father aloud and Meredith had apparently forgotten.

And then Arthur woke up in the morning, unsolicited proof that everything eventually carried on.

He woke to find Gillian's side of the bed empty, which was not unusual. While Arthur could be considered a morning person, Gillian was still usually awake first. There was a faint, lingering scent of her perfume, which was actually men's cologne. She wore a smoky, heady, vanilla-and-tobacco mixture that became sweeter over time—not pastry sweet, but meadow sweet.

Gillian knew the details of Arthur's relationship with Yves and Philippa and seemed to generically grasp its appeal, but both Arthur and Gillian were given to ritual in a way that seemed jointly pathological, born from some shared instability in their respective childhoods. At twenty-nine and thirty-one years old, Arthur and Gillian were already, as Eilidh had observed, almost fossilized in their collective behaviors. When they were in the same place, they always slept in the same bed, though they rarely, if ever, made physical contact. At first it had been a matter of devotion to aesthetics—a sort of paint-by-numbers conception of marriage, the wife on one side and the husband on the other. Which was not to say the optics were ever a nonissue, but over time the reliance on their customs made for a meaningful ease they both desired, like a fragile toddler's trust in rigid routine. A lack of conscious deliberation on which an altar of habit could be safely and predictably erected.

As Arthur often did each morning, despite being firmly instructed not to by several acclaimed self-help books that Gillian had given him in the past, Arthur picked up his phone and scrolled his notifications. (This would not be the day Arthur made his own internet go out, nor could he ever seem to disrupt his own cellular network, despite having done both to his father almost compulsorily over the course of his young life. The universe, it seemed, wanted Arthur to be in on the joke.)

Each morning, this ceremony filled Arthur with a disemboweling existential dread, and this morning was no exception. Arthur scrolled the headlines about his family, the reports of his points in the polls, the many comments to neither praise Thayer nor bury him. Arthur scrolled mindlessly past a chain of advertisements—THIS APP WILL MAKE YOU HAPPY! :), a tired promise like the whisper of a breeze, some unfulfilled change in season— and resurrected the familiar, ripening sickness in his belly, the nausea of being widely and unfavorably perceived. One post observed that Arthur's travel style was excellent; below it, the most-liked comment suggested that Arthur was singlehandedly responsible for the ongoing water crisis in Flint.

Arthur felt a pang of panic or hunger. Probably the latter. He reached into his nightstand for the bar of medicinal chocolate he had procured from Yves the following evening, relieved that he had thought to ask for something in advance. He checked the label for caloric content, giving up when he realized the label was something incomprehensible (God's note: Turkish). Then Arthur broke off what he considered a reasonably sized piece and popped it into his mouth, submitting to the near-instantaneous flood of relief. Ah, the singular bliss of numbness, which was so like ignorance! Arthur rose to his feet and began his day, bolstered now, albeit relieved Gillian had thought to safeguard the normal outlets with surge protectors.

Arthur's bedroom in the Wren family home was located in the same wing as Meredith's. Eilidh, who had always been more of a fixture than the other two, occupied the west side of the house, inside the thing that was essentially a turret. (Read: Eilidh, the princess, lived in the tower.) Arthur paused to look into Meredith's room, and then, finding it empty, wandered down the stairs to the kitchen, which was also empty, before wandering into their father's—dead father's—study, from which Arthur finally thought he heard a voice.

As expected, he opened the door to find Meredith inside, fully dressed, speaking rapidly into her phone in a brusque, impatient tone that was just her normal voice. She was pacing behind the enormous wooden executive desk, which sat some feet away from the built-in bookcase. The drapes on the floor-to-ceiling windows had been thrown open, gracing the room with a view of the redwoods outside and the reflective twinkling from the pool on the deck that was really just a fountain, not actually conducive to swimming laps.

Arthur wandered deeper into the room, feeling an odd tingle of rebellion at the mere fact of his presence. He'd never been allowed in here—Arthur *specifically*, who alone of the Wren children had an adverse effect on Thayer's technology, the functionality of his life's work. But Arthur had heard Meredith and Thayer argue from inside this room countless times, always with a sense of gallows envy. (Akin to gallows humor, but grosser and more hopeless. Grim, but also dumb.)

Recalling he could no longer be reprimanded—forgetting he was an adult—Arthur picked up one of the books that had been left out atop the decorative pillar, waiting patiently beside the leather armchair in the corner. There was an index card sticking out of it.

A bookmark?

Realizing this must have been the last book their father had read, Arthur was overcome with a strange, sickly feeling, like a large spider had just crawled out from somewhere between his lungs and forced itself into his throat. Thayer Wren would never know how the story ended. Arthur flipped the book over in his hands, preparing himself to feel something at the title; relieved again that he had thought to ask Yves for something relaxing, to keep the worst of the emotional spiders at bay.

The book was a biography of Napoleon. Arthur frowned, and then flipped to the inside, spotting the ex libris stamp he'd had custom made for Gillian two Christmases ago. *From the library of GNW.*

Never mind, Arthur thought, wondering why he'd even considered that the book might have been his father's. He had never once seen Thayer Wren sit down to read. In fact, he couldn't imagine Thayer actually sitting in this chair, which was ostensibly only there for decoration. Given that Arthur's family home had once been featured in *Architectural Digest*—an editorial that featured Thayer in various power poses beside the architectural features with particularly harsh lines—it made more sense, didn't it, that Thayer had just hired someone to give his life some shape?

Arthur looked up with a frown, testing a theory. The spines lining the shelves of the bookcase were arranged by color, all muted variations of bound hardcovers that prompted Arthur to realize they were largely unread, perhaps even unidentifiable. He marveled for a moment at his own failure to interrogate the brand of intellectual elitism his father so meticulously presented. Shouldn't Arthur, out of everyone, be able to tell what was real and what was fake?

Meredith looked at Arthur from where she stood between the bookcase and the desk, gave him the sour look of impatience that was really just her face, and continued her phone conversation.

"Where's Yves?" mouthed Arthur, setting the book back on the table with concerted effort to preserve Gillian's page. He had lost track of Yves again the night prior, at some point between deli pickles, medicinal exchanges, and the careful, parkour-esque motion of entering his childhood bedroom without accidentally making eye contact with the baseball trophies or the baseball lamp or the framed baseball photos or the baseball calendar or the reminder that hey, he had once liked baseball. Arthur was relieved, really, to find that Yves had no interest in partaking in nostalgia for whoever Arthur had once been. He had simply held everyone's hands for some meditative breaths before disappearing without explanation, and where he had deposited himself since then remained unknown.

Meredith, who was still pacing behind the executive desk, flashed Arthur a glare over the inconvenience of being addressed. "What? Arthur, I cannot understand you."

Arthur raised his voice, audible this time. "I'm just asking—"

"Can this wait? I am on the *phone,*" Meredith informed him sharply.

Then she scowled, huffed, placed one hand on her hip, and said, "Fine. Call me when you find out."

Then she ended the call, turning to Arthur again. "What is it, Brother Disruptive?"

"Sister Lunatic, as always, you're a gem. Have you seen Yves?" Arthur asked again, and Meredith flicked a hand in apparent disinterest.

"He's either with Gillian or with Cass. Theoretically someone is out getting coffee."

Arthur had learned the night previous of Cass's true identity—not Gillian's lover, as Arthur had been so initially certain, but actually Meredith's. Which, in its way, made sense, and yet delivered Arthur to another confusing blow of emotions, in that it was a nearly identical pairing of disappointment and relief. The inverse, he supposed, of his initial thought process when he'd thought Gillian might not only not love *him*, but actively love someone else. Even if the someone else in question was one who did, upon further consideration, seem much more suited to Meredith.

"Ah. Okay." Arthur looked up at the books again, moving toward them to pull one off the shelf. They were all missing their dust jackets—predictably, none of them were anything important or even relevant to their father's interests. A vintage cookbook. An encyclopedia of common show dogs.

"He hired someone," Meredith confirmed, sidling up to Arthur. "A bookstore, I think. Paid a ton of money just to create the illusion of leather-bound tomes."

"Do you think he was worried about not coming off smart enough or something?" asked Arthur, testing the weight of an encyclopedia volume marked *S*. "I guess it can be hard to carry around the title of genius. Must get heavy from time to time."

"I'm glad you've noticed," said Meredith. "I try my best to make it look effortless, but I'd hate for you to think it was as easy as it looks."

Arthur rolled his eyes, elbowing her in the ribs. "Did he ever talk to you about it?"

His voice had gotten quiet then, which was a little embarrassing, as it was venturing into an arena of sentimentality that Meredith did not like. She, like their father, did not have the patience for softness, though she tolerated it in Arthur, or at least did not comment on it as often as Thayer once had. "I mean, you and Dad did have a lot in common," he pointed out.

Meredith snorted in apparent disagreement. "In that we were both pig-headed, emotionally closed off, and incapable of meaningful relationships?"

Arthur shifted to face her. "I can't tell if you're joking," he said, "because yes, that's *exactly* what I mean."

"That's not true," Meredith said matter-of-factly. "I had Jamie. And," she added as an apparent afterthought, "I had Lou."

"You mean your ex-boyfriend and your ex–best friend, neither of which have been in your life for at least the past decade?" But the mention of Lou was too accessible, too tempting to overlook. For the countless time that day, Arthur felt the past like a door being opened in his chest, creaking from disuse. The awkward fumble of clothes, *Is this okay?*, *Yes it's fine shut up.* "You know, it's funny you should mention Lou." Funny, unfunny, devastating the way history was devastating. Had she been haunting Meredith as she did Arthur? "She's been on the mind lately."

"Mm," said Meredith with the feigned indifference she reserved for any mention of Lou. Arthur hadn't even realized Meredith could say Lou's name aloud without cursing it. Was this the result of age, time, maturity? Sadistically, he leapt at the chance to find out.

"Did you ever speak to her again? After you ruined her life."

"I didn't ruin her life," said Meredith mechanically.

"You narced, Death." Such was the verbiage appropriate for getting your best friend expelled, in Arthur's mind. Then again, he *was* widely reviled for his sinister complicity. "It's not actually up for debate."

"I didn't *narc*," said Meredith irritably, which Arthur considered countering with things like timelines and facts, but in the end he just couldn't hear the story again. It wasn't even a story, really, as Meredith did not have the means to tell it. She just had a list of blatant excuses that she recited like poetry—like *boring* poetry, which Arthur couldn't abide.

He supposed there was nothing new to unearth, no new-old secrets to share. He began to change the subject—to what, he still wasn't sure—breakfast, maybe—or the vulturous picking over of their father's things, which still needed doing—when Meredith abruptly spoke again.

"You know, sometimes she really seemed to prefer you." Meredith tilted her head in thought, gazing over the spines of their father's worthless books. Many of them, Arthur realized, were the equivalent of airport Westerns or dime-a-dozen mysteries. Then he realized Meredith was still talking about

Lou, which was unprecedented. Typically she slammed the gavel and court was tidily dismissed. "Sometimes," Meredith murmured, "I really hated being around the two of you."

Arthur thought about saying that wasn't true, that he was the hanger-on when it came to Meredith's relationships, not because he liked his sister so much but because his sister liked *him,* which seemed so rare and peculiar given everything about Meredith that Arthur found it kind of dementedly flattering, like being the prettiest girl in the small-town parade. He loved Meredith, even liked her a great deal, because they were both inadequate in their father's eyes; because neither of them were Eilidh, and therefore they were almost always on the same team.

Except when it came to Lou. Arthur remembered the old feeling of exclusion, the way it felt when Meredith and Lou would disappear together to discuss something in whispers, and the way that, in retaliation, Arthur liked to coax Lou into then doing exactly the same thing to Meredith, just so she would have to be the one left out. One of those lightly punitive things between siblings.

"Yeah," said Arthur. "Me too."

He wondered why Lou kept coming to mind, inserting herself into the conversation as if she'd existed in any meaningful way since the day she walked out of this house. A minor chapter in the Wren family gothic, or whatever she was to the pair of newly orphaned assholes idly rolling back her tomb.

Would she be able to fix it, any of it? She had once before.

But then again, that was before.

Arthur and Meredith stood in silence for a long time before descending back into small talk. "So, you said Gillian was out?"

"She mentioned picking up some things before the lawyer gets here at nine. Have you gotten any calls, by the way?"

"Calls?"

"Condolence calls, you know. *So sorry, such a good man,* blah blah." So Meredith did recall their father's passing, then.

"Oh, those." Yes, The Notifications. Not all of them were from faceless strangers on the internet. "I've been ignoring them." With the help of Yves's medicinal aids.

Meredith was blinking in a strange way, as if she had something in her eye, and she reached up before restraining herself.

"God, I'd kill you right now for a latte," she said, apparently having finished with the matter of grief. "Can you believe Dad doesn't have any coffee in the house?"

"I'm sorry, just to clarify," said Arthur, "your price for my murder is a cup of coffee, something you could procure by tapping a few buttons on your phone?"

There was an unexpected interjection from the doorway. "He was trying to drink less caffeine," said Eilidh, who nearly startled Arthur into knocking over the ridiculous pillar that was being used as a side table. (Now that he'd noticed the house had been designed by someone and did not express any sort of secrets as to who his father was or wished that Arthur would be, he considered it the height of excess. He and Gillian had not hired a decorator because that was absurd and wildly bourgeois. Everything in Arthur's home was a piece made by a local artist—Arthur's doing, although, come to think of it, Gillian was the one who'd sourced it all.)

"That's ridiculous," said Meredith instantly, as though Eilidh had suggested their father was in the process of converting to Anglicanism or currently blowing prostitutes on the moon. "As if he would have done anything to purposefully decrease his productivity. He ran this place like a machine."

Eilidh gave a gesture like a shrug, though it was stiffer than that. "He was doing wheatgrass shots every day. It was a whole wellness thing he was trying. He said it was helping with his energy levels."

"I'm sorry, he was doing wheatgrass? Grass, like a cow?" Meredith was frowning at her. It is of course very common knowledge that wheatgrass shots are considered wellness boosters, but try telling that to Meredith Wren.

Eilidh did, unwisely. "It's good for digestion. And concentration."

"Are you also eating grass now?" demanded Meredith.

"He wasn't *eating* it," Eilidh sighed, "and it's not *grass—*"

"So who do you think he left the company to?" asked Arthur, pondering it aloud on a whim. Eilidh and Meredith had forgotten him for a moment, and turned to him then as if he'd recently grown an extra head. "Do you think it'll be left to one of us?"

"This isn't a monarchy, Brother Delusional," said Meredith instantly—defensively? Perhaps. Arthur understood immediately that she'd been drafting contingency plans in her head since the moment Thayer passed. "It's merit based. Has to be. You can't throw five trillion dollars into someone's lap just because you share some DNA."

"Is that a fake number?" asked Eilidh.

"So you're ruling all of us out based on merit?" asked Arthur, who knew his sister too well to be personally insulted.

"I didn't say that." Meredith lifted her chin, pointedly overlooking Eilidh's unfamiliarity with Wrenfare's valuation (Arthur didn't know the exact number, but somewhere in the trillions sounded believable, and not simply because Meredith had said so with confidence). "I just don't see the point in phrasing it that way, as if he's some kind of mad king with the power to confer an entire company unto whichever of us he liked most."

"So you think it's Eilidh," concluded Arthur, prompting Eilidh to once again put on a one-woman performance of total indifference. Not that Arthur disagreed with Meredith on the matter of Thayer's favorite child, as there was no plausible margin of error there. "You think he was grooming her for the CEO job, then? I thought she worked in marketing."

"I'm right here," said Eilidh.

"Well, if he was giving up caffeine, maybe he was," scoffed Meredith, as if their father had wasted away to dementia rather than dying of a sudden stroke the previous day. "Who knows if he was even thinking clearly toward the end."

"But you told me on the phone that you thought it would be me," Eilidh pointed out, apparently torn between being grievously offended and undermining the logic of Meredith's argument.

"You did?" asked Arthur, who didn't disagree with that assumption, but hadn't realized Meredith could accept it.

"Just because I expect the worst doesn't mean I'm incapable of hoping for a better option," said Meredith, leaving Eilidh to blink very rapidly, as if processing a wide variety of thoughts. "There's still a chance that our father's absurd personal bias miraculously failed to compromise his better judgment, however slim that possibility might be," Meredith muttered, touching her eye again in that weird, slightly bothered way.

"Have you considered that he might have left it to me?" asked Arthur, pausing Eilidh's response—unclear what it would have been—and leaving her to turn to turn to him with a frown.

"You?" echoed Eilidh, an unspoken lambasting that Arthur read with perfect clarity. "But you have a job," she added, a flimsy effort at repair.

"Well, what if I preferred *this* job?" asked Arthur, light-footedly, as if it did not matter and had only just occurred to him sometime in the last five seconds. "I'm tired of Congress anyway."

"I did consider it," Meredith remarked, to everyone's surprise. It was a refreshingly generous position until she continued, "I *definitely* considered that our father might think it best to bestow his life's work and entire earthly purpose unto the one person in this family who has never set foot anywhere near the magitech industry."

"I suppose I shouldn't have to ask this," Eilidh sighed, turning to Meredith before Arthur could speak, "but are you saying you think the best option is you?"

"Of course not," said Meredith with a highly put-on indifference. "I'm saying the best option is whoever can best take the reins at Wrenfare, which might very well be a third party. I imagine—knowing as we all do the significance of the company to the industry as a whole," she pointed out, before adding casually, as if it were forgettable and unimportant, "and how much Dad cared about Wrenfare—his successor must be someone who has previously shown success as a CEO. I'm sure he must have considered any number of people who are currently head of a comparatively valuable magitech venture."

"So, you," Arthur ruled, as Eilidh nodded vigorously.

"I didn't say that," sniffed Meredith.

"Of course you didn't, Sister Subtle," said Arthur.

"I don't know what you mean, Brother Obtuse—"

"Could the two of you stop doing that when I'm in the same room?" said Eilidh.

"It's not like we're doing something profane," snapped Meredith. "Why should it bother you to be excluded? Neither of us knows anything about ballet and we don't ask you to stop talking about it."

"I have never once tried to talk to either of you about ballet," said Eilidh, again with Meredithian stiffness. "And I don't appreciate you both treating me like some little afterthought just because you think Dad liked me more than you."

"Have you ever stopped to wonder *why* he liked you more than us?" prompted Meredith, in a tone Arthur recognized as a prelude to Meredith's special brand of cruelty. Which was not to say he wouldn't agree with whatever came out of her mouth next, but that was the entire point. Meredith was cruel because she was honest, and even if that honesty was very, very selective and not particularly reflective of the situation in a more encompassing, healthy way, it was still impossible to pretend she had not said it, because there was no meaningful way to invalidate it once it had been said.

It was like Meredith had some magical quality to animate the worst thing you'd ever felt, and then once she brought it to life, there was no way to be rid of it. It just followed you around, mewling occasionally with hunger but mostly just sitting there in your periphery, never close enough to soothe but also never far enough away to forget. Arthur himself had at least four or five of those Meredith-creatures sharing every single space with him, which was not really Meredith's fault once you considered how many of them Meredith herself must have. But it still wasn't the best way to start a Tuesday.

"Did you say the lawyer was coming at nine?" Arthur cut in with a sort of heroic desperation, like lunging into a burning building. He did feel like a bit of a hero, actually, because when he met Meredith's eye, he could tell that she knew why he'd changed the subject and that she had definitely been about to be cruel, and was now glad she hadn't said the cruel thing. It had been unsheathed, though, which was still a problem. She could use it as a weapon any time now that she held it at the ready. But this moment, at least, was safe.

Safer, anyway. "Lawyer?" asked Eilidh, who was now being harmed by the fact that she'd had to ask. Honestly, it was too difficult to keep Eilidh from being hurt. She was the child in the back seat again in Arthur's mind, always a victim to youthfulness, to fragility. To the knowledge that for her, growing up would only make everything worse. "But it's already nine fifteen."

"Oh, fuck," exclaimed Meredith, looking down at her watch.

"Yes," agreed Gillian, who stood in the doorway holding an eco-friendly container of to-go coffees, each one printed neatly with a respective Wren sibling's name. "He's waiting for you in the kitchen right now."

# 15

We pause here to bring you the same Tuesday morning as experienced by Gillian Wren, a habitual early riser and woman of general emotional dexterity.

Gillian had actually had an extremely unremarkable relationship with her father-in-law, Thayer Wren, something that could not be said by anyone else thus far introduced to the narrative. As you already know, all three of the Wren children had experienced their father very differently, with each of them believing him to be a projection of some smaller fraction of what he really was, like widening the frame on the Mona Lisa and revealing her background to be something vastly different in each case (riding a centaur, for example).

For Meredith, Thayer was a source of inspiration: a driving, motivating force for everything she would later accomplish, his approval dangling like the proverbial carrot she could reasonably—even imminently—earn.

For Arthur, Thayer was a benchmark: a yardstick against which he would forever be measured and perennially fall short.

For Eilidh, Thayer was a kindred spirit: someone who shared her personal grief and sense of having been torn into fractions, equally split as she was into parts of before and after—multiple people living irreconcilably in one body, one mind, one everlasting taste of regret.

But who a person is to one's children can bear little resemblance to who they really are.

To Gillian, Arthur's wife and the hero of this story, assuming it is narrated by Gillian (it isn't, it is narrated by me, you're welcome), Thayer Wren had always been a relatively ordinary person. Meaning that he was a human being and therefore beholden to many strengths and, equally, many flaws. For example, he was a little bit racist and also quite a bit sexist, although no more so than other men his age, which was not an excuse so much as a bland generalization—a scale by which to judge the severity of his sociopolitical crimes. Thayer was very smart and quite contrarian, such that conversation over dinner was often a competition as to who could be the most incisive about a piece of media, usually one that was not designed to be torn apart so much as tasted, enjoyed, consumed. The lower the stakes, the more enthusiastic Thayer could become. He had a way of shifting the atmosphere of a room, resetting the perception of normalcy. Thayer could make concerns for a comic book franchise seem dire while determining a piece of critical legislation to have the merest, fleeting impact on the ordinary person's daily life, which on some occasions was a stance that felt both worldly and not inaccurate and on others could be almost breathtakingly self-absorbed.

That being said, Thayer could be a very entertaining dinner guest, and although he was not especially well-read, his intellectual curiosity was endless. He was not easily bored, nor did he seem to find most people boring. He had actually taken quite an interest in Gillian's research, to such a degree that she had developed a sort of liking for him—not quite fondness, nothing especially filial, but something that allowed for a neutrality she could use as a shield, because even when he was driving Arthur to madness, Gillian could recall that from time to time, Thayer Wren had not really been so bad.

That morning, she awoke as she usually did, her eyes opening as she lay on her back and wondered what had woken her. She determined that it was the degree of light filling the room, the shade that signaled a few minutes before six and was more of a suggestion, a bluish hint that did not say morning had broken but implied that morning would, at some point, break. She got out of bed quietly, in the way Arthur never could. Arthur was a very noisy person, almost as a personality flaw, although Gillian did not consider it to be one. To her, Arthur's noise was more an extension of Arthur himself. The way he seemed to hit upon every creaky floorboard in their mostly restored craftsman; the way every object he picked up or set down seemed to have its own auditory fingerprint. It wasn't that his voice was loud, or that he was disruptive, or really anything that was easy to explain. She supposed Arthur's noise was probably just what happened naturally when a person was not *afraid* to make noise, which is a very long-winded way of saying that Arthur wasn't especially considerate and that Gillian was, unusually so.

She made her way to the bathroom down the hall, her bag of travel-sized toiletries already unpacked and neatly spread across the bathroom counter.

Gillian, like two of the three Wren children, had had some exposure to one of the more folkloric forms of magic as a child—via her mother, who had a great fear of demons and demon-resembling powers the way many immigrants did, in what was more commonly viewed as pro forma superstition. To combat the possibility of interception by demon, jinn, rakshasa, or otherwise ill-intending calamity, Gillian developed a highly ritualistic nature, something she wouldn't have thought of as real magic but absolutely was. From experience, Gillian had learned that any disruption of a ritual would result in bad luck (though in truth bad luck simply exists with little in the way to stop it).

Gillian's devotion to ritual was a kind of wrangling in its way, a methodology for rightness. She wasn't as dedicated as Meredith to the many steps of skincare because Gillian wasn't as vain as Meredith, another thing the universe found worth rewarding. Comparatively, she had a threadbare three steps—wash, moisturize, protect. She did so that morning, then patted her face dry and took a deep, meditative breath, clearing her mind for a moment. Then she exhaled and put everything back.

She decided to put her dark hair in a simpler version of its usual elegant twist, then chose to tuck a black-trimmed navy blouse demurely into a pair of black trousers. It was cleverly done, Gillian's mourning, in that it was neither showy nor absent meaning. Nothing Gillian did was ever absent meaning, which would be exceedingly stressful to another human being. Actually, it was very stressful to Gillian, too, though nobody had taught Gillian about stress, so she didn't call it that, or even consider stress to be an actual possibility, much less an ailment. To Gillian, stress was something she lived beside, one of the demons she kept casually at bay with more rational tools like tactics and forethought. She would not be beset by darkness if she simply addressed problems as they arose.

For example: "Good morning!" said Gillian's husband's lover, or rather, one of her husband's lovers. The other, Gillian thought with an unhelpful twist in her stomach, was still due to arrive.

Yves Reza was sitting on the most formal sofa in the entirety of the Wren family home, which was saying something, as most of the house was unoccupied and therefore it was all excessively formal. This one was a stiff white leather, and the very last place Gillian would have sat for both fear of disturbance and because it looked extremely uncomfortable.

Of Arthur's paramours, Yves had always been especially mysterious to her, given that his personal behaviors were Gillian's opposite in nearly every way. Yves seemed, for one thing, thoroughly uninterested in ritual. He did not do anything (aside from her husband) routinely or even consistently. He didn't think about what anyone needed and yet still seemed to know it, offering it instinctively rather than with any sort of practiced hand. He was a natural at it, whatever it was. Existing, Gillian supposed. Loving and being loved. She thought the same thing of Arthur at times, though she knew Arthur too well to think of him as unburdened.

Yves seemed, to Gillian, very brave and quite wonderful. She didn't know him, of course, and couldn't be sure whether any of that was true, but she had never had to wonder why Arthur might love Yves, which was probably meaningful in its way. Yves made her ache with something she tried not to interrogate, much less name.

"Good morning," said Gillian. Her voice seemed suddenly very silly and formal and too deep and maybe too stiff and perhaps it sounded like she didn't want him there even though she didn't mind him, not at all. It was maybe a bit strange for him to be staying in the house—she'd already had to chase off a number of reporters, not to mention the many people contacting Arthur's political office wanting an official statement on his father's death— but the house was large, and anyway, it seemed unlikely that anyone would ask questions.

Well, it seemed unlikely that anyone would *specifically* ask the question "Is Arthur Wren having an affair with famous racecar driver Yves Reza in a situation that is known to both his wife and his other girlfriend?" and therefore Gillian simply did not think about it. Part of her concern at the moment was keeping Arthur relatively happy under the circumstances, which outweighed her need to protect his reputation from baseless (or in this case, true but barely believable) rumors.

Which was not to say the optics had not occurred to her, because optics occurred to her with a frequency that would give a more ordinary person a constant, irremediable headache, which funnily enough was a condition Gillian had lived with for so long that she did not technically know what it was to be without pain.

"May I ask you," Gillian broached to Yves, "if you have . . . well, a plan?"

"For what?" asked Yves, smiling peaceably.

For the day. For the week. For the funeral. For his life. Did a person who drove around a track for a living technically need a plan? Gillian had never met anyone so aimless, and now could not decide if that was true of all men who drove fast cars for money or if it was just this one, who never really seemed to be going anywhere or doing anything specific whenever she bumped into him.

Even now, Yves was sitting languidly on the sofa with no apparent goal in mind for his personal entertainment, nor any obvious intention to move. But surely he wouldn't be sitting there *all* day, would he? So did he have a plan for the arrival of Lady Philippa Villiers-DeMagnon, which could be, as far as Gillian knew, any given moment? Did he have a plan for avoiding the questions of the press? Had he given any thought to climate change, or the possibility of his eternal soul? Did he have a plan for whatever might happen if Arthur ever left him, and if so, would he mind sharing, just between casual friends?

"For . . . for breakfast," said Gillian finally.

"Well, I find this morning I would be very amenable to something smoky," said Yves, as if just now testing the waters of his appetite. "Either a very thick scotch or some salmon, depending on what is more readily available."

"Could you be convinced to begin the day with something more conventional?" asked Gillian. "Like coffee, perhaps?"

"There isn't any," came the voice of Meredith Wren, prompting Gillian to—well, not jump. Gillian was not especially jumpy and she never allowed herself to become so comfortable in any situation that she could lose her reflexive awareness of all nearby access points. But Gillian did betray a small blink of surprise at the presence of Meredith, who despite being a very immovable force in terms of personality had entered the room very deftly, like a tiger on the hunt. "I've gone through every cupboard in the house and there's nothing. It's like he didn't even live here."

Privately, Gillian had thought the same thing. Meredith was saying it spitefully, more a comment of insouciance than anything else, but Gillian had thought hm, it doesn't seem as if the owner of the house has been here for at least a week, based on her personal deduction. There was a pile of untouched mail, nothing perishable in the fridge, no open bottles of gin sitting on Thayer's personal bar as there usually were, and while there was no evidence of dust or the typical signifiers of absence—Thayer had a household staff, so everything was neat as a pin and criminally orderly—Gillian felt sure that if they turned on the TV, they would find that Thayer was behind in whatever prestige drama he was watching for the purposes of later informing a cast of obsequious Silicon Valley props was a damn waste of a hundred million dollars. She wondered, too, why Thayer had been at the office late on a Sunday night when by all accounts Thayer did not make a habit of stopping by the Wrenfare offices much at all. But of course these were not matters with which to burden the Wren children, who were either occupying different stages of grief or sampling different flavors of denial.

Meredith—whom Gillian liked because Arthur liked her, but also because Gillian did not wish to lose painfully in a battle of wills, undertaking something so profligate a waste of time as a grudge against (or even a low tolerance for) the human cyborg that was Meredith Wren—looked desperately in need of caffeine. Meredith was an extremely beautiful woman, almost painfully attractive for the first few minutes until she began to speak, at which point she remained beautiful but you were able to forget about it in favor of some other quality, like whatever Meredith thought or felt. Meredith had long black hair with one or two threads of silver beginning to invade her narrative of enviable volume and general high-quality maintenance. As mentioned, Meredith could be quite finicky when it came to her appearance, which Gillian deduced meant that the streaks of age were probably new. The fact that they had slipped Meredith's notice meant that Meredith had been distracted by something that wasn't her father's death—if Gillian had to guess, it was likely something to do with her company. Like Thayer, Meredith did not assign much value to anything that wasn't an extension of her work. She would consider it a waste of brainpower to dedicate even a few spare moments of anxiety to something trivial, such as emotional turbulence or a friend.

As Gillian was quietly wondering what was going on with Meredith, Yves had begun shifting the furniture around. He cleared a space in the middle of the sitting room, then sat down and began to breathe deeply, closing his eyes.

"There's a gym, you know," said Meredith loudly, before looking at Gillian as if only a wild animal would attempt a sun salutation in a formal sitting room. (Again, Gillian was inclined to agree, though she could just tell she was experiencing this thought in a different tone of voice.)

"This is the man my brother is sleeping with? One of them, I assume,"

Meredith added privately to Gillian, looking in no way perturbed by this information.

"This is the only man," said Gillian mildly, "to my knowledge."

Meredith stood beside Gillian, tilting her head as they both watched Yves transition from standing to a low lunge, then proceeding to enter child's pose. "As far as men go, this is a good one," Meredith admitted in an undertone, albeit not as quietly as Gillian would have liked. "What about you? Are you having any fun these days?"

"Within reason," said Gillian, which was either a lie or very true depending on how literally one translated the question. She was actually having a marvelous time with her dissertation, largely because she had always known from the moment she began that it was futile in a way, more like a hobby than anything else. There had been too many stakes in her previous job as a legal associate; a paralyzing sense that things going right or going wrong would have an impact on her future self, on her likelihood of making partner, on her ability to get through the day. Gillian liked her day to be filled with insignificant tedium that she could control—academic journals with readership in the scant dozens, papers authored by undergraduates who were taking her Napoleonic history course pass/fail. It was predictable and relaxing to Gillian, a ritual for self-care, and therefore a version of fun. It was not, however, sex parties or devoted polyamory, which was ostensibly the fun that Meredith had meant.

"Just know," cautioned Meredith as they both tilted their heads the opposite way, this time watching Yves step through from downward dog to an upright lunge, "that if you're ever not having fun, my brother will throw himself off a cliff. Which isn't to worry you or anything, that's just how he is." Just then Meredith's phone rang, and she glanced down at it with an obvious expression of loathing. "Fuck," she said, and answered it. "Ward, you had better not be calling with a stupid question. I'm busy grieving, for fuck's sake."

At that precise moment, Gillian became aware of a low pain at the base of her abdomen as well as an ache in her neck. It was, she knew instantly, her period. She operated with an extreme sensitivity to her own subtle shifts, like a meteorologist for the very, very niche. It wouldn't be an especially emotional one or she would have noticed that already, and her skin was no worse than usual, which meant it was either going to be a bloated one or a painful one. Physical, then, thank god. The worst of it was when Gillian's moods were subject to the shifts of her internal clockwork, leaving her to wonder for a week whether everything in her life was falling apart or if perhaps she just needed iron.

In this case, she could know that her general sense of dread was real and not a mirage of femininity. How wonderful for her. Perhaps she would feel better with some chocolate.

"Edward, please, you're being hysterical." Meredith had turned as if to take her phone call somewhere else, probably her father's office, but before she left she held one hand to her phone, vestigial to a prior era of technology. "Could you find a way to get some coffee?" she said to Gillian. "I'd send Jenny to go get some, but presumably the death of my father means I no longer have the means to direct his staff."

It was unclear to Gillian whether Meredith was trying to be funny or if she was genuinely disappointed. Also, the assistant's name was Dzhuliya, not that it mattered, aside from the fact that Dzhuliya had been very strange on the phone when she'd called to tell Gillian about Thayer's death, despite a very utilitarian approach to her job up to that point. Also, Dzhuliya had been the one to make the 911 call from the Wrenfare offices, which nobody had questioned given her position of employment there but was, in Gillian's mind, quite odd. Thayer was known to be eccentric, but would he have called his assistant into work on a Sunday night?

"Not a problem," said Gillian, who would also need to get Tylenol, and a hot water bottle, and some chocolate. "I've got a few errands to run. The lawyer is coming at nine," she added as Meredith nodded and flapped a hand that said something like *I know but that information is beneath me,* then disappeared down the corridor barking something about journalistic integrity.

From a distance, it was again possible to remember how pretty Meredith was, and Gillian took it in for a spell before turning to Yves, who lay on his back either asleep or in a deeply transportive savasana.

"Yves," said Gillian. "I don't suppose you'd like to join me to get some coffee?"

She wasn't sure what had come over her, really. Gillian didn't require company and she did not know what she was expected to say to Yves, who had seen her husband naked.

Of course, Gillian had also seen her husband naked. She had stripped him of his clothes and helped him into the bath when he'd gotten so sick during his first campaign that he'd nearly died of pneumonia. She'd been there many times to watch him strip carelessly down whenever she asked if there was anything he'd particularly like washed. She'd seen him in the minutes before he showered, the minutes after he showered, the conversations they sometimes had *while* he was in the shower, when she perched on the lid of the toilet and pulled at the skin of her elbow and laughed at his stories about his day, because Arthur was very funny, actually. She was there beside him every night, the quiet and unremarkable ones, the drunk and maudlin ones, the ones where Arthur said things like "The trouble with being young, generally speaking, is that you can't afford to do anything nice, and when you're old, you're too old to be bothered with any of it," and Gillian would say, "What if there was some kind of system where an auditor told you how much you were worth and they gave you that money as a loan while you're young, so you can spend your older years just paying it back in some kind of complex accountancy dystopia," and Arthur would chuckle and say "do you ever think about having children?" to which Gillian would softly reply, "I always assumed it would happen, you know, someday," and regret that her tone of voice made the whole endeavor sound distant because she didn't see it happening with him instead of sounding distant because she thought she'd eventually become comfortable with the process of child-making but it was taking an awfully long time to settle in.

So yes, she had seen Arthur naked, but not the same way Yves had done it, and Gillian supposed that what she really wanted was to absorb some of whatever Yves naturally possessed and see if it might work that way—if she could catch it like a virus. Or some benign bacterial infection that would make her suddenly long to be touched.

"I would be most honored to join you for an outing," said Yves, and Gillian wondered if she was remarkable to him at all, or if all the wives were like this, or if he looked at her and thought, *Oh yes I see, I understand perfectly why Arthur needed more,* or if maybe none of that had ever crossed Yves's mind because he was not in the habit of exploring the emotional depths of any given moment. She felt disgusted with herself for tipping into generalities again, and the low stabbing in her uterus was back. Everything would be fine so long as Gillian did not in any way lose control.

"Chocolate?" asked Yves, producing some from a small, zippered pouch he wore slung around his hips. Gillian blinked, wondering idly if Yves had read her mind, which, actually, he had in a way. Although that is not really relevant to the story now, unless you devote any substantial thought to the question of why Gillian did not simply voice her needs aloud, to which I would point out that most people aren't usually carrying chocolate around with them. Yves did as a habit, although the things Yves carried around were usually laced with something.

Which, of course, this one also was.

# 16

So anyway, the lawyer. Let's just say for purposes of general forward motion that the coffee-fetching errand went swimmingly, and that Yves and Gillian drove past four bus advertisements for Chirp that cawed THIS APP WILL MAKE YOU HAPPY! :) but did not compromise traffic safety or have any sort of wildly confessional chat in the car. Assuming that's true, or at least ignoring for the time being any plausible relevance to the story that such a conversation and/or minor traffic infraction might have, given that none of the Wren siblings—the main characters of this story, much to my chagrin—knew about it, then let's resume focus on the Wrens as we previously left them after they progressed to the house's kitchen at 9:15 AM.

"Hello," said the attorney for the estate of the late Thayer Wren.

"What are you doing here?" said Meredith.

"This is the lawyer," said Gillian.

"Like hell it is," said Meredith.

"Nice to see you, too, Meredith," said the lawyer. "What's it been now, ten years? Fifteen?"

"Was that school you went to even accredited?" said Meredith.

Eilidh, who as a rule did not speak until she understood a situation, found herself exchanging a brief glance with Arthur, who looked equally unsure which part of the scene to address.

"Public school isn't a crime, Meredith," said the lawyer, who was not someone Meredith had dated, Eilidh was pretty sure. Granted, Eilidh didn't remember all of Meredith's ex-boyfriends, but aside from Jamie they were mostly a predictable brand of milquetoast. This one was particularly divergent from the thread of Meredith's taste, given that he had a very polished appearance and Meredith was unwilling to take seriously any man who took an extensive interest in grooming. "I don't think I need to tell you that UCLA is incredibly highly regarded."

"I want to see your license," said Meredith, appearing to disagree.

"My license? To practice law?" asked the lawyer.

"No, to operate a hair dryer. Of course to practice law." Meredith seemed suddenly incensed by the presence of the lawyer, more so than she usually seemed to feel about lawyers in general. "Since when did my father hire you?"

"I really don't think that's any of your business," said the lawyer, before extending a hand to Arthur and Eilidh. "Hi. I'm Ryan Behrend."

"Ohhhhhhh," said Arthur, though it didn't help Eilidh at all.

"Nice to meet you," Ryan said to Eilidh, ignoring Arthur's reaction and gradually dismissing Eilidh as if she wasn't there. "Meredith, pleased to see you're as unpleasant as I remember. I thought for a second I might have to remain professional, but now I can see there wouldn't be a point."

He had very white teeth and was, Eilidh realized, not very old. Probably not much older than Meredith, if at all.

"Ryan," Meredith explained to the others through clenched teeth, "went to school with me."

"Kindergarten through eighth grade," Ryan confirmed. "So obviously Meredith's issues with me are salient and well-founded, and not at all a childish grudge."

Eilidh felt as if that remark was aimed specifically at her. It was true that Meredith had never gotten over a slight, and had a tendency to nurse a grievance overlong. Whenever there was a matter of contention, it was almost always Meredith's fault. Still, Eilidh wasn't sure why Ryan would attempt to sweeten her specifically, although he was very young and she had never met him before. She had sat in meetings with Thayer and his board and his administrators and surely his lawyers, though those were specifically the corporate kind. It didn't explain why Thayer had chosen someone Meredith's age to handle his last will and testament.

"Are we supposed to be going over the will right now?" asked Eilidh, feeling her heart kick with panic. She wasn't prepared to divvy up her father's life quite yet, though she knew in some elusive way that this was what they'd all come for. They weren't just staying in the house as part of their personal group therapy. She knew, distantly, that Meredith would want to get in and get out, and surely so would Arthur. Their time was limited, and unlike Eilidh, the other two had something to go home to. Unlike her, they had somewhere else to be.

Right on schedule, she felt the parasite uncoiling in her spine, snaking out in a line until it stretched from the top of her vertebra to the bottom. She'd woken it up again, the thing that seemed to live inside her chest, quietly lazing about, making a hammock out of every diphthong she spoke.

Eilidh had gone through a phase, shortly after the ceiling rained blood in her hospital room, where she'd become convinced that she had a real, actual parasite. She had requested every body scan known to man to prove that she had something alive inside her, something that had taken up residency the moment the possibility of dance had bowed out. Whether it wanted to please her, save her, or destroy her was really unknowable, unguessable even after five years. But it clearly knew that Eilidh was feeling something heavy, something that sank in the lowly caverns of her heart, and this time it sat waiting in the stiffness of her spine, as if all it would take to explode everyone in this room would be the tap of a button. Push to start, vroom vroom.

"You're not Dad's lawyer," Meredith was saying, waking Eilidh from her temporary sense of craving. "His lawyer is, you know, that guy, the one who came to all the Christmas parties. Cass met him last year, they spoke over punch."

"Right, that guy," said Arthur, which did not appear to be a joke. It seemed they both knew whoever "that guy" was, which sort of made sense, because Eilidh spent their father's big Christmas party hiding from people she worked with and becoming comprehensively inebriated, a tipping point where she could still avoid propositioning amicable colleagues or exhorting inexplicable feats of plague over the question of what she'd been up to since she got hurt but also fuzzy enough not to feel her own solitariness or the aftershocks of the question when asked. Ideally, she got just drunk enough to flirt outrageously with whatever young thing had been hired to tend the private bar, which was somehow always an aspiring actress or an aspiring playwright or an aspiring novelist and therefore someone much more interesting than Eilidh, who didn't have dreams anymore. Just sudden urges for destruction.

Just then the doorbell rang, and Gillian, who was still holding a pair of coffees—one labeled Arthur, the other Meredith—gave a slow, syrupy blink as if just registering the presence of other people in the room. "I'll get it," she said in a soft and girlish voice, like waking from a dream. Then she wandered slowly away, but returned almost immediately after she'd disappeared, flanked this time by a very, very old man (oh yes, thought Eilidh, *that* guy!) and a startlingly beautiful woman who filled the room with the overwhelming scent of aristocracy and freesias.

"Oh, Philippa," registered Arthur with a blink.

Philippa—or, as Eilidh and most of the internet thought of her, @LadyPVDM—breezed into the room after an air kiss to Gillian's cheek. "I found John waiting at the door, can you believe it? Hello darling, you look exhausted. Oh! Meredith, hello dear, you look radiant." Meredith, who was wearing an oversized men's shirt and boxers, did not look anything of the sort, and her reaction to being flattered was to scowl. "I don't believe we've met, you must be Eilidh. My god," exclaimed Philippa, "please don't take offense to this, but your aura is absolutely unhinged."

Eilidh opened her mouth to answer—what the answer would have been, she had no earthly idea—when her sister began to use concerning tones of argument, overshadowing anything Eilidh might have felt about being either harrowingly insulted or accurately perceived.

"This," said Meredith, pointing at the elderly gentleman with a hint of frenzy. "*This* is our father's estate lawyer."

"Yes," agreed Arthur, who was now contending with Philippa's apparent need to spritz him with rosewater. "This is the guy."

"Hello, dear," said the older lawyer to Eilidh kindly, which was when Eilidh realized it was her godfather, John. (Eilidh had come along in her parents' lives after they had already divvied up the godparent honors to the important people, so the man who had been Thayer's roommate for five years in the eighties and was now—or maybe was not—his estate attorney had been appointed Eilidh's godfather after Meredith and Arthur had been given three each.)

"Well, I assure you, I spoke to Thayer just last month about his will," said Ryan, the initial lawyer who was Meredith's sworn enemy for the time being. "Mine is the most up-to-date."

"Young man," said the now-squinting older lawyer who had sent Eilidh a nice card and a check every year on her birthday for as long as she could remember, "unless Thayer was half out of his wits when he hired you, you cannot possibly have the legal will and testament. Thayer Wren was religious with his estate planning, once a year on his birthday."

"Well, his birthday was two months ago," said Ryan, "so I win."

"I'm challenging this," said Meredith, before turning to Gillian. "I can challenge this, can't I? On the basis of my father not being stupid enough to hire any idiot off the street to represent his entire life and legacy?"

"Mm," said Gillian, who seemed suddenly very interested in her tongue.

"Meredith, didn't you drop out of Harvard?" posed Ryan conversationally.

"They parted ways mutually," said Arthur. By then, Philippa had swanned back out of the room, claiming something about the alignment of her chakras. "And anyway, she's right, whichever will John has in his possession is definitely the legal one."

"You do understand the nature of linear time, yes?" said Ryan.

"*Your* will—if it even exists," said Meredith, to which Ryan began to argue but which Meredith efficiently and loudly shut down, "could have been made under duress. Under false pretenses. He could have been blind drunk for all we know!"

"That's true," said Gillian thinly, as if from a very great distance. She seemed to be trying to remind herself of something at the moment, or possibly the statement was meant to be a personal reassurance.

Thankfully, before Ryan and Meredith could get into any further arguments about whatever Meredith might still be angry about—oh *yes*, recalled Eilidh, suddenly blinking with delayed cognizance, this was *Ryan Behrend*, the one who'd beaten Meredith at the science fair with a project he'd stolen from his older sister, something that had provoked Meredith into such an unexpected fit she'd destroyed nearly a thousand dollars in school property and been sent away to boarding school—oh *god*, thought Eilidh, how had she forgotten *that*?—the older lawyer stepped in to mediate the conflict.

"We don't want to disturb the family at this stressful time," he said pointedly to Ryan, gesturing into the other room. "Why don't we compare documents and discuss between the lawyers before subjecting the family members to any further distress?"

His words were extremely reasonable and gentle, Eilidh thought, but he had the browbeating tone of someone who expected to be paid exorbitantly and did not intend for any other outcome.

Just then, Eilidh's phone buzzed with a message. It was Dzhuliya, Eilidh noted with a brief lurch of surprise, notable for some added tingle of excitement. What, she thought, might Dzhuliya have to say to her this morning? They never spoke about work aside from Eilidh's crossover with Thayer's schedule, so really, possibility ran the gamut. Every other week or so there was a meme, or maybe a brief exchange of articles one or the other might like, usually the latest in reality TV recaps or group chat material about celebrities.

Then again, the latest in celebrity news was the passing of Thayer Wren, so never mind.

**Is the lawyer there yet?**

**Just checking!** Dzhuliya added in a hasty second bubble. **Wanted to make sure everything is going smoothly. Trying to take care of as much as I can on my end!**

Ah yes, Eilidh recalled, this was just Dzhuliya doing her job, or whatever was left of it. (How bad *were* things for the employees of Wrenfare? Eilidh often wondered about the Real World like a fairy-tale princess, never really conceiving of the possibility that she could ask.)

**Which one?** asked Eilidh in a joking tone that she realized only belatedly would not come across in a text message.

Immediately, as if Dzhuliya had been waiting for her response, a message bubble began typing in response, replies that came in quick, sharp succession.

**What do you mean?**

**Ryan's reached out to you, hasn't he?**

**He should be going over the will with you today.**

Eilidh felt a cool sensation wash over her, something she felt certain was dread. She couldn't say why, but if she'd learned anything about the things her body did to her recently, it was that ignoring them didn't help.

The will.

The will of her dead father.

The last thing her father would ever say to her.

Panic rose up, a mushroom cloud of atomic proportions. The thing in her chest buzzed like a hornet's nest, festering, swirling, cycloning in. She felt the presence of the swarm and knew her only hope was to dissipate it, give it the space to discreetly thin.

Eilidh needed to talk about this—she desperately needed to talk. Could she discuss any of this with Arthur, though? With Meredith? Absolutely not. They'd already made it plenty clear they would not be doing anything of the sort.

But there was Dzhuliya, wasn't there? Yes, Dzhuliya, an amicable colleague! And unlike Eilidh's siblings, Dzhuliya had spent all of Thayer's last days beside him. In many ways, Dzhuliya had known him better and more completely than Meredith or Arthur ever had.

Eilidh thought, then, of Dzhuliya's faithful presence within the radius of her father. She thought of the many scheduling messages on her phone from Dhuliya's familiar Wrenfare contact bubble; the little smiles she and Dzhuliya exchanged when they passed each other coming and going from Thayer's office; Dzhuliya pausing her conversation to wave to Eilidh from beside the tree of noxious flavored coffee pods; Dzhuliya asking Eilidh about her day whenever she answered Thayer's phone.

Then, inevitably, Eilidh's mind went to other things. The first wicked smile she'd clocked on Dzhuliya's face, that first little line of innuendo. The temporary relief of their hasty one-shot in the car, inadvisable and secret. Dzhuliya's shoulder, lean muscle and luminous glow, slipping out from beneath her navy hoodie. The shape of it, the way her sweat would taste.

Her sweat? Jesus Christ. The thing in Eilidh's chest seemed confusingly ravenous, holding three, four sensations at once, juggling them in turns.

**Do you want to meet somewhere and talk?** Eilidh asked Dzhuliya, telling herself gentle lies like it's fine, there's no agenda here. Amicable collagues talk all the time.

A message bubble appeared, then disappeared.

Appeared, then disappeared.

Appeared . . .

Disappeared.

**Sure,** Dzhuliya eventually said. **I can be there in like twenty minutes.**

# 17

Meredith Wren felt sure she was going to kill someone, as she often claimed to feel, though as Jamie had pointed out to her the day prior, all evidence suggested she didn't have the stomach for murder. This was meant to be a neutral statement on Jamie's part, but Meredith had taken it as an assault on her character.

"Of course I could kill you if I really thought it was necessary," she had told him in the car. "I could kill anyone if the circumstances were right. That's the thing, really. I'm just above any sort of moral absolutism. Sometimes the circumstances do prescribe an unlikely moral course of action, that's all I'm saying."

"Meredith, I think you're doing the thing where you just say words in any order to avoid voicing anything meaningful," said Jamie, which had set Meredith off again. But we don't need to focus on the conversation with Jamie right now. We'll inevitably come back to that.

At the moment, Meredith was contending not only with her stye, which was definitely worse today than it had been yesterday and she felt certain everyone else had noticed, but also the knowledge that she had placed all her eggs in the spineless basket that was her business partner, Ward.

That morning, Meredith had awoken in bed with Cass, picked up her phone to start her day as she always did—arranging her schedule and producing a to-do list that she would then attend to with a dutifulness that was borderline compulsive, like administrative zealotry—when she realized she had a string of messages from Ward.

> It's not out of the question Mer if he says he knows then he knows
> We don't need anyone looking into these allegations
> If he publishes we both go to prison
> No offense but I will absolutely turn on you Mer

Fuck they're going to subpoena our messages

You're going to look so guilty

I look bad obviously but whatever happens to me will be nothing
   compared to you

There's no legal precedent for this holy fuck it's going to be
   everywhere

Tyche will let you burn for sure

The feds will make an example of you

They'll charge you for way more than fraud

I could still get a cushy white collar prison situation out of this but you

There is truly no way out of this for you unless you get him to pull the
   article

Answer the phone Meredith

Holy shit Mer you have to do something you can't just say you have it
   handled

**YOU DO NOT HAVE IT HANDLED WE ARE FUCKED**

This, Meredith had thought upon waking, was exactly the kind of masculine hysteria she did not have time for. She proceeded to take Ward's call and explain to him in very clear, small words that he was to stop acting like an idiot and keep his shit together. Then, in a moment of extremely ill-advised panic, she had the brief, critically depressing thought that she wished she could have called her father.

Which probably made it sound like Meredith was sad about his death. She didn't think sadness was the right word. She had always wondered, after the severe impairment to her entire personality that had been the loss of her mother, if she would even register the splintering off of whatever her father was to her. She felt sure it would be simple, a little breath of relief maybe, perhaps a twinge of loss here and there at the man she had always wanted him to be, which he never was. In the past, when she had had problems with the company or needed help attracting investors or legitimizing her ideas, she'd made the mistake of saying things to her father like "what should I do" that had routinely proven counterproductive.

The last time Meredith had asked the great Thayer Wren for advice had been a real low point, possibly the dictionary definition of low point, almost exactly five years ago. Meredith had already been on the path to disaster by then, not that she clocked it at the time. Mostly she was concerned that accepting a deal with her father's nemesis might force her research in an un-savory direction, while rejecting it would mean watching her path to maxi-mum life achievement go up in smoke. That her relationship with her father had been irreparably damaged the moment she'd agreed to meet with Mer-ritt Foster—or that Lou had beaten her to the punch and sold her start-up to Tyche the year before—were personal matters, completely tangential, or so Meredith told herself all the time.

"I just worry," Meredith began, "that what Foster sees in Chirp is less about helping people than it is about—"

"Have you heard from your sister lately?" said Thayer, picking at a plate of hummus. Meredith had chosen the place, which was already a terrible sign. Thayer was incredibly particular, and already in a bad mood because it was one of those restaurants where you had to order from a menu that was just an enormous board behind the counter, which meant you were under intense pressure to pick your meal with the knowledge that at least a dozen people were waiting behind you. Meredith had thought a sun-drenched patio sounded nice, but Thayer, mostly in shape for his age but with a tendency to run hot, was dabbing irritably at his forehead with a napkin, visibly wishing he'd stayed home.

"No," said Meredith stubbornly, although she had looked at Eilidh's social media the night before, which was easier than actually speaking to Eilidh. The risk of a conversation was nearly always too much for Meredith. "The thing is," she continued, "I always knew there was going to be a tradeoff, you know, in terms of monetizing the product—"

"You get in bed with Tyche, you're never getting out," her father muttered gruffly. "They will own you. They'll buy you, replace you with someone more seasoned who'll do exactly what they're told, and then you'll do something else, Meredith, because that's how Foster does business. Fucking guy," Thayer added in an undertone before concluding, "Cutting that shithead loose was the luckiest thing that ever happened to Wrenfare." Which was, as the kids say, a blatant lie.

"So I should turn down the deal?" asked Meredith helplessly.

"Kip Hughes is an egotistical shit-for-brains who hates to lose. He'll outbid anyone else," said Thayer with the apathetic flap of one hand. "He's probably made sure everyone in the Valley knows you're Tyche's. They won't touch you now."

"But—"

"The problem with you," Thayer snapped, "is that you think you're smarter than everyone else. You think you know what you're doing, you always have. But they're not going to let you in, Meredith, not really, and they're certainly not letting you run the show, because nobody in this industry is going to take you seriously. I told you," Thayer said with an edge of warning, "get a degree, get some actual experience under your belt, *then* you can work for Wrenfare—"

"But you didn't get a degree." Meredith could feel her cheeks flaming.

"I also starved for a long time, Meredith. I groveled. I laughed at the shit jokes and I kissed the asses I needed to kiss for long enough that they trusted me—" (And here, what Thayer could not voice aloud: *And I had Merritt Foster, who had the Harvard degree I couldn't get.*)

"But why couldn't I have developed Chirp *for* Wrenfare?" Meredith demanded, failing as she usually did to hear subtext where it didn't pertain to her personal logic. "You told me my entire life that if I wanted to succeed, then I had to do the work, so I did."

"Exactly," said Thayer. "Do the work—*all* of the work. Which means learning to coexist with other people, Meredith, because nobody in this industry ever works without a team. It also means learning when it's worth holding your ground and when it's wiser to play the long game—to keep your head down."

"Why should I keep my head down?" Meredith could tell her voice was rising. A few people had already glanced her way, and Thayer was angling himself away from her, as if they barely knew each other. As if he needed plausible deniability, so that if anyone asked if this was his daughter, he could act like he hadn't the faintest idea what they were talking about. "You want me to be softer, be *less,* just so a bunch of old men don't get their feelings hurt?"

"People who lead this industry are worth learning from," Thayer said with a warning glare, getting as defensive as he always got when she suggested that his contemporaries were past their usefulness. "Everyone in this world gets where they are because someone else takes a shot on them. I got where I did because I wasn't a threat to the people who were willing to help me—and for that, it's my name on the company. It's me in the driver's seat."

"Okay, so which part about me do you think they find so terrifying?" pressed Meredith, who could feel herself getting emotional now. "My intellect? My ideas? My vagina?"

"Don't be crass," muttered Thayer with revulsion.

"Is it the fact that the average Silicon Valley CEO genuinely thinks I might be in league with 'the Chinese'?" snapped Meredith.

"Let me ask you something," Thayer said, levying a piece of pita in her direction like he'd just unsheathed a sword. "What did you say when Kip told you?"

"Told me what?" said Meredith with only the slightest stumble, in lieu of saying she had yet to speak personally to Kip Hughes, the founder of Tyche, who had been a thorn in Thayer's side for as long as Meredith could remember. Which Lou had also known when she signed with Tyche, by the way. But as usual, Meredith shoved all thoughts of Lou aside.

"When he gave you the propaganda, the red pill speech. You know—'this idea of yours could change the world, you just have to think bigger.'" Thayer did an absurd impression of Kip, as if the CEO who'd shaped magi-tech commerce from the ground up was a child and not a grown man no less than ten years Thayer's junior. "I'm guessing he used the words 'revolutionary' and 'disruption' in there somewhere," Thayer added with an air of spiteful mockery.

Actually, it had been Kip's adviser—the same adviser who'd once been Thayer's. *A product this revolutionary would be the disruption Big Pharma has needed for decades,* had been Merritt Foster's exact words. *You just have to see that your market goes beyond the simple delivery of SSRIs. What you have is a product that could change the way every human being moves through the world, and Tyche could help you do it.*

*Oh,* Meredith had breathed, and Cass, sitting behind Foster in the conference room, just to the left of the presentation screen, had smiled at her.

"I . . . said I'd think about it," said Meredith.

Thayer gave her a fleeting look; the kind that reminded Meredith how infrequently he actually looked at her. Normally it was like there was something in her that he couldn't stand to see—something that jumped out and tied the two of them together. Like he looked at her and saw something weighing him down, some shadow he couldn't shake.

She knew then that he wasn't going to help her. He was going to ridicule her, and he was going to do it in a way that sounded like caution, even though it felt like criticism. He was going to call it love, even though it was only ever disappointment.

"It's a strong offer," said Meredith to her hands. "I really thought you'd be proud."

Later, she would wish she hadn't said it.

"If I thought your product was worth anywhere near as much as Tyche was offering," her father told her without even a moment's hesitation, "I would have outbid them by now."

Meredith shook herself free of the memory and thought, in a very cold, firm internal voice, he's dead now. Lots of incredible people had shitty fathers. Lots of people worked hard because they had something to prove. Really, she ought to thank him. She could put his body in the ground and step over it, outpace him, use his legacy and the memory of his disappointment to raise herself back up.

She shouldn't have had the thought *What would my father do*, because the answer was that her father would never have been in this predicament. Her father wouldn't have been swayed by someone telling him he'd done something brilliant, patting him on the head and practically leading him by the hand. He wouldn't have been so desperate to have the resources, the money, the reach. He wouldn't have cheated, and if he knew that Meredith had, he would cut her off from everything. His estimation. His legacy. Whatever he claimed to be his love.

His last will and testament. She shivered a little, wondering what would have driven Thayer Wren to draw up a new will with a new attorney a month ago; whether such a thought somehow concurred with a larger shift in the zeitgeist, riding the same invisible current that had driven Jamie to suspect her of flying too close to the sun. How long had everyone been mobilizing against her? She felt like the butt of the joke; that her months—years—spent waiting for the shoe to drop were not only earned, but worsened by retrospect. She'd done nothing but scour the sky and still she'd failed to see it falling. Was it because success was never a real outcome—had that always been doom in her future, the thing she'd misread as brightness the whole time?

The glass cliff, thought Meredith, searching around for some justifiable anger. It meant the phenomenon of women being awarded captaincy over men only when a company is in trouble, when leadership is more likely to fail. It meant letting a woman win the battle only when she was sure to lose the war. Philosophically, Meredith could intellectualize the inequity of this, falling back on the reliability of her sociological, systemic rage—the one where she'd been doomed from the start by the narrative, by the institution, by a deep, patriarchal flaw.

As always, though, her darker thoughts were quick to whisper *Not you, though, dummy!* You've *deserved this all along.*

Inevitably, Meredith thought of Lou again; of what a typical Tuesday might look like in Lou's current life. Meredith had always imagined it would go something like this:

7:00 AM: Awaken sweetly beside long-term partner, perhaps to morning cunnilingus.

8:00 AM: Accept an award.

9:00 AM: Throw the first pitch for the season opener at Tyche Stadium.

10:00 AM: Cure cancer, uninvent childhood hunger.

11:00 AM: Throw darts at an effigy of Meredith.

12:00 PM: More cunnilingus.

1:00 PM: Board meeting for whatever magitech venture Lou was pursuing lately (curing cancer being more of a philanthropic hobby).

2:00 PM: Burn aforementioned effigy of Meredith.

3:00 PM: Receive secret document detailing Meredith's many professional failures; laugh maniacally.

4:00 PM: Engage sudden craving for complex souffle; bake perfectly.

5:00 PM: Nap.

6:00 PM: Wake up.

6:15 PM: Contemplate Meredith's destruction.

6:19 PM: Suddenly recall that Meredith did not need any help destroying herself, on account of being a complete and total hack.

6:30 PM: Forget about Meredith completely, attend Posh Gala with Handsome Celebrity.

And so on. Leave it to Meredith to not know baseball season was well underway.

In any case, before Meredith could linger too long down that particular spiral, Ward called again, freaking out about the investors this time—*They must have heard by now, they're asking for more clarification on our testing parameters, nobody would ask for this unless they really knew—THEY KNOW, MEREDITH, THEY KNOW*—and then, around ten that morning, her phone buzzed with a message.

**Coffee?** asked Jamie Ammar.

Meredith stared at his name on her screen, wondering why she wasn't surprised. Shouldn't she be? She thought about Cass, who was working up-stairs from her bed. *Their* bed. He'd asked her how yesterday's spontaneous drive had gone and she said fine, she'd tried to talk Jamie out of publishing the article and he'd refused, so now it was over.

"Tyche will bury it if it's any legitimate threat," Cass had said with a shrug, because he didn't understand that actually, Thayer was right; that Tyche would use this as an excuse to toss Meredith aside, to bury *her* under the weight of their misdeeds because everyone was just waiting for her to fail. There was no love for her in this industry. If Jamie published an article proving Chirp to be an insidious con, in all likelihood, Tyche still profited. Jamie couldn't take them down without taking Meredith down harder, end-ing her career, making her the sacrificial lamb, the obvious agent for Tyche's financial crimes while Kip Hughes and Merritt Foster settled easily out of court. While they kept selling the thing she'd spent decades trying to make, only to warp it beyond recognition the moment her check had cleared. Pos-sibly long before that.

Because she'd taken the money. Her hands were filthy, with no way to walk that reality back. She knew who she'd gotten in bed with. No one had said anything when Tyche was accused of tracking users' data. Nothing had changed when people criticized the conditions of Tyche's factories, their his-tory of labor abuse, the thousands of workers who were undertrained and injured on the job. People still bought their products, still used their ser-vices. The only difference was that now everyone knew it was bad, Meredith included, so everything she said yes to was just another bite from the poi-sonous tree.

All of which Thayer had pointed out to Meredith. Not in the context of her own ethical responsibility (irrelevant) but to point out the reality that despite Foster's multibillion-dollar offer—despite Meredith's ability to stand (attempts to stand) on her own merit—she still had not actually won. Be-cause it was Meredith that Tyche would happily slaughter if it meant keeping her product—and their means of monetizing it—alive.

Thayer had known it because for all intents and purposes, he *was* Kip Hughes—he'd been the man at the top all his life, which Meredith could never be.

Thayer was right about her all along. And now Wrenfare, the thing she'd tried so hard to be good enough for, would transfer breezily to someone else.

Not that it mattered at the moment. Not that this feeling was grief, or that grief was merited under any circumstances. Not that the ache in her chest was any reasonable form of loss.

Meredith stared down at her screen, pondering what to say to the man who was first and foremost a traitor before he could be considered her ex.

What changed your mind? asked Meredith.

I didn't change my mind, said Jamie. What made you think I'd changed my mind?

You mean you're still publishing the article?

Yes

Even after hearing everything I told you yesterday?

Especially after that, yes

You seriously think I'm okay with you doing this?

No, I don't imagine you're ok with any of it. Nor, he added pointedly, am I ok with you trying to brainwash me, just so we're clear

Right, this hasn't been mentioned yet, but in case it's crossing your mind that Meredith, who can change the brain chemistry of her test patients magically, might also be willing to alter the mind of her investigative journalist ex-boyfriend who may or may not be about to destroy her, the answer is yes, she did try that. Unfortunately (for Meredith), the reason she and Jamie Ammar broke up in the first place has a lot to do with how far Meredith will go to keep herself on top.

Meredith rolled her eyes. If you think I'm trying to brainwash you, why would you want to have coffee with me? And why would I want to see you again when you clearly have every intention to ruin my life?

No logical reason I can think of, replied Jamie, but when has that ever stopped us?

Fair enough, thought Meredith with a sigh. She thought again about Cass, about the glasses he wore when he used his computer, about how he looked shirtless, about how he promised her in very soothing tones that everything would be all right despite the fact that no, it wouldn't, because her father was dead and nothing would ever be right again.

Then she hated herself no more or less than usual when she typed back, Fuck you, I'll be there in five.

# 18

Even from a distance, Dzhuliya did not appear to have slept well. She was waiting for Eilidh in her car by 9:55 AM, double-parked behind the carport at the bottom of the drive, and was staring into space as Eilidh made her way from the house's staircase and over the stretch of creek ambling beside the empty single-lane road. In one direction was the winding trickle back to the center of town, the city equivalent of a country lane with its sleepy coffee shops and overpriced tourist traps; in the other, a steady climb into the woods, traversing nimbly from concrete lane to steep, well-trodden tendrils of redwood-lined trails. Eilidh considered her options, then rapped on the driver's-side window.

"Hey," said Eilidh when Dzhuliya rolled down the window. "Fancy a hike?"

Dzhuliya's brows furrowed a bit, traveling from Eilidh's leather sandals and thick, woolen socks up to the bun she'd piled messily atop her head. "Won't that be hard for you? You know, with your back and everything."

Ah, so she did remember that Eilidh had something of a life-altering injury, how marvelous. "I can handle a reasonably paced climb, provided you don't need me to do any pirouettes. Come on, get out." Eilidh stepped back into the road, letting Dzhuliya clamber out of the car with a slight grimace. She was wearing an oversized T-shirt, gym shorts she usually wore for twice-weekly rock climbing (not that Eilidh was keeping track of Dzhuliya's workout accoutrements; it was just that they'd run into each other once in the bathroom on her father's office floor when Dzhuliya was changing out of her work clothes for the gym, so, you know, amicable small talk)—and sneakers, Eilidh noted, so she shouldn't be complaining.

For a moment, Eilidh wondered again what her feelings ought to have been about Dzhuliya—Could they, in certain lights, be considered friends? Was it normal, under the circumstances, to be friends? Perhaps not, given

Dzhuliya's less-than-enthusiastic reaction—when Dzhuliya suddenly turned a sheepish smile on Eilidh that was equal parts youthful and horribly aged. "Sorry I'm so out of sorts," she said. "I just can't believe he's gone, but of course it must be so much harder for you."

Eilidh ignored the sharp prod of a parasitic tail.

"Everyone grieves differently," she said, thinking of how her brother's version of grief involved having his wife and both members of his throuple around to coddle his problems while her sister seemed completely unaffected, prompting Eilidh to wonder yet again whether Meredith might actually be a complete psychopath. "Honestly, I don't think it's fully sunken in."

They walked in companionable silence for a bit, the road crunching beneath their feet as they left the lane behind and ventured onto a foothill trail. Their strides were well matched; Eilidh was about the same height as Dzhuliya, though she didn't slouch for vocational reasons and Dzhuliya now seemed to curl uncharacteristically into herself, folding in like there was a hinge in the center of her breastbone. Like one of those mahogany easels that hold picture frames.

The creek burbled a little as they went, the continuous sound of water a soothing monotony as Eilidh ran through a droning series of thoughts in her head—still desperate to talk, yet now wondering where to begin. The thing living in her chest was particularly present, sharp as hunger pangs. Not that Eilidh ever really knew what it wanted from her, but today it seemed particularly opaque, and everything seemed heightened by the mere fact of Dzhuliya's presence.

The thing in Eilidh's chest tightened like a cyclone around the very idea of Dzhuliya, pointing like an arrowhead, the buzz of a glaring neon sign. As if finally resolving the question mark of Dzhuliya (amicable? professional? perhaps something better or markedly worse?) might give Eilidh a sense of necessary clarity, maybe even a feeling that could be considered satisfaction, like finishing the Sunday crossword after wrestling with it for two years. There was a nagging sense of betwixtness for Eilidh when it came to the constancy, and mystery, of Dzhuliya; something not technically forbidden but not quite acceptable, either. Eilidh knew in an indeterminate way that her father lived in close proximity to whatever the answer was, and the thing in her chest gleefully wrung confusion from every battered pulse of her agonized heart.

Even that was bewildering—the way the occupant of her chest seemed at all times to have an unexpected aftertaste, part sweetness of longing, part violence of feeling. Some of it was about Thayer, probably even most of it, but it was Dzhuliya who was here now, and so for better or worse, it was Dzhuliya unto which the thing latched on. It throbbed and thudded with craving, with bestiality and zeal. Did she want to hold Dzhuliya's hand or throw her into a river? Did she want to vanish Dzhuliya into smoke or float her gently on a cloud of her own making? Was this vengeful thunder in her chest or was it claggy, sickly sweetness?

What had sadness wrought inside her, and why wouldn't the damn thing let her go?

"So, as far as Wrenfare goes," Eilidh managed to say after a moment. "Is that . . . I mean, are you—would you want to . . . stay?"

Dzhuliya looked at her, a mark of hesitation in her brow. Perhaps because Eilidh had phrased a human resources question as casual chitchat between friends. "I only mean to ask whether you see yourself . . . you know . . . pursuing any particular advancement opportunities within the company. Because under the circumstances, I'm quite sure I could put in a good word." Dear god! Eilidh thought. Without realizing it, she'd affected some kind of contrived musical accent, like she'd gone briefly aristocratic. "I just know how highly my father thought of you," she attempted again, and felt even worse. What was she doing, promising Dzhuliya some kind of promotion? From what to what? And with what power? "I don't know what I'm saying," Eilidh concluded, which was worse and yet somehow better, because at least it wasn't a lie. "I just want to tell you that I'm here for you, whatever happens next. Whatever . . . changes. Whoever takes my father's place." With that, Eilidh remembered what she had actually wanted to talk about, though she'd traversed too far from things like feelings, having entered the conversation through the dumbest possible side door.

Luckily, Dzhuliya seemed willing to overlook the majority of Eilidh's mind-numbing inability to communicate, gingerly sidestepping the potholes and landmines. "Is something going on with the company? I thought you'd have heard who was inheriting Thayer's shares by now."

Which reminded Eilidh of her father's apparent change of heart—a matter of relevance, if not the thing she'd actually hoped to discuss. "You would have known that he changed his will, right? You handled all his appointments," she remarked, as if Dzhuliya would not be perfectly aware of her daily responsibilities.

Dzhuliya cast her another uncertain glance, this one more dismissive. She had begun to huff slightly as the trail grew steeper—perhaps, Eilidh thought, from all the sudden stress and slouching. "I can't imagine you want to talk about that right now. Do you?"

Well, that was true, Eilidh didn't want to discuss *that*, necessarily, whatever "that" was—her father's unexpected secrecy, she supposed. Or was it unexpected?

She reconsidered it now, realizing she still hadn't taken the temperature of her feelings on the matter. She supposed that for all Thayer often spoke to her about the intricacies of her job, they very rarely discussed the details of Thayer's. She hadn't realized she could consider herself uninformed about his work until just now, upon registering that maybe he *wouldn't* have mentioned a meeting with his lawyers, because he didn't really burden Eilidh with specific trivialities. Not in an elusive way—if she asked him about things like layoffs, he simply dismissed her concerns outright, assuring her there was no truth to the rumors. He mainly focused on the private matters of his life, reliving memories with Eilidh as a sounding board, and he usually wanted to talk about her—or, very often, her siblings.

The thing in her chest fluttered, the sudden launch of pigeon flight or psychological indigestion. Eilidh still hadn't decided what the worst possible outcome would be when it came to the matter of Wrenfare's inheritance. It was Meredith's practice to be prepared for the worst, but Meredith was also incredibly talented at projecting disaster. Meredith's worst case was easy: Wrenfare would become Eilidh's, her father's chance to prove at last that Eilidh was the favorite. But Meredith had always been hard on their father, and she hadn't known him very well in his last years. This will would have come from the Thayer Eilidh had known best—the one she felt had become a different person, perhaps a little softer. Maybe filled with a little more regret.

"Do you know what he changed?" asked Eilidh, and Dzhuliya shook her head.

"I actually thought you'd know, if anyone, but—" She began to speak again, but then stopped. When she spoke, it was to say with grim finality, "I do think it's possible your siblings won't like it."

What was Arthur's worst case scenario, Eilidh wondered? Meredith's was easy, but Arthur's was less straightforward to predict. Until that morning, Eilidh hadn't thought it possible that Arthur might still want to be their father's chosen one. Arthur seemed to have changed so much, to have become so many different people, first Gillian's husband and then the congressman and then the strangely craven lothario that now seemed to occupy the space where her brother had once been. All that was familiar or even recognizable about him now was the unexpected and eccentric, the thing he denied as being important—the occasional uncontrolled spark that made Eilidh long to ask him how different the two of them really were.

Arthur had always been a mystery to Eilidh, more so than Meredith, because Meredith was mean and that was actually quite simple as far as human characteristics were concerned. Meredith was consistent and predictable. Arthur was charming but malleable, sharp enough to be loved by Meredith and therefore a bit of a threat to Eilidh, who never really knew where he stood.

Surely he would want their father's money. What politician didn't want money? But did he want Wrenfare? And if so, would he try to wrest it from the others, even away from Meredith—even away from her?

Eilidh had seen what social media said about Arthur's political agenda and thought it to be untrue. She believed, perhaps delusionally, that she knew him better than the faceless mob. But maybe she didn't! He said he'd grown tired of Congress, but was that true or merely convenient? Was Eilidh projecting her anxieties onto Arthur, or had they always shared something Meredith hadn't?

Eilidh thought again of the tremor in Arthur's hands, the shower of taillights like falling stars, his uncanny death and resurrection. Wasn't that a version of her apocalypse, in a way? Or was she looking too closely for something that didn't exist?

"Your brother and sister are vultures," Thayer had said to Eilidh some weeks ago. Was it around a month, when he had drawn up the new will? Come to think of it, it might have been. "I can't say I blame them. They spent more time with your mother; they're more like her than you ever were. I never could stand it when they were young, and I suppose I took my pain out on them."

Thayer almost never spoke about Persephone in explicit terms, something Meredith actively held against him and that Arthur seemed to agree was cowardly in some way. Eilidh always felt her siblings were too hard on Thayer, that perhaps regret was harder to face than anything else, even loss or grief. After all, Persephone had died while Thayer was still hard at work expanding Wrenfare, and to Eilidh, Thayer had always carried around an awareness that someone could have saved his wife. Someone who could, theoretically, have been him.

Eilidh's memories about her mother were hazy, or rather, clear in a way that suggested they weren't memories at all but just stories she'd been told to ease the fact that she hadn't really had a mother in any of the ways that counted. People had always seen it as her tragedy—prior to her actual tragedy—and even written about her performances as if pain was something she carried in her soul, something intrinsic. That she could dance so beautifully was an extension of a lifetime's search, her story playing out on the stage in a way that could be shared, as if the real art was always the act of communion.

Eilidh had never wanted to admit out loud that this was utter bullshit, because she couldn't feel sad about something she'd never had. If anything, she found Persephone kind of cruel in her own way, a cruelty she must have taught to Meredith, which left Eilidh with the sense that she was mainly angry at her mother. Because wasn't it reasonable to feel annoyance, given that Persephone had had not only the resources but the responsibility to treat herself better, to make better choices, at very least for the sake of her children, who were so vulnerable and young? Eilidh, meanwhile, kept on going; she ate food even when she was depressed, she exercised for the illusion that was her health, she went to the doctor even though she didn't really care whether the horrors befell her. All of which made her feel a bit cheated, because wouldn't it be nice to simply give up on herself, as Thayer seemed to feel Persephone had done?

And now Thayer was gone, too, which left only Meredith and Arthur, their dark little bond, and anyone their lives happened to touch, for better or worse. The world carried on, senseless as usual. Eilidh hadn't expected her siblings to grieve Thayer's loss the same way she did, but it would have been nice if they could share one single thing, such as the fact that they were now orphans. Orphans! Adults, obviously, but still. Their children, if any of them ever had any, would not have grandparents. There would be no reason to gather during the holidays—Meredith already hardly found the time to call Eilidh back. They had lost something, some foundational cornerstone on which the three of them were built, and now all that was left was . . .

Well, something like a trillion dollars, depending on what happened with Wrenfare.

And the possibility that her father had left everything to her.

The thing in Eilidh's chest did a kick-flip that felt like whiplash. Eilidh exhaled sharply, pausing for a moment in the middle of the trail as the creek burbled gently below them. She felt the parasitic flutter of nausea, the sense that whatever lived inside her was in a grotesquely pleasant mood, the kind that led to pestilence. "I really don't want to dwell on the . . . the *commodification* of it," Eilidh managed to say aloud, trying not to burp up a plague of boils. "But I suppose you're the closest I've got to an objective source. When it comes to my brother and sister," she began, uncertain how to proceed, and then she paused.

A pause that became a full stop.

"He never spoke of them directly," said Dzhuliya. "Never outright. Certainly not in any detail. He was—"

"Private," Eilidh confirmed, and then winced. "Professional." Thayer was adamant about keeping skeletons in the closet where they belonged—he would never have discussed family matters with someone he worked with. Especially not someone he considered beneath him, Eilidh thought uncharitably, for which she was punished by another thing-driven sting.

Dzhuliya hesitated, then tilted her head. "I'd say he was protective."

"Right, yes. Protective." That was a better, more generous word.

"He understood you were all very vulnerable from a young age," Dzhuliya pointed out, which struck Eilidh as notable. It was true, obviously, but she'd never considered this, the specific possibility of herself existing in Dzhuliya's eyes as someone with the erstwhile potential to be created or destroyed. "He's always been very careful to keep any scrutiny on himself, especially as things got—"

"More difficult," Eilidh finished for her, and paused.

In her head she replayed the last few weeks, the things that had seemed to weigh on her father's presence. She knew he'd gruffly dismissed an email requesting a comment on what he called "fucking clout chasers," or the series of labor-related lawsuits against Wrenfare; the closest he'd gotten to angry with Eilidh was when she brought up a recent seminar on brand reinvigoration, which Thayer seemed to interpret as a personal attack despite its obvious relevance to her field. He had actually suggested the Vermont retreat shortly after that, determining that Eilidh needed a shift in perspective.

Dzhuliya paused, then, too; a pause that seemed equally meaningful.

"He *did* seem to feel that your siblings had already inherited whatever they needed from your mother," Dzhuliya said, and broke off, or trailed off. Eilidh was too distracted to tell. The thing in her chest had become very alive, animated like a vaudeville performer, or maybe Eilidh (the thing's external cage) had begun to feel very numb and fearful and dead. Something inside her seemed out of sync by whatever metric was used for the existential weight of being.

Maybe there *was* a worst case, she realized. Because what would she even *do* with Wrenfare? Well, easy, whatever her father wanted done, which was perhaps the most persuasive reason so far that he might have elected to leave it with her. Meredith would change things to suit her personal agenda, as would Arthur, but Eilidh had never wanted any of this. Perhaps for that reason she could be considered the safest one to carry out a legacy, because she would not deviate from the plan.

But of course, if that was the case, then Thayer had sentenced her to a lifetime of being despised by her brother and sister. Meredith would probably fight it, tying the whole estate up in legal trivialities for years, and then what? She'd disappear, most likely. They'd be estranged, which was mere breaths away from whatever they were now. The thought of it made Eilidh sick—sick*er*, like a plague of perpetual darkness. It made her desperate to call her father, to ask what he could have possibly been thinking. Maybe he *hadn't* been in his right mind.

"The problem with Meredith," Thayer said in Eilidh's ear from the recesses of her memory, "is that she will always choose herself. It doesn't matter whether she's the right answer. It doesn't matter if she's made a mistake. She gets it from her mother—Persephone was always like that, and she spent the most time with Meredith." He was clutching a martini the size of a punch bowl. "Meredith will choose Meredith and take everyone else down with her. I'd call it admirable except she's still young, which means she's reckless in addition to ruthless. She's a bad judge of people because she still thinks this world is fundamentally fair, that people who work hard get rewarded, that the cream eventually rises to the top. But she's wrong, and someday someone will prove it to her in a way she can't come back from—and as for Arthur." Thayer laughed again, this time splashing a little liquid from his drink onto the edge of the table, which he ignored. "Arthur doesn't have a single real conviction in his entire body. He'd say whatever he needed to say just to stay in the light, just to keep people's eyes on him. I can't decide whether to be impressed he found a way to make it work for him or just guilty for raising yet another worthless politician."

Eilidh wondered why, in her memory of the moment, which seemed so oppressively, brutally clear, Thayer wasn't meeting her eye.

Then, belatedly, as if suddenly recalling the circumstances of a dream, she remembered that none of that had been said to her. Thayer had said it to someone else while drunk at the Christmas party, and Eilidh had been lingering nearby, hoping he would say something nice about her. Hoping he wouldn't say her name at all.

So much for protective, she thought with a sideways lurch, the earth tilting slightly to the left with a sense that she hadn't been looking at anything correctly; that she had missed something from where she was standing, too busy was she trying to do exactly as Arthur was doing and stay in the light. But Thayer wasn't a monster. No, she knew him. She understood him. It was a bad moment, a dark day. If Thayer loved her more than the others it was only because she, unlike them, had forgiven him his weaknesses, and never forsaken him for his mistakes. Eilidh alone had understood that her father, like everyone, only wanted to be loved, and the elder two of his children had been too struck by the loss of their mother to actually do it. If they had been loved unequally, then surely that was Eilidh's doing, not Thayer's fault.

Wasn't it?

"Eilidh?" prompted Dzhuliya tentatively, and Eilidh turned to her with the feeling that her eyes were wild, that the creature in her chest was cradling her heart in its hands, quiet and urging. She felt the presence of it again, of doomsday's comfort. The other side of this feeling, behind a fragile, wispy veil, was carnality and blood, and Eilidh didn't need to witness it to know for sure how that would taste. That it would be in some way satisfying—that what had driven her mother to self-destruction was magnified exponentially in Eilidh, spreading outward like avaricious craving from Eilidh's chest. Everything, the stasis of her life stood balanced on the thinnest, sharpest edge, held aloft by nothing but her personal suspension, her ability to keep darkness at bay—which only grew more and more insubstantial as time went on and she failed to grow or change.

But thank god there was Dzhuliya, the evergreen problem of Dzhuliya, which wasn't a problem at all so long as Eilidh didn't have to face the

answer—so long as Eilidh could just repeat the question to herself ad nauseum, never adequately persuaded to make up her mind.

Amicable colleagues! A father who loved her!

"I'm fine," said Eilidh, shoving the thing back down, keeping it locked
tight.

# 19

Somehow, shortly after the lawyers had convened to speak in private, Arthur got stuck with the job of greeter, the task of consoling the politely inconsolable, perhaps just because he was very friendly looking, such that people couldn't bear to hold in an emotion whenever he was around. Whatever the reason, by ten thirty there had formed a sort of receiving line, which, given the state of his father's landscaping and the height of the stairs, almost looked like a pilgrimage. Beneath the canopy of trees, Cascade Road was its usual moody tranquility, patches of sun shining for only minutes at a time on each of the supplicants who had begun their holy ascent to the home of Thayer Wren.

"Such a shock to lose him like that, no warning! I brought a casserole," said the neighbor from down the road, handing it to Arthur before taking his face between her hands. "We were all so fond of your father. Don't let anyone tell you otherwise."

"Hell of a businessman, Thayer. People will do anything to dredge up the past, lot of envy in the industry. Thayer Wren, a real once-in-a-lifetime genius," said one of Thayer's previous board members, wiping a dry eye and unloading via his personal assistant a fruit basket that, in life, Thayer would never have touched. "Plenty of antioxidants in there."

"He was so thoughtful and down to earth, given everything," said one of Thayer's golf buddies, a statement that would be echoed several times by Thayer's fellow hobbyist cyclists, with whom he rode habitually on Sundays. From them, Arthur and his siblings were gifted a fascinating mix of expensive liquors and fancy mixed nuts. "We never believed the rumors, by the way. What a great guy."

Everyone, Arthur noted, seemed eager to be witnessed. They were all very eager to receive something from Arthur as well, which Arthur was surprised to find was not a mystery and indeed, came very easily to him, probably because he understood that nothing being said was sincere or even sort of conceivable the way that rumors were, in some spiritually inaccurate but believable way, true. Thayer Wren had chosen at first chance to exempt himself almost completely from public consumption, and only seemed to participate in social rituals as a way of reminding himself what a relief it was to not be other people. It seemed to Arthur that even the fastidiously obsequious could not have genuinely enjoyed Thayer's company any more than he himself had, which made all the ritualized compassion seem somehow—paradoxically— very real.

He patterned back their sadness, mimicked their expressions, like some kind of sentient mirror. At first he'd never felt more ridiculous in his life, but then eventually he began to actually hear himself—to genuinely hear the words coming out of his mouth—and then, as if they were being spoken by someone else entirely, to believe them. He *was* sad. He was *devastated* to lose his father. Thayer *had* been a great guy, in fact a *genius*! What a *loss* it was, chanted Arthur in his head, tiny minion voices saying *loss, loss, loss* until he felt it, an emptiness in his stomach that he later diagnosed as hunger. Then he consumed some antioxidants and mindlessly scrolled his notifications (he caught the words "only son—" and ate a little more of Yves's chocolate) and felt slightly better, at least until he heard himself say again how terrible it all was, such a shock, gone far too soon.

Arthur was the only sibling at home—eating a handful of premium mixed nuts, purely to maintain stamina for all the grieving and consoling—he and the visitors seemed to be passing it back and forth, hot-potato style, with no one in complete control of either for too long at the risk of seeming indecent— when the lawyers emerged unexpectedly from the cave they'd made in his father's office. Both looked slightly haggard, which surprised Arthur. In his experience the only lawyers who looked like that were the underpaid ones, which surely neither of these two could have been.

"Should I go get my sisters?" asked Arthur, finding himself struck once again by the weaselly little face on Ryan Behrend, who deserved a quick shot put to the nuts. Arthur remembered, fleetingly and punishingly, that he and Lou had once put together a curse for Ryan, fully playacting their intent to enact it, until Arthur had hesitated because what if curses were real and then Lou had said well, good and Arthur had said but it's less fun, though, if it actually happens. To which Lou had said this is why I prefer your sister, and Arthur had thought okay, fair enough, me too.

"I'm afraid we haven't reached an agreement," said John, the older lawyer who looked a bit shaken, which was probably bad news. He seemed like he had been semiretired for at least a decade, so maybe it was just the necessity of having to lawyer at all. "It appears we're going to have to bring in a judge to arbitrate, which means it might be another day or so before we can reveal the contents of the . . ." John trailed off, looking briefly at Ryan, who seemed no less smug even if he did appear to have lower blood sugar. "Will."

"I sort of thought this whole thing was very straightforward," said Arthur, more to himself than to either of the lawyers. "How different can the two wills possibly be, if they were only revisited a month or so apart?"

A month. A month ago Arthur had been exactly the same as he'd always been, except accidentally shooting sparks and therefore far more likely to lose his reelection campaign. Well, and around that time he had first conceived of Riot—or the possibility of Riot, anyway, which changed the scope of practically everything. Suddenly Arthur *had* something, something that his father had always suggested that Arthur was incapable of understanding. A legacy. And not just something silly like a bloodline, but a reason to feel there was some purpose left to reach, an answer he hadn't realized he'd been asking for all this time. Riot! Riot Revolution Wren. There should be *blood*, Arthur thought, then reemphasized it in his head. There *should* be blood. Then the words lost all meaning and Arthur felt as if something was missing, like he'd come here for something but couldn't remember what it was. He looked between the lawyers but still couldn't figure out what it had been.

"There are some details to sort out, some of which—" Here, John again shot a look at Ryan. "Some of which is less concerning legally than ethically."

"We'll have it sorted," said Ryan, reaching out with one hand for a masculinely aggressive clasp of Arthur's before striding out of the room.

John flashed Arthur a parting glance that was impressively both *I've got this* and *help.* "If you could just let me confer with the judge—"

Their voices vanished almost immediately as they left the room, swallowed up by the thickness of the walls, the acoustic dominance of the house. Again, Arthur had the sense that he was missing something, which in this moment was the presence of sound. Thayer had always been very particular about sounds.

During the brief period in which Persephone had lived here, the house was monastic, at least to Arthur's memory, though perhaps she had just lost her zest for homemaking by then and they had simply not unpacked over the course of the single year. Arthur remembered watching the shadows shift and change, the sounds gobbling each other up just like the people inside it. He thought of Lou again, of the way she said the house was creepy, the way she'd looked at him after they slept together that first and last time when it was clear that it had all been an act of desperation, doomed to never be repeated or mentioned aloud.

"Try not to get a complex from this," Lou had suggested.

"Why wouldn't *you* get a complex?" Arthur said, feeling something he already understood to be unmanly (he didn't always need Thayer there to point it out).

"Oh, it's just as much a possibility for me, I just don't have room for another one," Lou replied.

"Darling," interrupted Philippa, and Arthur jumped, having been lost in thought. "Do you know, is the beef in the fridge slaughtered humanely? I like to believe the cows at least had a pleasant thought before the end."

"Christ, Pip, you scared me." His heart was thudding in his chest, probably a result of having been temporarily transported to a much quieter, lonelier past. "Sorry, what was the question?"

Philippa stepped between his feet, gazing up at him in her disarming way. She was wearing one of his shirts, a pair of woolen trouser socks on her feet, and nothing else. "If it helps," she said gently, "I don't think we're necessarily doomed to the shape that our parents make for us."

Arthur had never really considered himself doomed so much as he had worried about the opposite. Doom felt like fate, a presence of something, a solidified prophecy. Arthur felt he was several pieces with maybe a little bit of scattered air, something to be compiled over time, though he thought he'd have figured out the entirety of the shape by the time he had to put his father in the ground.

"Oh god," said Arthur suddenly. "Is his body just lying somewhere? Like on a slab?"

"Arthur, these are not images conducive to a healthy reality," said Yves, who wandered into the room in the inverse of Philippa's outfit: no shirt, a pair of thick woolen lounge pants, and for whatever reason, one of Arthur's winter hats that he occasionally used for hiking. "By the way, Art, you neglected to tell me what a jewel your Gillian is."

"Gillian?" said Arthur, realizing that was the missing thing—the presence of Gillian. He hadn't considered that he didn't usually have to look for her, because she was always just there, like an idea hovering at the back of his thoughts.

"She's very chatty, isn't she?" said Yves.

Almost never, actually, though it was hard to argue with something once Yves had absorbed it as reality. "I suppose she can be," said Arthur in a very diplomatic lie, before asking, "Where is she, by the way?"

"Darling," said Philippa, taking his face in her hands. "You look so tired."

Arthur glanced distractedly at her, realizing she was finding something on his face that he didn't think he had put there, although the likelihood that it might be true felt reasonably possible. "Do I?"

"Don't you think he looks tired, Yves?" Philippa asked, and then Yves was there, scrutinizing Arthur with a long and medical glance.

"Well, we did come for a reason, didn't we, love?" said Yves.

Philippa took Arthur by the hand, leading him out of the room and up the stairs, winding a perfect route to Arthur's bedroom. It was impossible to believe she had only been there a handful of hours. The house had already begun to smell like her, woodsy and almost acidic, biting like too much freshness. "Ouch," said Philippa, retracting her hand suddenly just as they reached the threshold of Arthur's room.

Arthur looked down, realizing he had shocked her, and elsewhere down the corridor a light had flickered and gone out. "Oh," he said, and the memory of Lou pressed in on him again.

"My grandmother says this kind of thing happens when someone like you doesn't practice for a while," the ghost of Lou was saying to him, and suddenly Arthur was seventeen again. He could practically taste the orange sports drink in his hand, the way he was sore and tired from baseball, and the way he felt instantly stupid, realizing yes, she was right, he should practice harder, practice more. That's what his father always said, what Arthur always did whenever he got the yips. Work harder, Arthur. Work! "Not that kind of practice," said Lou with a roll of her eyes. "Lola says if you don't use the magic, the magic uses you."

He felt Philippa's hands undressing him, Yves's mouth on the span of his shoulder, the place where his neck ended and all the weight began. Arthur closed his eyes and thought about things that weren't Lou, which was almost everything in his life now, given that it had been over a decade since he'd last seen her. And even then, she had only really been a brevity, a little hiccup of something he hesitated to call peace, although in his mind, that was what it had been.

Because really, to Arthur, Lou was an imaginary thing, someone who had frozen in place right where he'd left her, which is what often happens when someone who is capable of moving on moves on. Add to it the hubris of believing oneself to be bigger than another person, to be living a more interesting story, and you have precisely the danger of Arthur Wren, a person who believes himself to be generally good with bad pieces here and there instead of a person who confuses goodness with inaction. I am purposely not telling you where Gillian is or what she's doing, because it's important to understand that at this moment, Arthur has forgotten that he ever wondered where she was. Actually, at this particular moment, Arthur is about to have sex in his dead father's house, which is something we can get into if you really want to. I can describe Arthur's body to you. It's the body of an athlete, sculpted in its way to become useful, an entire musculature that has done as it was bidden for the sake of performance, to be measured for its worth based on how far it can throw a ball. In recent years, Arthur has been going to the gym routinely, almost religiously, because pain is something he considers a necessary part of being alive. He is sore almost every day, he deprives himself (in some ways) in service to nourishment, or what he thinks is nourishment because he has never known what it is to behave like a bear, to do nothing but eat and sleep rather than running in circles just to have abs that look like that. He played baseball, and has devotedly kept the glutes.

Arthur Wren is a beautiful asshole, like something Michelangelo sculpted with devoted hands. Arthur's hair is thick and swept from his eyes in waves and there is an artfulness to him that reveals itself most noticeably in motion. It is extremely important to the story that you understand that although Yves Reza is famously one of the most handsome men in the world and Philippa Villiers-DeMagnon is lovely enough to feature prominently in all the British tabloids as well as multiple devoted fan accounts, it is Arthur who is always the most beautiful person in the room. And yet right now, absurdly, Arthur is thinking to himself how lucky he is to be in the room at all, which *could* strike you as very sad but should really be kind of annoying.

I mean, think of it from my perspective—you know, omnisciently. What does Arthur actually care about? Does Arthur really know? Not to say Thayer Wren was a saint by any means, but he kind of had a point.

Anyway, you can go back to being in Arthur's head now, which is for all intents and purposes blank. Arthur did enjoy a certain amount of roughness in the boudoir, but he was finding that impossible to conjure in the moment, knowing how precious Philippa's body now was to him, how powerful and divine she suddenly seemed. The first time they had slept together, Arthur had enjoyed taking her hair in his fists, pulling on it lightly until she made a sound, her particular sound of enjoyment that thrilled him because it was like getting an A, like a triple play, the "attaboy" he so desperately needed. His love for Philippa the woman was nothing compared to his love for Philippa the mother; Philippa the dreammaker; Philippa whom Yves could still call Babe or Mouse but whom Arthur could only call out for as he would a goddess, a god. Beseechingly, or as to Athena—someone wrathful, spiteful and envious, who could hold his entire world in one delicate hand.

She tried to pull him on top of her, and Arthur murmured back no, no, shouldn't be on her back, he'd read it somewhere, bad for the baby. Instead he switched places and pulled her up to him, shimmying down until his lips met the curves of her thighs. He could look up at her then, properly, though when he slid his tongue along the lovely, decadent slickness of her and looked up to meet her eyes, he found them closed. Silently, he begged. *Look at me.*

She didn't. The track lighting overhead sparked. Philippa moaned, and Arthur closed his eyes.

# 20

Meredith Wren met Jamie Ammar during the early days of a crisp New England fall. It was doomed, probably, or so she told herself in retrospect. It was impossible not to fall in love in autumn, something about the colors, or the way death and rot were such powerful erotic motivators. The way the desperation to be outside was so sensual, an atavistic longing to be one with the earth, to commune with nature, to fuck and be fucked. She had been without Lou for nearly two years by then or she would have said something like that to her, and Lou would have said my god, you're so goddamn pretentious, I love it. You don't need to explain adolescent horniness to me like you're Robert fucking Frost.

The details about the day were unsavory. Meredith typically forced herself to block out the circumstances, but for purposes of setting the scene, I'll tell you what had happened: Meredith had done a search for Lou that day, discovering that Lou's paper on experimental technomancy—authored by Lou as not only an undergraduate, but a mere *sophomore*—had recently been published. Meanwhile, Meredith had failed to impress a professor for the first time.

It was a class on rhetoric, a general education course in the philosophy department that Meredith considered a profligate waste of time, because Meredith was a biomancy prodigy. She had gone to Harvard because they had the biggest, most lavishly funded lab in the country. She was destined, as her father had been, to be named an industry genius, to earn a place in the magitech revolution, not to perform on command for the whims of *general education*. (Similarly, although Arthur technically had the greater proficiency for magic, Meredith was more devoted. Meredith focused harder. Meredith cared more.)

But then her philosophy professor told her point-blank that she wasn't talented. The word he used was, literally, "talentless."

As in, "For someone so essentially talentless you have an extremely unproductive attitude," then bestowed upon teenage Meredith verbatim.

As in, "You act as if everything we do in this class is beneath you, Miss
Wren, but nothing is beneath you. You are below everything. You are a worm,
do you understand this? I don't mean you exclusively, everyone your age is a
worm—you are meant to be learning things, not deciding at first glance what
does or does not matter."

As in, "Okay, so you are very promising at something this university considers valuable, that's wonderful. So you will go on to make this university
lots of money, how wonderful for you. But I am trying to teach you how to
*matter,* which you will never do so long as you continue to believe that you
*alone* are the source of value, that you exist in any heightened significance;
that intrinsically you are worth in some way more than anything else that
lives on this earth."

As in, "Either you will learn that lesson from me, Miss Wren, or I will
give you the grade you deserve for failing to learn it, and perhaps you will
hate me and nothing will change, which is fine by me. Because I already
know that you do not matter, and I will forget you the moment you exit this
room."

Jamie was an English major with prelaw aspirations, and taking the class
as a junior because he was just a few credits shy of a secondary concentration
in philosophy. He was in the room when the professor said all of that to Meredith. It was obvious that Meredith was supposed to respond haughtily, or
that the professor had assumed she would, or maybe the professor had only
said it because it was a rhetoric class and Meredith was meant to respond, to
argue. Instead, Meredith had blinked and then nodded, and then she caught
Jamie's eye just before she walked out of the classroom. As far as Jamie could
tell, she'd had no reaction to what was an unquestionably vicious undressing
of her entire existence and self. And then Meredith came back on Monday,
seemingly unchanged.

Jamie saw Meredith at a party a few weeks later, holding a red cup in one
hand and frowning distractedly as a boy rambled drunkenly in her ear. Jamie had a girlfriend at the time, although things were not going especially
well between them because he was finding that his girlfriend enjoyed life
in a way that seemed somehow insane. Like, she just sort of went about her
day, and when good things happened to her she celebrated them and when
bad things happened to her she was bummed but then she moved on. Jamie

wanted more conflict in his life, presumably, or what else would have led him to Meredith Wren?

"Hi," he said, walking right up to her. The boy who had been talking to Meredith gave Jamie a possessive look, which Jamie ignored. Jamie was focused on Meredith, who glanced at him with that same furrowed frown, as if he were no different to her than the other boy currently next to her, which was fair. "I'm in your philosophy class," Jamie explained.

"Oh," said Meredith.

"I don't think it's true," Jamie added. "The thing that Professor [purposefully redacted from Meredith's memory] said to you. I think he's incredibly mean-spirited and probably a little misogynistic."

Meredith took a sip from her cup and tilted her head at him. She glanced at the boy next to her, then back at Jamie. "Are you single?" she asked Jamie.

"Oh. Um, no," said Jamie.

"Oh. Okay." Meredith set her cup down on the bar behind her and left the room. The boy looked at Jamie with something like murder in his eyes, and would later report this incident to his friends as an unsportsmanlike cock block.

Jamie, however, followed Meredith out of the room in service to something that was most closely considered impulse. "Hey, wait—"

"Are you single now?" asked Meredith without turning to look at him.

"You mean between five seconds ago and now?"

"Yes." She had her arms folded over her chest as she walked and Jamie wanted to give her a jacket, but he wasn't wearing one. This was momentarily very upsetting to him.

"No," said Jamie, "I'm still in a relationship."

"Then stop following me," Meredith advised.

"I'm not following you," said Jamie, who then stopped, because he realized that yes, he was absolutely following her. "I mean, okay, sorry. I just wanted to talk to you, that's all."

"I can see that," said Meredith. She walked a few steps, then stopped, turning to face Jamie. They were a few feet apart on the sidewalk, such that a very tall person or a small crime scene could lie between them. "But I don't really want to talk to you if I can't have sex with you."

Jamie was very taken aback by this, probably because the era of sex positivity had not yet dawned. This sort of attitude would later be branded something-something manic pixie when really, as Lou would have pointed out to Meredith, it was merely horny, which was natural, literally. It was fundamentally tied in with nature, and it is very important that you understand that for this moment alone, Meredith is not to be blamed. Parenthetically, everything else is fair game.

"What would happen if I were single?" Jamie said.

"What if, indeed?" said Meredith whimsically, although because it was Meredith, it did not read as whimsy. Then she turned and kept walking.

"Wait," Jamie called after her. Poor, poor idiot Jamie. "Can I walk you home?"

"No," said Meredith without turning around.

Eventually she disappeared from sight, and Jamie broke up with his girlfriend, and another week or so went by. They all went home for Thanksgiving and then they came back, and Jamie stopped Meredith outside of their philosophy class.

"Do you want to study for the final together?" he asked.

"I don't know if you've noticed, but I'm not very good at this class," said Meredith with another of her slight frowns, which was actually just her face. "If you study with me, you're probably not going to get anything out of it."

"But I would, though," said Jamie. "Because you'll be there, which is kind of my only goal."

"I like that we're developing a real rapport," said Meredith. "But I do actually need to study, and unless you're single now—"

"I am," said Jamie, a little breathless. "I mean—not that I'm, like, suggesting anything—"

"I'd actually prefer it if you'd suggest something, and quickly, because I really need to study for this class," said Meredith, who had been reading about Lou again. Lou had won some kind of award. Lou was very good at college. Lou, as Meredith had always known, *wasn't* talentless, not that it matters to the story.

"I do actually think that most of the things I think about are more valuable than this exam," Meredith qualified, "and I don't really like to waste my time, but I still don't want to fail."

Of course, there wasn't really a way to avoid failing, because by definition, not caring about the class was defeating the class's entire purpose. Jamie told Meredith this, and she considered it, and by then things had emptied because most people had gone to their next class or to lunch or wherever they were going, but Meredith stood there contemplating what Jamie had said, and also the possibility that a department-mandated curve meant that someone was going to fail, and dear god, it might be Meredith, who couldn't actually care about this no matter how hard she studied.

Which was ironically the inverse of a problem Meredith would later have, although right now, what's important is what Meredith said to Jamie, which was, "I do really want to have sex with you, although I don't think it should be especially drawn out given the time constraints."

Jamie felt destabilized by every single word out of Meredith's mouth. He felt the beginnings of an obsession, the little prescient stirring in his gut that everything in his life was about to revolve around Meredith. He was about to see her constantly in every crowd, he was about to memorize the divot between her brows, he was about to create an invisible, personal mood ring that would only change color depending on what Meredith did, said, or thought. He did not, however, realize that the feeling would follow him well into adulthood, so that later on, when Meredith lied to his fucking face and he knew it, because he had already learned so long ago how to read her, because he had once considered the mere act of knowing her to be a reward in and of itself, he would suffer the simultaneous thrill of hatred that married with the violence of loving her passionately, without respite.

She was so fucking *unlikable,* that was the thing! She was so fucked up it was addictive, because he could never make it stop, this wanting to understand her that was already impossible. It was exactly the perfect inverse paradox of failing a class because you couldn't care about it. He loved her because he knew he could never actually know her, and for fuck's sake it was paralyzing, breathtaking. What calmer love could ever compare?

So they went to Meredith's room in Adams House and had sex, and then because it hadn't taken too long, they had sex again, and then Meredith studied and Jamie studied next to her because he didn't want to leave, and then Meredith had to eat and so Jamie went with her to the dining hall, and then Meredith had to sleep so Jamie slept beside her, and then Jamie had to go home and take a shower but then Meredith called him so Jamie came back, and days just kind of kept going like that for a long, pleasant buzz of time, and then Meredith went home for Christmas break and when she came back Jamie realized it had been like he'd held his breath for four weeks. Like time had stopped and then she was back, and everything was alive again.

And then Meredith went away again, and time stopped again for Jamie Ammar. Though he hadn't necessarily noticed until he saw her on the Tyche stage, because it was easy to become accustomed to suffocation when it happened glacially over time. After twelve years, you can almost forget what kind of madness lives in your chest until it shows up again to destroy you.

# 21

It wasn't a long walk to the coffee shop in town, though it was long enough for Meredith to feel eight different forms of dread before eleven. That was impressive for Meredith, who was single-minded enough to feel only one at a time, intensely, usually. She stopped and turned around to go back to her father's house several times, at least four or five. But eventually she made it to the coffee shop because physical space had limits. Eventually, destinations were reached.

Jamie was already there, sipping a coffee in the public plaza that was the central part of the town. Meredith recognized him immediately, just as she had when he'd first introduced himself to her in college. She had told herself then that she was never going to speak to him, firstly because he was so attractive it was physically crushing her chest, and secondly because he had heard the professor call her a failure and Meredith felt certain that Jamie knew, somehow, in a mind-reading way (Jamie can't actually read minds) that Meredith agreed with the professor, and that it wasn't even the first time she'd heard it, because Meredith's father called her talentless all the time. Not in those exact words, because Thayer wasn't usually so explicit. But she did understand after eighteen years of routinely suggesting she become a different person that Thayer didn't like what she actually was, and that was its own version of being called talentless.

And then Jamie had spoken to her because he felt sorry for her and Meredith had the wild, extremely upsetting thought that she would like to have him on top of her anyway, just lying on top of her looking like that, looking at her, being him. Which was obviously so distressing she had needed to leave the room then, which was also what she wanted to do now, because now they were adults and *she* was the one who wasn't single and yet she still wanted him to lie on top of her and look at her like that for the rest of her life.

Even though he didn't look the same as he did when he was twenty—

actually, he looked better. And once again it crushed her chest and not at all in the way she wanted.

"Hello," she said in her coldest voice, sitting down across from him and determining this instantly to be a mistake. He had such a strong jaw. She couldn't look at him, he was too perfect.

"Meredith, a pleasure as always." He made her name sound beautiful whenever he said it. Not like Cass, who was always bastardizing it, calling her Mer. Why was intimacy so disgusting? Why couldn't Cass have remained a mystery, never using the bathroom with the door open or cutting her name into stiff paper strips? Why couldn't she simply revel in Cass's usefulness, his magnificent way of existing so stably, which she had envy for, which sometimes felt like desire, like she wanted to peel off parts of him and make them hers? God, what she wouldn't give to wear Cass's calmness, to put his practicality on like another skin, and yet she sat there and wanted silently to lick the span of Jamie's earlobe, to bless him tenderly with the tips of her fingers, to do unspeakable things with him tied to her bed.

The fucking carnality of him, it was relentless! She needed a coffee and ten beers.

"Here," said Jamie, pushing a latte toward her. "I have no idea how you take your coffee anymore."

"Thanks," said Meredith with a brief, all-consuming madness that flashed in front of her eyes like a sudden wash of red. "So, what are you going to do after you destroy me?"

"Hopefully wind up with health insurance," said Jamie. "Maybe see the dentist."

His teeth were perfect and the latte was exactly right, the sort of thing Meredith never allowed herself to drink. Sweet and creamy, like a day spent in bed. FUCK. "I just don't understand why you had to come for me," she said. "You could have written about anyone."

"Ah, but you're the only one pulling off such an amazingly sociopathic con." He drummed his fingers on the table.

"I'm not a sociopath," Meredith pointed out. "If anything, I'm a psychopath."

"No, you're capable of empathy," said Jamie. "That's what makes it all the more insane."

"Again, assuming any of this was true, it wouldn't be *insane*," said Meredith irritably. "It would be purely a means to an end."

"An insane means," said Jamie, "to an objectively toxic end."

"Journalism is never objective," countered Meredith, "or you would have given the article to someone else."

"I want the money," Jamie argued. "Actually, I need the money. I'm thirty-three years old and still paying off debt."

"You could have been partner in a law firm by now," Meredith reminded him. "I never stopped you from doing that."

"Yes, true, I could be overpaid to do absolutely nothing of value," said Jamie. "Or I could actively destroy society, good point." He gave her a barbed look of significance as he sipped his own coffee, which was black. Meredith resented now that he'd doused her with sugar. "And you wonder why I developed such a so-called obsession with you."

A series of obscenities reached Meredith from a deep, profound well of rage.

"I will never be able to explain why dating me made you a *better person*," said Meredith exasperatedly.

"I know," said Jamie. "Which is exactly why I loved you so much."

They both sipped their coffees as Meredith remembered that she could leave at any moment. She had left before, which made her the leaver. She was actually very good at leaving, she had so much practice at it, *and* she had the motive to leave as well, because according to a bunch of HR paperwork in Tyche's corporate offices, she was in a relationship.

Her phone buzzed and she glanced at it. Ward again. She shook her head and dismissed the call.

"Do you remember?" asked Jamie. "The night you showed me."

*Did she remember.* She could slap him across the mouth just for that. Motherfucker, did he really think there was any detail she had forgotten? That anything between them had ever evaporated into the ether, slipping carelessly away? For a while she had managed to forget the digits of his phone number, but only in the sense that she had to think about it for a while before it came back. Every year on his birthday she wandered around for the day bereft, like she was missing an organ. Like he'd physically stolen one of her lungs.

"I obviously shouldn't have," Meredith muttered to herself. "Which is, again, a compelling reason for you to stop calling me," she added, louder. "What if I'd sent an assassin here, hm? If you're dead, the article is dead. Nobody but you would even suspect I was capable of doing something like that. If, allegedly, I even did."

"Again, I appreciate the effort, but I'm ninety percent sure you're not going to kill me," said Jamie. "And you can also stop acting like you didn't do it, because I'm one hundred percent sure that you did."

Meredith was pleased she retained a ten-percent chance of homicidal tendencies. That was a real relief, all things considered.

"I didn't do it," she said, and then, because it was bothering her, "Are we having an affair?"

"Right now?" asked Jamie.

"Yes."

"I, personally, am having coffee." He sipped from his cup to prove it. "I have absolutely no idea what you're doing."

"How's everything with your mom?" asked Meredith listlessly.

"How's everything with your dad?" Jamie replied.

She longed for the shorthand of sex. There was so much that could be telegraphed with contact and motion that she could never—*would* never—say out loud. She knew that if she fucked Jamie right now, he would know exactly how she felt about her father's death, and he would know why she had lied, and he would understand that it wasn't a grift, it was another utterly talentless act of cold-blooded certainty, a mistake that she would make again and again and again if it meant she could still claw her way forward, so long as there was a finish line to drag herself across. Maybe if they had sex, he wouldn't publish the article? Maybe if they had sex, he'd feel it all like it had been born in his chest and he'd know, of course he'd know. All of this sitting around and talking, it was such a waste of time, unless you considered time to be an accumulation of moments you'd rather die than go without.

Though if that's how you saw time, then holy shit, yeah, this was an affair.

"I never really liked my dad much," she said.

Jamie gave her the same look he'd given her when she met his eye that day in philosophy class, after the professor had finally taught her something. It was actually just a really effective example of pathos, rhetoric used to appeal to an emotion that was already felt, and in the end, Meredith got an A– on the exam.

"I know, Meredith," Jamie said. "I know."

# 22

When Arthur awoke in a haze sometime in the late afternoon, he found he couldn't move his legs. Or his arms. Or lift his head. Or move his fingers. Alarming. He was unsure whether he could actually find the means to panic, though it did appear his lungs were theoretically within reach. He considered screaming and didn't. The energy for it, usually conjurable under these or any circumstances, simply did not arrive. He awoke to his thoughts in a sequential way—*I'm awake, it must be afternoon, oh shit, my legs*—before they began to creep outward, weblike and familiar, per Arthur's usual patterns of thought. He began to have several thoughts at once, about the well-being of unborn Riot and the loss of his father and the drowsiness that accompanied a post-orgasmic haze. He still had not heard from Gillian, although in fairness he seemed to have fallen asleep. He would check his phone as soon as motion returned to him.

He did not, at the time, doubt that it would, and this faith was rewarded when eventually a sticky pins-and-needles sensation crept around from his spine to his toes, radiating outward. He did not feel confident that he would be able to stand, but did manage to turn his head toward the alarm clock sitting there on the nightstand, a totem of his youth. It blinked 12:24, which meant that was not the correct time. Arthur impressively moved his pinky.

"There you are, Brother Slothful," said Meredith, bursting into his room just as Arthur summoned the feats of strength to lift his head. "Did you get the email from the lawyers? Absolutely ridiculous. Did you bring a suit? I'm assuming Gillian brought one for you . . . I don't see it. Ah, there it is." She was riffling ineffectually through his wardrobe. "Can I ask you something?" she remarked into the custom armoire, a question presumably directed at him.

"Mm," said Arthur inconclusively.

"How hard would it be to have someone, you know, eliminated?" Meredith turned to look at him then.

"In a squash tournament? Very simple," said Arthur.

Meredith squinted at him. "Is this you being funny?"

"Not successfully, it seems." Arthur became aware of a cottony feeling in his mouth and pondered whether Meredith might procure him some water if he asked nicely or flatteringly enough. (For purposes of theoretical exercise: "Sister Murderous, you have never looked so righteously vengeful, might you grant me a libation, please?")

Meredith looked thoughtful.

"It's funny," she mused, "I don't really want to kill him, but at the same time I feel like he'll respect me less if I don't at least try." She glanced down at her hand, where apparently her phone was buzzing. "It's Ward again, the little weasel. He's going to have a meltdown and call the Feds himself at any moment, I swear to god. Anyway, forget about the assassin, it was really just a whim. What now?" she barked into her phone, and thankfully was gone.

She had pulled a suit out of the wardrobe, which did bear markers of Gillian's handiwork. Arthur had forgotten to ask why he'd be needing a suit for whatever occasion Meredith seemed to know was on their agenda for today, though he supposed it didn't matter. Meredith had set it out for him, and so he put it on.

At this very moment, since I'm sure you're dying of curiosity, Gillian Wren was in the woods, woolgathering. By then it was nearly three, a solid eight hours since Yves had offered her a bit of medicinal chocolate, theoretically long enough for Gillian to regain some sense of her usual executive mastery, though it was well into the hike before she realized she wasn't wearing the proper shoes for such an outing. They were a pair of black ballet flats, which of course were filthy now, all soiled around the toes. She had also been thinking in silence for almost forty minutes before Yves said something to her.

"Hm?" Gillian said, blinking to cognizance. Something was wrong with her, she deduced. And not just the drugs, although yes, drugs.

"We will have to go back soon, I'm afraid," Yves repeated. "There is a gathering this evening in honor of your father-in-law."

Gillian faintly remembered that Meredith, upon returning to the house at some point midday, had spoken to exactly one grieving pilgrim (a friend of Thayer's from primary school) before throwing her hands in the air and saying there would no longer be any allowances for coming and going—anyone who wanted to grieve would do so at one time, conclusively. "Where the balls is Eilidh?" Meredith had added, before stomping off muttering something about Daddy's little princess.

At which point Yves had turned to Gillian and suggested they go for a walk. "You know, I sense I could teach you something," he said, "if you were interested in the matter of sensuality we discussed earlier."

Gillian hadn't the faintest idea what Yves was talking about. She was discovering that there were some holes in her memory of the day, not unlike the time she'd torn her calf playing lacrosse in high school and had been forced to take a muscle relaxant. She had spent the day with her high school boyfriend, and had later received a message online that he was sad she felt that way and hoped they'd be friends even though she'd apparently made it clear to him that she didn't want to be. She didn't have any idea what she'd said or why she'd said it, though mixed into her distress was some tiny, glowing ball of relief. Her father had always liked that boyfriend. Gillian thought he could be a bit of a bore.

"Okay, a walk sounds nice," said Gillian. Some of the lethargy was beginning to fade by then, and so the menstrual pain that she'd forgotten about for a while had returned. Still, she felt a kinship with Yves that hadn't been there before, as if whatever he'd said that didn't make any sense actually did make sense if she really thought about it, though when she thought about it, she just found a sort of big empty space, so a lot of this was really just a feeling. "But I don't want Arthur to worry."

"Oh, Arthur is fine, we will not be gone long," Yves assured her, shutting the front door behind him in a way that Gillian realized meant they had already begun to walk, descending the long staircase from the house's front door to the private drive below. "Chocolate?" Yves offered again as they wound their way downward, withdrawing some from the small pouch he'd been wearing earlier.

Gillian glanced at the unfamiliarly marked bar of chocolate with the feminine sense of danger she'd been unwisely lacking earlier, when Yves had first offered it. "What's in that?"

"Only a little recreational marijuana," said Yves, "as well as some mild intoxicants. You needn't worry, I have a very good mixologist. He has almost all the licenses."

"Am I on drugs?" asked Gillian then, wondering why she wasn't more bothered by having to ask such a question.

"Oh, no!" Yves laughed. "Or yes, depending. They are really more like herbs. Would you like more?"

"I'm okay, thanks," said Gillian. Then she became curious what Yves had meant by the "matter of sensuality" they had apparently earlier discussed, noting privately the irony of descending literally into temptation as they disembarked the house's stairs. "When you say, um, *teach me* something, did you by chance mean—?"

"Oh, you would like to start now? Well, let's see, I suppose as a baseline we will need to establish your comfort level. How is this?" asked Yves, coming to a sudden halt to face her, placing both hands firmly on her waist.

"Oh. Uh." Gillian looked at his hands, which were objectively very attractive hands. They were big and masculine but artful, as if he could do many magnificent things with them. She imagined them hunting a very large animal or gathering vast amounts of wheat. She tried to picture them painting or sculpting and found that she could do that as well. Then she tried to imagine him undressing her with them and she suddenly felt very cold. "I don't think I like that."

"Wonderful. How is this?" Yves shifted one hand to her face, stroking her jaw with his artful thumb. It was very intimate. Gillian was forced to look him in the eyes, which despite the heavy precision of his brow were lovely, very lovely. His eyes were a very interesting shape, and they were an extremely dark brown, almost black, set back within the shape of his eye so that she could see the entire circle of his iris. They were very unlike Arthur's. Arthur's eyes were a cool, grainy amber he had gotten from his father, and they had the effect of appearing larger, softer. Less penetrating, but more unearthing.

"I don't really like this," said Gillian, squirming. It was strange, as she was sure she felt some kind of philosophical attraction to Yves, and certainly she liked him a great deal. She also did not feel any sort of moral guilt, since she knew Yves had done all of these things to Arthur and therefore there was nothing inherently wrong with being touched. It was more of a fundamental wrongness, like oil and water—like her feelings of attraction sat on top of the feeling of discomfort, instead of relieving or dissipating it.

"Yes, okay," said Yves cheerfully, and leaned in.

Gillian immediately withdrew, turning her head so sharply that she was sure it had to read as repulsion. "I'm so sorry," she said, though she didn't turn toward Yves again until he had fully retracted his sudden closeness. "I don't mean to act like . . . like you disgust me or anything, it's not *that*—"

"Oh, Gillian, I am only finding your edges," said Yves, his mood undiminished. "I have to learn before I can teach. Although in this case, I do not think there is any teaching to do."

"Oh," said Gillian, who was hearing that she was a hopeless case, which was what she had already sort of understood about herself. "Right, okay."

"Would you like to keep walking?" said Yves. "We don't have to touch. I can stay this far away from you," he said, leaving a space of about two or three Arthurs between them, "or perhaps this far," he attempted, squeezing in an additional Arthur.

"I think here would be fine," said Gillian, excising the fourth Arthur, which seemed excessive. Arthur had very broad shoulders, broader than Yves's.

"Excellent," said Yves, popping a bit of chocolate in his mouth. "And now, we walk."

It was about four by the time Arthur later regained the motion with which to partially dress, unaware that his wife had been out with his boyfriend in an attempt to explore the constraints of her sensuality. His girlfriend, however, had reentered the room in time to join him at the mirror.

"Oh, I've always thought it would be so romantic to tie a man's tie," said Philippa, slipping an arm around his waist. "Unfortunately, I haven't the faintest idea how."

Arthur chuckled as Philippa folded into his embrace with an ease that would have filled Gillian with longing, for reasons entirely unrelated to the presence of another woman. "I could teach you now, if you wanted. We could make quite a portrait of domesticity."

"As tempting as that would be, I think adventure suits us more." Philippa smiled up at him and Arthur bent to kiss her neck.

"Well, I suppose that adventure is about to change, isn't it? A very domestic adventure, such that tie-tying might not be totally out of place." His lips traveled to her clavicle, to the place she wore a locket with a filigreed *M*, for Mouse. "It's nice, isn't it? Having so much time," said Arthur, winding his hands into her hair, which Philippa currently wore loose and windswept and golden. Arthur's father's death had created an interesting pocket universe where time no longer mattered and everything felt suspended, hung low and swaying on an existential breeze.

"I suppose we'll have more of this soon enough," Arthur realized. He could certainly afford a few months to bond full-time with Riot, and surely

Philippa would want to continue her charity work, so perhaps it would make more sense for Arthur to stay home. "What do you think about me taking a year off, or maybe more than that, when the baby comes?"

"Ouch," said Philippa, withdrawing to look up at him with a little pout. "You stung me."

"I did?" asked Arthur, confused. Normally he was more aware when things were going awry. "Like a static shock, you mean? I'm sorry." The electrical malfunctions had been confined to work situations up to then, a slip for which he felt a genuine guilt. "I suppose it's my father's death—everything's just a bit off." Even more so than usual, and the "usual" of the past few weeks had already been less than ideal. "You know, when I woke up this afternoon I couldn't even move, like one of those weird paralytic dreams," Arthur remarked, before recalling, "Where were you, by the way?"

Philippa was plucking lint from his collar. "Oh, I was just—"

"Brother Indolent," announced Meredith, bursting once again into the room. This time she wore a black dress that looked some years off trend, her hair in severe, precise curls that she had pulled into a ponytail, and at her side, with one hand tucked into hers as if he were a prop, was Cass. "Do you intend to conduct your indecencies in a public way," Meredith asked Arthur, "or would you like to track down your wife?"

"I'm here," said Gillian in a small, efficient voice, bustling past Meredith in the clothes she'd been wearing that morning. Arthur moved instinctively to let go of Philippa, then realized Philippa had already withdrawn from him, busying herself with her hair. Gillian met Arthur's gaze in the mirrored surface, pausing him for a moment. She was looking very intently at him, more so than usual. Gillian had the most remarkable eyes, thought Arthur. He supposed as a practical matter they were brown—that was what it said on Gillian's passport, brown eyes, brown hair—but there was something of an earth-shattering quality to looking at her, a burst, like watching a flower bloom before his eyes in an effervescing time lapse.

"Are you all right?" Arthur mouthed to her.

Gillian turned her gaze from his in the mirror. "Fine," she said in her usual perfunctory way, reaching up to untie his tie with characteristically brutal efficiency. She had taken offense to his usual Windsor, as she often did, but this time, as she began tactically reconstructing the double Windsor that was, to Gillian, as significant as the Oxford comma, she hesitated a moment, for the first time ever doing so that Arthur could remember, and simply paused there, as if she were temporarily confused—no, the opposite. As if she'd had a revelation.

Then her eyes lifted sheepishly to something over Arthur's shoulder, an odd expression alighting on Gillian's cheeks with a flush that Arthur had never seen before.

From the mirror, Arthur caught Yves's insouciant presence in the doorway. Then he spotted Philippa's narrowed gaze, which lingered on Gillian's back.

From where they rested uneasily at his sides, Arthur's knuckles tensed. Overhead, the lights resumed flickering, one bulb sharply burning out.

"Hello?" said Meredith in a voice that was pure infuriation. "Did I not make it clear that you're all running late?"

# 23

By six thirty that evening, Eilidh had done what she customarily did at social functions and disappeared. She sat alone in the chair behind the desk in her father's home office, ignoring the muffled sound of partygoing mourners outside the door while staring up at the painting on the wall. It was a Degas, one of the paintings of the ballerinas, which Thayer had purchased at great expense in honor of Eilidh, assuming she would love it. She didn't, and not because it made her nostalgic, or even sad.

Actually, it was one of the rare things in her life that made her feel better about having lost ballet. She had never told her father how sinister that series of paintings felt to her, how insidious they seemed, the way there was a male presence lurking in them, the idle sense of depravity to the girls being placed on display. How young they were, the dancers—how *girlish*. Pretty things in pretty clothes. Ballet was both delicacy and contortion. Like girlhood, ballet was art meant for consumption; it was virtuous because it was beautiful pain.

Eilidh learned later that her instincts were right—that at the time Degas painted, ballet was actual entrapment in its way, with the girls plucked off the street too young to say no, usually forced to engage in sex work for their patrons. Ballet had always been a little bit cruel, the way that at the highest levels it deformed you, hurt you, broke you. Eilidh had thought that was something she and her father had in common. The brokenness, which made Eilidh harder to love, actually, than Meredith.

Eilidh thought of her affairs, her liaisons with other dancers; the way that they, too, were just bodies to her. Means to an end. Which was not to say it hadn't been consensual, but Eilidh only knew how to live for an audience. What she did with her lovers was never sacred because there was always the implication of a performance. Her intimacy was a lie that lived in the lurking presence of some higher desire—at the time it was ambition, her craving to shine on the stage. It was a hunger that Eilidh still felt, but no longer knew how to satisfy.

The thing in her chest snapped with an unquenched thirst for vengeance, like biting the inside of its cheek and flooding the Nile red.

"Oh. You're already in here."

Eilidh glanced up sharply to find Meredith standing in the doorway of Thayer's office, looking annoyed. Meredith hesitated, then shrugged and closed the door behind her. "Fine."

It was Meredith's usual treatment of her, as if Eilidh were something she wished would disappear, an inconvenience or a blemish. Something that would, eventually, go away if she simply outlasted, which Meredith usually did. But Eilidh didn't currently feel like giving in.

"I don't like them either," Eilidh pointed out, gesturing to the people outside. "Are you drunk?" she asked in matronly disbelief, noting Meredith's quick stumble over the corner of the office rug. To Meredith's answering middle finger, Eilidh sighed, shaking her head. "Dad would hate this," she muttered, now sounding all of six years old.

"Disagree," Meredith countered, toasting her with a bubbling glass. "Or rather, irrelevant. He's gone."

Eilidh said nothing.

"I think he'd find it funny. Champagne for his real friends," said Meredith in an ironic toast, draining the glass and then moving as if to drop it on the floor.

Eilidh leapt up from her chair. "Don't—!"

"You're so easy." Meredith gave Eilidh a look of actual loathing, something worse than her usual lukewarm irritability. "Such a fucking daddy's girl."

"Oh, I'm sorry, is my inconvenient grief obstructing your natural talent for spitefulness?" snapped Eilidh, the thing in her chest rearing up with an apoplectic glee. "There are a million other rooms in this house. Go destroy his things in those."

The door opened and they both stopped talking. The thing in Eilidh's chest slithered up in her throat, ready to fling itself out like a toad. Then Arthur slipped inside, so Meredith again gave Eilidh the finger.

"Oh good, something exciting in here," said Arthur, falling into the chair opposite the desk and propping his feet on top of it. "All's well, Sister Spiteful?"

"Stop it." Eilidh nudged his foot away.

"Yes, Brother Negligent," mocked Meredith, "be very careful with Daddy's nice things."

"Shut up. Just shut up." Eilidh felt she was being unexpectedly commanding, which she must have been, because Meredith feigned indifference and shrugged, turning toward the floor-to-ceiling windows. "Again, I can't believe I have to say this," Eilidh snapped, addressing both her siblings, "but it's not unreasonable for me to feel sad that Dad's gone. Not that that has anything to do with me not wanting you to wreck his things for no reason."

"You never know, they could be my things," said Arthur with a tipsy twinkle in his eye, as Meredith whirled around with a scoff.

"More likely he left all his stuff to some obscure charity," said Meredith, with a tone of unspeakable annoyance. "Or to Eilidh, which is basically the same thing."

"We already did this," said Eilidh, fuming a little. The demonic thing inside her chest began to chirp like a baby bird, begging for the opportunity to spread its wings, to swallow up her anger and then use it to douse the room in flames. "And believe it or not, I don't really care if you're mad that he was closer to me. I don't think it would be very surprising if I got everything, given that you never gave a shit about him."

"Everything," Meredith echoed with a sudden darkness. Eilidh felt it, the sudden dampening she'd always known and quietly dreaded. Meredith's natural state was a simmering impatience, but her real rage was cool, cavernous, and black.

"Hey, hey." Arthur was on his feet, stepping between them. "Dad had his moments, but he wasn't actually unfair. You're getting worked up over nothing."

"Dad was *absolutely* unfair," snapped Meredith. "And he was petty, too."

"Which must be where you got it from," muttered Eilidh.

"And," Meredith added, ignoring her, "let us not forget that *he changed his will*, apparently so drastically that two lawyers can't even agree on which one stands." She turned to Eilidh again. "And if anyone would have any idea why that is, it's you. But apparently you don't see fit to share with us your privileged little secrets."

Meredith was fucking impossible. "Unlike *you*," Eilidh seethed, "I didn't think of my father as a source of inheritance. I loved him because he was a person, because he was my father, and because he was the only one there for me when my entire life ended in *a single day*—"

"Oh, grow up," snapped Meredith. "You got hurt, Eilidh, your life didn't end. You can move on anytime you like, you know, and try actually doing something with yourself. God," she snarled, "you've always been such a martyr."

Eilidh had always known that Meredith lacked the emotional competency for sympathy, but hearing herself painted as a failure was like a slap to the face; like learning that the worst thing that could happen to you was real; that all the cautionary tales were actually true. "I'm sorry, did *you* train for your entire life to do one thing, only to get the thing you love most ripped away from you?"

But Meredith was eternally uncompassionate, unfailingly so. "You're still one of the richest women in the world, Eilidh, for fuck's sake, you can still do *literally anything you want—*"

"Okay, so by that logic, what do *you* need Wrenfare for?" demanded Eilidh, stung by the reminder of her privilege, her wealth, all of which she'd give away in an instant just to dance again—the money that was also, by the way, something Meredith would have easily inherited if she'd just stayed at Harvard like Thayer asked, instead of throwing it all away to create something nobody needed so that a tech company financed by their father's number one personal nemesis would give her the funds to fuel a petty grudge. Just so some heartless industry would take her seriously, because Meredith, a *productive* member of society, could be given vast, universe-altering sums of money to do frivolous, meaningless work that would feed, cure, and house absolutely fucking *no one*. "*You're* the one who never lets us forget you've already got ten billion dollars—"

Meredith threw her hands in the air. "I don't *have* ten billion dollars. I have a company *valued* at ten billion dollars, none of which I actually have—"

"Why?" asked Eilidh. "Because your product doesn't work?"

The room got cold again, but this time it didn't scare her. This time, Eilidh wanted her sister to look her in the eye and say, explicitly, that Chirp could not make anyone happy. That *Meredith* could not make anyone happy, including and most importantly herself. That Meredith was a miserable, miserly person for whom all the money in the world would not recreate her mother's love or her father's affection, and that yes, maybe Eilidh was still suffering from something in her body that had gone wrong, but at least she had something that Meredith would never have, which was the knowledge that for at least one person on this earth, she was enough.

And even *that* wasn't happiness! Because nothing could invent happiness that didn't exist intrinsically, in a way that was deserved. Especially not Meredith Wren.

"Death," warned Arthur thinly.

"Not now," snapped Meredith, her eyes still locked on Eilidh's. It was unclear to Eilidh what would happen next, only that whatever it was, she would return it, blow for blow. If her sister actually hated her, if those words would be painful to hear, so be it. The thing in her chest was awake—no, not just awake—acute, *alive,* thriving. The worst thing Eilidh had ever thought about herself was already true. Nothing Meredith could say to her would cheapen her own carefully cultivated self-loathing. Nobody could hate Eilidh Wren like Eilidh Wren.

"Death," said Arthur again.

Irritation sparked in Meredith's eyes, temporarily disrupting her stare-off with Eilidh.

"Arthur, I swear to god, if you don't stay out of this—"

Then there was a thud, and Eilidh and Meredith both turned to find Arthur lying motionless on the floor.

# 24

"You know, if you do decide to kill me, you'd probably be doing me a favor," Jamie had remarked some seven hours prior as he and Meredith had sorted the refuse of their coffee paraphernalia, the recyclable lids in one bin and the compostable cups in another. "I sometimes think I'd do just about anything to get away from my completely diabolical ability to like you."

"That's demented," had been Meredith's only available reply.

"Yeah," Jamie agreed, sounding genuinely sour. "It is, and so are you."

It floated through Meredith's mind as she knelt down beside her brother's unmoving body for the second time in twenty-four hours. Specifically, the illogical thought that maybe Arthur had died just to get away from her, which was frankly believable in the moment. It was the only thing that made sense, because the alternatives—that Arthur had died from grief, or that he was somehow at risk for repeated heart failure at the tender age of twenty-nine— were flatly impossible. It seemed to Meredith, particularly with the way Eilidh had just looked at her, much more likely that Arthur's death was an act of desperation, and that he had said her name as he went made it all the more unmistakable; cosmic requital for her personal sins.

But, of course, beside her, Eilidh was hysterical. "Oh my god, we killed him again," Eilidh was saying. "He was asking for help and we just ignored him!"

"What, pray tell, were you going to do?" said Meredith, attempting to slap Arthur awake. He again had no pulse, but historically, brutality sometimes worked. Or at least it had one time before, which under the circumstances felt statistically significant.

"This is my fault," said Eilidh in a quietly agonized voice. "I did this somehow, I know it."

"The world doesn't revolve around you, Eilidh," snapped Meredith, despite having had the exact same thought moments before. "Unless you physically pulled the trigger that killed him, let's just stop fixating on you for *five fucking seconds*—"

Eilidh, who had been pacing, pulled up short. "Oh god. I know what it is."

"What?" As in *What are you talking about*, not *I'm so intellectually curious about your thoughts in this critical moment*, though Meredith lacked confidence in Eilidh's ability to recognize the difference.

"Firstborn sons." Eilidh went pale. "That's one of the plagues."

"What? Jesus." Eilidh was unsurprisingly useless in a crisis and always had been. Meredith was running through her head for anything magically relevant that Lou had ever taught her, though she had never had a strong grasp on physical things. Arthur could do them, Lou could do them . . . Meredith was really only good at mental things, ideas. She was trying to think but she couldn't, because now the ghost of Lou was standing judgmentally in her periphery again and Eilidh wouldn't shut up.

"Sometimes it happens when I'm not fully keeping it at bay, and I *was* really angry—"

"What the hell are you talking about?" demanded Meredith, ripping her attention away from her brother's body to look up at her sister's colorless face.

"There's—there's this thing," Eilidh said hesitantly. "I don't know if . . . I don't know how to explain, really, but—"

"Eilidh," Meredith seethed, her vision a blinding white starburst of impatience, "would you *get to the point*?"

"I make apocalypses happen!" burst out of Eilidh's mouth. "I'm sorry, I don't—"

"What?"

"Apocalypses . . . doomsday things." Eilidh was ringing her hands, beginning to pace. "The ten plagues of Egypt, you know, with the firstborn sons—"

"What?" said Meredith, who was feeling increasingly ill with frustration.

"I don't know if they happen in any predetermined order—they don't seem to? The first time, when I was in the hospital, I made the sprinkler system rain blood. Yesterday my plane was going down and there were locusts—"

"What?"

"I once made all the sea animals come up on the beach in Mallorca!" Now Eilidh was wailing. "I don't know if it was *all* of them, but I don't really understand if there's any, you know, doomsday *exactness*—"

"Firstborn sons," Meredith repeated, and felt a sudden stab of rage. "You're telling me multiple millennia have passed and we're still gendering the apocalypse?"

"So *you'd* rather be dead?" said Eilidh in piercing disbelief.

"I'm just saying it's absurd that I'd be passed over! Even the monarchy evolved!" shrieked Meredith.

"Sister Hysterical," said Arthur, "you're crushing my legs."

Both Meredith and Eilidh screamed, rising abruptly to their feet as Arthur sat up, swaying a little from apparent dizziness.

"But you were—" Meredith stopped, pressing one hand to her racing pulse as Eilidh scrutinized her hands as if this, too, were somehow their doing. "But I swear, you really were *dead*, like actually *dead*—"

"I did wake up from a nap today unable to move," commented Arthur.

"You didn't think that worth mentioning?" asked Meredith.

Arthur shrugged. "I thought it was one of those weird dream paralysis things."

"That's never happened to me. Has it ever happened to you? Or to anyone outside of a horror novel?"

"Well, Sister Rational, at the time it was unclear," Arthur said.

Something about his tone of voice was soothing, almost hypnotic. "I appreciate how calm you're being, Brother Pragmatism," said Meredith, her mouth dry. A headache pulsed behind one eye. Lou's ghost remained in the haze of her periphery—scowling, middle finger up, something Meredith's vision couldn't clear away. Fucking stye.

"Thank you, I think I'm handling everything really well—"

"Hello?!" said Eilidh, who was still there, despite Meredith's intention to ignore her. "How can this be a thing that keeps happening?"

"Unclear," Arthur replied.

There was a crash of glass bursting from the chandelier overhead, a bright stream of sparks falling below to catch on the edge of their father's Turkish-style rug. "Oops," Arthur said, and attempted to reach for something to rise to his feet before frowning. "Wait. Can't move my legs yet."

Just then the office door opened. "I smelled fire," said Gillian, holding a champagne flute in one hand and surveying the scene with one efficient sweep before spotting the smoldering edge of the office carpet. "Yes, fire. One second." She disappeared again, then reappeared, handing Meredith a glass of water. "That should do it. I'll let you get back to whatever this is. Are you all right, Art?"

"Mostly," said Arthur.

"Well, good luck, I suppose." Then Gillian was gone.

Meredith, having very nearly lost her hold on reality, took a steadying glance at the very real, extremely concrete glass of water, contemplating the more ineffable things that had occurred in her chest. From the edge of her vision, the specter of Lou was still staring intently. Meredith considered asking what she wanted, but then again, she already knew. Ghost-Lou was only ever there to prey on Meredith's weakness, and this was definitely one.

Meredith didn't think of herself as a person suffering from undue loss, but it turned out she really didn't want to look at the people around her as things that might be gone from her at any moment. Having now lost Arthur twice, however temporarily, she was beginning to diagnose some feelings of deep-seated anxiety, almost as if she were approximately nine years old.

She did not like it, Meredith decided, when her brother died. Even when he came back to life, it was really very unpleasant.

"Something will have to be done about this," Meredith commented to herself as she doused the rug with the glass of water. The fire petered willfully out as she bent to check the damage, blinking away the ghost in her mind's eye and deducing with a sigh, "Well, there's only one plausible solution. I should have known. I've thought about her at least three times already this week. That's portent." Meredith shook her head. "Even she would say so."

"No," said Arthur, looking concerned as he flexed his hand. "You don't think—?"

"Who else would know what to do?" countered Meredith, who despite the minor catharsis of submission to the inevitable was never one to relish the taste of seeking help. The fact that she disliked it less than she disliked watching her brother die was really saying something. "You have a problem that can't possibly be natural. We can't tell a doctor you've fucking died twice. Who else are we supposed to ask?"

Arthur seemed to be battling similar feelings, though what he said aloud was, "Do you even know where she is?"

"No, but how hard can it be to find out?" Meredith's pulse quickened. Her fingers itched.

"Who are you talking about?" Eilidh interjected, which the other two ignored.

"I don't know about this," said Arthur. "The last time I saw her . . ." He shifted uncomfortably. "We parted badly."

"How do you think I feel?" said Meredith. "To say we parted badly is an understatement."

The child-ghost in Meredith's head stayed nine years old for a reason. It was safest that way, with Meredith's betrayal not yet a glimmer in either of their minds.

"Wait," said Eilidh. "Are you two talking about—?"

"I really don't want to," said Arthur. Except he did.

"Neither do I," said Meredith. Except she did. "But you need to stop dying, and apparently Eilidh is some kind of apocalypse maiden, which as usual is somehow my responsibility now."

Eilidh made a sound of juvenile ingratitude. "I *never said*—"

"Do you think she'll even talk to us?" said Arthur. "I'm pretty confident she hates us."

"Oh, definitely," Meredith agreed. "She thinks we're fucking assholes. But can *you* think of anyone else who could possibly help?"

The three of them looked at each other then.

The ghost of Lou that had been lingering in Meredith's periphery was gone.

Why stay? They'd already invoked the real one.

"All right," sighed Arthur. "Then I guess let's go find Lou."

# Another Brief Note from God

I may not have been completely honest with you about my position of objectivity in the narrative.

# The Life and Times of Meredith Wren

- On December 16 at 9:00 AM sharp in the midst of an unseasonably warm wind, Meredith Honora Liang Wren is born with wide, incisive black eyes, a shock of black hair, a helplessness to her parents' slavering Anglophilia that will only be exacerbated over the years with other, more intense commitments to aesthetic, and a healthy wail of indignation. The world rejoices, for thusly an earth-shaker walks among us! Blessed are the eldest daughters for they shall inherit the generational burdens, et cetera, et cetera—what can possibly go wrong!

- Meredith begins to walk at the tender age of eleven months. Shortly afterward, on November 21, her brother, Arthur, is born. Meredith says her first word a month later. It is "no," and seems to apply generally, without specification.

- When Meredith is four and Arthur is three and both have grudgingly become used to the presence of the other, their sister Eilidh is born on a lovely spring day in early May. Meredith immediately assumes her rank as family lieutenant and is assigned (by herself) care of the brand-new infant. Eilidh is a quiet baby who doesn't walk until she's nearly two, partially because Arthur keeps pushing her over and partially because Meredith insists on trying to carry her, but also because who in Eilidh Olympia Liang Wren's position would deign to walk, like a common peasant, when offered so many fortunate alternatives?

- It's summer when Meredith's mother dies, hot and bright and forever undermining Meredith's childlike belief that bad things can only happen in bad weather. By then the family has moved from their home in Palo Alto to the gloomy, shadowed house on the forest floor in Marin County and their father has begun to withdraw from the daily mundanities of Wrenfare Magitech, choosing instead the remoteness of being willfully unreachable for his tyrannical captaincy of the ship. By the time Persephone Wren is discovered post–heart attack by their housekeeper, nine-year-old Meredith is waiting patiently for an adult outside the bedroom door as if to guard her mother's enchanted sleep. It is unclear to the housekeeper and to Meredith's father whether Meredith understands what has happened to her mother, though if Thayer had been paying attention, he would have known that Meredith was so advanced in school that her parents had been advised to advance her through both the first and second grades. Persephone declined on both parents' behalf, stating that just because her daughter was precocious didn't mean she was necessarily ready for the realities of life. When Thayer Wren is called in for Meredith's parent-teacher conference that year in the weeks following his wife's demise, he is advised to advance Meredith from fourth grade to fifth, so that a more challenging curriculum might coax her out of her grief. He agrees. Meanwhile, Arthur's teacher advises that although Arthur has an incredible aptitude for schoolwork, it might be best that he stay back and repeat the second grade, just to catch him up with the other kids emotionally—Arthur is dealing poorly with the loss of his mother and has begun to hit and kick the other children and occasionally himself in moments of frustration. Thayer declines, instead enrolling Arthur in baseball camp, to more pragmatically deal with his hypermasculine rage. Eilidh is, of course, a perfect angel. Why wouldn't she be?

- At the local Marin elementary school, all of the children hate Meredith—except for one.
- Her name is Maria Odesa Guadalupe de Léon and there are two main things wrong with her. One, she is ugly. Two, she is poor. Okay, three, her clothes are shabby and too big and for boys, because they belonged first to her mother's older cousin's baby, who coincidentally is now fifteen. Four, she brings food to school and it smells weird, not like pretty Meredith's neat little prepackaged lunch that Thayer oversees in a managerial way, from on high, but doesn't personally pack. Five, she keeps calling herself a witch and cursing the other children, to the point where the teachers are concerned she has developmental problems. She should have

outgrown behaviors like that by now and her parents have been called in multiple times but her mother is always working, her father is no longer (perhaps never has been?) in the picture, and her two grandmothers who hate each other attend these meetings together and proceed to bicker in separate languages the entire time. It's impossible to tell which grandmother speaks better English or is more, you know, reasonable. They are both very Catholic and almost identical, so it's unclear why they don't get along.

- The answer, in case you're curious, is that Bernila's beautiful whore of a daughter has always been too good for Lupe's precious bastard boy-king of a son, or something along those lines. As the teachers and administrators correctly observed, the two grandmothers have nothing in common except everything—their hatred of each other, their fear of eternal damnation, and the fact that they are too old, too brown, and too insane to work productive office jobs and so instead take on various positions of domestic labor, nannying or cleaning or cooking or caregiving whenever there's cash on the table. And, of course, the daily task of caring for their granddaughter, who has unfortunately bound them to each other for life. She is Lulu to her mother, Marisa Lou to her Lola, Lupita to her Abuela, Maria to the teachers who can't understand why a child would have so many goddamn names. But most importantly, she is Lou to Meredith Wren.

- When Meredith asks Lou why she doesn't have a dad, Lou asks Meredith why *she* doesn't have a *mom*. Because my mom is dead, says Meredith. Oh, that's sad, says Lou, if my mom was dead I'd definitely bring her back. How? says Meredith. Well I'd have to ask my Lola, says Lou, but she and Abuela both say I'm a really good witch for my age so probably I could figure it out. Are you really a witch? says Meredith. Yes but it's not really special, anyone can be a witch, says Lou. Oh that makes sense, says Meredith. Yeah, says Lou, anyone can learn to do it but it's definitely real, I don't know why nobody believes me, they could just do it themselves and find out. I'm not a witch but I'm a genius, Meredith says, that's why I'm in this grade and why the other kids don't like me. I'm pretty sure the other kids don't like you because you are kind of mean and weird, says Lou, but it's cool that you're a genius. If I teach you to be a genius, says Meredith, will you teach me to be a witch and bring my mom back? Yeah I guess so, you can come over to my house after school if you want, I'm not really busy on Wednesdays, says Lou.

- Bernila, Lou's maternal grandmother, doesn't necessarily take to Meredith right away, but when Lupe says very explicitly to Bernila's daughter (Lou's mother, Daniela-called-Dani) that she does not like Meredith and should no longer allow Meredith in their house because she's a very bad influence on Lou, Bernila is morally obligated to take the opposite stance and instead become very attached. It is Bernila who teaches Meredith how to soften a person's heart, how to change their mind, to find the pliable part of a person's soul and weave them into submission, which forces Lupe to take Meredith aside and tell her that Bernila is just a stupid village witch who doesn't know anything except how to raise whore daughters who corrupt precious boy-king sons, and that real magic is something you call upon like a spirit to do mainly the same thing Bernila said it did. Meredith asks how such things can coexist with Catholicism and both grandmothers tell her to be quiet unless she wants to go to hell. Lou is mostly just happy to have a friend.

- Together, Lou and Meredith read *The Count of Monte Cristo* and plot revenge on their ribbon-plaited bullies; they research spells on the early innocence of Meredith's father's internet. Meredith, Lola observes in private to Lou, has terrifying amounts of will-power. Meredith can mind-over-matter all day, to the point of near nonexistence—to the point where she is more stubbornness than girl. But *Lou,* Lola says, is a little bit more well-rounded—for Lou, everything is within her grasp. It all depends on how badly she wants to reach it, which is something Lou must decide for herself.

- Arthur, who now has to spend a lot of his day playing sports but not *all* of his day, notices that Meredith is doing something secretive that she doesn't want him involved in. At first she tells him to go away, but then he nearly kills himself in the crossfires of an unexplained electrical surge and thus, at Lou's urging, Arthur is grudgingly permitted to tag along. Lupe instantly adores him, so Bernila takes the position of harboring a lifelong grudge. (On her deathbed, she tells Lou not to ever get involved again with That Demon Wren Boy, who will surely lead her astray—Bernila can tell because she knows these things, she's just blessed. "Okay, well, I haven't spoken to Arthur Wren in about seven years," Lou tells her, and Bernila uses the last of her strength to shout "GOOD, DON'T.") During this time, Eilidh does ballet.

- Meredith's middle school teachers recognize that Meredith has an incredible aptitude for math and science, and particularly the burgeoning field of biomancy, which is a growing area of biomechanics that marries with the supercomputational advancements of magitech. They suggest a boarding school, the Ainsworth Academy, which is a Harvard feeder school and has an excellent reputation in the biomancy field. They add that Meredith seems abnormally interested in childlike things, like the use of magic for "spells," and after Meredith has an altercation with another child (Ryan Behrend, a little shithead who had it coming, but still, the district has rules), they suspect it will be best for Meredith's future if she gains some distance from her childhood home; her emotional growth seems to be stunted by the early loss of her mother. Thayer mainly hears "boarding school" and says oh hell yes.

- You should come, Meredith tells Lou. I can't afford it, Lou replies, having become aware by then of her position in society, which is to say her general irrelevance. Let me ask my dad if you can come with me, says Meredith.

- Thayer says who the fuck is Lou? Followed by Grow up, Meredith, you have to learn to be on your own. People will always try to ride your coattails because you're a Wren. You're not supposed to be like other people because you're not like them. You'll make new friends at your new school.

- Meredith, a genius, fills out paperwork on Lou's behalf and forges Lou's mother's signature. Lou gets a full ride scholarship to the Ainsworth Academy and doesn't realize that from then on, Meredith's philosophy will be *I gave you a future, so now you owe something to me.* But Lou is grateful, her mother even more so, and Lou says a tearful goodbye to her family while Meredith waits in line for security with someone from the airline, holding her back very stiff and straight like her father always tells her geniuses do.

- Lest this make you feel sorry for Meredith Wren, let me remind you: Lots of children lose their mothers or have fathers who don't really care. And many of those children do not go on to become white-collar grifters—although, statistically speaking, many of the ones born to billionaires do.

- Meredith and Lou both excel at cryptography, computer science, and biomancy, though neither ever publicly confesses their secret dabblings in witchcraft, which despite the awe-inspiring age of Magic™ is not viewed with any more legitimacy than magic ever was before it became commercialized for corporate use. Magic the unofficial version continues to refer to individual practitioners in lesbian astrology communes or third-world immigrants who pray to the god of their colonizers. Meredith and Lou never speak of what they are taught by Lupe and Bernila, though they both guiltily know to whom they owe their talent, their proficiency, and their love.

- Lupe dies of cancer from lifelong exposure to asbestos (in the walls of her Guatemalan primary school, the ceiling of her first American apartment, the many buildings she was hired to clean that were never up to code) during the spring semester of Lou and Meredith's sophomore year, the same year Arthur attends an all-boys' boarding school called Canongate Hall, some thirty minutes from the Ainsworth Academy. Meredith flies back to San Francisco in the aisle seat with her hand in Lou's, Arthur on Lou's other side staring quietly out the window. Eilidh is now considered a ballet prodigy, though the idea of something so unproductive now feels so distant from Meredith's world of ambition and academic elitism that she no longer knows what to say to her, except to note with some suppressed envy that Eilidh is too skinny, like their mother was.

- Meredith excels at tennis, playing in the national championships every year, lacing up her fancy, powder-white running shoes every day, pushing herself for trophies and the occasional approving look from Thayer. Lou has no time for extracurriculars, because free tuition doesn't mean free books or free housing or free food or the right clothes to avoid the sniggers from the other kids in the halls. She shoplifts from time to time until Meredith catches her doing it and asks if she needs money. After all, Meredith points out with her ivory tennis pleats sharp as teeth, it would be a waste of time bothering to get Lou into Ainsworth if she just got herself kicked out.

- If Lou hadn't been sixteen years old, she probably could have understood that Meredith, who has never had a friend except for Lou and the annoying brother Meredith pretends she can't shake because it's easier than acknowledging that she actually adores him, does not want Lou to jeopardize her own future. But Lou is getting tired of being told about Her Future, about how bright it is, *if*—and *only if*—she says the right things and ignores the parts of her background that are unsavory, the pieces of her heart that don't contribute to anything Productive, the position she holds in society and the capital importance of her Getting Out. Out of what—*Marin*? Lou has been the poorest fish in all the most opulent ponds, kept afloat by the quicksilver charity of rich people, and the fuckery of it is that she actually does long for their approval. She *likes* being told that she's special. She doesn't mind the threat that if she doesn't succeed, she'll go back to being nothing, as if "nothing" is a thing she has honest-to-god once been. The truth is that to Lou, her mother's life, the lives of her grandmothers, her absent and constantly down-on-his-luck father—it *is* scary! It *does* seem pointless and worth fearing! The idea that she could fall from grace, it *terrifies* her. So even when the townies mock her for being a rich person's pet and the rich people mistake her for being a cheap townie, she can ignore it because The Future is calling. Someday, Lou can afford things her mother never could—that her grandmothers could barely have dreamt of—if she just meets *their* metrics, if she follows *their* rules. If she simply jumps when she's told to jump—if she does it perfectly, the best jumper in class—then how can anyone ever deny her? A graduate of the Ainsworth Academy goes to Harvard, then they work on Wall Street or something, Lou doesn't know and doesn't care. She knows that Ainsworth means money, which means safety, which means freedom. She will never have to worry about how to pay the rent. She will never have to wonder whether a cough is bad enough to see the doctor. She will never have to hear a landlord tell her he'll call ICE if she complains about roaches, about the gas line that seems to constantly leak, about the way a fleeting whim can suddenly make their shitty house untenably expensive. Poverty is in a thousand ways a death sentence, and Lou, who's had a happier childhood than Meredith, understands this deep in her soul, and it's a bone-chilling fear, the idea that if anyone ever casts her out of Eden, nothing she knows how to do is of any real value. The fear that being gifted only matters if you, yourself, are the right gift.

- But Lou is sixteen and Meredith's being a bitch, so when someone offers Lou a lot of money to write an essay, Lou uses it to buy new shoes that don't squeak in the halls, and then a hoodie that has the right label, and then a pair of jeans that make the right boys look more closely at her Rubenesque third-world ass.

- Meredith's eyes look a little glazed over when she says *What if we could invent something that could actually make people happy.* "You said you were a witch," Meredith says in a quiet voice, "and you promised you would help me bring my mother back." Which wasn't spiritually true, because Lou was like nine years old when she said that and even magic has its limits, but more importantly, it's just so fucking morose. They've been drifting apart ever since Abuela died, maybe because it's becoming more real to Lou, the idea of mortality. The idea that she has to cash in this golden egg for something—that she has to make it worth it, fit in, find her way to The Future, because otherwise she's just a dumb girl who wasn't there when the grandmother who raised her died alone, still working, still scrubbing floors on her hands and knees. At the time Meredith says it, Lou is late for a date with the football captain who doesn't look her way in the halls but tells her he loves her under the bleachers, when her bra is off, while Lou tries to feel something like desire, which is a sexier form of fear. Desire is desperation; it's looking for signs; it's if you look at me right now it means you actually *do* love me, you're not just using me, you wouldn't touch me like this if I was nothing to you, if I was actually nothing then wouldn't I know? Choose me and it means everyone else was wrong, I am choosable! Pick me and it means that somehow, by some ineffable metric, I win!

- So Lou looks at her best friend and says Meredith, I thought you were over this? Get over this, Lou says, people die. Lots of people die. Grow up.

- She doesn't know that Meredith knows about the cheating. She doesn't know that Meredith knows about the football player, that Meredith is sure that Arthur, too, is in love with Lou, that Meredith feels like Lou is evolving and Meredith isn't, because she's still chasing something, a different ending than the one her mother got—a better, sweeter fate.

- But anyway, this is Meredith's story, so there's a lot of more important things to talk about, like what happens when Meredith walks, as prophesied, the hallowed Harvard halls, or what happens when Meredith breaks Jamie's heart as well as her own, or how Arthur calls Meredith ten times in a row and she doesn't answer because she knows it's about Lou, who's back home now, in El Cerrito, where her mother now lives because Abuela is gone and Lola is sick and Lou is going to have to get a job to help out, and sure, maybe Meredith feels badly about it, but who can really ever tell with Meredith? There's obviously a story to how Meredith ends up lying about the deal she's made and releasing a product she already knows is a fake, a fucking forgery, and what is she even supposed to say, that she once had a friend whose grandma was the actual, literal village witch? That it turns out the Garden of Eden isn't the Ainsworth Academy, and it isn't Harvard, and it isn't Silicon Beach or Silicon Valley or the magitech economy or the 30 other assholes Under 30, and what if it isn't even Wrenfare or her father's approval, because the truth is you could fall from grace at any time, before or after thirty, which is a completely arbitrary number, and you're never safe from a fall unless *you are* because you were *born* safe, actually, and if you have the wealth of Thayer Wren and Persephone Liang behind you, then all you have to do is be happy with what you have without tearing down the only person who really *loves you,* but you can't be happy, not really, because you're still trying to be in Eden, when the whole time it turns out that Eden is just a fucking lie?

- But I don't really feel like talking about it anymore. So, you know, let's move on.

**Maria Odesa Guadalupe de León**

*"Do your worst, for I will do mine!"*

**Maria Odesa Guadalupe de Léon**
El Cerrito High School
HONORS: Class Valedictorian, Summa Cum
Laude, Most Likely to Succeed
"Do your worst, for I will do mine!"

# WEDNESDAY.

# 25

Meredith awoke in a cold sweat, the dream still thundering through her head. It was the usual one, the first day of school and she hadn't registered for classes, except the school was actually Tyche's campus and her feet wouldn't move, they were stuck in place, the halls labyrinthine and unrecognizable. All she had to do was get to the registration office, to tell them what courses she wanted, she'd take anything at this point, whatever they had to give. But instead of a registrar it was Kip Hughes and Merritt Foster and Lou, and they were all saying they needed Meredith's data right away, right now, it was late and if she didn't give it to them she was going to be eaten. Unclear if it was jackals or a cannibalistic ritual. She simply understood that the situation was dire, and yet her fucking feet wouldn't move.

"The industry, it's very 'fake it till you make it,'" Cass had said to someone at the cocktail party (as it had inevitably become) last night, someone who had golfed with her father or built model cars with him, who could say. Meredith had been tiptoeing around in the kitchen at the time, trying to get more alcohol without anyone seeing her, wearing their not-so-covert expectation that she fall to her knees and weep. "The whole deal with venture capitalism is that it's a race to prove that the thing you make is both necessary and worth a lot of money, which isn't always true. In reality, sometimes things underperform for a while. But it doesn't mean everything is shit, necessarily."

"So you think Tyche will survive the risk?" said the old golf dude, who was apparently an old industry dude.

"Oh, Tyche will be fine," Cass replied. "There's always a margin for failure built into any product gamble. Not that I'd count Meredith out quite yet."

Meredith looked over at Cass now, his peacefully sleeping face. The traitor. Sure, he'd been upbeat enough, but he wondered, too. He wondered if she would fail. Every day it was I believe in you Mer, everything will be fine

Mer, you'll figure it out. But what he really meant was Mer, if you fail, it makes no difference to anybody. We all cleverly planned for the likelihood that you were never actually going to succeed.

Glass cliff.

Meredith picked up her phone, glancing at the screen. It had an address in the East Bay, where Lou now lived, unless this was outdated. It was someplace to start, at least.

Meredith hadn't had to look too hard for Lou, because this wasn't her first rodeo when it came to checking up on her former best friend. Meredith already knew Lou had graduated from public high school the year Meredith had graduated from Ainsworth. She remembered Lou posting her yearbook quote, a line from *The Count of Monte Cristo*, on a now-defunct account, something that Meredith had, at seventeen, been quietly, desperately sure that Lou had only posted for Meredith's benefit—a message to her, sentimental for its pettiness. Because who else but Meredith would have known what it meant?

From there, the personal updates got fewer, farther between. Lou graduated from UC Berkeley the same year Meredith was supposed to have graduated from Harvard. Lou didn't have a professional page of any kind—she was too successful for that, and likely didn't need the many start-up vultures hunting for her private line given that she'd been valued in the hundred millions by the age of twenty-five—but she was still listed on the website of Cal's technomancy school for the many influential papers she'd published throughout her schooling.

Lou was probably working somewhere else in the magitech economy now, maybe just didn't care for social media. She didn't have any personal accounts and Meredith couldn't find any record of her after she'd sold her first start-up to Tyche (at least two years before Meredith would later do the same, making Meredith's fingers itch), but maybe she'd gotten married. Maybe her name had changed. Meredith tapped on the Berkeley page again, lingering on the first academic paper that had borne Lou's name—or, well, technically the name that everyone else had used for Lou. Maria de Léon.

All the time between them seemed scattered grittily across the floor, like it had spilled out from an hourglass. Meredith looked at the address again, and the phone number.

Then she tapped Jamie's name in her messages.

"Look, I already know the story about your mom," Jamie had said to

Meredith in the car two days ago, "and I know you already had the idea for Chirp when I met you. You told me about your friend from high school and the things she taught you to do. Which means I already know everything, basically, except for one thing I can't figure out. Why'd you do it?"

By "it," he meant turn her subcutaneous magitech-powered mood stabilizer into the profit-deriving go-button of a brainwashed corporate shill.

"As both a theoretical exercise and a refreshing change of pace from you asking me the same question in different formats," Meredith had replied, "why don't you tell me why you think I did it? Since you're probably the only investigative journalist who doesn't find it plausible that I did it for the sake of pure, unadulterated greed."

"You'd think you'd be a little more grateful to me for that," commented Jamie.

"Well, it's not my fault if you look for zebras," said Meredith.

"You mean because I hear hoofbeats?" He looked skeptical. "You really think there was any possibility it was a horse?"

"I think any reasonable person would assume it's a horse." The horse being the usual reasons anyone did anything.

"So you're saying that's it, you did it for the money?"

Meredith then gave him as long a look as she could manage without driving them off the highway, which she hoped conveyed the extent of her irritation.

"Fine." Jamie was quiet then, considering it. "I think," he said slowly, "you did it because you're ambitious. You're, you know, hungry. The hungriest person I've ever known." He stopped. "I do think a lot of it was for your mom," he admitted. "That was my first thought, that you never really got over losing her, and you wanted to fix her even though you couldn't. This was the closest thing. But the scale of it, the betrayal, the fact that you chose *these particular* corporate overlords . . ." He trailed off. "That part doesn't sound like you."

Meredith thought about the sweat of it. The heart-crush of it. The way she'd stood in a room full of people she'd hired at twenty-four years old and promised them they could trust her as if she wasn't just an idiot teenage girl playing dress-up in a fancy suit. All those mothers and fathers with children to feed. The people who needed this job to pay their rent, to keep a roof over their heads. The people who expected her to be a genius because everyone she'd ever met had told her she was a genius even though she was pretty sure she was just an idiot teenage girl. She read eight different books about impostor syndrome. *You go, girlboss! You are smart and capable!* But surely not everyone who read the books was *actually* smart and capable. The book was only printed with the assumption that a bunch of stupid, incapable people would buy it. If only the worthy read those words, then publishing as an industry would collapse. Maybe impostor syndrome was real, but not for her, an *actual* impostor.

"Everyone takes the money," said Meredith, realizing she was parroting her father's words back to Jamie. "Couldn't this whole thing have been a natural consequence of an industry built on pretense? Everyone who takes the money has to show success that doesn't exist yet—that isn't technically possible until it is. I'm not the only one who doesn't want to fail."

Jamie didn't say anything.

"Why didn't you tell me you called off your wedding?" blurted Meredith.

"What would you have done about it?" said Jamie.

Meredith didn't say anything.

"Yeah," said Jamie darkly. "That's what I thought."

Meredith shook herself of the memory from the car, typing out a message.

U up?

Very funny, said Jamie.

That's not a no

I'm proofreading the article to send to my editor. Could be free later

After you destroy me, you mean?

Yeah, after that.

Meredith picked at her cuticle and blinked, then blinked again, struggling to clear her vision. The stye was still going strong. She looked over at Cass, then back at her screen.

Do you think we should just have sex and get it out of our systems?

No, said Jamie, but I could do coffee again if you want. Or a drink?

Assuming she found Lou today, she was definitely going to need one.

Okay, said Meredith. See you later for a drink.

# 26

Arthur woke up to motion in his hands and feet, which signaled in a way that had recently become noteworthy that he had probably not died overnight. He rolled over and felt the presence of warmth beside him, opening his eyes to see that Philippa's hair was swept across his pillowcase, golden and honey-warm.

"Where's Gillian?" said Arthur, and Philippa's eyes snapped open.

"Well," she said. "That's one way to greet someone."

"Sorry, I just—" He shook himself, reaching over to pull her closer, which was something he very much enjoyed doing. He had always loved waking to Philippa; the way Philippa curled into him like the slice of a crescent moon, all soft contentment and gentle narcissism, a kitten wanting to be stroked. But usually he had a mental space for waking up next to Philippa and/or Yves, and a very separate one for waking up with Gillian, and he had thought it was going to be a Gillian day. "I thought you'd gone to bed with Yves."

"He's up early this morning, as is your wife." Arthur had the distinct impression that this word was meant to punish him somehow, although it didn't seem reasonable. His arrangement with Philippa had always been rooted in Philippa's distaste for the conventional, though he supposed it didn't get more conventional than sleeping next to someone in accidentally matching pajamas, which was not his fault. For one thing, life among the middle-aged had given both Arthur and Gillian certain middle-aged ("mature," they liked to tell themselves, since they could no longer envision themselves at the proverbial club) creature comforts. Besides, they didn't coordinate; they just happened to like the same colors and brands. One Christmas they had gifted these pajamas to each other, him to her because she'd commented that the material was so soft and hers to him because she knew he'd like them. It had been one of the times Gillian had laughed so hard she started to cry, which was something that happened when Gillian thought something was really, gorgeously stupid. Usually, Arthur prided himself on a Gillian laugh-cry three to four times a year.

The point is that the pajamas were very comfortable, but hardly a comment on the institution of marriage.

"Gillian is a very early riser," Arthur decided to say, which was true. Gillian was most productive in the hours before most people were awake, although there were technically no times when Gillian was unproductive. The thought gave him a strange wrenching sensation, so he reached into his nightstand for a bit more chocolate, breaking off a piece and tossing it into his mouth. His phone screen flashed with a string of headlines: WREN (D-CA) NOTABLY SILENT IN CONGRESSIONAL HOUSING DEBATE AFTER CLAIMING MARKETS "UNAFFORDABLE" FOR WORKING CL . . .

ARTHUR WREN IS RIGHT—THE EAST BAY IS UNAFFORDABLE AND IT'S HIS FAU . . .

"Are you getting enough sleep?" Arthur asked tangentially of Philippa, who by then was nestled comfortably into him, a veritable pea in a pod. "Or enough . . . vitamins?"

"I wonder where we go when we sleep," said Philippa, turning over her shoulder. "Do you think our consciousness runs into each other?"

"Gently, I hope," Arthur replied, "but almost surely."

When he and Philippa had first met, Arthur had dreamed of her and Yves constantly, as if he were longing them into being. He had always been particularly watchful of his dreams, a conscientiousness he owed to Lou's grandmothers.

Lou again.

"I had a friend once," Arthur began telling Philippa, "who told me our dreams were sometimes a meaningful communion with the fabric of nature, the connectedness of our spirits to things in this world and beyond. But other times they're just neurological snapshots, like all our thoughts were poured into a bottle and shaken up. She said that things became unrecognizable when we saw them from a different perspective like that, as if they'd happened inside someone else's heart."

(Yes, Lou had been a person once, not just a marionette ghost who existed only to remind Arthur of his failings. Not that Arthur had made that distinction yet.)

"Imaginative friend," Philippa commented, turning to look at him. She was so terribly arresting in the mornings, like intimacy incarnate. Arthur hated to make a mistake and ruin it, the fragility of it all. The delicate nature of perfection.

"I'm going to see her today, actually." Arthur reached down for Philippa's hand, stroking the valleys between her knuckles. "Meredith and I can't decide whether it's better that one of us go alone, so we're all going together."

"In a pack? That can be quite threatening," said Philippa.

"Well, Lou and I didn't part on the best of terms," Arthur said. It felt strange to be discussing Lou with Philippa now. Not solely because he and Philippa didn't typically undress the details of each other's lives—she was more intellectual than that—but because he'd done such a marvelous job of conserving Lou to the recesses of his memory, preserving her in the usual dark places for shame and regret. "But Meredith and I disagree on which one of us she'll be angrier with."

"Did you both sleep with her?"

"No. Well, I don't think so." Granted, he didn't really grasp the difference between platonic sisterhood and the erotic closeness of girlhood. Among the things he did know about Philippa's early life were some fascinating anecdotes of her own relationships in boarding school. The experience of being sent away for schooling had been formative to both their sexual tastes, though Arthur hadn't acted on his for a very long time. Yves, however, had gone to the local school in the small village where he'd lived with his father, his mother, his father's wife, his half-siblings from his father's marriage, and all of his mother's first cousins. Which, Yves pointed out, was not really a thing their village was known for, but rather an eccentricity for them personally. (It was unclear how or when Yves got the introduction to cars, but Yves did have a way of making things seem quite reasonable without providing any actual reasons.) And as for whether Meredith and Lou had ever been involved romantically, Arthur doubted Meredith would spell that out for him. Though she had certainly seemed upset when she'd discovered what Lou and Arthur, in her absence, had done.

"Did you wrong her terribly?" asked Philippa with a small flutter of her lashes. "One of your juvenile mistakes, this Lou?"

"No, actually. Well, not that I know of." Arthur quieted a moment, remembering the day he'd snuck Lou into this bedroom, lain with her in this bed. "But I must have," he admitted. "She just stopped talking to me after that."

"Ah, an unsatisfied conquest," Philippa teased.

"No. Well, I don't know if she was satisfied," he said, feeling forgivably embarrassed for what his teenage self hadn't yet understood about the clitoris, "but she wasn't a conquest. I loved her. I was in love with her."

*You could fall in love with anything,* Lou had said to him. *A light breeze. A good idea. The smell of cookies in the oven.*

*I do love cookies,* Arthur had said.

*See?*

"I guess it just wasn't enough," Arthur finished, and cleared his throat.

"Oh, poor thing." Philippa stroked his cheek with one of her lovely hands. "Is she the one that got away?"

"Oh, I don't know about the one. Lots of people have gotten away." Never because he let them. True, people had the tendency to float in and out of his life, but not for lack of connection. Never because he hadn't cared.

"You say that like you've lived a lifetime pining in the shadows," said Philippa with a slight wrinkle of her nose.

Arthur laughed. "I've never wanted for sex, if that's what you're worried about. I didn't have an awkward adolescence." Unless, dear god—what if *this* was his awkward adolescence? Given the headlines, he was certainly starting to feel like he was aging out of his appeal.

But the loss of his youth was not such a sacrifice, he remembered, picturing Riot again. Her mother's golden hair was probably unlikely, given Arthur's half-Asian genes, but even a Punnett square left room for the implausible. There was always a little magic, as Lou used to say to him. The impossible was never entirely out of reach if you knew where to look.

Arthur placed a hand on Philippa's stomach, stroking a line from her navel with his thumb.

"What are you doing? Stop it." Philippa smacked his hand away lightly, then caught his fingers with hers, bringing them up to her lips. "What are you going to say to this lost love of yours when you find her?"

*Hi Lou, sorry about the sex, can you help me stop dying?*

For a politician he really should be better with words, but then again, he was about to be a displaced one. Arthur was very good, he realized, at being loved for a brief window of time; in the honeymoon space where nobody really had to know him. The reality of him was disappointing, irreconcilable with the person that other people's imaginations routinely built him up to be. It was no wonder Meredith felt she should come along.

"What do you think I should say?" asked Arthur.

Philippa tilted her head, deep in thought. "Pragmatically it might be worth pointing out that you've recently come into a vast sum of money," she said. "It's gauche, but depending how artfully you put it, probably a real conversation starter if you don't want her to slam the door in your face."

"Well," said Arthur reasonably. "Can't argue with that."

# 27

Ryan Behrend hadn't done especially well in law school, but he did know a secret that Meredith Wren never figured out: after a certain level of acceptance, you really don't have to get good grades.

Sure, it mattered up to a point—looking good on paper was a necessity for many reasons, academically speaking. Around sixth grade (or maybe earlier, depending on how early your school begins to gauge the giftedness of its students) you began to be separated out from your classmates on the basis of your potential ($^{TM}$). Strong performance on preliminary evaluations led to placements in honors classes. Meeting or exceeding the benchmarks in honors classes led to placements in APs. High AP scores got you out of university classes and gave you extra points on a transcript. More APs meant higher GPAs, higher than any comparable students in schools without advanced resources or competitive test scores. It helped to be good at the SATs, but what also helped with the SATs was expensive private tutoring. Good scores, good grades led to good universities, which was when things started to *really* shift. The better and more famed the university, the harder the administration worked to prevent you from falling. What could be more embarrassing than a high dropout rate, which for all intents and purposes was like saying the oracle got it wrong? Think what you will about the virtues of merit, but Harvard and Yale do not let their students fail.

It's true, even in the magitech age that has so reshaped the landscape of what is possible, that high-minded dignities remain intact for certain jobs despite the fact that nearly anyone can do them. The law, for example, remains an attractive profession in the United States, even though I've met countless smarter people driving taxis than any I've watched sign off on contracts for an industry standard quarter million a year. The world is oversaturated with lawyers—or rather, with people capable of memorizing law. Though unless you can get into one of the top twenty law schools, don't bother. And true, unless your grades are good, the big law firms won't look your way, and even if they do, you'll likely be laid off in lieu of promotion, because a fresh, hungry law school graduate has the fire (and the motivating student loans) that all those hundred-hour weeks took out of you, and they'll do it for half the cost of your raise.

But once again, all institutional legacies pad their stats, and a law school isn't giving you a C or lower unless you're comatose, maybe even dead. If you've got a pulse, you're managing a decent set of passing grades, and so Ryan Behrend skipped the readings and went to the free cocktail hours; he slept with every woman under forty in his section and didn't miss an episode of his favorite network drama; he gained a respectable tolerance for excessive alcohol and perfected his golf swing in the name of networking; and then he went home to work for his father, not bothering with the effort of being good enough for Three Random Last Names Here.

It sounds relaxing, doesn't it, that life? Hard to believe that for some people, that's reality. Some people really think they've been through the ringer; that because they danced the right dance in the correct order, they deserve what society tells them they've faithfully earned.

Which maybe they have, because I can promise you right now that Ryan Behrend has laughed at a thousand jokes that weren't funny, which I personally could not do if you held me at gunpoint. Still, if it seems like certain talents should be rewarded more generously than others, you'll have to take that up with some other narrative god.

In any case, Ryan Behrend awoke that morning after a cushy eight hours; he looked at his heart-rate-monitoring Tyche watch for the time, and then went back to sleep for another hour. By the time he emerged from his bed, it was close to eleven and he had several messages from John, the elderly lawyer who had worked for the Wren family up until Ryan had casually bumped into Thayer Wren at his usual restaurant, the place Thayer Wren went every Friday night as some kind of personal ritual, after having spent the day at the golf course with his usual crowd of acolytes, which coincidentally included Ryan's father.

But let no one claim Ryan was without drive! A golf joke, but also the truth. He'd had a drink with Thayer Wren, and then another. Over the course of several weeks, Ryan ingratiated himself slowly with Thayer Wren on the hunch that the man might one day be poachable—because Thayer's own pet lawyer was too busy golfing, again with Ryan's father. Ryan was nonthreatening, he was one of the boys, he was ambitious and golden and a symbol of what the titans had all wanted to be when they were young (fuckable), and Ryan understood that Thayer was at a point in his life where his priorities were changing; where his thoughts on his own legacy were cast in a different, more troubling light.

Again, Ryan was not untalented. He was just *also* dealt a favorable hand, which in this case was a natural fluency with the inner lives of rich old men.

"The judge wants to see us in his chambers at two," said John on the phone, sounding tired. No doubt he'd been wandering the house at 4:00 AM, thinking idly of his prostate. "I've already gotten in touch with the Wrens. We'll pass on the judge's decision this evening."

John was reasonably threatened by Ryan. (And do you know *why*, Meredith Wren? Certainly not because of the grade Ryan got in Contracts!) "As I've said," Ryan smoothly pointed out, "I already know the will we drew up last month is sound."

"The personal details will be . . . difficult to deliver," said John. "It's a sensitive matter. I'm sure Thayer thought he'd have more time to explain his decisions to his children."

("It's my money," Thayer had said to Ryan, "and I'll do whatever the fuck I want with it.")

"The Wrens have already received the trusts their mother left for them," Ryan pointed out. Persephone Liang Wren had left her family fortune in equal parts to each of her children. They were plenty wealthy. "It's not as if any of them are being left destitute."

"Still. I have some concerns about the corporate decision as well," John fretted aloud. "The board will still have a say in the matter I'm sure, so it's not as if it's final . . ." He trailed off. "But I have to admit, I'm surprised."

"You're really surprised he'd leave the family business to his daughter?" asked Ryan mildly. "Seems quite a standard inheritance to me."

"Maybe surprised isn't the word. But still, the circumstances, the things he felt the need to change, it's all a bit . . . fishy," said John. "We spoke every year and he never changed much of anything, not since his wife passed. It's just very unexpected, that's all."

Ryan knew that John was going to contest whether the will had been made while Thayer was in sound mind. But there were no medical reports suggesting that Thayer was ailing—he'd died from acute causes, a stroke, not something more prolonged. He wasn't drunk when he made the will, nor was he under any duress. Imagine Ryan Behrend being a source of duress! He would *never*. So really, the existence of the new will wouldn't have been fishy at all if the timing of Thayer Wren's sudden death hadn't been so . . . coincidental.

But it was, of course. A coincidence, that is.

"Well, if that's all," said Ryan cheerily, with all the leisure of someone whose time was billed by the hour, this phone call included. "I'll see you in chambers this afternoon."

"Yes," said John, who was probably sorting his medications or contemplating the lasting effects of his accomplishments or seeing his much younger girlfriend, as so many of Ryan's clients were. Coincidentally, of course. "I suppose I'll see you then."

# 28

Eilidh had not initially been invited on Meredith and Arthur's excursion into the East Bay, which was infuriating. *She* was the one with the apocalypse problem, which, last she checked, concerned everyone. Wasn't she part of the reason Meredith had decided this excursion was even necessary to begin with? Instead, Eilidh had caught Arthur and Meredith bickering about who should drive and then realized that Gillian was there, making it clear this visit hadn't been limited to those who'd known Lou in the past.

"Why does Gillian get to go and not me?" Eilidh demanded.

"In case we need a stranger," said Meredith, who was wearing a pair of sunglasses so enormous that Eilidh wanted to slap them off her face. The thing inside Eilidh's chest barked a warning, like a hiccup. An image of the current flowing from east to west, the blanketing of the San Francisco Bay in vengeful waters becoming a distant but not implausible outcome. A stirring of something primordial, a deep, maternal well of disappointment, threatened to swallow Eilidh's better judgment. Being twenty-six and past her prime was starting to feel incredibly hellish.

"We don't know how Lou is going to react to seeing us," Meredith continued. "And Gillian's very good at this sort of thing."

"Lou doesn't know who *I* am, either!" Eilidh snapped. She herself only sort of remembered Lou, though what she remembered more clearly was Lou's absence. Eilidh and Meredith had never really been close, but there was a time when Meredith was slightly more present in Eilidh's life, and it was when Lou was gone and Meredith was bereft, lacking in sisterly feeling.

Meredith had never had another female friend, or another friend, really. But Eilidh was busy with the Academy by then, beginning to grow her reputation, being watched for sponsorships in a way that made her eyes become starlit and bright. She could instantly date every picture of herself from that time—she looked young and beautiful, and vibrant. And alive. And some of

Meredith's calls had gone unreturned, and so Meredith, never one to suffer indignities, eventually stopped calling. By the time Eilidh had room in her life to share it more equitably with her sister, Meredith no longer picked up the phone.

"Oh, just let her come," said Arthur exhaustedly, as if no one on earth had ever been so tired, as if he had suffered so many days and days and days of this, as if his blood was scattered across the dusty floors, as if he'd traveled here over the span of countless millennia and found it wanting, as if all of mankind weighed upon his immortal soul, as if he could now not dream of drawing breath for anything shy of expiration. "We've got to be back for the lawyers."

"We're not supposed to hear from them until later this afternoon," said Eilidh. "It's an hour away at maximum. How long do you expect this to take?"

"Let me ask you something," said Meredith, with an air of preparation to launch something intolerable at Eilidh. "When you spent the last five years secretly amassing the power to destroy the earth, did you think it could be resolved in a day? Besides, it's a fucking weekday, traffic will be hell on the bridge. Get in."

She held open the back seat, where Gillian was already sitting on the driver's side. Arthur had climbed into the passenger seat, apparently having lost some unspoken game with Meredith as to who in this situation was the alpha. Which of course meant Eilidh was . . . well, very low in priority. Frustrated, she got in.

Eilidh watched Meredith in profile as her sister slid into the car, her jaw set in its usual position of stubborn authority. Her sister, the genius. Her sister, who was smart enough to ruin anyone's life.

Briefly, Eilidh thought of Dzhuliya and the way their conversation the previous day had ended. "I'll do everything I can to take care of things for you and your family this week," Dzhuliya had promised in parting, before adding with a grimace, "though I have to admit, Meredith scares me."

Eilidh felt another grip of loyalty to Dzhuliya, something protective and part obligation. Was this an amicable feeling? she wondered. Then she dismissed it once again.

Eilidh glanced at her sister-in-law Gillian, who was looking out the window. She wondered what Gillian thought of all this; if Gillian was ever bothered by Arthur and Meredith the same way Eilidh was. If Gillian would be on her team when the time came. Feeling Eilidh's eyes on her, Gillian turned and gave her a small smile. "I'm sure it's fine," said Gillian, which didn't seem within Gillian's capacity for knowing. Still, it was effective, probably because it was kind.

Eilidh breathed out. Only a few more hours now and they could put it to bed, and their father to rest. Or Eilidh could, anyway, when Meredith inevitably spat on his name. Eilidh realized she should record that somehow, legally, in case she needed it. To make it clear that Meredith and Thayer had been estranged at best for years, and that Meredith had always been deceitful in her filial piety. She always expected something from him and Eilidh never had, so if Thayer rewarded her for that, was it really so unreasonable?

Somewhere on the Richmond bridge, Eilidh drifted off as the thing inside her chest began to sooth, unfurling in submission to the space of her momentary calm like a dog's tongue from a yawn.

When she woke again, it was because Meredith and Arthur were arguing. The car was in the parking lot of a strip mall that must have recently been turned into a more modernized shopping center. There was an attempt at a glossy contemporary aesthetic, and a fountain, though aside from the Wrenfare storefront and the Demeter grocery store—THIS APP WILL MAKE YOU HAPPY! :), chirped the advertisement in the window—there was nothing noteworthy, no reason to stop.

"This is what it says," said Meredith brusquely, shoving her phone at Arthur. "Did you put it into the GPS correctly?"

"Of course I did—"

"Well, obviously there's been a mistake—"

"That doesn't make it *mine*—"

"Fine, give me back my phone—"

"I'm doing it, give me a second!"

"Brother Intolerable, I said *give it to me*—"

Suddenly Arthur slumped against the seat, unmoving, and Meredith inhaled sharply.

"Arthur? Arthur." Her voice shook a little. "Arthur, you can't be serious."

"Again?" asked Eilidh, her heart faltering in her chest. She leaned forward, reaching to check Arthur's pulse, when he suddenly sighed and slapped her away. "Oh my god, *Arthur*—"

"What?" he said with a shrug. "Got Death to stop yelling."

"I will *kill you*," shrieked Meredith, just as the back door slammed shut.

Meredith twisted around, as did Arthur, in the same moment Eilidh realized that Gillian had somehow commandeered the phone in contention and already gotten out. "What's going on?" asked Eilidh, who was still a bit disoriented from her unintended nap on the drive over.

"She's probably just going to the bathroom," said Arthur.

"The address we have for Lou," huffed Meredith, who was apparently now speaking to Eilidh to avoid acknowledging Arthur, "is this Wrenfare store."

The irony hit Eilidh (who, if you've been dozing off, is one of Wrenfare's titular Wrens) with a low, disbelieving thud.

"Oh, wow," said Eilidh. "That's, like, a very weird joke."

"My feelings exactly." Meredith was clearly very angry with Arthur for pretending to die if she was speaking cordially to Eilidh to avoid him. "I swear, she must have done this just to mess with me."

"It's not like the internet public record knew we were coming," Arthur pointed out.

"So? You remember her yearbook quote," snapped Meredith. "Who knows how long she's been putting this particular gag in motion!"

"What, on the off chance you *happened* to look for her? She's not *that* obsessed with you," Arthur countered.

"It's a *Wrenfare store*," Meredith said hotly. "This is exactly what Lou would find funny!"

"You haven't spoken to her in what, thirteen years? More?" said Arthur. "Maybe you don't know what she finds funny anymore."

"And you do?" groused Meredith.

"No," said Arthur. But it wasn't the beginning of the argument, Eilidh observed. It wasn't even particularly irritable. It was really just . . . sad.

Meredith didn't say anything.

After a few minutes, Gillian emerged from the shopping center. She pulled open the door to the back seat and handed Meredith back her phone. "Here," she said. "The manager wasn't confident about who I was asking for. They said Maria de Léon doesn't work today, but this is the address she has on file."

"They just gave you her home address?" Eilidh asked, watching Meredith frown at the screen.

"For legal reasons it's really best if you don't press me on my methods," Gillian replied, to which Arthur nodded before looking up in thought.

"Wait, manager of what?" asked Arthur. Meredith continued staring hard at the address on the phone in silence.

"That Wrenfare store," said Gillian.

"Which one?" asked Arthur.

"That one." Gillian pointed.

"I don't understand," said Arthur.

"Well, all I know is that a woman named Maria de Léon works at that Wrenfare store, so unless your public record search was for someone else, then this is probably the work address for the woman you're looking for," Gillian said in such earnestly informative tones that Eilidh wondered how she could even be alive. Had Gillian ever received a concept with any sense of its inherent comedy? Not that Eilidh knew Gillian well, but she was so wildly, impossibly indifferent to the absurdities of any given situation that it occasionally seemed like she couldn't be experiencing life in real time.

"But Lou is a genius," said Meredith, scouring the parking lot with a look of unfiltered venom, waiting for the producers to suddenly appear and announce it had all been a prank. "She went to one of the best technomancy programs in the country. She sold her first start-up for almost a billion dollars. *And* she can do magic nobody else can do."

"That's true," said Arthur, nodding vigorously as if someone had asked him to fact-check Meredith's statement.

"So then maybe this isn't her," Gillian suggested, seemingly undimmed.

Meredith made a face that was equal parts repulsion and bemusement, like she had just been told that if she thought about it hard enough, she could set fire to something with her mind.

"Maria is a common name," Gillian pointed out in a secondary attempt to be helpful.

"But . . . a Wrenfare store," said Meredith, with no change in tone.

"Maybe she has a gambling problem," suggested Arthur. "Or she's an alcoholic?"

"Maybe," Meredith said, sounding soothed by the possibility that a genius working retail might be suffering from prodigious personal catastrophe.

"Or maybe it's not her, and the whole thing is just a coincidence," Gillian repeated. "Would you like me to drive? I'm happy to just go to that address and find out," she added. "I don't want us to get back too late. You know, because of the lawyers."

She said that last bit as if it was very important, which Eilidh felt they'd already established wasn't the case. She didn't know what else Gillian would be in a hurry to get back to, though, and didn't comment on it except to add, "I agree, let's just go."

Eilidh wondered if she had a personal opinion on any of this. It did curdle something in her a little bit to hear that Lou, whom both Meredith and Arthur thought so highly of, might be depressingly underemployed at a Wrenfare, but it bothered Eilidh specifically because *she* was depressingly underemployed by Wrenfare, and now—for fun—she got to really understand that her siblings, despite vying for ownership of the very same company, considered that level of employment to be a fate worse than alcoholism. A tragedy, that's what it was to them, and a waste. And the fact that Eilidh knew exactly how they felt about it meant that it was exactly how she saw herself.

So it was a punch to the gut, and Eilidh couldn't decide whether she wanted them to be wrong—for this whole day to be a waste of time because *of course* Lou was someone important, some president or CEO or something who couldn't be found by public record because she had paid for that sort of thing to go away—or for them to be right, so that Eilidh could ask her what went wrong and how to fix it.

*Fix me,* she imagined asking this woman that she did not know, the woman that her genius sister Meredith considered the most magical, intelligent, arcane-knowledge-having person on the planet. *Teach me how to exist.*

*I dunno,* said the imaginary Lou cheerily, *can I offer you a deal on a Wrenfare Creative Suite subscription? Six months free if you sign up now!*

It couldn't be her. The thought gripped Eilidh madly, desperately. The address was wrong. This wasn't it.

"Let's go," said Eilidh.

Wordlessly, Meredith put the car in drive.

# 29

The house was small, with another small apartment building around back, such that they weren't sure which building was intended to represent the address they were given. The house was a stucco Spanish revival, a gray or beige or simply dirty white, though it had a big window out front that was shaded by a mature oak, its front yard mostly sundried dirt with patches here and there of passionless grass. It wasn't ill cared for, exactly, though the houses beside it were overrun with flora, such that vines from the neighbors' yards had crept out onto the sidewalk, rendering it unwalkable. Meredith parked the car and got out, and then Eilidh got out, and then Arthur said I thought Gillian was going to handle this and Gillian said yes I can do that and Meredith said I just wanted to get out of the car Brother Micromanager calm down. But it was clear they all wanted to get closer to the house; to sniff it out and see if it had an air of something. Magic, maybe, or the opposite. Whatever it took to make errant magic behave.

As Gillian took the initiative to walk up to the house, Eilidh lingered by the car and Meredith hung back to take a phone call, beginning to pace along the sidewalk as she answered in clipped tones. Arthur, meanwhile, stood in front of the house and pondered it.

It occurred to Arthur that the place Lou had grown up—an apartment on the outskirts of Mill Valley with two bedrooms, one shared by Lou and her mother and the other by her two grandmothers—had probably not looked dissimilar, though in Arthur's memory it was warmer, homier than this. He remembered the feeling of walking inside, uncertainty mixing with hope that an answer might be waiting for him, left on a gentle simmer on the stove.

In this era of leapfrogged maturity and responsible home ownership, Arthur could see the house before him needed tending to; that it was one of the only affordable places still remaining in the Bay; and that from where

he stood on the street he could see bars on the bedroom windows, a surefire
sign of neighborhood crime. He remembered that Lou's mother had had
her car broken into several times while they were growing up, which always
cost her more money to fix than the value of anything the thieves had taken
from the car's interior. Lou's Lola, who hated Arthur, had still taught him
how to reconfigure the wiring for the new-old detachable radio unit, and
afterward Abuela told him that it was because Lola could secretly no longer
do that kind of magic herself—she was getting too old to hold it on her own,
and he was a good and clever boy who listened well. Then she fed him rice
and beans until he couldn't comfortably sit down.

"Cahhhhhhhh!" exclaimed a small voice.

Arthur was still staring at the house when he realized someone was waiting on the sidewalk for him to pass. A boy, no more than two or three, was
holding hands with his mother, pointing at the vehicles lining the street.
"Oh, I'm sorry," said Arthur vacantly, and stepped aside.

"Lost?" asked the mother.

"Oh, no, not really. Well, no." Arthur looked down at the boy, who wore a
vibrant green T-shirt that read DINOSNORES. He was dark from late summer
heat, bruised around the knees, tufts of sun-lightened copper dappling his
chocolate-cherry hair. "That's some high-quality weaponry," Arthur said,
pointing to the bow and arrow in the boy's hand. The tips of the arrows were
suction cups.

The boy instantly hid behind the mother's knees, peering up at Arthur in
wide-eyed silence.

"They're not really military grade," offered the mother. "More for feats
of strength."

"Makes sense," said Arthur. He took a longer glance at the mother, whom
he had not really been paying attention to until then, noting only that she
seemed near his age; she had shoulder-length black hair and wore an oversized Cal T-shirt. The boy resembled his mother strongly, although his eyes
were a different color, hazel or maybe green where hers were deep and dark.
She wore a faded black baseball cap on her head, a faint look of amusement
playing idly around her mouth.

"Are you anticipating any sort of tournament?" Arthur asked the boy.

The boy said, firmly, "Dahhhhhh."

"I think probably a quest," the mother translated.

Arthur smiled. "For treasure?"

The boy got shy again, leaning against his mother's thigh.

"He's not really ready to talk about his quest preparations," the mother said as the boy buried his face in her denim shorts, looking stressed in the way young children sometimes did. Arthur wondered if Riot would do the same thing someday; become mired in the existential anxiety of her quest preparations. Hopefully not. Hopefully she would be firing arrows because she understood the world didn't wait for you to take the time to draw.

The mother patted the little boy's head. "You're fine," she informed him. "Don't worry. Arthur won't be staying long."

Arthur blinked with surprise, then looked more closely at the mother.

"Oh my god," he said.

"Yeah," I agreed, because yes, it was obviously me. "This is really embarrassing for you."

"Dsdjhbkebrbu?" said Monster, looking up from my shorts.

"This is Mommy's friend from a long time ago," I explained to him.

"Mommy?" asked Arthur before he could stop himself.

I looked up at him, and the moment our eyes met, Arthur couldn't believe he hadn't placed me sooner. To him, I looked exactly the same, as if no time had passed, and at the same time, I was so much older. I'd grown into my cheeks. The shorter hair suited me. So did the lack of aggressive straightening that had been such a sign of the times.

"Am I to assume you're looking for me?" I asked, and for a moment, Arthur couldn't bear to admit that he had wanted something from me— that he had actually thought I might even give it, even though we hadn't spoken in over ten years and I was a mother now and probably married and he didn't know anything about me—didn't know who my husband was and whether he made me laugh; didn't know whether I knew that Arthur had gotten married, too; didn't know that now Arthur had one of those fancy stand mixers on his kitchen counter. Not because it was a symptom of adulthood, but because he had really, genuinely wanted one.

"This is your house?" said Arthur. "What a weird coincidence!"

"Well, Lou's not home," announced Gillian, unfortunately choosing that moment to retreat from my front porch. "Assuming she actually lives here."

"She does," I confirmed, as Gillian blinked, acknowledging my presence and then making adjustments to her tone as only Gillian was capable of doing (a thing I hadn't learned yet, but would soon enough).

"Oh, hello," Gillian said, extending a hand. "I'm Gillian Wren, Arthur's wife."

I glanced briefly at Arthur before taking Gillian's hand. "I won't consider surrogacy for anything less than a million dollars," I said to Arthur, because there are only so many things a married couple wants from an estranged woman that one of them once knew. "No, two million. No, actually, I've reconsidered. You couldn't pay me."

"Mygfiuosjbfjth?" asked Monster, who hasn't been formally introduced yet. (He was ostensibly now "Lou's son" to Arthur.)

"Yes, of course, sweetheart, go play," I said, leaning down to kiss his forehead with such crushing fondness that Arthur felt a pang of something he told himself couldn't possibly be jealousy. Then I straightened and said, "And if this is a weird threesome proposition"—I didn't know yet about Yves and Philippa—"then you should know that the third person is supposed to be a stranger, not someone you fucked once when you were in high school."

Monster, who hadn't run off quite as quickly as I'd hoped he would, looked up at me.

"It's a root vegetable, like beets," I offered in explanation for my language.

"Cahhhhhhhhh," said Monster, and then he began shooting arrows at the house's front window, apparently satisfied with that explanation.

"That's not the first time I've slipped up and dropped an f-bomb," I admitted in an aside to Gillian. "I assume that at some point he'll stop believing me, if he even has a clue what I'm saying now. But he's a little behind verbally, and you wouldn't believe how much he hates beets."

"I've never cared for them either," said Gillian tactfully.

"They're a real faff, but they turn smoothies pink, and for the longest time he wouldn't—well, anyway." I turned to Arthur, scouring his face for a moment. "Well, congratulations. You didn't peak in high school."

"Thank you?" said Arthur.

"Also, your knuckles are doing that thing again. That streetlight just popped," I observed aloud, and then tilted my head. "Ah, I see, that's why you're here. You have a magical problem."

"No," said Arthur loudly. "I was just—"

"Oh wow, Lou," said Meredith, who had hung up the phone by then and joined us. She said it as if I were a public monument of some kind, or the thing she'd been digging around for in her junk drawer. "Did Arthur already tell you about the weird magical problem he's having?"

I gave Arthur a sly, knowing smile before turning my attention to Meredith. "Hello to you, too, Meredith," I said, seeming to Arthur quite impressively unmoved by the suddenness of her presence. "What's it been, twelve years? Thirteen, give or take one or two instances of irreconcilable betrayal?"

"Thirteen, I think," said Meredith.

"Great. Auspicious. Congrats on the app," I added. "I see ads for it all the time on the bus."

"Thank you," said Meredith, a little uncomfortably, and with an air of surprise.

"I hear it doesn't work," I remarked with an obsequious smile.

Meredith's expression stiffened.

"We're having a bit of a problem," Gillian cut in, helpfully redirecting the energy of the conversation. "Arthur seems to be going a bit . . . awry. And Meredith felt sure you were the only person who'd know what to do," she added, selecting the tactic of flattery. Arthur was unsure as of that moment as to its effectiveness, which might have succeeded on another person, and perhaps *might* work on me, although it was difficult to say. "So we thought we'd try to see if we could find you."

I fixed a glance at Meredith. "My phone number is the same."

I said it in a conclusive tone. Meaning, *You could have called me and you didn't, and now you can fuck off because I—and I can't emphasize this enough—don't care.*

Meredith said nothing.

"Oh," said Arthur. "I see."

"I don't know how to fix you anyway," I added flippantly, brushing him off like a harmless fly. "I don't really do that anymore."

"You work at a Wrenfare store instead?" said Meredith. Her voice was edged with something flimsy, airy. Mockery, Arthur thought.

Then I turned to her in a slow and predatory way.

"I know what you're doing," I said to Meredith. "And you know that I know."

Meredith lifted her chin.

"And you still thought I'd help you?" I prompted.

"What are you doing working at a Wrenfare?" snapped Meredith.

Gillian glanced at Arthur, her polite smile marred slightly by a divot of confusion in her brow. It was true that the conversation was escalating, but Arthur wasn't sure how to reroute the momentum, nor did he really know how to telegraph that in a way Gillian could understand. He made a vague gesture, intending to express the conclusion that they should just keep a careful distance from the friction between Meredith and me. Gillian nodded as if thirteen years of conflict had been effortlessly translated and perfectly understood.

"What else should I be doing, hm?" I asked Meredith, crossing my arms over my chest. "Making weapons? Defrauding investors? Franchising my grandma's fried chicken?"

"I didn't do this to you," Meredith said, unconsciously—or so it seemed to Arthur—leaning away, as if to calm an oncoming tiger. "You went to Berkeley. And you were a star, a fucking prodigy, just like you were at Ainsworth when *you* fucked yourself over. I didn't ruin your life, okay? You did this to yourself."

"Excuse me?" I said, dangerously.

There was a bang as my little boy shot an arrow into the house's front window. Arthur jumped, I blinked, and Meredith stood stonily, still braced for a fight. Arthur already knew that I wouldn't give her one. The only way to beat Meredith in the ring is to abandon her to it, and regardless of how much time had passed since the two of us had seen each other, that had never stopped being true.

"Okay, so you came for redemption," I ruled aloud to Meredith before turning to Arthur, "and you came for help. Bummer," I said in a bored voice. "Looks like you're both leaving with nothing."

"Actually," came a voice behind us. "I have something as well."

It was Eilidh, obviously. Arthur had forgotten about her in the midst of all the tension, and had already realized—the moment he failed to know me on sight—that I wasn't going to help him, no matter what he said. The errand was a waste, so now the only thing left to do was see how the rest of the interaction played out.

I regarded Eilidh with a slow sweep of carefully restrained surprise. "I forgot about you."

"Yeah, that happens a lot," Eilidh said with a shrug. Arthur recognized that Eilidh was performing, but I wouldn't have known that. When I had known Eilidh, she was still a tiny blob of nothing in a leotard and a hairline-destroying bun.

"So what's your problem?" I asked, performatively squaring my shoulders. In reality, it was undermining my obstinacy, Arthur realized, not knowing how to fight back against this particular Wren.

And he was right. I can't say now whether I regret it, but at the time, Eilidh was the tipping point. I'm like a lot of people, in the end. I respond positively to curiosity. I can't hear the words "I keep accidentally causing apocalypses" without wanting to ask more questions. Also, I'd realized that Monster had stopped shooting arrows and was watching me at the time.

I don't really know what I want my son to think I am. I didn't then, and I still don't. But it seemed important to me at that particular moment to not be the kind of person who lets one unsavory situation rule the rest of her life.

Raising a boy is really hard, actually. You have to teach him to be a man, the kind of man who doesn't reject things just because they might be humiliating or painful. Regardless of what kind of human you choose to be, you make choices. You own them.

When the world presents you with an apocalypse, you fix it with the tools that you have.

"Your son is very cute," Arthur said after I agreed, grudgingly, to see what I could do—to *consider* helping. Not right then, I added—the following day, when Monster's daycare was no longer dealing with some flooding issues, and he could get back to his routine.

"What's his name?" Arthur asked me.

"Archimedes," I said.

"Is it really?" asked Gillian, incredulous.

"No," I said. Then I walked away, calling Monster into the house, and it became apparent to the rest of them that they had been dismissed, and would now have to return home to speak to some lawyers.

They all turned to the car, Meredith handing the keys to Arthur without comment. He climbed into the driver's seat, Meredith into the passenger seat. She looked out the window the entire drive, and didn't say anything until they reached the Richmond bridge.

# 30

"You could have been nicer," said Arthur. "We did need her help."

Meredith didn't reply. She crossed her legs, jiggling one foot and thinking about the existential itch she'd felt while looking at my house; at the extra weight I now carried around my hips. At the life Meredith had been sure I'd wanted desperately to get away from—wasting my brilliant mind on the same tragedy that had befallen my mother and grandmothers. The curse of domesticity, underemployment to make ends meet.

"How could Lou even have a baby at this age?" Meredith demanded. An absurd question, but she was suddenly furious with me; with the choices I must have made to throw my whole future away. (Meredith's brain, with a shriek: *What happened to Eden?*) "It's demented."

"You're both, like, thirty," said Arthur, pronouncing the word "thirty" as if it were "geriatric" or "dead." "It's really not out of the question."

"But Lou's only thirty-one," said Meredith instantly, wanting to express that I, like her, had not yet crossed the finish line into obscurity, was not yet completely irrelevant. Was still, if you squinted, a prodigy. She rubbed her eye, capable only of the single thought STYE STYE STYE. "How could she have a full-grown toddler? Was she some kind of child bride?"

"That kid was basically just a baby," Eilidh pointed out from the back seat. "He couldn't have been more than two years old."

"So?" said Meredith, turning in the passenger seat to glare at her sister. "Now you're an expert in child development?"

"She's saying it's not exactly a teen pregnancy," Arthur pointed out. "And don't be mad at Eilidh just because she's the one who convinced Lou to help."

Meredith reeled backward, stung. "Wow," she said to Arthur in a snarling, hollow voice.

("I don't understand," Jamie said later that evening, when Meredith met him for a drink at the bar downtown that had an atrocious greenhouse effect, leaving Meredith sweating profusely and ultimately twice as drunk as she'd set out to be. "You're angry because you think Arthur took Eilidh's side? But it sounds like he was just trying to be diplomatic."

"You weren't there," insisted Meredith, who didn't want to express in words that Arthur chastising her unexpectedly when it came to Eilidh was the equivalent of shooting her while her back was turned. Their alliance relied on a pact—an unspoken one—that Meredith was always more right than Eilidh, even when she was mostly wrong. "You didn't hear the way he said it.")

Eventually they made it back to the house, despite some rerouted traffic in downtown Mill Valley. They parked the car and ascended the stairs in silence.

"How was it?" asked Cass, who was in the kitchen making a frittata. The fridge, Meredith realized when she opened it, had been fully stocked. Instead of gratitude, she felt a deep, inexplicable pulse of loathing, mostly toward herself. Arthur wandered away, probably to find his circle of sexual deviants. Eilidh stretched out on the sofa and closed her eyes.

Meredith looked up at Cass, imagining for a moment that they were married. The wedding would probably be a small affair, an elopement. He had been married before and she had a number of other things to do. They'd probably do it in the morning at the Beverly Hills courthouse on a Wednesday and then go for lunch after, maybe get a little bit drunk just for fun. They had the same taste in movies. They both liked to read before bed to unwind. He never suggested she should finish her college degree; he always told her he was proud of her. He did not hold her to invisible metrics that she could neither identify nor parse. Their sex life was routine but not unsatisfying. If she told him the truth about Chirp, he would help her. He would help her. She could accept his help.

He would remember it forever, though. The score. They both would. Maybe it wouldn't come between them—maybe it would make them stronger? But it would always mean she defaulted to his competency. That she couldn't be trusted. That she was a fuckup, actually, and maybe it would never be discussed, maybe it wouldn't even matter, but someday, maybe twenty years from now, maybe a few months, maybe tomorrow, he would look at her and she would know that he was thinking about how he had saved her. She might have been a genius, but he would be a hero. She might be a star, but he was still a man.

"What?" he said.

She leaned over the fridge door and kissed him soundly. She put both hands on his face, then pulled him close until only the butter, the jangling of the glass-jarred condiments stood between them. He shifted, breaking away to come around the door, to press her back into the cold, cold fridge, one hand hovering over the goose bumps on her midriff. She traced the shape of his neck, deepening the kiss, pressing herself against him until the only natural follow-up was sex. She took his hand, led him to her bedroom, and pushed him down on the mattress.

"Thank you for the groceries," she said, and unbuttoned his trousers.

("I see," said Jamie, after Meredith told him how she and Cass had spent the afternoon. "And how did he take it when you told him about the article?")

"You seem like you're trying to prove something to yourself," Cass remarked when they were finished.

"Do I?" asked Meredith, staring at the ceiling.

("I still haven't told him the details," she admitted.

"I see," Jamie said again.)

Cass rolled over to look at her. "I was married before," he said.

"I know."

"I've been here before."

She looked at him.

"The thing is," Cass said, "I like you a lot, Meredith. And I love you. I think life with you is something I could easily do forever."

"Are you breaking up with me?" She wondered if she wanted him to. If that would ease something for her. If she'd finally become safe, impenetrable—successful enough, valid enough. Something that a little casual rejection could no longer destroy.

No, she realized. No, it would still hurt. Everything would always hurt. *You're perfect,* Cass had said to her once, and she knew that what he'd meant was that she fit perfectly into his life, because she was independently wealthy and she was smart and a riveting conversationalist and she would not hurt him because she wasn't really capable of hurting him, because they didn't love each other like that. They loved each other like you loved a really good electric toothbrush. The way you loved the perfect cashmere sweater. Because it kept you warm when you were cold.

But she wanted to be perfect; that was the kind of love that, in her better moments, she thought she might deserve. That maybe love was something she could be good at, that she could conceivably do correctly, that she could earn, that she could win. From the beginning she had understood that success amounted simply to mind over matter—that if she could put aside the pain, she could do anything. She could do anything.

("Why are you here?" asked Jamie.

"Please don't run that article," said Meredith. "Please don't be the one to ruin me. Please, I can survive it. Just let it be anyone else but you."

Jamie looked at her for a long time.

"You almost had me," he said after a moment, and clinked his cocktail glass against hers.

"Yeah," she sighed. "Well, it was worth a try.")

"No, I'm not breaking up with you," said Cass. "Actually, I'm proposing to you."

"Oh," said Meredith. "Really?"

"We'll sign a prenup," he promised her. "You keep your money, I'll keep mine."

"That's not really my concern." Well, not completely. She couldn't honestly say the idea of money hadn't crossed her mind, but there was something both unromantic and yet deeply sexy about him bringing it up right away, as if he was promising to uphold her agency, her personhood. As if to say *what's yours is yours,* which wasn't wholly unwelcome even if it lacked the wholesome shine of *what's ours is ours.*

"I figured not, but I wanted to be up-front." Cass shrugged. "I told you, I've done this before."

"When you proposed before, what was it like?" asked Meredith. She leaned over to run her fingers over his chest, over the tattoo of SPQR, like a Roman gladiator. He said he'd gotten it when he was twenty, in Italy, too busy being romantic about being a battler, about his willingness to fight to the death.

"Well, we were in Paris," said Cass. "I brought fresh bread and a bottle of champagne and I got down on one knee while the lights were twinkling on the Eiffel Tower. And afterward we went to have dinner at this beautiful place. Had the best steak of my life."

"Best sex of your life?" asked Meredith, like shoving her finger in a bruise.

"No, that was a threesome in Bali." Cass smiled vacantly at nothing.

"Stop reliving it." She jammed a nail into his rib cage. "I'm right here."

"I like sex with you. Hence the offer to do it forever." He rolled to face her again. "But you're younger than I am. Hungrier. You still have a little romance left in you."

"No, I don't," said Meredith. "I'm old, really. Very crone-like."

He reached over. Eased a thumb over one bare nipple. "I beg to differ."

("We should really have sex," Meredith told Jamie. "Just to get it out of our systems. Then we can fight, which we're obviously going to do, and you can send the article to your editor in a fit of rage, and I can call up my personal contract killer and have you taken out."

"I already turned in the article," Jamie said.

Meredith rolled her eyes. "You're bluffing."

"I'm not bluffing. I sent it over today. Why else would I have been proofreading it this morning?"

"You don't honestly want to destroy me."

"No, I don't, but this is my job. And I keep waiting for you to tell me the truth, but you won't do it. So yes, I'm publishing the article as a matter of public interest. It's not just about you, Meredith, it's about Tyche. About corporate ethics."

"But it's my name you'll be printing."

He took a long pull from his glass. "Yes."

"But you love me," said Meredith, stung.

Jamie looked her pointedly in the eye.

"So?" he said.)

"Do you really want to be married to me?" Meredith asked Cass. "I have a feeling I'm only going to get worse as I get older."

"Do you really want to be married to *me*?" Cass countered. "There's a nonzero number of women in the world whose answer to life with me was absolutely fuck that."

"Did you not think I deserved Paris?" asked Meredith.

"I'll take you to Paris if you want," said Cass. "Honestly, you deserve Bali."

"I don't actually care," she admitted. "About the ring or the steak."

"You should. The steak was the best part."

"The sex must have been terrible."

"The sex was great. I just happen to really love steak."

"The sex couldn't have been great."

"It was great, I remember it."

"Really?"

Cass paused. "Fine, I don't."

"I told you."

"But the steak," Cass repeated, "was sensational." He picked up her hand and kissed her knuckles, giving her a look that she understood was safer and better than passion because it wouldn't fade. Because it was honest and self-aware, and could be trusted. "And I will love you forever if that's what you want."

"And forget me forever if that's what I ask?"

She wasn't sure why she'd said it.

"Yes." Cass looked at her with a trace of a smile on his mouth. "Which is kind of better in its way, don't you think?"

("I'm not going to let you destroy me," Meredith said to Jamie.

"I keep telling you, I know that," said Jamie. "You're going to save yourself, Meredith, because you can, because you always do. And don't you understand, I really do love you for that? You're a phoenix, you're a fucking . . . I don't know, a fire-breathing dragon. You're Meredith Wren and you will save yourself. And you'll do it in a way I can admire but not respect." He drained his glass. "So I will love you, but not choose you."

"Christ," said Meredith, after a minute or so had passed. "I really, really want to have sex with you."

"I know. I'm pretty sure I've been hard for the last forty-five minutes." Jamie glanced at her with half a tipsy smile on his face. "Meredith Wren," he said.

"James Ammar," she replied. "Are we done now?"

He shrugged. "Unless you do something else I have to investigate."

"So we can meet up for drinks again, after I take someone else's money?"

"Speaking of," he said, "how'd things go with your dad's lawyers?"

Meredith scoffed. "Why do you care?"

"No reason." He gestured to the bartender to close his tab. "I've just heard some things about Wrenfare."

"What kinds of things?"

"Investigative things." He winked at her. By then he was definitely drunk. They both were, not that Meredith cared to interrogate her state of mind at the moment. "Look, take it with a grain of salt," Jamie said, and looked genuinely pitying. "I know how badly you wanted Wrenfare. And you deserve it more than anyone, but he's doing you a favor in the end. Whoever takes over at this point is fucked, full stop. Wrenfare's in a downturn and has been for years—ever since your father replaced Merritt Foster with a re-volving door of Harvard's finest ass-kissers." He waved a hand dismissively. "Face it, Meredith, nobody's steering that ship to safety."

Meredith fiddled with her glass, telling herself the pang in her chest was a normal one, a melancholic heart-pluck of wine rather than pride. "I hadn't heard that."

"You sure?" He gave her a look, which she chose not to respond to.

"So then what's your advice?"

"My advice?" He leaned closer, brushing her hair over one shoulder. "Take Thayer's money and run. Use it to deal with your own legal battles if Tyche makes you take the fall. You're Meredith fucking Wren." He rested his forehead against the side of her head, like a nuzzle between two car-toon lions or the drunk lean of a man who felt guilty, morose. "Meredith," he murmured, "you deserve more than your father will ever give you. He wasn't a good man, he was barely even a smart one, and you don't need his approval in death any more than you did in life. You turned out the way you are in spite of him, not because of him."

"Don't," whispered Meredith in a mortifying, wobbly voice.

"Okay," said Jamie. Then he kissed her forehead, and then he left.)

"So?" said Cass. "What do you think?"

Meredith's watch buzzed with a message from Jamie. She glanced at the screen. **Drinks at 8?**

**K,** she typed back.

"Sorry, Ward again. Yeah, okay," said Meredith. "After the funeral. Maybe next—oh, no, never mind, I've got that thing," she said, skimming her calendar. "The week after?"

"Sure. I'll schedule something at City Hall and get it in your calendar," said Cass.

She smiled gratefully at him. Groceries. Calendar invitations. Assuming she didn't go to prison, life would be so easy. So sweet.

Then there was a knock at her door.

"Ah," said Meredith, blown over by a tide of inexplicable relief. "The law-yers must be here."

# 31

When Eilidh came into the kitchen, Gillian was staring blankly into space. She had one foot curled around her calf, one knee knocked casually to the side, and for the first time, it occurred to Eilidh that Gillian had probably done ballet for some substantial period in her youth. It was always a bit cruel, the realization that some people had simply stopped dancing instead of having dance robbed from them.

The thing living off to the side of Eilidh's rib cage gave a small ruffle of indignation and there was an itch in the center of her palm, the place she might curl around a dagger. Her heart quickened with a rush of something, the primal hunt for something untrackable, adrenaline that could drive her to the ends of the earth. But the feeling was about Gillian, so it was too light to really be mean-spirited.

Then Gillian blinked herself to cognizance. "I feel nothing resembles my ethical failings more than a desiccated brie," she commented aloud, angling over her shoulder for a fleeting glance at Eilidh before turning her attention back to the cheese plate she appeared to be preparing, presumably for the lawyers. Eilidh looked down and realized that yes, Gillian had been excavating cheese from well below the rind, leaving a gluttonous margin of edible scraps that would now likely go uneaten. She was snacking, apparently, on this and stray cuts of a sourdough baguette, which seemed somehow very odd. (Bears snacked, not Gillian.)

"Well, as symbolism goes, you could do worse," said Eilidh, sidling up to her and stealing a grape. Gillian had selected a beautifully curated variety of textures and flavors, the sort of hospitality expertise that Eilidh assumed people didn't naturally accumulate until they were much older, in their forties at least. "I feel like I need to take a class on adulting, or whatever skills you need to do things like this."

"Oh, this isn't skill, Eilidh, it's just money," replied Gillian, just as there was an indication from the security system that someone was climbing the steps up to the front door.

Eilidh and Gillian both watched the little screen show an obviously laborious Dzhuliya, who was dressed that day in the trappings of magitech business casual (jeans and a half-zip performance fleece). The thing in Eilidh's chest rose up on tiptoe at the sight of her, a lovely little relevé of carnal appetites, which Eilidh was forced to both tamp down and obscure when she sensed Gillian wryly observing her expression.

"I didn't realize Dzhuliya would be coming for this," Eilidh remarked, which was true. She'd taken away the understanding that she'd probably see Dzhuliya again shortly, albeit not this soon.

"I asked her to," replied Gillian with a shrug. "I thought we could benefit from having all hands on deck, at least until the funeral."

They continued watching in silence as Dzhuliya paused to catch her breath on the second stairway landing.

"Hm," said Eilidh, unintentionally aloud, and Gillian nodded as if she'd perfectly understood.

"She seems different, doesn't she?" commented Gillian. "Granted, I normally don't speak with her more than once or twice a week—"

"Once or twice *a week*?"

"—and I see her in person far less frequently, but still, there's something off." Gillian began thoughtfully placing slivers of dried apricots beside a miniature tureen of honey. "What do you think it is?"

"I don't know." A partial lie. Not that Eilidh *did* know, but nobody who worked for Wrenfare could be characterized these days as "on." "Maybe stress? I mean, without my dad—" A small, temporarily forgettable lump in her throat. "She doesn't really have a job, does she?"

Gillian made a sound of diplomatic disagreement. "Certainly she could be stressed, but to this degree? It's not as if Wrenfare won't still need administrative assistance. Besides, she's very qualified. Whatever happens, she'll land on her feet." Then she turned to the fridge, withdrawing a selection of cured meats. "I think she's pregnant."

"*What?*" burst out of Eilidh with a suddenness that jarred the thing in her chest. It had curled tightly around her ribs, playing them like a cello.

"It's just a hunch," said Gillian, shrugging as she returned, meat-laden, to her culinary preparations. "It's something about the fullness around her face, and look, she's exhausted." She pointed to Dzhuliya on the screen. "She's gone up about ten steps and she's already fatigued. Which isn't a judgment," Gillian rushed to add, "but isn't she some sort of rock climber?"

"It's a lot of stairs," said Eilidh, though it was true that Dzhuliya was an exceptionally active person. Once again, Eilidh mentally replayed their halted tryst, the firm lines of muscle beneath pliant softness, the familiar lure of Dzhuliya's bare shoulder. Eilidh was intrinsically drawn to athletes—something about their discipline, their tolerance for pain, the way they didn't mind a little (or a lot) of sweat.

"I was always quite good at guessing when my mother was pregnant." Gillian paused again, staring into space for another extended period of time. She didn't say anything for a very long time, and Eilidh was about to ask how many siblings Gillian had or something else along those lines—polite small talk, essentially, though there was something else to the statement, some suggestion that maybe Gillian's childhood had involved the need for unceasing vigilance that was a sad but clarifying insight to Gillian's adulthood—when Gillian suddenly shook herself free of whatever thought had gripped her. "Well, we'll offer Dzhuliya some forbidden soft cheeses and see what she says."

Dzhuliya's anxiety about Wrenfare could certainly be justified by the financial stress of an unborn child, Eilidh reasoned internally. And Gillian was right—a personal crisis would better explain Dzhuliya's odd behavior, her visible tiredness, the sudden purchase of a larger car. Before Eilidh could say anything, though, they were interrupted.

"Maybe your radar is misdirected" came from behind them, and Eilidh glanced over her shoulder to see Arthur there, looking rumpled but fortunately still—for now—alive. "Maybe someone else in the house is giving off pregnancy hormones and you're just trying to find the source," he evasively teased.

"We're women, not werewolves," said Eilidh, as Gillian shook her head with a slightly anxious laugh. She seemed nervous, Eilidh realized, at the appearance of Arthur. Or perhaps not nervous, but a little . . . silly, like a girl with a crush.

"Well, I think we can rule out Meredith," Gillian remarked in the tone that people usually used when speaking of Meredith, which explained the laugh—it was, Eilidh agreed, a very stupid suggestion by Arthur, the possibility that Meredith could do something unplanned or, even more unlikely, make an intentional plan that required the nurturing of something other than herself. "And Philippa certainly isn't, either," added Gillian with a shrug.

"Oh, definitely not," said Eilidh, who hadn't warmed to @LadyPVDM over the last few days of shared habitation. Not that there was anything to actively dislike—Philippa was nice enough, if a bit . . . *much*—but the thirst for attention that Eilidh read into Philippa's social media posts felt noticeably sinister in the context of real life.

Maybe that was Eilidh being too conventional, finding it inappropriate for Philippa to even be present in their father's house at this particular moment—though, fair enough, Eilidh didn't really understand the rules of polyamory—but Eilidh had the sense that if Philippa had any intention to have a baby, it would quickly become content, something dressed up and trotted out to be slowly eaten alive. Consumed, literally. Philippa had an energy of swallowing things up, making them part of her own story, taking ownership of it for her feed. (Why was all of social media about eating?)

Eilidh had the sense that Philippa looked at all of them through one of those virtual reality masks that assessed the usefulness of every situation, clocking every possible weapon or the coordinates of a potential attack, except she was also very unguarded, so it wasn't a matter of privacy or defense. It was more like she sized them all up for some secret thing that might be revealed later, or might not. Sex? Social capital? Maybe some ongoing game she was playing with herself as to their rankings . . . ? Maybe those weren't entirely unrelated things for Lady Philippa, which would probably explain the way Eilidh's voice had sounded at the mention of her name.

She must have been unintentionally derisive—Arthur's look of pleasantry seemed suddenly very forced. "Oh?"

"What do I really know, though?" said Eilidh, a bland attempt to smooth things over.

"It's true," Gillian added quickly, and generically, much in the same way Eilidh had, an apology for not finding Arthur's mistress an ambrosial delight. "We're just over here making up stories anyway. Unless *you're* pregnant," Gillian added playfully to Eilidh, who, when applying the theoretical exercise to herself, temporarily couldn't remember how such a thing even happened. Biologically speaking it all seemed so unlikely, borderline absurd. A penis, in this economy?

Before Arthur could answer, however, his phone rang. "It's the lawyers," he said, and left the room to answer it.

On the security screen, Dzhuliya had nearly reached the front door, so Eilidh decided to simply go and meet her. It felt a little bit cruel, really, just to watch her huffing toward the top.

"I didn't realize you'd be coming today," Eilidh said, pulling the door open as Dzhuliya rounded the last sharp turn up the steps. She realized she'd erred tonally again when Dzhuliya's face faltered, and so quickly adjusted her tone. "Sorry, I meant that more like . . . what a pleasant surprise! So lovely to see you! I didn't think you were coming today!" Eilidh clarified in a horrifying singsong, which was markedly worse.

"Oh, just felt I hadn't had enough torture for the day." Dzhuliya's smile was thin, more of a grimace. She was sweating profusely. Eilidh didn't know much about pregnancy (she would have assumed something much more horrifying was causing the fatigue if not for Gillian) and so didn't know what else to look for. Dzhuliya's skin looked a bit worse, Eilidh thought, unless that was just some sort of internalized misogyny? Or envy? Dzhuliya was extraordinarily pretty and Eilidh knew it, and so did the thing in Eilidh's chest, which was now somewhere approximating arousal, making itself comfortable in the knowledge that Eilidh hadn't been laid in a very long time. Like a hornet's nest, abuzz.

It didn't matter, Eilidh thought. It wasn't relevant. The possibility of pregnancy or . . . hornets.

(Amicable colleagues!)

"Is the lawyer here?" asked Dzhuliya, as Eilidh stepped back to let her into the house's mud room. Dzhuliya was obviously winded, which Eilidh didn't comment on. She merely looked over her shoulder into the kitchen and exchanged a loaded glance with Gillian, who was opening a bottle of wine.

"Well, bad news," said Arthur, jogging down the stairs with a trouserless Meredith in tow. She wore crew socks, a man's shirt, and nothing else, looking tousled in a way that Eilidh considered a personal attack, given her own brief wrestle with amorous craving nary a moment before. "Lawyers aren't coming today. They're still stuck in chambers."

"What?" said Meredith. "For this you dragged me out of bed? Brother Monster." She turned with the intention to storm away, then thought better of it. "Wait, why did they call you?"

"What?" said Arthur.

Meredith looked at Eilidh, which always caught Eilidh off guard even though Eilidh was technically aware that she was (1) a person and (2) not invisible. "Did you get a call?"

Eilidh shook her head no, and Meredith turned back to Arthur. "So why did they call you?"

Arthur shrugged. "Alphabetical order?"

"Penis," said a still-struggling Dzhuliya. (God, thought Eilidh, wasn't that the operative word!)

"Right," Meredith agreed in a surly voice. "It was a rhetorical question, Brother Oblivious. Why are you here?" she asked Dzhuliya, doing the Meredith thing where she changed the subject so abruptly it felt like a guillotine falling.

"I just . . . Gillian mentioned there's some administrative threads we should tie up before Friday?" Dzhuliya was uncharacteristically girlish, wide-eyed, like she was frightened Meredith might yell at her.

"Dzhuliya's helping me with the funeral arrangements," Eilidh cut in quickly, instinctually. Dzhuliya had a perfectly reasonable explanation of her own, but Eilidh felt it more worthwhile to mediate preemptively, as an amicable gesture. "Plus I thought she might be helpful here with the lawyers, since, you know, we're probably going to hear from the Wrenfare board soon."

Meredith rolled her eyes but shrugged in implied acceptance. "Fine."

"We *have* heard from the Wrenfare board," Arthur pointed out. "A lot of them were at that little grief soiree you threw last night. I think they expect the new CEO to come to a shareholders' vote, pending Dad's distribution of his majority."

"The most reasonable outcome is your father passing on his shares to the three of you equally," Gillian agreed, sounding very lawyerly. Eilidh routinely forgot that Gillian had once been a lawyer, except that whenever she remembered, it all made perfect sense. "They'll likely try to sway the three of you to the CEO of their choosing."

"Assuming Daddy Dearest didn't leave all his shares to just *one* person." Meredith was now looking at Eilidh as if Eilidh had threatened Meredith with a knife. "In which case that person could very easily tell the board to fuck off, assuming they had the balls."

"Well, yes," Gillian mildly agreed. "That's an alternative outcome."

Arthur looked at Eilidh; Meredith looked willfully away.

"I don't think there's much point to speculating about it until you know for sure," said Dzhuliya, in an apparent attempt to pacify the situation. Unlikely she could grasp the full extent of the tension or how constant it was, but Eilidh appreciated the effort all the same. It made the thing in her chest give a little flutter, an insect thrum. "Did the lawyers say when they'd get back to you?" Dzhuliya asked Arthur.

"They said they'd call tomorrow," he said, gesturing to the phone in his hand. "Apparently they should have a judgment in the morning and then they'll let us know in person." His phone buzzed again, the screen lighting up as he glanced at it. Half a smile quirked across his face, which Eilidh noticed that Gillian did not miss. She wore another thoughtful look, though it was substantially more focused this time. She was no longer thinking into the ether, but somewhere much closer to earth.

"Oh, you're all here!" exclaimed Yves, who bounded into the kitchen shirtless from the front door. He was chipper and gleaming, a little sweat-slicked. "I have just been running among the trees. Have you seen them?" he asked, presumably of Eilidh, who was closest to the door and whom he was looking at directly.

"The . . . trees?" Eilidh echoed.

"Yes!" said Yves, beaming.

"Any specific trees?" demanded Meredith.

"No, no, I couldn't possibly choose favorites. Oh, thank you!" he said as Gillian held a glass of water out for him, which she had apparently just poured. "Oh, you should try this," he added to Eilidh as he sidled past her, reaching for the glass from Gillian's hand.

"Water?" asked Eilidh, again bemused, as Yves downed the entire glass in one prolonged gulp. She glanced at Arthur, who was busy typing into his phone.

"Ahhhhhhhhhh!" declared Yves, like a toddler or a commercial spokesperson.

"Anyway," Meredith announced, "if that's all, can we circle back on this at a later time?"

"Lawyers aside, there's still the matter of the funeral," Gillian pointed out, handing Yves another glass of water. She looked a little flushed as Yves gave her a slavish look of gratitude.

"Okay," said Meredith doubtfully. "Anything specific?"

"Well, I know Eilidh's the executor, but it's likely there will be a lot to arrange," Gillian said. "It might be more productive to divvy up all the relevant tasks."

Meredith shrugged. "Fine. I can handle it."

"Dzhuliya can help," said Eilidh quickly, spotting an opportunity. The more they kept Dzhuliya involved, the more natural it would feel to reward her with job security regardless of who took over. Which, by the way, was Eilidh's only goal for keeping Dzhuliya around! Certainly no ulterior motives.

Probably. "Right?" Eilidh asked, giving Dzhuliya a plaintive look she hoped read as helpful.

"Oh . . . yes, of course." A funny, slightly wary looked passed from Dzhuliya to Eilidh for a moment, but then Dzhuliya reached tentatively for Gillian's cheese plate. "May I?"

"Of course," Gillian said in an unusually purry voice. "Brie?"

"My goodness, Arthur, you should have woken me!" came the voice of Lady Philippa from the corridor. At the sound, the thing inside Eilidh reached up to somewhere in her jaw—she grit her teeth, attempting to remain well-hinged. She tried to hide the effort for Arthur's sake, though Meredith characteristically made no effort to conceal her own eye roll.

"Gillian," Philippa said, "you truly have a gift, you're a natural hostess." At least Philippa did seem genuine in her praise, although what room would there have been for inauthenticity? It was true, Gillian was blessed by the cheese plate gods. Eilidh had hardly noticed when she'd begun reaching for handfuls of candied pistachios, absentmindedly snacking away.

Dzhuliya's hand brushed hers, ever so lightly, beside the tiny brioche toasts. The thing in Eilidh's chest roared incongruously, as if Dzhuliya had pinned her to the counter. As if Dzhuliya had pressed a cheese knife coolly to the inside of her thigh.

(Amicable! Colleagues!)

"Oh, it's really nothing," said Gillian, looking the way she did when someone else was praising her research. Not that Eilidh had taken much of an interest in Gillian's dissertation, but Thayer had always made a point to bring it up whenever they were all together.

It occurred to Eilidh then that, actually, Thayer had quite liked Gillian. He hadn't at first—he'd assumed Gillian was some fleeting whim of Arthur's and regarded her with suspicion, interpreting her completely ordinary

economic background as something of a gold-digging threat, particularly
when it became clear that she intended to stop working as an attorney—but
even he came to understand that whatever Gillian could insidiously want
from Arthur she either already had or could get on her own. As far as Eilidh
could tell, Gillian was a much-lauded star in her doctoral program, and as
politician's wives went, she was utterly flawless. During the year of Arthur's
unexpected rise in popularity (followed by his million-to-one win), Gillian
Wren was a celebrated figure in American media—none of which remotely
changed her. She did not, it was clear, *need* Arthur, and as soon as Thayer
had understood that, he'd come to see his daughter-in-law for what she was:
a whip-smart, elegant young woman who seemed to genuinely like his son.
"Of course, what specifically she sees in him I haven't the faintest idea,"
Thayer had told Eilidh during one of their lunches.

Eilidh assumed he had been joking. "Everyone loves Arthur," she reminded him, and it was true. Arthur had never been short of girlfriends to
Eilidh's knowledge. That was before Yves, of course, and therefore before
Eilidh knew that Arthur had never been short of boyfriends, either. If anything, knowing what she knew now only exacerbated the point. "Even you,"
Eilidh added to her father, "when you decide to cut him a little slack for not
being like you. Or like Meredith."

"He's lazy," said Thayer dismissively. "He's not hungry. His life was too
comfortable—everyone was too soft with him."

"I'm comfortable," said Eilidh, unsure what line she was treading.

"Yes, but you've got that spark, that drive. You've got focus."

"Lot of good that did me." Eilidh instantly felt guilty about descending to
self-pity, but Thayer only shook his head.

"You were injured. That's not your fault. You and Arthur aren't the
same." He gave her a look as if to say please don't make me explain what you
already know, though in fact Eilidh *didn't* know, and wasn't sure in what
way she was so different from her brother except for knowing that everyone
loved Arthur and only Thayer loved her.

"Of course we aren't the same. I work nine-to-five for my father," Eilidh
said bitterly, thinking of a conversation by the proverbial water cooler that
had stopped completely the moment she entered the room, "whereas Arthur
is the youngest congressman in—"

Again, Thayer flapped a hand in demurral. "That's Gillian's doing," he
said. "She made a man of him. I should be more grateful to her, really." He

had a lost look in his eye then, not unlike the thoughtful look that Eilidh had just seen on Gillian's face.

Eilidh realized the conversation had been about a month ago. Had Thayer decided to include Gillian in their inheritance? Was it possible he'd weighted the shares in Arthur's favor, purely by virtue of the marriage, toward the woman that even Eilidh agreed deserved a reward?

But then she remembered there had been more to the conversation. A hollowness grew out of her gut, a tiny maelstrom of sorrow, or worry.

Worry. *Don't worry about it,* Thayer had said. "Arthur performs for applause. He thrives when he's in the sun, but the moment the crowd stops clapping, he falls apart."

On some level, Eilidh knew that was true. Arthur didn't like to fail; hated to do so publicly. Meredith was the same, except Meredith didn't fail, because Meredith picked the right battles, the smart battles. Meredith was a genius. Arthur was a different kind of genius, something potentially more singular, but less . . . not to borrow a word from her father, but less focused.

Still, the problem with drawing any sort of distinction between herself and her brother seemed obvious to Eilidh. "The crowd isn't clapping for me anymore, either." She glanced down at her hand, the way it guilelessly held a salad fork. She had set it down when she realized she was about to pay thirty dollars for a head of lettuce.

No, not her. *Her father* was paying the check, which was unspeakably worse. No wonder nobody commiserated with her at work unless they had something to gain.

(Except of course for Dzhuliya, who had been in the background of the conversation somewhere; Eilidh could feel her presence in its quietly evergreen way. Arriving with the town car, sending an email on Thayer's behalf, her eyes meeting Eilidh's so naturally over Thayer's shoulder, her name sluicing the blackness of Eilidh's idle phone screen.)

Thayer, unconcerned, had reached across the table and patted Eilidh's hand. "Don't worry," he said. "You're not done yet, my Eilidh."

"Eilidh," said Gillian then, startling Eilidh back to the present. "What about you?"

"Hm?" asked Eilidh.

"Would you like a glass?" Gillian asked with an air of repetition.

Eilidh realized that Meredith was gone. Yves was spreading honey sensually over a piece of bread. Dzhuliya was on her left, nibbling, kitten-like, on a cracker. Gillian was holding a bottle of wine, a corkscrew, a handful of glasses.

"Oh," said Eilidh. "Sure."

"Wonderful," Gillian said, and withdrew an additional glass from the cupboard.

Arthur, Eilidh noticed, had looked up from his messages as Gillian poured. She handed one to Eilidh, then poured the other two, sliding one across to Philippa and offering the final glass to Dzhuliya. "Would you like one?" Gillian asked, with an impressive lack of noticeable agenda.

"Oh, no, I've got to drive soon," Dzhuliya demurred. "I don't want to overstay my welcome."

"Nonsense!" exclaimed Gillian, who was probably too young to be exclaiming things like "nonsense" in situations that weren't utterly contrived. "Are you sure we can't tempt you?"

"No, not tonight—"

"Well, then . . . Yves?" asked Gillian, and proceeded to hand the glass off to an unfailingly delighted Yves while Eilidh took a sip from her own glass, the thing inside her unfurling for warmth like a thirsty lizard's tongue.

It was a grippy, fruity wine, red but still light, a characteristically perfect selection by Gillian although it was probably chosen by Thayer, by virtue of whoever Thayer chose to select his wine. Eilidh felt a pang of sadness, reminded suddenly of being young and taught things by her father, like what to look for in a glass. The color, the opacity, the thing Thayer called legs that Eilidh thought of as drips. She watched the liquid cling to the side of the glass, the slow, treacly evanescence of the wine as she swirled it with one hand. For a second, she was gripped by the knowledge that he was really gone; that all that was left of Thayer Wren was his wine and his work, and his untold promises.

And, Eilidh supposed, her.

She shoved aside the pang of distress, the tasteless sensation of loss. She looked up from a swell of feeling to find that Arthur was gone now, and so was Philippa. Yves and Gillian had moved into the living room, looking up through the shadowed skylight at the canopy of trees.

As always—wasn't it always?—it was Dzhuliya who remained. She was perched uncomfortably on a stool beside Eilidh, looking longingly at nothing, one long leg wound atop the other. There was an unclaimed glass of wine, the one Gillian had poured for Philippa, which looked at first glance to be untouched. But then Eilidh noticed that Philippa had left legs behind, the sheen of at least one sip. There was that for Arthur's laughable pregnancy candidate, Eilidh supposed, which left Gillian's—admittedly the only valid theory of the two.

Eilidh looked at Dzhuliya again. And looked. And looked. For signs? It was true, Dzhuliya was a climber. It showed in the frame of her shoulders, the toned muscle of her back. Dzhuliya, always Dzhuliya, inseverable from Eilidh's memories of Thayer in some idle, nascent way. When Eilidh pushed thoughts of Thayer aside, it was Dzhuliya who remained.

(Buzz, buzz.)

"You're not dating anyone," Eilidh observed aloud to Dzhuliya, who glanced up at her with a jolt, knocked unexpectedly out of her reverie. Eilidh had meant to phrase it as a question, but then again, it wasn't. After all, if Dzhuliya was always there, then so was Eilidh. She would have noticed if there was someone else.

So much for amicable colleagues.

"No," Dzhuliya confirmed. She held Eilidh's eye for a meaningful stretch of time, then looked down. A quizzical, ironic smile played across her lips. "Does it matter?"

Lack of romantic attachment didn't rule out the possibility of pregnancy—Eilidh wasn't a total square. Then again, it was possible this had become a separate line of questioning, deriving evidence for some other hypothesis that was tangential, perhaps even irrelevant to Gillian's.

The constant question of Dzhuliya. But what if it wasn't a question? What if her constancy had been the answer all along?

"One drink probably wouldn't hurt," Eilidh commented. "I won't tell," she teased in a conspiratorial tone, realizing that she hoped for something. For Dzhuliya to say yes, that was clear, although what did it matter to Eilidh whether Dzhuliya misbehaved?

Oh, but it mattered profoundly, Eilidh realized when Dzhuliya met her eye again. Not as to the matter of Gillian's hypothesis; something much more Eilidh-centric instead, swirling inward like a lure. The thing in Eilidh's chest felt wild and devilish, a circling void. What was it about grief, the eroticism of sadness, the desperation not to be, how else to put this, alone?

"You could just stay here for the night," Eilidh said in an undertone, and added before she could stop herself, "With me, if you wanted." It was all suddenly so clear, like fucking crystal. How do you solve a problem like Dzhuliya? You put it to bed.

(The thing in Eilidh's chest was *alive*, baby!)

If Dzhuliya noticed the sudden huskiness to Eilidh's voice, she carefully made no allusion to it. "Oh, I don't think your sister would like that. I'm pretty sure she hates me."

"She does," Eilidh confirmed (the thing in her chest was inattentive to all but its own thirst), "but trust me, it's a compliment. Or, I don't know, normal. Meredith hates everyone."

"I know it's stupid, but I just really need her to like me." Dzhuliya gave Eilidh a grimace. "It's diabolical, I know."

"Believe me, she has that effect on everyone." An incredibly intimate thing, a truth Eilidh had never intended to share, because she didn't want to be honest. She wanted, put frankly, to be naked. The thing in her chest was being very clear about that. But in that particular moment, it felt natural to tell Dzhuliya the truth, and to imply by way of that truth that by *everyone* Eilidh clearly meant *me*.

Dzhuliya seemed ready to acknowledge the choreography of the tension, the patterns of a familiar dance. Her eyes met Eilidh's in a more meaningful way, laden with significance.

Then she looked away. "I didn't realize," Dzhuliya began, and trailed off. She reconsidered, then said, "You made it seem like the first time between us was a mistake."

"Things were more complicated then." False! They were amicable, a word only used for someone with whom you should not have sex.

Dzhuliya gave a little snort of a laugh. "I'd argue they're more compli-cated now."

"Then let's argue," Eilidh suggested, her eyes pointedly drifting. "Make your case and I'll make mine."

"I don't think we should," said Dzhuliya, in a way that sort of, maybe whispered *I want to.*

The thing in Eilidh's chest migrated south, filling her with heat. "Oh?"

"Funerals . . ." Dzhuliya trailed off. "Sex is a biological compulsion when people die. You know, a member of the herd gone, the need to reproduce. For the preservation of the species."

Biology again. It sounded fucking filthy to Eilidh, who was obviously too far gone to think with the thing in her head. She had the sense that if she touched Dzhuliya just then, a thunderstorm of fire would erupt. No, no, she told the demon in her chest, I don't want plagues, I just want a normal, contained amount of friction.

"And anyway, like I said." Dzhuliya looked away, and Eilidh thought no, no, wait. "I should get home, and I definitely shouldn't drink if I'm going to drive—"

Maybe Dzhuliya was right to bring up their sexual history. What had come between them before, why had they stopped? Eilidh had always been attracted to Dzhuliya, that was the source of the problem, who in turn had always seemed to look at her *like that*. Eilidh remembered, vaguely, the first time she'd seen Dzhuliya two years ago; that Eilidh's father had been trying to set her up then with someone named Justin. As if Eilidh could date a Justin—as if she could feel attraction to a Justin—as if she could call out JUSTIN!!!!! erotically, in bed. Dzhuliya had straightened then and caught Eilidh's eye and smiled, and then a few weeks later there they were, in Dzhuliya's dinky little hatchback trying to find some leverage, to make some room for their long legs and the sense of inadequacy that lived eternally in Eilidh—the feeling that if she crossed the line arbitrarily drawn at her father's pretty assistant's zipper, she would be uninvited to Thayer's weekly lunch.

No crowd for Eilidh, no applause. Except her father's.

(Her father, who was gone now. Her father, who, for better or worse, no longer got a say.)

"Dzhuliya," said Eilidh, her voice low enough with want that she knew Yves and Gillian couldn't hear her, though she didn't care if they did. "Have the wine or don't, but I would really, really like you to stay with me. Call it a second chance," she said, knowing that in fairness, she owed Dzhuliya after last time. Honestly, fuck *leverage*—that had always been such a terrible excuse, a real putrescent blow of cowardice. Even Eilidh Wren, eminent prima donna, didn't require king-sized luxury for an orgasm. The clitoris was simply not that complex. "Or hell, call it grief," Eilidh compromised, because yes, sex would be better than sadness. That much she knew for sure.

Dzhuliya had a familiar look on her face. Eilidh remembered it, the same look from sneaking out of the dorms, meeting someone in the practice rooms. The look of *We'll get in trouble* that only made things more delicious in the end.

"Okay," said Dzhuliya, and Eilidh felt exuberance, felt guilt, felt the loss

of her father in a new way, for the first time in a way that felt less like emptiness than like relief. A different kind of vacancy, more exhalation than loss.
Eilidh held out her hand and Dzhuliya looked around for a second but took
it, like a schoolgirl passing a note.

How long had she been holding her breath like this, and when had she
started, and what might shatter if she stopped?

# 32

A few months ago, public opinion polls showed Arthur struggling for the first time against his right-wing opponent. A couple of months later, it became steadily clearer that Arthur's momentum was slowing down, that he was starting to—might very likely—lose. After his campaign team broke down the poll results from August, Gillian had set a cool hand on his arm, wordless (disappointment? pity? regret?), and out of a sudden desperation for escape, Arthur had called Philippa and Yves and asked them to meet him in the Hamptons. Arthur had conveniently been invited to a fundraising gala thrown by the one percent, which was part of the problem. If he didn't go, he snubbed his donors. If he went, he snubbed his base. Election costs were climbing, spiking, his septuagenarian opponent driving PAC contributions left and right, solidifying Arthur's many, many enemies. He wanted to cry on someone's shoulder. He wanted someone to draw him a long bath and lie in it with him. To sink into the depths of his misery beside him, hip to hip.

Yves had been sympathetic, soft with him. Yves stroked Arthur's cheek, kissed the edge of his jaw, spoke sweetly to him. Philippa, meanwhile, seemed agitated, fidgety, irritated with him, with both of them. She sat them down when Arthur was halfway through a bottle of champagne, his cheek slicked to the bare skin of Yves's waist, his lips traveling aimlessly, gratefully. He felt drowsy with relief, with the impending catharsis of quitting, giving up; capitulation like a distant orgasm that might finally revive him, bring him back to life. He could be done with it. He could run away with his lovers, disappear into this bed.

"I'm pregnant," Philippa announced, jarring Arthur from his syrupy contentment, his postcoital haze. She wore the sheets around her body, her hair floating around her shoulders. She looked like Aphrodite rising from the foam, and Arthur loved her. When she said it, bracing herself for something,

Arthur didn't feel fear. He seized her face in his hands and kissed her, and reached out one hand for Yves and kissed him, and felt a moment of blissful certainty, of having found his family, of holding his whole world in the crooks of his arms.

"Yes," said Arthur dizzily, overjoyed, suffering the kind of happiness that felt unearned and undeserved, like maybe in another life he'd had to fight for this; like maybe it had taken countless tries to get it right. Like this was always the answer he'd been waiting for, the words he'd been wanting for so long to hear, as if they could mean *Welcome home* and *At last, I found you* and *I'm finally done searching, it's here, it's always been here.* He remembered the feeling, as if from a dream, of "Yes, yes, yes—"

"Oh Arthur, don't be ridiculous," snapped Philippa now, from the shadowed cavern of his adolescent bedroom. Moments before, over Gillian's finely crafted cheeseboard, Arthur and Philippa had exchanged glances in wordless, telegraphed argument until Arthur had finally led her up the stairs to calmly chat.

Philippa sighed at him with impatience as if he were some little frivolity—a shoe that didn't match, a fraying cuff. "Is there something so terrible about accepting a glass of wine when it is offered? We don't have this silly fixation with alcohol like the rest of you American puritans. One glass is harmless. I barely had a sip!"

Later, when Arthur asked me for my seasoned postpartum opinion, I confirmed that this was, by technical constraints, true. Obstetricians, especially if they are old-school, are generally less strict about wine than they are about caffeine, although I was allowed one precious cup of coffee a day to contend with the lifelong wrestle of my own brain trying to kill me (migraines).

Of course, just because something is true doesn't mean it answers every question. The problem was that after Gillian had been so certain—and Gillian was never wrong—that Philippa couldn't be pregnant, objective perinatal clarification wasn't what Arthur was hoping to hear.

Which was, admittedly, an Arthur problem.

# 33

I suppose you might be wondering at this point how I know all this. It's not complicated: They told me. Everyone wants to tell you their story if you just, you know, ask. And I asked pretty much everyone important in this story, aside from Thayer Wren. Though he did meet with me about a month before his sudden demise.

# 34

Anyway, where were we? Oh yes, Arthur was arguing with Philippa.

"Arthur, be reasonable. I'm not the host for your holy sperm," Philippa continued on, after pointing out that a glass of wine was not such a sin, "and by the way, it's still my body. I'm not just some vessel destined to incubate a future possession of yours. Or do you think you should have a right to control everything I do, ad nauseum?"

"That's not what I'm saying, that's not what I'm saying at all," said Arthur, seeing only flashes of things, colors behind his eyes, mainly red but occasionally white. Had Meredith been there, she might have pointed out by virtue of her A– in university rhetoric that the device Philippa had just employed is called a "straw man logical fallacy," which is when a person distorts the original point (in this case: Why are you drinking wine if you're having a baby, which you are definitely having, correct?) to make it easy to refute. But Meredith wasn't there, and Arthur was finding it difficult to blink, and then there was a little burst of light from his periphery, and he thought *Oh fuck no, not again.*

And then when he woke up, he was on the floor and Philippa was bending over him.

"Oh, Arthur," she sighed when he opened his eyes, speaking before he could fully break the rigor mortis. "Dying just to manipulate a woman is highly frowned upon, just so you know. Very gaslight-y behavior."

Then she straightened, gave him an admonishing look, and sauntered out of the room.

Arthur closed his eyes and opened them. He thought about magic, the way it seemed to be ruining his life, more so with every passing minute. And hadn't it always been an inconvenience? Why, then, had he ever wanted to do it? Why had he even learned?

Because of me, of course. Because I had loved it; because it was taught to me by my grandmothers, who had loved me. Because when I taught it to Meredith and Arthur, he'd felt something like love, too. Like the joy a person could feel making art, or preparing for their loved ones an elaborate, painstaking meal.

"Meredith's scope of interest leans too pragmatic," I once told Arthur, probably fifteen years earlier, in what Arthur had then felt was a disapproving, semi-bored tone. "I want to have a little fun with it."

"I like fun," was what Teenage Arthur told me then, although he would have told me almost anything at the time.

Guiltily, Adult Arthur thought now of the way he could make the lights dance if he wanted, the surge of electricity he could conjure in his fingers— the things he occasionally did just to do them, like loving just because it felt nice to love. He thought of the times he and I used to sit shoulder to shoulder researching obscure spells on the internet, looking up anything that seemed even remotely like it could work.

He thought, as he had been doing almost obsessively lately, of me.

He reached for his phone as soon as motion returned to his fingers, returning to his messages.

Specifically, to mine.

# 35

It had been me who'd texted Arthur earlier that day, when Eilidh had caught him smiling at his phone. I'm not totally sure what had driven me to contact Arthur specifically, since all three of them—and Gillian—had given me their numbers. I guess I couldn't be casual with Meredith; I didn't really know Eilidh; Gillian was a total stranger.

So I had texted Arthur: By the way this is going to cost you

He found it amusing. How much?

Depends on the results

Arthur: If there are no results then I'm not paying

Me: Why are all rich people so cheap?

I thought you were a rich person now, Arthur admitted. I saw the announcement all those years ago about the software you sold to Tyche

I opted not to tell him yet about the details; the things that both were and weren't loss. I'm not NOT a rich person. I own a house. That's something

Arthur: You own that house? As in, you bought that house on purpose?

Me: Wow, the snobbery!

I shot him an eye roll and added, It's close to my mom's job. You missed her today, she was at work

Arthur was overwhelmed with sadness at the image of my kind and pretty mother still bent over a floor, scrubbing the grout with a toothbrush like fucking Cinderella. She's still working?

Me: Of course. She's only in her late fifties Arthur, we don't just drop dead once we become unfuckable

Arthur smiled to himself. How do you know she's unfuckable?

Gross, I said, and meant it.

Arthur: I just hope it's not too hard on her

Me: What, accounting?

Arthur: What??

She's an accountant, I said. Has been since I last saw you

Really??? said Arthur, who despite his progressive, aspirational politics had still managed to forget about the concept of upward social mobility.

Me: She went to night school and got her degree while I was still at Ainsworth. She paid for my books and the first year in the dorms at Berkeley before I moved home and commuted. I lived with her until I sold my first start-up to Tyche. And it's really only thanks to her that I could buy a house at all instead of spending every penny I had on my loans.

Arthur correctly identified that I was telling him this for a reason. You're worried about what I think of you?

This is a good house was all I said in response.

I'm sorry, Arthur said, considering saying many other things but didn't, and I didn't reply.

Then Arthur watched Philippa drink wine, and had a momentary seizure over the possibility that Riot would suffer, or that he wouldn't be able to give Riot every single opportunity she deserved, or that Riot had never even existed. Which was the worst of several dismal options, because it meant so many other things about what Arthur believed to be real.

So, after he died and spontaneously resurrected, he reread the messages I'd sent him. He thought, again, of me.

And then he said, What's your son's name?

Aristotle, I replied.

Arthur: No! Is it really?

Me: Absolutely not you pretentious fuck

Arthur: Who's his father?

Me: Some guy, probably

Arthur: Are you fucking with me?

Who can say? I replied from where I was leaning on my kitchen counter. Monster asked me for some juice and I told him no, no more juice, he'd just brushed his teeth.

Arthur, meanwhile, stayed on the floor for a long time before saying what he wanted to say, which was Can you meet me in the morning?

It's Thursday and I have to work, I pointed out, a fundamental truth that was easily forgotten by the generationally wealthy.

Take the rest of the week off please. I'll pay whatever you think is fair, I promise

I just have a lot of problems, Arthur added. This dying thing is really inconvenient

I personally find Eilidh's apocalypse problem more interesting, I replied, mostly to be curmudgeonly, which unfortunately Arthur intuited, because he's very intuitive that way. Monster asked me again for more juice and I said no again. Then Monster asked me to read him a book, which really meant four books, so I didn't see Arthur's reply until much later, after my son had fallen asleep.

It said don't tell anyone but I wish my dad had liked me

Oh Arthur, I said. Literally everybody knows that.

# 36

You already know that at that particular moment, Jamie and Meredith were meeting for a drink.

"What would stop you from publishing that article?" she asked him. She was fiddling with her glass, trying not to look at Jamie. Blood in the water. She knew he'd smell it, but she didn't have to look him in the eye while she drowned. Or whatever.

"Nothing," he said.

"Seriously, nothing?"

"Seriously, nothing." She flicked a glance at him to watch him take a long sip of his drink. "I mean, I'd love to make you more sympathetic. Anytime you want to tell the truth, just let me know."

"The truth?" echoed Meredith.

Jamie nodded once, stoically. "The truth."

She looked at the liquid in her glass and tried to imagine being someone different. What would a real genius do—one that was not a fraud?

Not this. "It scared me," she confessed. "When I was with you. The person I was willing to be for you. I didn't like what it said about me."

"What did it say about you?" Jamie asked gamely.

She didn't answer. "I was nineteen and barely treading water in everything but biomancy. I was supposed to be brilliant." She slid a carefully manicured nail down the sheen of condensation on her glass. "I couldn't make myself not care."

"Nobody asked you not to care."

"I hated it," she admitted. "Failing."

"Were you failing?"

"I was to me." *And to my father,* she didn't say.

Jamie shrugged. "Everybody hates failing."

"But I wasn't supposed to fail. I was a prodigy." She paused. "You were distracting me."

"Was I?"

No, he wasn't. Only in the sense that he existed, and she always wanted him more than she wanted to jump through hoops for Introductory Bullshit 101. She couldn't fight the sense that her time was being wasted, that her likelihood of singularity was receding—all of which was her fault, not his. She just wasn't *good* at it, not as good as she should have been. Everything was so much harder than she'd expected. And it hurt, perfection hovering eternally out of reach.

Only Jamie had been easy. Only Jamie had felt right.

So she said, "I loved you too much. I was afraid to miss a single moment of you. I picked you over everything, over and over again, and it was stupid. I got a C on a midterm because I wanted to spend the night with you instead of studying. I thought about you," Meredith said through partially chattering teeth, "incessantly. The human brain isn't made for that kind of puppy love, it can't adequately perform."

"Puppy love," Jamie echoed hollowly.

"Yes, puppy love, because if I'd been a grown-up, I would have done things differently. I'm not an idiot, Jamie. I know the choice I made back then was immature and it was childish. I dropped out because I didn't like that things didn't come easily, naturally, like they were supposed to. I left you because I knew eventually you'd leave me, and I just couldn't take the stain of it, I'd already failed so many things." She took a long pull from her glass of wine. "I thought if I cut you off first, then I could suck the poison out."

"That's what you thought I was? Poison?" For the first time, Jamie sounded wounded.

"No, Jamie, but I'm a fucking liar and I lied to myself. And then—" Meredith felt her voice shake. "And then we got older and I was right, it was self-fulfilling, because whenever we fell back into it, you didn't stay. Whenever I woke up in the mornings you were gone. And I said okay, he doesn't love me, I knew he would have a life without me and I can't have one without him and that's embarrassing, it's so stupid and fucked up and I'm supposed to be—"

"A genius," Jamie said in a wry tone of insouciance.

"Someone," Meredith clarified. "Something. There were all these metrics for it, these things I had to do before I ran out of time—"

"Who said you were running out of time?"

"It's the thirty *under thirty*," Meredith scoffed into her glass. "You think it's my fault I couldn't envision life on the other side?"

"So you're blaming society?" Jamie sounded patronizing, unconvinced.

"No. I'm telling you I'm sorry," she said, watching him pause with his glass partway to his lips. "I'm telling you I'm older now, I'm different. I'm telling you that if you ask me to run away with you now, I'll do it. If you ask me to marry you, settle down, disappear into obscurity, shop for groceries with all the other moms in yoga pants and graphic tees, I'll do it for you." Would it really be so bad, eternal boredom, if success only meant underattended tech talks, colleagues who didn't trust her, investors who threw her to the wolves? Success was a myth, a sharp cliff—couldn't she at least be unsatisfied in a way that felt less hollow, more like a life?

THIS MAN WILL MAKE YOU HAPPY IF YOU JUST, LIKE, CHANGE! unfurled like a scroll in Meredith's mind.

"If I could do it all over, I would choose you, Jamie." Meredith exhaled, closing her eyes. "If someone gave me another chance, I'd choose you instead."

She heard Jamie set his glass down on the bar and let her eyes flutter open, waiting. Jamie was quiet for another few minutes, long enough that Meredith finished her drink.

"Nice try," he said eventually, "but that's not the truth I was asking for."

She breathed out a sharp laugh, like someone had punched her.

"Damn," she said. "I really thought that might work."

# 37

"Try it again," suggested Gillian, and so Yves bent his head and kissed her softly on the side of her knee a second time. She repressed the urge to kick him in the face. "No," she said with sigh, "never mind, I must have imagined it."

Yves caressed her calf gently and this time she did kick him away, albeit in the shoulder and not very hard. "I suppose it's probably just hopeless," Gillian said.

The day before, when Gillian and Yves had gone to the grocery store, Yves had confessed a number of things to Gillian in the car under the influence of what was essentially an edible. Gillian had been very, very focused on driving the car through the steep, winding roads of Mill Valley and so had listened sort of absentmindedly to Yves's soliloquy, which did not necessarily rise to the level of diatribe but felt spiritually significant in a similar way.

"The thing is, she didn't realize at first that it couldn't be mine," Yves said, "because I use male birth control."

"Do you?" asked Gillian, impressed.

"So then the whole thing essentially backfired," Yves said cheerfully, "or I think it did, although she is not being very forthcoming about the whole thing, which I suppose is understandable because she is not one to give up the game so easily. More chocolate?"

"No thanks," said Gillian, who was feeling . . . not a lack of clarity, exactly. She felt *exceptionally* clear, which was kind of the problem. Gillian required a certain degree of haze in order to get through all her rituals for the day without the interruption of unruly thoughts, and now she was having all sorts of them. She realized, for example, that Yves had just confessed something quite personal to her, and now she was meant to confess something personal back, which was a condition she would have picked up on under normal circumstances—Gillian had a militaristic awareness of social cues—but in this case, she felt oddly compelled to rise to the challenge in a way she might not otherwise have done.

"Do you love her?" asked Gillian.

"I love love," said Yves. "And Mouse is quite a person."

"I love Arthur," said Gillian.

"Of course you do," said Yves.

"No, I love him," Gillian repeated.

"Yes, Gillian, that is—"

"I *love* him," she half screamed, and then suddenly she was crying, like, actually sobbing, full-on weeping, which was not a thing she ever did. She was crying so hard she stopped the car right there in the street, in the middle of a very steep road, because she couldn't see. It was shocking, actually, the sheer vastness of emotion, which Gillian made an effort not to identify or feel, because Gillian was quietly filled with a horrible, trying ugliness. She'd had so many siblings, so many siblings, all these children relying on her, her mother who needed her to process everything quickly and move on, her mother's latest marriage that seemed to follow the same trajectory each time, everyone needed something from Gillian, everyone, everyone, it was so fucking exhausting all the time being Gillian, or it had been until she met Arthur.

Arthur! Whom she had liked right away but not realized she would love, and when she married him she thought she was safe now, she wouldn't need to worry anymore because Arthur would take care of her and she'd take care of him and it would be pleasant and transactional and she honestly wouldn't mind if he had sex with other people because she didn't really understand what all the fuss was about with sex and he would never force himself on her, god, he wouldn't dream of it, so she had this image of them growing old in a fond, contented way, and she would help him and at the same time be able to focus on her studies, to center her passion on academia itself. She would have no thoughts in her mind about nurturing anything aside from her work, which was what she really loved.

And then, for the love of god, Arthur! He was so noisy, so essentially full of noise, he was always so physical, always in motion, but he knew she liked a certain amount of distance and he never subjected her to anything she did not like. He spoke about the future so beautifully, so poetically that she believed him, oh god, she believed him. She *believed* him! Arthur Wren said the world could be better, that it *should* be better, and Gillian listened with glistening tears in her eyes and wanted to make everything softer for him, softer and sweeter, kinder and better, she loved him! Fucking Christ, but she loved him! She wept and wept until she was sure she'd be sick, she'd throw up over the side of the car, directly out onto the street until it blew into the face of the officer who'd gotten out of his vehicle and stood there knocking on her window, oh fuck.

"Ma'am," said the cop, but Gillian couldn't speak, she was too busy crying. She was a danger to herself and others because it was too late now, Arthur didn't know and she didn't know how to tell him! How do you express to someone that you didn't necessarily love them when you said so at first but now, years later, after you have already made it perfectly acceptable for him to love other people because *you said you didn't need it,* that now you want him to devote himself to you on bended knee? Not even, and that was worse! She didn't need anything from him! She was completely content to love him this way, heartsickly, for the rest of her life and it made her gag, she retched into her palms, the police officer looked alarmed and Yves was negotiating from the passenger side as if over the crimes of a terrorist and Gillian didn't care. She loved her husband so much she was physically *in pain,* how could anything else possibly matter?

Eventually the cop helped her out of the car and drove away, and all the while she was hiccuping with effort, doubled over on the side of the road and struggling not to fall down one of the staircases that led into town, which she couldn't properly see because her eyes were swimming. Oh fuck, the pain of it! And the policeman had called her "ma'am," like she was eighty fucking years old! It was wretched, everything was catastrophe, Gillian Wren was having a mental breakdown and her heart was in shredded slivers in her palms, death by emotional papercut!

"I," she gasped, "love," another gasp, "him," and of course the part of the sentence she couldn't complete was I love him *but I can't touch him,* or I don't really want him to touch me, or maybe it's both, I'm not sure exactly, but it seems kind of a problem, logistically speaking.

"Oh yes, I see," said Yves worriedly. "Shall we do a little practice, then? I could teach you, if you wanted?"

Gillian nodded her head with great difficulty, as by then she had a terrible headache. She had cried more in that one breakdown than she had for several years, and for the rest of the day she was unusually subdued, to the point where it almost seemed like a good idea to let Yves be some sort of substitute for Arthur, the man she loved so fiercely it pained her, who did not really notice her because Philippa was there. And truthfully, Gillian did not dislike Philippa. She envied that Philippa knew what Arthur liked, what Arthur wanted, but Gillian also knew she loved a man who honored her love, or whatever he knew of it, which wasn't very much, which was what made it altogether more painful. Because she wanted him to be happy and if Philippa and Yves made him happy then who was she to judge? OH GOD, THE PAIN!

But now it had been a couple of days and Gillian was acutely aware that she liked Yves, she liked him a great deal, she could see why Arthur would love him, could even see why Arthur would want him, because Yves had sensual hands and was, even for someone not especially won over by the concept of sex, a person who exuded it. Sex, that is. It seemed to come so naturally to him.

For example: "Arthur's particular language of love is most certainly touch," Yves told Gillian now, redwood branches rustling in the dark above the glass skylights. "He likes this; it means something to him."

He stroked the place behind Gillian's ear and she was mortified by how thoroughly she hated it.

"Well, I think it's hopeless," she replied, sitting back on the sofa with a sigh. Arthur was somewhere in the house with Philippa, Meredith had snuck out (not very successfully, considering they'd both seen her go), Eilidh was with Dzhuliya, and while Gillian didn't know me very well yet, she knew I existed somewhere with a toddler in El Cerrito, and felt a profound pang of envy for me that she couldn't yet explain.

"Maybe the problem is not you," Yves advised, taking a seat beside Gillian and affectionately patting the air above her hand. "Maybe the problem is that *I* am not Arthur."

True, there was a glow of something from inside Gillian when she thought of Arthur touching her. Not a long embrace necessarily, but the moments their hands brushed when she fastened his American flag pin, or the way his eyes met hers whenever he heard something funny, a little crinkle of laughter that she supposed was not technically a touch, although it felt like it was. It felt like the sort of sweetness she wanted to dunk the whole world in until it came out better, more lovely, just for him.

None of which seemed worth mentioning aloud. "I thought you'd be spending more time with Philippa," Gillian observed tangentially.

"No, things with Mouse have been fading for some time," said Yves with a shrug. "She and I, we want different things. I expect I will have to tell her soon."

Gillian felt a shock of unkindness. "You brought her here just to break up with her?"

"I didn't bring her here," Yves corrected gently. "I came to be with Arthur. Mouse decided she wanted to come along, and who am I to stop her? Although I do not think she is being truthful with him."

"But what happens to the three of you, then, if there's no you and her? Wait, sorry," Gillian added belatedly, "I'm sure that's very personal, and I'm afraid I don't know much about, you know, ethical non-monogamy—"

"Oh, Gillian, this is hardly a shining example," Yves told her with an ironic look that was almost unendurably handsome. "Arthur may love both of us and we may both love him, but the circumstances for us being together has never been what I would call unimpeachable."

"What?" asked Gillian, feeling shocked.

"Oh darling, it's nothing to be upset about," Yves assured her, misunderstanding completely in a way that made Gillian feel disturbingly fond. "It is only that Mouse hates me passionately but cannot relinquish the person our relationship has made her."

"What?" asked Gillian again, slightly squeakier this time.

"Mouse's family is very poor, Gillian," Yves said solemnly. "Well, not truly poor, not in the sense that she could ever be impoverished in any meaningful way. But in the fashionable scheme of things, you know, she is . . . How to put this? Completely destitute."

"What?"

"And unfortunately Mouse is getting on in years and has very little to show for it," Yves added with a genuine tinge of sadness, as if he hated to say it but couldn't not, as he was under oath. "If I do not marry her then she will be thirty-two years old and unmarried, which is, you know, unacceptable in her circles."

"What?"

"I did think Arthur would do the trick for a while," Yves admitted. "I thought Mouse and I could put aside our difficulties and share in our affection for him for quite a profound stretch of time, which I suppose we did. He is such a lovely person, very lovely—but you already know this." He nodded sagely at Gillian, who was still trying to do very complicated math in her head. "Unfortunately, such a thing is not fair to Arthur. And while it pains me what our separation will mean for him—the lies, the deceit, the sense at various moments that Mouse would like to stab me with the nearest butter knife . . . I simply cannot do it anymore. My heart is, you know, not vacant, but hugely uninspired. It is tired," Yves determined eventually. "The problem is that my heart is very tired and needs to rest."

That part made sense to Gillian, so she did not ask "what" for the fifth time even though she wanted to, retroactively, about several other factors in the conversation. It was such a sadness that she felt she wanted to express something to Yves in a way he would understand, and so she carefully, very carefully, with extreme and meticulous slowness, reached over to brush his hair from his forehead. His eyes shut briefly as if she'd caressed him, and Gillian felt an unsteadying lightness, a slow leak of affection.

He made as if to lean forward and kiss her cheek, then to Gillian's great relief he didn't. He smiled and rose to his feet, wandering elsewhere in the house to be alone with his thoughts, or to use the bathroom.

"I see you two are getting very cozy." Gillian looked up with a start to see Philippa standing in one of the darkened corridors, the one that led away from Arthur's bedroom. Her arms were crossed tightly over her chest. "I suppose you think you're very saintly, don't you? The perfect wife."

I'm ninety-six percent sure I had a psychological breakdown yesterday, Gillian thought about retorting, but knew that tactically it wasn't a very choice maneuver. Gillian had never been very good at these kinds of wars, but she understood at least one thing about Philippa, which was that fear was a very strange motivator, and one rupture—however small—could send the dominoes cascading.

Already, Gillian felt sure that something was coming undone. Secretly, she felt responsible for what was happening to Arthur. She had broken her routine, she had done things differently, and now Arthur was starting to die, things were collapsing all around her. She reached for the grip of fear and it was easy, terribly easy to find. For Gillian, it never really left.

"Would you like a drink, Philippa?" asked Gillian.

Philippa's eyes narrowed. "I can't," she said with an air of weaponry. "I'm pregnant."

"Are you?" Gillian countered coolly.

"Yes," said Philippa. "It's Arthur's."

For a moment, at the possibility of such a thing, that something so precious and transformative could be treated so casually, Gillian felt a stab of pain. Not the same kind of pain that she'd felt over loving Arthur, because that was a deeper ache, something worse and more corrupting; it was a pain she acted on daily, because love was an ailment she couldn't cure. Philippa was trying to use jealousy as a weapon, but Gillian refused to cut herself on any blade she hadn't forged herself. Besides, she knew what pregnancy looked like.

"I've seen this one," said Gillian quietly.

"What?" said Philippa.

"With my mother," Gillian continued, louder. "A few times. A lot of different versions. She loved soap operas. Though I have to say, a baby? With times as they are, politically speaking, you really shouldn't play around with that kind of thing. Reproductive autonomy is very important to Arthur." Gillian felt increasing pain when, after mining the entire contents of her marriage, she still could not be sure if a baby was something Arthur wanted. He had never brought it up to her, as they did not usually engage in reproductive activities, so Gillian didn't know if it was something that mattered to him, which felt worse than any tactical miscalculation. The idea that maybe it did and she'd let him believe something else about his life and the things he was allowed to have in it was suddenly iron-wrought and cold.

"I'm not lying," said Philippa.

"Okay," Gillian generously allowed.

Philippa let out a heavy sigh, then fell sulkily onto the sofa beside Gillian. "It wasn't a lie at first," she said, and then grimaced. "Damn. You really are a good wife."

"And you are a terrible mistress," said Gillian, miming a toast.

"I'll drink to that, if you won't tell Arthur."

Ah, the pain was back. Because how indeed to tell Arthur—how, now, to soften his world as Gillian wanted so badly to do? It was a constancy, the difficulty. It was so . . . unsexy, the tenderness she felt, the raw wound that was her love for a grown man who already understood the nature of life and disappointment. If only personal success would salve it; the longing to set everything right, like tending a garden so it always bloomed, evergreen and everlasting.

"Be careful with Arthur," Gillian said.

"Because he's fragile?" asked Philippa, sounding dryly amused.

No, because he's mine, thought Gillian. Mine to love, mine to care for, mine to lose.

But Gillian had a keen sense for when a situation wasn't about her. So while Philippa shamelessly unburdened herself of a month's worth of lies, Gillian fixed them a companionable pair of drinks, ever the selfless hostess. Gillian had never cared for melodrama, personally; considered herself well above it, choosing instead to regard the woman who had lied to Arthur as a sympathetic figure, even a friend.

"So you see, the problem is and has always been the patriarchy," Philippa concluded with a conspiratorial sigh, to which Gillian offered a nod of reflexive feminism, participating in the call and response of womankind. You go, girlboss! Yaaaaas, queen!

But couldn't Gillian have an agenda, too? She'd been so good for so long. What could it hurt to try a tiny little ultimatum, as a treat?

"Tell him the truth," Gillian delivered to Philippa with a tactical sip, "or I will," and then neither woman spoke again.

The next day, when Gillian woke up in the bed she shared with her husband, she reached out to brush his hair from his forehead. By then, that particular show of physical affection had been adequately rehearsed and a degree of performance anxiety had meaningfully eased, given that it had worked once on Yves and might very well work again now, when it counted, on Arthur. Her fingers were nearly unfurled when she realized, cruelly, that Arthur wasn't there.

She thought for a moment she might have overslept. Then she checked her clock and saw that no, she hadn't, it was six thirty just as it usually was, and it was Arthur who had risen unusually early.

Gillian felt a stab of dizzying confusion, the hurt of a broken routine. The peril of it, the unknown. Who was she when she woke after Arthur, when his toothbrush was wet in the sink before hers? It was like pigs flying. What had Eilidh said about plagues, about apocalypses? Gillian felt one now, overrun by the terror of whatever unplanned calamity was to come.

Which would only get worse when she realized that Philippa was gone.

# THURSDAY.

# 38

Meredith was still asleep when Cass's phone rang with a call from Ward, Meredith's CTO and business partner. Ward and Cass rarely spoke, as Cass made it his business to stay out of Chirp's inner workings, firstly because he was dating Meredith and secondly because he was too high up in Tyche's leadership to be on call for anyone at Chirp, no offense to them. The fact that Ward was calling Cass's personal cell now meant he'd leapfrogged over Cass's staff and junior associates, the ones who ought to have been dealing with whatever a subsidiary CTO might need from Tyche's operations department.

Cass looked over at Meredith's sleeping form, and the way she seemed so small and delicate whenever she was at rest. Sometimes Cass looked at the woman in his bed and could imagine, astral projecting through time and space, the girl that she had once been.

On the phone, Ward was saying, "My friend at *Magitek* told me the piece is set to run in their online edition first thing Monday. Look, Cass, you're a good guy. I just want you to know before all this shit comes down on your head that Meredith lied to all of us about Chirp's development process. And before you go down for any of it, I really think you should talk to her."

How noble of you, thought Cass wryly. Before Meredith Wren, nobody in tech had thought much of Edward Varela. Whatever she alone had seen, she had used to spectacular effect.

"So what do you propose I do, Ward?" asked Cass, wondering if he really needed to hear the answer.

"Cut and run," Ward breathlessly advised. "It's what Meredith would do."

# 39

On a tangentially related note, Arthur received a text early that morning from Philippa.

**Ask your wife why I left.**

# 40

Of course, Arthur didn't get that text because he was with me. Monster had woken me early that morning by kicking me several times in the diaphragm. His motor skills are really something.

Monster got his nickname by the usual means. He was a nightmare child right from go; from inside the womb, even. Did you know that during pregnancy, a woman's body changes so drastically and miraculously, so fast and so dangerously that her eyeballs change shape? A common symptom of pregnancy in the second trimester is chronic nosebleeds. Did you know that? Sure, you know about the nausea and the vomit, and maybe you know about "baby brain," the thing where your body slows production on your brain cells so it can offer those resources devoutly to the baby instead, like some kind of deranged patriarchal tithe. For almost a year of my life I was so incredibly stupid that I had to take pictures of everything I did, just in case I forgot where I was parked and had to sit down and have a little cry about it, which everyone ignored, because contrary to popular media-driven belief, most people don't give a fuck about your pregnancy. When you're just an unfuckable woman wandering around undesirably, it's amazing how many men can see right through you, as if you magically don't exist.

The full extent of my vocabulary never came back, either. I routinely forget the word for . . . the thing, the thing in the kitchen, you know the one. And then, after the sciatica and the expensive year's supply of daily contacts I could no longer wear and the nausea that lasted the entire time (some people *don't* get their energy back in the second trimester, FYI) and the carpal tunnel that formed my fingers into claws each day like a badly transformed velociraptor, then Monster, an incredibly active fetus, tore out of me an incredibly sleepless baby who did everything in his power several times a day to merge his body back with mine. He would only sleep if he was on top of me, wrestling with me every time he woke up like he was trying to shove himself back into the womb. His father—yes, Monster has a father, though obviously I didn't tell Arthur that right away, purely for the giggles—was useless, through no fault of his own. Monster only wanted me.

And for that I love him to the point of insanity, to the point of emergency. To the point of invention. It was for Monster that I started working in magitech again after I swore it was all a waste of time, which it was. Participation in capitalism is its own form of doom—it can only end pointlessly no matter what you do, we all go into the ground. I know this isn't new, because before this there was industrialization and the likelihood we'd all die of asbestos in a factory fire for an overlord we'd never live to set eyes on, and before that we could have all been peaceably going about our lives until some guy showed up in a boat and started shooting off cannons and throwing smallpox our way.

Makes you wonder, doesn't it? What the point is of anything. If I hadn't had Monster, I probably would have just kept working at the Wrenfare store because honestly, why not? I owned my house, with my mom's help I could afford childcare and put food on the table, and hey, at least I had health insurance. There's nothing quite like the question of whether a sickness or injury is bad enough to merit the cost and wait time of the ER, and for so much of my life that was the tipping point I'd always known, existing beside my doom on the lancet of a needle.

Anyway, I figured I had woken Arthur prematurely because of the message I sent around five in the morning instructing him to meet me, a trickle-down effect of toddler-induced sleep deprivation. And I didn't question it when he replied that he'd only need twenty minutes, because how much time do men really need? It turned out, though, that Arthur hadn't slept at all. He'd gone to bed early, alone, though instead of falling asleep he'd just lain there thinking about death, and then eventually someone crept in and Arthur held his breath, thinking for a second it might have been Philippa coming in to finally tell him the truth, or possibly even apologize. But instead it was Gillian, in her usual pajamas and the silk hair wrap that made her look, to him, completely and utterly glamorous, like some kind of 1920s movie starlet who was born to be in the pictures. She'd laughed when he first told her that, a very Gillian laugh where she covered her mouth and seemed to mostly twinkle around her eyes. Arthur felt a pang of something at the thought, loss and affection and the usual intestinal twist of agony. But oh well, what did it matter, things were what they were. And then he couldn't sleep. He picked up his phone and scrolled his social media, the one thing he knew he shouldn't do under circumstances of debilitating malaise.

CRITICISM OVER EAST BAY HOUSING DEBATE INTENSIFIES AS WREN ABSCONDS T . . .

@FRANKIE267 TAGGED YOU IN A POST: WREN PRETENDS HE CAN'T ACCOMPLISH ANYTHING HE PROMISED BECAUSE HIS HANDS ARE TIED BY CONG . . .

So he was awake when he got my text, and he rose quietly, more quietly than usual, hoping not to wake Gillian because if she looked him in the eye—if she asked him even one single question—he would blurt out something inadvisable, and there was really no telling what it would be. I'm leaving you for Philippa and Yves because they love me in a way I understand, because they want a family in a version that my silly little brain can actually imagine? I'm staying right here with you because I still want something from you that I'm not sure you'll ever be willing to give, but selfishly I still want to try? Either way it felt more like levying a threat, which wouldn't help matters for either of them.

Fundamentally, the question that Arthur wanted to ask was what does our future look like? Because by some definition he could see it clear as day, matching pajamas for a lifetime, Gillian with laughter lines around her eyes, him losing the hair at the crown of his head just like his father had done. But there were pieces missing, a fogged-up window through which Arthur couldn't see outside the house. Were there children playing? A dog, three cats? Did they live on a farm or somewhere dotting the San Francisco skyline? When he lost this election—and he was almost certainly going to lose this election—would he still be enough for her? Had he *ever* been enough, or was it always just the promise of what he, Arthur Wren, was born to be? Potential! He wanted to scream it, as if through a hysterical laugh. *Gillian, I know you chose me for my future, is it turning out the way you thought it would? Gillian, was my father right, did you gamble it all on a choker, is this a roadblock or is it the yips—did life deal you a really bad hand when it presented you with me?*

"Jesus, you look terrible," were my first words to Arthur when I met him in the parking lot of Muir Woods, not long after sunrise had broken. The first thing Arthur noticed about me was my worn Berkeley crewneck, the same one I'd been wearing the previous day, and the child on my hip currently resting his head on my shoulder. Arthur felt a sudden wave of envy, followed by recognition of what I'd just said.

"Was I supposed to look pretty for our hike?" he asked me. My expression didn't change, though he'd been hoping to make me laugh.

"Yes," I said in what Arthur considered a guarded tone. Arthur turned his attention to Monster, who was chewing on his thumb. He'd never used a pacifier, simply wouldn't take one. I was the only thing that would ever calm him. Me and my flesh.

"What's his name?" Arthur asked, gesturing to Monster with his chin. As if I might have somehow been confused as to who he was talking about.

"Socrates," I said.

"Stop it," said Arthur.

"Aeneas."

"Stop. What's your name?" Arthur asked Monster, who turned to bury his head deeper into my shoulder.

"The *g* is silent," I said.

Arthur sighed audibly and gestured us forward. "Into the woods, I suppose."

"Into the woods," I agreed, hoisting Monster higher up on my hip. I had intended to leave him with my mother, and I'm still not sure why I brought him on that particular morning. Sometimes I just really like to be with my son, even when it annoys me that he refuses to walk because it means I'll have to carry him, and it's not like he's tiny anymore. I used to carry him everywhere in one of those little baby wraps, partially because it was the only way I could get anything done when he was a newborn. He would cry for multiple hours a day, who knows why, though at the same time I understood completely. I used to strip us both down and walk around naked with him on my chest. The doctors call it skin-to-skin bonding but it shouldn't even have a name, it's that primal. There is something animal about motherhood, about the way that the first thing Monster did when they handed him to me was shit all down my bare tits and I didn't mind. In fairness, my perineum was split completely in half, what was there to mind about a little shit?

I was grumbling a little at Monster, which Arthur noticed because he was thinking about Riot—Schrödinger's baby, who both existed and didn't exist. Riot would enjoy hiking, Arthur thought. Riot would probably love the feeling of being out in nature, exploring the wild deep. This part of Muir Woods probably wouldn't be enough for Riot! There were too many tourists, you couldn't do witchcraft here. Arthur was thinking about how Riot would want something that felt more undiscovered, or maybe she'd want to visit the tide pools at Stinson Beach. Arthur was thinking again about what Gillian said about Philippa not being pregnant, and about the fact that it was feeling increasingly likely that Philippa had lied to him. Had Yves known that already? It wasn't often that Arthur felt like the stupid one among the three of them, but he supposed he was. It had been a while, he suddenly realized, since the last time he even saw Yves and Philippa together outside the context of sex. But if he accepted that what Gillian had said was true, then Riot would go away, back into the ether, and Arthur couldn't do that to her. In his mind he was carrying her, she was sleepy and he was taking her from the car up to her bedroom and she had her arms around his neck, and she was his, and he just couldn't let her go.

# 41

Meredith woke up to find Cass sitting on the edge of the bed. She couldn't see what he was looking at—only that he was curled around himself, probably scrolling on his phone. She sat up and crept toward him, resting her chin on the edge of his shoulder. He turned and kissed her forehead and she thought, to her own massive disappointment, *You don't smell like Jamie.*

From this angle, she could see there was nothing on his phone screen. He hadn't been scrolling. He'd just been staring into space.

"You've been neglecting Ward," Cass said. Meredith rolled her eyes. She'd ignored several of Ward's calls the previous evening, mostly because she no longer knew what to say to a man who couldn't keep his house in order.

"My father died. Ward isn't a priority right now."

"Meredith." Cass turned to face her, cool air splitting them as he shifted to look her in the eye. "Ward is going to turn on you."

Right. Well. She certainly hadn't chosen Ward for his impressive feats of loyalty. "I see."

Cass looked like he was contemplating what to say next. He seemed to have been thinking about it for a long time.

"Kip knows the difference between what he bought and what he brought to market," he eventually said. "The possibility that the ax might fall on Birdsong was always a consideration."

There it is again, thought Meredith, reminded of the partially filled Tyche auditorium. I'm not a genius. I'm just a face. (THIS APP WILL MAKE YOU HAPPY AS LONG AS HAPPINESS MEANS 50% OFF ORGANIC PEANUT BUTTER AND BOGO CONFLICT-FREE LEMONADE! :) )

"But I don't think he realized the extent of the data you and Ward covered up," Cass continued, running a hand over the stubble on his cheeks. "Now that Ward's on the record blaming you, once the article goes to print, I think

Tyche's neatest course of action will be to remove you as Birdsong's CEO, or—" He grimaced. "*Incentivize* you to step down."

"I didn't," Meredith began, and stopped. She didn't know why. She'd had every intention to keep going, to say that nothing had been covered up, to insist that this was ridiculous and that everything involved with Chirp was sound. Instead she said nothing.

"Yeah," Cass said in apparent agreement. "Save it for Kip, or for whoever is putting out the article in *Magitek*. Is it the journalist you were talking to on Monday? Your ex?"

"Yes." It stung a little more now, knowing that Jamie was done with her, that the article was going to print, that there was nothing more she could do. Well, not true, her career wasn't necessarily dead yet. There was a long, arduous distance from an accusatory article going public and whatever burden of proof it might require for Tyche to point the finger at her alone. She could sue Jamie for libel; that would tie him up financially for long enough that nothing dire would happen to Chirp. It wasn't ideal that Ward was turning on her, but she'd seen that coming a mile away. He'd been waffling on the whole thing for the last five years, and why shouldn't he put some distance between his reputation and hers? She'd have done it if she had the choice, but even if she'd blamed him first, people would find some way to make it her fault regardless. She was the woman in charge. She should have known better. The woman always knows.

She felt a small deflation in her certainty then. *Kip knows the difference between what he bought and what he brought to market.* What Cass meant was the same thing Thayer had once told her. *Kip knew that if you could be bought, you could easily be sold.*

Blood in the water. She couldn't even blame them, any of them. She knew what it was to be a shark.

"Well, get a lawyer," Cass said reasonably. "Your ex did right by you that way, he gave you enough warning to assemble a defense. You've got someone in PR on staff, right? They can put together a statement for you. Tyche will release one as well, but as far as I know they aren't aware what's in the article yet, so you can make sure yours is ready first."

"A lot of talk about me and mine when you were all about we and ours yesterday," Meredith observed dully, even though that hadn't even been true.

Cass shook his head. "I think it's better if I use my eyes and ears at Tyche to help your defense," he said. "I think that's far more valuable to you right now. You'll need someone advocating for you, trust me."

"Why?"

"Why?" Cass sounded surprised that she'd ask, though she supposed he had a right to be. "Come on, Meredith. You know why."

Because Kip would let her drown. Because Ward would hold her head underwater himself just to make sure she drowned alone. There were a couple of women on the Tyche board, two or three in the company's leadership, but they didn't like Meredith, never had, and the men found her abrasive for the mere fact of her existence—her success, which somehow took inherently from theirs.

Her father's voice came back to her again, unhelpfully. *You have to learn to play the game, Meredith.* It was never enough to be smarter or better, to run farther or faster. In the end there would always be an easy victim, and in order to not become one, you had to fight alone.

"Your father's death buys you some time," Cass pointed out. "Nobody will blame you if you don't mobilize right away. But Thayer Wren wasn't universally beloved, especially near the end, and a lot of people will be plenty happy to see the billionaire's daughter take the fall."

Meredith thought about what Jamie had said about Wrenfare, about whoever wound up with the reins ending up with the blame for bad investments. Even Meredith could admit Wrenfare's profits had publicly flagged over the last five years, maybe longer, though a good portion of the attention she'd paid her father's company had been jealousy, hate-watching the performance of the thing she had wanted for herself. Oh god, and she had wanted Wrenfare! With Thayer no longer alive she could finally admit that to herself, that Wrenfare had always been the finish line. To inherit the house her father had built with his bare hands while he was still invincible to her—his *real* house, where his true artistry lived—had always been the dream.

When their father's legacy crumbled in Eilidh's hands, under the leadership of Meredith's little sister, whom everyone liked because they had no reason to hate her, how would Meredith feel then? It would all be Eilidh's fault, Eilidh's doing.

Suddenly, Meredith felt a surety that she could not, *would* not, go down without a fight.

"*Magitek* is a niche industry magazine with limited subscribers," Meredith reminded herself. "Nobody pays attention to it, at least not in any significant way." Even if the article went viral, so few people would know what to make of the accusations therein that the damage would fade, like all trends faded. Cass nodded, so Meredith knew her reasoning was sound. It would be bad for a few weeks, fine, but then everyone would move on. It wasn't the same as an investigation by the *Times* or the *Post*. "I'll get a lawyer," she said. "And I'll hire a third-party PR manager. Not someone who represents Birdsong or Chirp."

"Good idea," Cass said.

"And at Dad's funeral . . . I should look devastated, right? A total wreck."

"Might be meme fodder," said Cass blandly.

True. Meredith shuddered to think what they might do with her face if they could control it. If she looked vulnerable, if she looked sad, how would people puppet her, how might they put words in her mouth? "Private, then. Really private. We'll get someone to be an insider source or something, some anonymous voice." Probably Ryan, that lawyering son of a bitch. He'd take the payday in a second.

She turned to Cass then, realizing something. "Are you going to leave me?"

Cass looked blankly at her.

"I'm a stain on your reputation," she said. "At least until all of this goes away."

Cass said nothing.

"You haven't even asked me why," Meredith realized with a bitter laugh.

"I don't have to." His voice was characteristically calm, the way it always was. "Everyone fakes it until they make it. Your data was always too perfect, it skewed impossible right from the start, but what you created is profitable. It made us a lot of money. We recouped our investment the moment you said yes to the partnership with Demeter." *Corporate sleaze,* said Jamie in her head. *Jesus, Meredith, you sold out, it's all over you.* "Mer, by any corporate measure you've already succeeded. The job is high risk, and there are always losses. All things considered, yours isn't that bad. Assuming you don't go to prison for fraud."

"Ha," said Meredith, dully.

"You won't," Cass assured her. "A good lawyer will make a good deal. You get what you pay for when it comes to defense attorneys, but you've got the money, especially now. Tyche will make sure the article gets enough holes poked in it that nobody takes it seriously, you'll do what you can, then eventually this will all go away and you'll rebrand and move on to your next idea. That's what geniuses in this industry do. It's what Kip did, it's what Thayer did, and it's what you'll do." He sounded emphatic, devoutly capitalist, like reciting a childhood prayer by heart.

"Cass," said Meredith, "I invented a way for Tyche to make more money off people who just wanted to be happy. I not only said yes, I manipulated the data to make sure it would happen."

"You invented a product that sold for a lot of money because everyone could see the value in its success," Cass corrected, or maybe paraphrased. "I don't need to ask why you said yes, Mer, because I make my living in this industry too. Philanthropy for the sake of philanthropy doesn't pay the bills. It's about compromise—getting to do a little more of what you want each time you play the game correctly. You think corporate operations is what I dreamed about doing as a little boy?"

Meredith hadn't the faintest clue what Cass dreamed about. She had never considered the possibility that once upon a time, he had been innocent or young. "You still want to marry me? I'm telling you explicitly that I'm a criminal."

"Mer, listen to me when I tell you this," said Cass. "I already knew you were lying about something. Whether or not that's a crime depends on you."

Meredith wanted to laugh or something, maybe throw up.

"I'm going to spend my life with a man who loves me because I'm a bad person," she informed the air. "And Dad, you said it couldn't be done!"

"Look, maybe you need a minute to yourself." Cass rose to his feet, wiping his hands on the tops of his thighs like there was grime on them, probably her corporate sleaze. "And by the way, I don't love you because you're a bad person. I love you, and you're a person. If I were in your position I'd have done the same thing. It's not easy, and not everybody gets it. You climb every step of this tower and then you lock yourself inside—because this is it, Meredith. This is the top, and there's no other way to make it. It might be lonely once you get here, but nobody chooses it for the company. They choose it for the view."

He leaned forward and gripped the back of her head with one strong hand, pulling her forward to press his lips to her hair. "Meredith Wren, you're a fucking genius," he said. "You don't have to be anything else."

Like a good person or a fair person or a person that Jamie Ammar could possibly love.

She nodded and didn't say anything. Cass grabbed a pair of navy joggers, some socks, and she watched him until something occurred to her.

"Do you know what Wrenfare was working on?" she asked, and Cass looked up with a blankness, bemusement. "The talk of lawsuits, the bad investment rumors," she explained, and he nodded with delayed recognition. "I never wanted to look into the details of my father's work before, but . . ."

She trailed off, and the look Cass gave her was more pitying than she expected.

"As far as anyone at Tyche can say, a lot of what seemed to be killing Wrenfare was the culture—I can't comment on that, I wouldn't know how true those rumors were. But on the product side there were just too many big ideas, a lack of corporate focus. Expensive stuff, you know, space race, deep sea shit, VR. And there was also—" He stopped.

"What?"

Cass shook himself. "A neuromantic chip," he said. "That was one of the things they were rumored to be working on."

Meredith blinked. "What?"

"A chip," Cass repeated. "Something to help with neurological disorders, schizophrenia, that kind of thing. About a month ago your dad was in talks to buy a start-up that was in direct competition with—"

"Chirp," Meredith supplied, mainly so Cass didn't have to.

*Your product,* Thayer said in her head, *is unsound.*

*Your idea won't work,* a seventeen-year-old version of me reminded Meredith in her head. *If you really want it to work it's gotta be from—I don't know, fucking* inside *the brain or some shit, not subcutaneous. That shit won't stick.*

Cass looked at her with pity, like he was throwing dirt on her open grave.

"Mer," he said. "I'm sorry."

"Don't be." She forced brightness into her voice. "Do you know the name of the start-up?"

Cass shook his head. "Some Berkeley technomancy grads were shopping the concept around for funding. It crossed Kip's desk because they'd sold to Tyche in the past." Something tore inside Meredith's chest; a small thing, like an artery. "It's proprietary, so we weren't able to vet much. A generic name, probably a shell corporation."

"Ah. Did the sale go through?"

"I don't think it was finalized or we'd have heard about it, so either Thayer passed or it's still on the table."

"So then it's Eilidh's problem now," Meredith murmured to herself, wondering what her sister would do with the opportunity to compete with her—or destroy her. What *she* would do to Eilidh if the tables were turned.

Cass shrugged again, pulling on his sweatpants. "Maybe. Maybe not." When he was dressed, he put a hand on the doorknob and then stopped, turning over his shoulder to face her. "You okay?"

"Yeah, yeah. Just gonna call a lawyer, get stuff together."

Cass nodded. "Okay. I love you."

"Love you." Meredith waited until he was gone, then she looked down at her phone screen. She selected my contact file and typed in a message.

**You fucking bitch,** she said. She thought about my yearbook quote, the fact that it was Dumas, from our favorite revenge story. **How long did you plan this?**

But like I said, I was in the woods, so I couldn't respond.

# 42

Eilidh awoke to Dzhuliya trying to sneak out, but Eilidh knew every creak of every beam in the turret and Dzhuliya didn't, so achieving the necessary degree of stealth was always going to be unlikely. Eilidh opened her eyes as Dzhuliya struggled to put one leg in her jeans, nearly toppling over as she attempted the other. She wrestled with the button, giving the air a pained look before she finally managed to fasten them. Then Dzhuliya exhaled and stared down at her stomach, looking at it with a slight foreignness, as if she'd never seen her own navel before.

"Good morning," Eilidh remarked with amusement, watching Dzhuliya wince at her own surprise. "Love 'em and leave 'em, huh?"

"I have to . . . follow up on the arrangements we discussed," Dzhuliya said, clearing her throat and fiddling with her hair, which had been hastily scraped back into a ponytail. "Funeral things."

Eilidh felt the sinking reminder of her father's loss, followed by the floating recollection that he wouldn't waltz into the room that moment; that she would never have to see whatever expression might cross his face after she told him what she'd spent the night doing with his assistant. Former assistant. Whatever.

"What's on the docket for today?" Eilidh asked, sitting upright. She realized only belatedly that she'd thrown on a white pointelle sleep set without a bra, looking like a small French child apart from the near-transparent material. Her nipples were paying rapt attention to the conversation at hand and she nearly covered them up until Dzhuliya's eyes drifted longingly down.

Which was, in a word, interesting. (The thing in Eilidh's chest bloodthirstily agreed.)

"We're not going to tell anyone about this," offered Dzhuliya tangentially, "are we?"

"You mean you don't want to have breakfast with my entire family?" Eilidh replied. "Right now, this instant?"

Dzhuliya gave a long sigh, adjusting her jeans. There was the barest, slightest curve to her belly, which Eilidh had run her fingers down and slid her tongue over several times the previous night. If this was the gestational body, then from an outsider's perspective, it was highly underrated. Dzhuliya's breasts were full and sensitive, tender to the (frequent) touch. Eilidh had chosen not to ask questions, largely out of the hope that Dzhuliya would not ask any herself.

"I thought I'd take care of the ashes this morning. Save you a trip," Dzhuliya said. "Although I'm not entirely sure what urn your father would have wanted."

"Probably one of those red cups," said Eilidh. "Or a genie lamp."

"His coffee thermos," suggested Dzhuliya. "Or the cup he used to use that kept the coffee warm all day. You know, instead of just drinking it."

"Oh yeah, my other sibling," Eilidh said, and Dzhuliya laughed. A husky, morning-after laugh, like lovers did—an unsolicited thought. Eilidh managed a playful, "Maybe one of those little vodka bottles you get on planes?"

"Probably more than one of them, I'm guessing?"

"Yeah, like a treasure chest of those."

Dzhuliya came around the bed, idly tracing the material of Eilidh's quilt with the tip of her finger. "I can't tell if this conversation is wildly inappropriate or just . . . some kind of coping mechanism."

"Both," said Eilidh.

Dzhuliya was quiet for a moment, perching delicately on the edge of the bed and staring down at the quilt before locking eyes with Eilidh. "I'm sorry," she said.

"For what? Not last night, I hope. Because I'm definitely not sorry." Eilidh reached out to run a finger over a light bruise on Dzhuliya's neck. "Even though I maybe should be."

Dzhuliya leaned into Eilidh's touch for a moment. "I meant . . . your father, I guess. I don't know. Everything." She exhaled. "I'm not sure last night would have happened if you weren't . . . you know. Vulnerable." She gave a sidelong search of Eilidh's face. "I can't help feeling like I should have turned you down."

"I'm grieving," replied Eilidh with a shrug, not wanting to engage with what it might mean if Dzhuliya was right. If last week's Eilidh would have clung to the lie of amicable colleagues forever, then had her father always been the only thing in the way? Were Eilidh's current feelings the mirage or was it the person she'd tried so hard for so long to be? The thing in her chest flicked an admonishment, like the tongue of a deadly asp. "There are basically no rules right now."

"*I'd* have done it a long time ago, you know, without the grief excuse. For the record." Dzhuliya looked squarely at her then. "I didn't think you were interested, given how things went last time."

The abbreviated tryst in the car, she meant. And all the months of circling each other since then. "It's not that I didn't want to. It's just . . . this isn't a priority for me," Eilidh said with a wave of her hand to gesture at the boudoir and its realm of recreation—something that felt both true and easy to explain, or maybe the easiest version of a heavier truth. "And I've been pretty stuck the last couple of years. Longer than that, really." The thing in Eilidh's chest seemed to take profound offense. "I just don't think I had the bandwidth for whatever this was. Is. Could be." Eilidh grimaced at the uncertainty in her voice, the way she didn't seem to be answering the question, if there had even been one. "Is it okay if I don't choose my verbs wisely just yet?"

Dzhuliya looked as if she might say something, but then changed her mind. "It's fantastic, actually." She leaned away, straightening her shoulders with a renewed sense of purpose. "But I really should get going." She stood, seeming winded just from the effort of rising.

"Do you want me to come?" asked Eilidh. The question surprised her, having manifested from nowhere. If someone else had asked her if she wanted to pick out her father's urn today, at this very moment, she'd have said absolutely not, thank you very much. "It feels like, I don't know, maybe a cathartic exercise. Plus, I'm executor, right? And I'm kind of going crazy just waiting around for the lawyers to tell me what to execute."

"Are you sure? I thought it might be . . . difficult for you," Dzhuliya said. "Emotionally."

Eilidh shrugged. "You'll dry my tears, won't you?" she joked.

Dzhuliya hesitated, wrestling for a moment with her response, and Eilidh wondered if she was doing it again. Being the boss's daughter, crossing the line that should have stayed firmly in place. She was perpetually looking down from her vantage point of untouchable safety, making her out-of-touch, amicable jokes.

"I thought we weren't specifying verb tenses?" Dzhuliya said. "Emotional labor seems pretty grammatically defined, relationship-wise."

"I didn't mean . . ." Eilidh trailed off. "You're right, I'm sorry."

"Although you're not wrong about taking someone with me. Meredith and Arthur might want to weigh in, too," Dzhuliya seemed to realize aloud.

"No." Eilidh shook her head. "I doubt it. They never really understood him." She meant to say that her siblings hadn't understood their father's decorative taste, but that phrasing worked just as well.

Dzhuliya must have heard something different, something else. "Maybe you *should* come, then." Dzhuliya was looking at her watchfully, overlong. "For practical reasons."

"Makes sense. I can dry my own tears," Eilidh agreed.

"No." Dzhuliya's intensity then surprised her. "No, I'll do it for you, if you want."

Eilidh had an odd sensation of lightness that she realized was the absence of heaviness. The thing that usually sat somewhere around her clavicle and had, up until that moment, been lazing around her shoulders like a shawl seemed to have temporarily lifted, the usual tension evaporating from her skin like midsummer rain. Not gone, but with a satiated presence somehow, as if it had eaten a filling meal and drifted off.

There was a buzz from the floor, where Dzhuliya had set her purse. "Oh, sorry, hang on." Dzhuliya dug around for her phone, a pained expression crossing her face as she answered. "Hello?"

An explosive feminine voice began to rant from the other end of the call. "Oh, um. De Léon, you said? Yes, I think . . . I think so, maybe." Dzhuliya was silent as the other voice picked up, growing more and more agitated as they spoke. "I can check his calendar if you want, but he did have a few meetings with someone who meets that description. I'm not sure what they discussed." More intensity. "Right, I'll check on it for you." *Blahblahblah!!!!* From the other end. "Okay. Okay, bye."

Dzhuliya hung up and gave Eilidh a vacant look. "Your sister is really quite the charmer."

"Oh," said Eilidh, shuddering. "Oh, god."

"Yeah." Dzhuliya rolled her eyes. "It seemed unwise at the moment to add fuel to whatever that was."

"Did you say de Léon?" Eilidh asked, recognizing my surname. "That's my sister's ex–best friend."

"I know," said Dzhuliya. "Your dad met with her three times over the summer. He was interested in something she was developing. As far as I know, negotiations were tentatively moving forward until, you know. This." She waved an unsteady hand at the sharedness of their circumstance. "But he had Legal draw up an offer, which is currently in his inbox awaiting approval. If he intended to pull the trigger, he would have done it this week."

The answer was so coolly informed that Eilidh was a little taken aback. "Really? But you just made it sound like—"

"I told you, I didn't think it was in anyone's best interest to make Meredith angrier. Nothing I just told you is public knowledge, and if she wants to ask her friend about it, she can." Dzhuliya's tone and expression appeared intimately informed, the air of someone—like many of the people Eilidh worked with at Wrenfare—with a shrewd awareness of the industry.

Eilidh felt another pang of fundamental wrongness, though she couldn't say why. She had always known Dzhuliya was part of Wrenfare's ecosystem in a way Eilidh wasn't; the entire purpose of Eilidh's amicable shield had always been that Dzhuliya was a Them and not an Us. (Which of course begged the question of what remained of "us" without Thayer, the answer being something Eilidh couldn't bear.)

There was also, again, Eilidh's inability to imagine Dzhuliya separate from Thayer in the context of his life, while being equally unable to imagine herself *with* Dzhuliya without the necessity of his death. The three of them triangulated inexplicably in Eilidh's head—though perhaps the real concern, less urgently, was the realization that Dzhuliya knew and understood Thayer's business in a way that Eilidh, despite the possibility of being tasked with it, never had.

"You won't say anything," Dzhuliya posed hesitantly, which was sort of a question, Eilidh noted, but also not.

The thing in Eilidh's chest woke up again, gleefully cavernous, ready for any passing excuse to swarm. For the first time, Eilidh wondered just how closely Dzhuliya had worked with her father—whether Dzhuliya's level of familiarity was somehow Eilidh's loss.

"Of course not," said Eilidh, shaking herself. Thayer had always been a father first when it came to Eilidh, and unlike Meredith's tendency for obsessive micromanagement, Thayer's long reign meant he barely deigned to open a file without an assistant's help. Of course Dzhuliya would know more than Eilidh, if only by osmosis. She handled Thayer's calendar, she booked his meetings, she voiced his correspondences. Obviously Dzhuliya knew things that were never meant to be Eilidh's concern—she probably understood countless things about his daily life that Eilidh didn't, purely by virtue of circumstance, not design.

Unless—

Eilidh reconsidered what Dzhuliya had said, the lies she'd told Meredith about Thayer's potential willingness to go into business with me. If Dzhuliya knew who I was in relation to Meredith, that meant Thayer must have been aware of it, too. But that knowledge wasn't administrative, it was personal. And the possibility that Thayer would go behind Meredith's back, maybe even betray her—was that something he would do?

Eilidh realized she didn't know the answer. She hadn't the faintest idea whether Thayer's intentions could have been to taunt Meredith or punish her. Eilidh knew only what Thayer would do for her, which was protect her. Shelter her, go so far as to ensure she never felt a moment's worry or pain or doubt, and yes, that was different than anything he'd do for Meredith or Arthur. But either Meredith and Arthur were right and Thayer hadn't actually loved them—this Eilidh didn't believe; it didn't fit with her understanding of him, nor her understanding of *them*—or the lengths Thayer routinely went for Eilidh, the things about his life he was willing to divulge to his assistant but not his daughter, those were driven by . . . something other than love.

Suddenly the thing in her chest felt grainy, minutely particulate. Eilidh tasted disintegration on her tongue like floating ash, the shattering of an old illusion.

"Are you going to get dressed?" Dzhuliya ventured, her gaze lingering slightly southward.

Abruptly, Eilidh remembered the pointelle fabric, the louche triangulation of her breasts as she lounged in bed, waging an endless war of loyalties with her sister.

"Right," she said, leaping to her feet. "Just give me five minutes, and then let's go."

# 43

Monster had recently become very interested in balance-related exercises. He was constantly trying to tightrope on things, like a very preliminary gymnast, although he was not especially talented in this regard. Thus, Arthur and I were forced to make our way very slowly through Muir Woods along the initial two-mile loop that was accessible via carefully placed wooden beams. Monster held my hand, setting one foot carefully in front of the other, making a reasonable effort not to topple sideways into the clovers, or onto the delicate tangles of redwood roots plaiting the forest floor.

Arthur, meanwhile, was silent at first, thinking about children, about progeny, and about the time he'd once had sex with me, which if I haven't already mentioned was the height of adolescent awkwardness. For Arthur, the day had been one of semi-enchanted suspension. He remembered it all in terms of sensations, the rain that fell on the skylights of his room, the way he had always felt his father's house to be a sort of glass cage. The relief of not being alone; the piercing joy of a moment with me that did not involve Meredith. He was running the tips of his fingers up and down my bare arms, thinking about how everything would soon be different. He had an image in his head of defending me to Meredith, of becoming my knight in shining armor, of taking a broken situation and righting it, clotting the wound and thus being forever cocooned by love and gratitude or whatever Arthur expected to find whenever sex was involved.

I don't think I need to tell you that Arthur and I had very different experiences that day. Though, for the record, it was my first time, too. I never told him that because Arthur has a way of assigning meaning to things unnecessarily. It's very preternaturally witchy of him, and/or slightly OCD.

"Interesting choice of meeting place," he told me as we made our way slowly over the beams, beneath the canopy of trees. "Reminds me of . . . you know."

Oh god, I thought, having then forgotten about Arthur's habit of assigning meaning. Like I said, I remember the day in question very differently. I remember thinking how fucking insane Arthur's sheets were. Why did a teenage boy have such nice sheets? The boys at Ainsworth all had excellent bedding, better than anything I'd ever slept in, though to me, my sheets were softer for being more broken in, for smelling as much like my mother's house as they possibly could without the constant presence of platanos frying or adobo simmering on the stove.

"It opens early and I could take Monster," I told Arthur. "Don't make a thing of it."

In his head, Arthur was totally making a thing of it. He was thinking about the women in his life, the love he felt for both Philippa and Gillian, how different they were from each other, how different they were from me. He projected in his mind the imaginary future he and I might have had together, which admittedly I had thought of many times myself in the past.

There was a time I would have given anything to be a Wren—absolutely anything. Meredith was my first friend, Arthur my first love, or maybe it was the other way around, I don't know. Even after everything fell apart I still frequently imagined it, although my renditions of what it would take to be a Wren grew increasingly vindictive. I stopped marrying Arthur in my imagination and started simply beating Meredith. As Dumas put it, "How did I escape? With difficulty. How did I plan this moment? With pleasure." I thought about saying that one day to Meredith's face, looking particularly hot for no reason other than to rub it in, the proof that *I* was the phoenix, that *I* was the once and future Wren, because I was actually so much better than they were. For years that single thought, that crystalline desire drove me constantly through exhaustion, pushed me limitlessly through pain. I was only properly motivated when I imagined the chance I so plainly deserved to laugh, laugh, laugh in Meredith's fucking face.

I had to stop putting it in those terms, though, because the more my fantasies revolved around Meredith, the more agonizingly obvious it became which Wren sibling I had actually loved most.

In any case, to lose Arthur and Meredith in one fell swoop was easier to do once I was angry. I don't think I could have given either of them up if not for Meredith running me over with her proverbial car, and where would I be if she hadn't? Would I now be Arthur's politician wife? And what about Meredith—what would I have been to her? Wouldn't we always have drifted apart until I was no different from any other sorority sister she couldn't bring herself to call?

I don't see any of it anymore, even when I try, probably because Monster doesn't coexist with the possibility of that branch of lives unlived. The thought of uninventing him pains me, it literally pains me, somewhere deep in my chest. So I guess I've taught myself in recent years that the chips simply fall where they may—which sounds an awful lot like I'm getting an A in therapy, so hearty congratulations to me.

"Mama," said Monster. "Ball. Ball. Ball. Car." (To Arthur, this sounded like "bahhhhhhhh" and "cahhhhhhhh," which is fair, as he is less fluent in Monster's particular dialect.)

"Yes," I said. "Totally."

"Car," said Monster.

"Yes, car, very good. What do you see, honey? Trees? Can you say 'tree'?" Monster thought about it.

"Car," he said.

"He's a little behind, verbally," I explained to Arthur, having forgotten I'd already said that. Arthur, meanwhile, had a faint smile on his face. His hands were tucked into his pockets, his eyes drifting upward, to the trees framing the gray sky overhead.

"Behind what?" Arthur asked.

"Behind other theoretical children," I said. "Or, I don't know, something."

"I think he's perfect," said Arthur with a shrug. "What does he need to talk for? He knows they're trees. It's cars we've left out of the conversation."

I'd been wondering why I'd ever felt so painfully in love with Arthur Wren, right up until that moment, when I remembered.

"So," I said, to cover the embarrassing possibility that maybe Arthur would know what I was thinking, although I think I've made it clear that he was consistently very dense when it came to identifying the devotion of others, "you've got a case of the deaths."

"I do come back, though, which is nice," he said.

"Okay, so what's the problem?"

I meant it as a joke, but Arthur took it very seriously. He turned his chin up to the sky again and—I cannot emphasize this enough—he is better looking than he has any right to be. It's no wonder he has eight girlfriends and ten husbands. Or whatever. Let's not focus on my opinion of this moment, though. It's unproductive.

Arthur was thinking about *the problem,* as if I had said it in proper noun terms. *What's The Problem?* is what Arthur heard me ask him, even though, again, I was only joking.

"Do you think it's possible to be in love with more than one person?" he asked.

Yes. For example, both the Wrens simultaneously, in troublingly inseverable ways.

I said, "I think we have a lot of different kinds of loves."

"I might be having a daughter," Arthur said, "named Riot."

"Great name," I said.

"That's what I thought!" He turned a sunny glance at me. "Riot Wren."

"Alliterative."

"I know. What's your son's name?"

"Michael Jordan."

"Stop. Do you think Riot Revolution Wren is overdoing it?"

"Absolutely," I said. "That's a solid ten steps too far."

Arthur sighed heavily. "Damn." The beams of the path creaked beneath his foot. We were winding our way through the woods at a glacial pace, though we had come to a bridge that crossed over a stream to another path on the opposite side.

Sometimes Monster liked to run back and forth across bridges. "Want to cross the bridge?" I asked him, hoping that might divert him from his unsteady gymnastic pursuits.

He considered it with a pensive frown. Then he returned his attention to the balance beam without a word.

"Okay," I said a little glumly.

Arthur laughed.

"As for you," I began, returning to the subject at hand and to the wording I'd found strange until I'd gotten distracted by the name of his theoretical child, "what do you mean you *might* be having a daughter?"

"Oh. Well, my . . ." Arthur looked around, checking for any eavesdropping reporters before turning back to me. "My girlfriend might be pregnant." He told me briefly about Yves and Philippa, about the way they'd met, about how much he loved them both, and the thing about Philippa being "beautifully difficult," like that was a novelty and not just a description of his sister. Or me.

"You really have a type," I sighed.

"Yves is different, though," he said, defensively. "And so is Gillian."

"Yeah, but they're not the ones you're considering part of the problem, are they?"

"I don't think that's fair." Arthur sounded troubled, his brow knitting pensively, precisely the way Monster's had done at the earlier prospect of switching to another activity. "And it's not like it sounds, you know, the whole sleeping-with-other-people thing. It's not an affair, not in the clichéd sense. It's different."

That sounded a lot like what everyone who sleeps with other people says and I told him so.

"Well, okay, fair." Arthur did feel more shameful than he usually did, explaining his lifestyle to me. Normally, people (chronically online people, but I digress) just accepted that it was progressive and sexually fluid and entirely within his rights as a human being who wanted nothing more than to combat loneliness, to be alive, which Arthur usually felt a sort of smugness over when it came to his own precocious liberality.

But I wasn't really moving my face very much, and he had the sense that I had probably had polyamorous relationships of my own—which I had, for a brief period of time, not that it's worth getting into. The point is that Arthur could tell while he was talking to me that everything he claimed about the forward-leaning grandiosity, the utter *profundity* of love in his relationship was, you know, bullshit-resembling.

"You always make me feel so conventional," Arthur told me, apropos of nothing, while scraping a hand through his hair. We had been silent for a while at the time, because Arthur was thinking about what I thought of him and I was thinking about whether Monster could be convinced to eat tacos for lunch. And, yes, I was also thinking about Meredith.

"I don't think I'm the one making you feel that way," I pointed out.

"Because it's not like I'm cheating on my wife," he insisted.

"Sure," I agreed.

"She knows about it. She supports it. Our relationship is, you know—"

"Progressive?" I guessed with an undertone of irony.

Arthur heard it. He turned to me with a sudden burst of energy.

"I *am* progressive," he said.

"Okay," I agreed.

"It's not my fault I can't get anything done. Politics is fucked, Lou, it's just *fucked*. Sorry," he said to Monster, who had certainly heard worse from his own mother's mouth. "I came into office and I tried to change things but two years is . . . it's nothing," he ranted, beginning to pace across the wooden trail. "It's just absolutely nothing—in two years I accomplished fuck all and now they're pulling me from office and I'll just forever be this *blip*. Just some nepo baby who said oh sure let's regulate magitech and let's get rid of the guns and let's make things safe for immigrants and of course I'm pro-choice and then in the end, I'm just, like, another guy." He said that last word with unbelievable derision, which was so funny to me that I snorted a laugh. "What?" he demanded, hurtfully. "And anyway, what do they want me to do? 'Nepo baby' this, 'nepo baby' that—should I just kill myself, is that the only way to solve the ethical issue of my existence? Should I stop breathing, is that what they want?"

He was breathing hard, like he was on the verge of tears.

"Whoa, whoa," I said loudly, pretending to cover Monster's ears. "Profanity is one thing, but I draw the line at intrusive thoughts. And anyway," I added, changing tack because Monster was annoyed that I was doing something other than helping him on the balance beam, "I think we may have stumbled upon the source of your little death problem, Congressman Wren. You're just sick to death of other people."

He exhaled, deflating like a balloon.

"That's not true." He folded his arms over his chest. "I like the idea of people."

"Unfortunately, though, we're not an idea," I said. "Nor are we a *good* idea. Not the time for it, but my personal theory is that we're God's starter universe. He seems to have messed up somewhere, maybe even right away, with the chromosome problem where all mammals sunburn, and now I think He's not only *not* an interventionist, He's actively left the building. He's like, you know what, bro? I'm trying again! Milky Way can suck a dick, the end."

"Ball!" said Monster excitedly.

"Is this your way of telling me I'm being overdramatic?" asked Arthur, with a deep sigh.

It wasn't, but since he seemed a little more subdued, I felt I was achieving a breakthrough, however incidentally.

"So what if you're just some guy, huh?" I asked, poking him in the shoulder. "What's wrong with being 'some guy'?"

"I said 'another guy,' but thanks for making it unbelievably worse," said Arthur.

"Why? I'm just some lady. I'm some fucking *mom*, Arthur, I mean. Can you imagine?"

"But that's amazing," Arthur insisted.

"Sure, to you, because you know me. But to my congressman, am I anything? Am I anything to the ruler of Dubai? Am I anything to the man at the deli counter? I will answer that question for you now—unless I'm wearing mascara and a pair of tiny athletic shorts, forget it. I am absolutely some guy," I ruefully bemoaned.

"Do you know who your congressman is?" asked Arthur.

"The problem isn't the election," I said. "Which you haven't even lost yet."

"I'm going to lose." He sounded so maudlin I laughed aloud.

"Imagine," I said performatively to Monster, "being the youngest congressman in the history of the United States and you're still mostly in kindergarten."

"Car!" said Monster. "Car, car, car—"

"It's not the election," Arthur said insistently.

"I know, I just said that," I reminded him.

"It's a *magic* problem," he said, showing me his hands. "I keep starting fires!"

"I haven't seen you do anything weird since yesterday. And why did you come to the fucking redwoods if you're a fire hazard?"

"I—" He seemed pained again. "Jesus, what am I doing?"

He looked around, as if for an exit, which clearly there wouldn't be, because we were only a quarter of the way through a two-mile loop. "Arthur, you're fine," I told him. "It's fine. If you burn down Muir Woods, I'm sure that will have no effect whatsoever on your reelection chances."

"Stop," he begged, helplessly.

"Your marriage does seem genuinely problematic," I said. "You were always, you know, a little physical."

I flushed, which led Arthur to think I was referencing our teenage tryst. I hadn't meant to, but unfortunately I *was* thinking about it. Abuela had always said Arthur was especially good at kinesis, the physical magics, because there was something primally physical in him. He was connected to his body, to his being, in a way that Meredith wasn't, and in a way I only sometimes was. When we slept together that one time, which I hesitate to discuss without sounding like an absolute creep, I understood that for Arthur, touch was magic and magic was touch and everything was very real that way, very grounded. Existential thoughts, fleeting fears of disapproval and being forgotten by time and space, they just evaporated for him. They just didn't exist, not the way Arthur existed. Also, he could do a fun trick with his fingers, which we'd looked up on the internet a few hours before because what can I say, we were teenagers.

"What I mean is that I don't think you can go on as you are," I told him. "It's fine to have different relationships with different people. But not a whole bunch of people who are lying to each other about what they want. Honestly, it's a cesspool."

"His eyes are lighter than yours," Arthur noted, fixing his attention on Monster for a moment.

"He has two sets of genetics, Art, he wasn't a virgin birth. And are you listening? I'm not saying your problems aren't magical, but your magic definitely won't work if your heart is broken."

I hadn't meant to use those words. I meant more like his soul, or his being. I don't know why the word heart came out except that Lola had put it that way before she died. *You are my heart and I am yours, my magic is your magic and you are mine, and that is why, hija, I will never leave you.*

So basically, what I meant to tell Arthur was: Your magic won't stop malfunctioning if you don't get the rest of your shit together. But that's not what he heard.

"It's just," Arthur said with a sigh, "that I want Riot to be outside the window, and if she isn't then I don't think I can stay."

He said it with such overwhelming misery that I had to look away from him then. I didn't want to get pulled back under. I was a grown woman now, an adult with a child, I understood how to pay taxes and which fabrics went with which setting on my washing machine. It wasn't my job anymore to make a sad, motherless boy laugh.

We were entering Cathedral Grove, home to the highest redwoods in Muir Woods. Patches of pale blue sky were breaking through in shards, the grayness of morning fog threatening to give. Imagine the tallest trees, the puffs of your breath in the air, the sanctity of the silence. It was, I thought, missing my grandmother, a very physical place.

I joke about the abandonment of my personal experimental God, but really, you have to give it up for nature. It's almost better if it's all a breathtaking accident. It's a reminder that from chaos can come peace.

The balance beam had ended and Monster darted ahead, over to the benches facing the running burble of the stream. Arthur and I lingered, looking up at the trees.

It was so, so quiet. Birth of the universe quiet. Arthur was looking at me, thinking about all the time he'd missed, the people I had been in all the phases of my life that he had forgone, the times he'd thought of me at the very same times I thought of him, the togetherness we hadn't shared and couldn't know. He was looking at me with nostalgia, with fondness. With love that was softer because it was worn.

He was looking at me, and I could feel his eyes on me, and I hadn't told him yet, but I was just so *angry* that morning. I was angry about my mother's diagnosis; about the people in life you are given just to lose. I was angry about my son's pediatrician heavily implying that I was a bad mother because I still pulled him into bed with me whenever he wanted me to, because I didn't like to hear him cry, and because verbally he was still a little behind. I was angry that I could never really shake the fear that someone might consider Monster's dad a better alternative to me, that he was a better father than I was a mother because he came from money, because his father was a lawyer and his mother was a lawyer and there were lawyers all up and down that family lineage like a fucking life achievement waterslide. I was angry that Arthur Wren had come back into my life at a time when I was still a little too weak not to love him. I was angry that I could love my life so dearly, cherish it so completely, just to see its reflection in Meredith's sunglasses as a mirage of the ways I had failed. I was angry that I had lived my life so freely for so long, so fearlessly, until my son was born and then I realized how small I was, how fragile, how very full of terror I'd become. I had to stay alive for him, I had to be happy for him, I had to be fucking *happy* and Meredith Wren still hadn't figured out how! I was angry, I was bitter, my life was full and yet, somehow, my heart was still broken—had been broken for over a decade, unfixable still. I was angry, and for fuck's sake, I was tired. I have a toddler, okay? I was *really fucking tired*.

So, in the middle of nature's church, I tilted my head back and I screamed.

# 44

That morning, Meredith called a defense lawyer, one she knew had done good work in the past; a woman with a keen eye for employment-based discrimination.

She called a few different PR firms, then chose one who'd made tidy work of a defamation case in tech some years back.

She read the transcripts of her previous speeches to try to pull together a cohesive narrative, a ready-made defense, and watched her phone, waiting for me to text her back.

She called her father's lawyers and they said just a little bit longer, Ms. Wren, not long now, we're just waiting for the judge's decision.

She called Ward, whose phone was off or maybe he had blocked her number, she didn't know which but either way she understood what that meant. He wasn't on her side anymore, and who cared? She'd turn on him too if she had to, and by every imaginable definition it seemed like she would, indeed, have to. She loved Ward for his mind, always had, but even he must have known he had more enemies than friends when it came to the industry, from top to bottom. He worked his employees too hard, he was anxious in a way that demanded not just perfection but absolute acquiescence to his constant interference, he chose stick over carrot every single chance he got. To his peers he behaved like a little Napoleon, rubbing his successes in the face of his haters, judging any little win to be the equivalent of an empire. Meredith had always known what she'd done when she chose a business partner even less likable than she was. She'd always had the tools to bury him to save herself, and to his credit, Ward was smart enough to know it. It was no wonder he'd put himself one step ahead.

She was staring at her phone screen, legs pulled up onto the chair in her father's study, waiting to see my name when her phone finally rang and she snatched it up.

"Hello?"

"Meredith." Jamie sounded carefully toneless. "I heard you lawyered up."

Meredith's throat felt dry. "News travels fast."

"I've had feelers out for a while. Took you longer than I thought it would, to be honest."

"Look at you, investigative journalist." She wanted to scream at him but sensed it would be unproductive. "Did you call to gloat?"

"No. To give you an update."

"You're pulling it." She held her breath. "Don't tell me the lawyer scared you."

"I've had a lawyer of my own since I started writing this. I knew that if not you, then Tyche would come for me. I'm not scared."

"Of course not, you'll win a Pulitzer. I hope you thank me in your speech." Meredith could taste the bitterness on the tip of her tongue. It warred with her ongoing desire to cry.

"Look, Meredith, my editor got a call this morning."

"From who? Tyche? I told you this was insanely stupid." She wanted to heave a sigh of relief. Thank god!

"Not Tyche." Jamie cleared his throat. "The *Times*."

(SILENCE.)

"So you're getting a promotion," Meredith wryly observed.

"I'm a freelance writer, Meredith. And that's not the point."

"What's the point?" Don't do it, she thought. Just don't.

"The article isn't just running in *Magitek*." Jamie sounded far away for a second, like he'd turned his head away. "It's Monday's cover story in the *New York Times*."

Meredith hung up and threw the phone away from her, breathing hard. She stared around her father's office, looking at the painting of the ballerina on the wall.

Fuck, she thought, fuck fuck fuck.

Then she picked up the phone again and called Jamie back.

"Meredith, I'm sorry."

"Come say that to my face." She sounded breathless, barely over a whisper.

"I'm on my way," Jamie said, and the relief in Meredith's chest, it was icing. It was just the fucking cherry on top.

# 45

Eilidh hadn't spent much time in the interior of the funeral home, but she knew the cemetery well. It was the same one her mother had been buried in, or rather, it was the place where her mother's tombstone was. Persephone Liang Wren hadn't designated any burial plans in the event of her death, so Thayer's more traditional impulses took over. Eilidh supposed Persephone didn't—couldn't—care, but she remembered Meredith frequently berating their father over his handling of their mother's life.

Eilidh didn't remember what Meredith had said, only that her sister's face had been streaky with preadolescent rage. At that age, before Lou, Meredith had seen a therapist once or twice, after her teachers had called her "unusually defiant." Thayer had told Eilidh about that on one of their visits to Persephone's grave, which wasn't often. But Thayer was a man of ritual, and on holidays and anniversaries, he paid a visit to his wife.

"Meredith took the whole thing badly," he'd told Eilidh once when she'd come with him. "As if it wasn't hard enough. For a while I thought I was going to have to sedate her."

"I thought you said Meredith didn't cry when Mom died," said Eilidh, though she couldn't remember if Thayer had said that or if that was just how she remembered it. Meredith had been stone in all the pictures from the funeral, barely even human.

"She was acting out," Thayer said with a shrug. "She stopped eventually." He looked up at the trees, then glanced back down at the Celtic shape of the grave marker bearing Eilidh's mother's name. "Arthur cried a lot. Started wetting the bed again, regressed right back into babyhood." He glanced at Eilidh. "You wouldn't let me out of your sight, but all you wanted to do was sit with me. You just hugged your little doll and sat there holding my hand."

He had seemed so pleased, so fond. Thinking of it now—aware now of something she hadn't articulated then, the sudden sentience of an amorphous monster—Eilidh wanted to interrupt in retrospect, to ask, *Excuse me, Father, am I perpetually trapped for you in girlhood? Am I your favorite because I never grew up?*

But she didn't like the way that thought tasted, so she shook it away.

"Luckily your father was very precise," the director was saying to Eilidh, "and there isn't much work for you to do." He paused for a long moment before saying, "I know the circumstances are odd, but I have to say, I remember when I first met you. You were so astonishing, the way you handled your mother's loss so young. I never forgot it."

He looked at Eilidh through kindly eyes, and perhaps because Eilidh was so eager to displace the odd, adult-tainted doubt in her father that she'd been struggling to fit back into the void from whence it came, she said, somewhat fishingly, "Oh, I couldn't have been that memorable, could I?"

Dzhuliya turned away, observing urns in various colors and shapes, as if to offer Eilidh some semblance of privacy.

"You told me the most remarkable thing," said the director, smiling at the memory. "Oh, I wish I could remember it now, how charmingly precocious it was. Something about finding the way back when your mother couldn't. I thought, what clarity for someone so young! Most of us just fall into our lives, or drift into them. Not her, I thought. Not this one."

He seemed to have collapsed into the memory then, pulled away on a lazy river of nostalgia.

"You know," he said, shaking himself free, "I wasn't surprised when your father said you were the only one of his children who could handle his loss. I think, between the two of us, that it was easier for him to be fond of your sister—that she was simply easier to love because she required more nurturing, and he never had to question where he stood with her—but you." He leaned forward with a little twinkle in his eye, like a magical toymaker. "You were the one he really trusted."

"He said Meredith was easy to love?" asked Eilidh with a faint sense of confusion.

All of a sudden, the twinkle vanished.

"I might be wrong, of course," the director said hastily. "I only spoke with Thayer a few times about his family, so maybe I didn't get the details quite right."

But only a moment ago he had said he recalled it all so clearly.

"Oh," Eilidh realized dully. "You thought I was Meredith."

The thing in Eilidh's chest coiled tighter around her heart, a death-squeeze. She felt the flick of rage, the asp again, the sharp pierce of her tongue from the wreckage of revelation. The director hurried to say something, to make it sound as if this was something he could play off, and Eilidh waved him away as politely as she knew how—*Don't worry about it, I get that all the time.* Meredith was nearly a foot shorter and she had the most naturally bitchy face in the world, but sure, easy mistake to make.

The director hurried to excuse himself, replacing his presence with that of a lackey, the kind of person they likely would have dealt with anyway if they weren't discussing the final rites for the great Thayer Wren.

*He never had to question where he stood with you.*

Wasn't that a good thing? Wasn't it a wonderful thing for Eilidh that in her father's final moments, he had been assured of her affection, her gratitude, her love?

*You*—Meredith—*were the one he really trusted.*

And why wouldn't he? Meredith had been the one he had allowed to become an adult. He disliked her as he disliked any other colleague. As a person worthy of being taken seriously. Someone who stood on her own two feet, even when he tried to push her around.

What did Thayer Wren actually value, in the end? Which version of him had been love?

Eilidh felt a hand on her shoulder, realizing Dzhuliya was there and that her father was gone, and she could never ask him okay, so did you mean it? Did you like me more but respect me less? Did you confide your real concerns in others while sedating me with praise, anesthetizing me with false assurance? Was it easier to love me because you could control me, because you could send me on silent retreats and I wouldn't argue, because every time you sent me away you knew that inevitably, helplessly, I would come back?

Now, Eilidh understood something she hadn't before. If Thayer left all or most of his money to Eilidh, that wasn't a reward. It was a failsafe.

But whoever got Wrenfare got his legacy—the thing he had actually loved.

"Is there any chance he left his shares to me?" Eilidh asked Dzhuliya, who opened her mouth to answer, but then Eilidh shook her head. "Don't lie. Don't soften it."

It changed things, Eilidh thought, observing Dzhuliya's sudden hesitation, the flicker of obvious discomfort when Eilidh issued a warning. Before, Dzhuliya might have been happy to let Eilidh think whatever she wanted, whatever would make her feel better—Eilidh hadn't been the only one with a crush. Now she was having to answer with the truth, which was that she'd gotten more insight into Thayer in two years than Eilidh had had all her life.

"I don't know the corporate details, Eilidh, sincerely, I don't. I do think," Dzhuliya said slowly, "there's a reasonable chance he split the shares equally among his children."

So then why had Dzhuliya seemed so concerned when she'd brought up the will? Well, equal shares meant Arthur was the tiebreaker, which was like not having a tiebreaker at all. More like having two Merediths. Wouldn't Thayer have known that? Wasn't he always telling Eilidh how well he knew them all?

Had she ever really thought it would go to her? It hurt to realize that even days ago, even hours, that answer had honestly been yes. But the real truth, the hard truth, was that Eilidh wouldn't know the first thing about leading a company—which Thayer would have known, because it was as much his doing as it was his fault. Thayer may have kept her close, but he never actually taught her. He never trained her. He protected her.

How could he trust her to succeed when he had never let her fail?

Eilidh closed her eyes beneath the weight of it, the thing that was back, the thing she'd carried around with her, the grief that far preceded her father's loss. She'd lost herself five years ago; the world had already ended for her when she put away her pointe shoes for the last time. Every plague, every incremental step to doom was always slouching toward the inevitable. The threats of blood and pestilence were nothing in the end but warning signs—paltry aches for which nothing but total annihilation could ever suffice.

Meredith was right—Eilidh had never gotten over it. She had never gotten over it, and Thayer had never asked her to. He'd never needed her to move on—move on to what?—and of course it was easy to love her, she stayed put! Not like Meredith—growing, changing, *innovating* Meredith.

Meredith, who didn't need to be easy to love because who cared about ease when there was genius—honest-to-god *genius* underfoot?

The brief thrill of sex, the rotting sensuality of intimacy that had subdued Eilidh for a few hours that morning faded away then, capitulating to the clawing, shrieking feeling festering unstably in the ricocheting of her pulse, her noisy, battered heart. It was loud, and more than that, it was *big*, it was infinite, stretching beyond the confines of Eilidh herself, bursting free like sweat from her temples, like radiating beams of light.

*Did you think I was too soft to really be tested?* raged Eilidh's heart. *Did you think I was too weak to pick myself back up?*

The answer, when it came to her, cruel as it was, should have been in Meredith's voice. Because *of course* the answer was yes! Hadn't Eilidh proven to everyone that the answer was yes every single day for five years? Every day that she had considered each breath more pointless than the last was the same thing as a slow submission, sinking deeper and deeper into the ground. She had always heard everything mean in Meredith's voice, but was any of it really cruel, or was it just honest?

Eilidh saw the look in her father's eyes, the one she had so long considered love that had probably always been pity. The thing in her chest clawed for release, for the sweet collapse of rock bottom, and Eilidh wouldn't, couldn't hold it back.

The dam broke, apocalyptic. Through the skylights of the funeral home, the sky overhead turned black as if someone had blown out the sun, and Eilidh Wren didn't notice.

Instead, she buried her head in Dzhuliya's shoulder and cried and cried.

# 46

You'll recall that when you last left me, I was screaming.

Arthur was taken aback, firstly because of the sound—always alarming when a woman begins to scream—but more so because he was an athlete, and therefore respectful of things like hierarchy and rules. I screamed for so long that he became sure the police would be called, that someone would soon see him and say hey, aren't you my congressman? And then he would be forced to say yes I am, sorry about this screaming woman, I slept with her once when I was seventeen and I'm only here now because my dark occult witchcraft is malfunctioning.

But then he started to consider me as something else, something aside from just a girl he had once known, and realized that, seeing as I was now a woman—a woman living in the same country he had been trying so hard over the course of the last two years to fix—I probably had a lot of problems. (Monster, meanwhile, seemed largely unaffected. We had already established by then a practice of saying, "Mommy needs two seconds to freak out, okay? I'm going to step over here and howl into the void, but then after that we'll have yogurt.")

Eventually I ran out of scream. Then I turned to Arthur and said, with much invigoration, "You should try it."

"Oh, I don't know," said Arthur, whisper-quiet. "It's, you know, a cathedral."

"Well, then we know God is listening," I said. "Which is great, as you clearly have a bone to pick."

"I don't want to disturb Her," Arthur joked.

"Oh, come on." I don't know that I actually thought ill-advised scream therapy was going to do either of us any good, but Arthur had always assigned me more competency than I actually possessed. I don't know if it was because I was older or because I was friends with Meredith, but he'd always lent me a lot more deference than he should have, and I took advantage of it. "You'll feel better."

"I don't really have a scream in me," he hedged.

"Oh come on, of course you do. Maybe I just need to be more specific." I turned again to the grove of trees, directing my complaints to management. "I FUCKING HATE WHEN PEOPLE SAY THEY'RE SOCIALLY LIBERAL AND FISCALLY CONSERVATIVE," I said, enunciating clearly to be sure it was filed in the correct department. "HOW CAN YOU SAY YOU CARE ABOUT SOCIAL PROGRAMS IF YOU DON'T SPEND ANY MONEY TO FUND THEM?"

"What she said," Arthur said, a little bit louder, but not much over his usual speaking voice.

I turned to glare at him. "FUCK RESTAURANTS THAT MAKE YOU ORDER BEFORE YOU SIT DOWN BUT YOU HAVE TO READ A HUGE MENU IN TINY WRITING AND EVERYONE BEHIND YOU IN LINE JUST WAITS AND MAKES YOU FEEL LIKE AN IDIOT UNTIL YOU PANIC-ORDER A BLT BUT YOU DON'T EVEN LIKE BACON," I said.

"Who doesn't like bacon?" said Arthur.

"I HATE ARTHUR WREN," I snapped.

"Oh, come on, I just—"

"CAR!" said Monster.

"See?" I crossed my arms. "Even he gets it." When Arthur still looked unconvinced, I gestured around at the park guides who were definitely not coming to arrest me. "Do it or I'll keep yelling. I HAVE CRAMPS," I yelled. "GOD IS FAKE, BUT HE'S ALSO DEFINITELY A MAN! WHY ELSE WOULD BEING A WOMAN *SUCK—SO—HARD*?"

"AHHHHHH!" said Arthur, which startled me. I had been really focused on shouting my God theories, but it seemed now wasn't the time.

"AHHHHHH*HHHHHHHHHH*!" Arthur elaborated, and a small group of tourists came toward us as if to shush him, but I glared daggers their way.

"I JUST WANT TO BE LOVED!" screamed Arthur.

"SAME!" I bellowed.

"I JUST WANT TO DO SOME GOOD IN THE WORLD!" Arthur wailed. "AND I HATE THE INFINITE SCROLL!"

"Ooh, good one," I said.

"Thank you," Arthur said, exhaling with relief. "Are we done, then?"

"I LOVE MY SON!" I said. "I HOPE HE DOESN'T GET SHOT AT SCHOOL!"

"Whoa, dark," Arthur gasped.

"The world's a dark place," I informed him, adding, "I THINK PEOPLE WHO GET BORED EASILY ARE THE WORST!"

"I WISH I'D MARRIED A WOMAN WHO COULD LOVE ME LIKE I LOVE HER!" said Arthur, which felt like something real.

I wanted to acknowledge it somehow, but I wasn't sure what to say that wasn't obnoxious and pitying, so instead I turned to Arthur, looked at him for a long time, and then said, "I HATE THAT MY MOM IS GOING TO DIE SOMEDAY!"

His eyes were wide, tragic, honest. He looked back at me, then screwed up his face like he was about to say something repulsive.

And when he said it, I guess I wasn't really that surprised.

"I JUST WANTED MY DAD TO LOVE ME, AND NOW HE NEVER WILL," said Arthur Wren to the grove of heavenly trees. To the indifference of nature and a universe who hadn't put him into motion in any particular way; hadn't given him the fate it did for any particular reason.

We studied this in biomancy, the profound accident that was heredity, and life. There is a randomness to the universe; you can find it everywhere, from physics to biology. Oh, there is definitely elegance in this world, mathematics mainly, the things you can do with magic once you understand the nature of communing with something larger than yourself. But there is only so much order. Most of that beauty comes from somewhere broken, from something accidental. In life there is no narrative, no neatness to the ending. Your mom might forget who you are someday, even if you're the reason she's done everything since the moment you first drew breath. Your dad might have three children he cannot love equally. He might love you the most unfairly because you're some weird mirror-sliver of himself. Because someday, he might be gone and you're what will be left, and perhaps he has always been too selfish to imagine a world without him in it.

Arthur's voice broke then, after admitting out loud the thing his father had never given him the space or the tools to say, and suddenly he dropped away, and I thought maybe this was an example of him dying. I thought whoa, I know he said this was a thing, but I really thought he was joking.

But it turned out he had just sunken down to sit on the bench, holding his head in his hands.

Monster, who had been really excited while we were all yelling, was alarmed by the sudden change in the game. He reached for me, and I picked him up and kissed the palm of his hand, and he stroked my arm and then kind of smacked my face, and I said no, no hitting, and kissed his hand again. Then I sat down next to Arthur, and Monster wriggled away to go look at a stick on the ground.

Arthur was silent for a really long time, so I figured I'd give it a try. The stakes were low, anyway. Whether he felt better or not we probably weren't going to have a lot of time together after this. If he never spoke to me again, so be it. I'd already lost him once before.

"I think your dad probably loved you," I said. "But even if he didn't, you can't control how he felt. You can only control how *you* feel, what *you* accept. So you can accept that he was really inept at his most important job, and you can hate him for that if you want. It doesn't matter, he's dead. But you could also just decide you don't need it—his approval or whatever. And you can keep on living, because you have to do that anyway." I shrugged. "You're the only one left, so you get to decide."

Arthur's eyes were brimming with tears that he didn't want me to see. He was thinking about all the things he'd never hear Thayer say, but also the things that Thayer would never see. Because Arthur was grateful to Thayer for the things that had made him, but also, he was grateful to himself for the things that hadn't unmade him. He might be just some guy, some has-been, some failure of a politician, maybe one who ended up divorced and alone, but even some guy is allowed to live a normal life with normal problems. If it wasn't this, Arthur reasoned, it would be something else.

Arthur reached out for my hand and I gave it to him. I don't know, I guess I decided that being together in that moment was more important than staying mad about something that happened half a lifetime ago.

I'm not totally sure what I was mad at him for, anyway. Not the sex, that was consensual, and the feeling of emptiness I carried around with me afterward wasn't his fault. It was that I had done things for the wrong reasons—things that preceded him. I had given my girlhood away in stages because in my quest for my amorphous future, I thought it was already gone. I had loved the wrong parts of him; I wanted a version of him that I had imagined for myself, a person whose love was more like a metric, because I was innocent and heartbroken and young. Meredith I could definitely still hate, she'd had agency all the way down, but Arthur I had closed the door on that day because I thought I was understanding something about, I don't know, class solidarity—the way the rich always choose themselves. And they do! Don't get me wrong, we should absolutely eat the rich, and I think what made me so furious with Arthur for so long was the specific way he had wanted to help me; like Meredith's ability to discard me meant she had the means to ruin me; like because my fancy education had fallen away, then my potential, too, was gone. To Arthur, I was the despoiled one, the one cast cruelly out of Eden, and I believed it then, too—but what was Eden, in the end? The father who didn't love him? The prison of a life built on external validation? On what photo filter or idea of a person the public could guilt-lessly love?

"You know," I said, "Meredith's app, that Chirp?"

"Oh, that," Arthur said with a sigh. "I tried it. I really wanted it to work, and not just for her sake. I just . . ." He shrugged. "I just wanted it to *work*."

"Yeah," I said, "me, too."

He looked at me with surprise, so I nudged his shoulder with mine.

"I just want to be happy," I admitted.

"I just want to be happy," he agreed.

Then Monster wandered over to us and solemnly handed Arthur the stick he'd found.

"For me?" he said, with genuine surprise, as if it was too rich a prize for him, unearned.

"Degoydegoydegoy," said Monster. "Tcheeeyyyyyaaa!"

"Oh, for sure, dude." Arthur smiled faintly, touching Monster's cheek before Monster ran away again, this time crouching down to look for rocks.

"What's his name?" Arthur asked me in a quiet voice.

"Tripp," I said, just as quietly.

"Really?"

"Absolutely not, asshole." I rose to my feet, holding a hand out for his. "Come on," I said. "Let's finish this hike and do some spells."

# 47

Meredith met Jamie at the old mill, near the children playing on the swings. She was staring out at the creek when he sidled up to her, handing her a cup of coffee without a word.

"I think I might be marrying someone who isn't you," she said, accepting it.

"Mm. How does it feel?" Jamie asked, sipping his coffee.

Meredith considered it. "Safe," she said. "But also, kind of like I want to swallow hot poison and die."

"Yeah," Jamie agreed, half smiling at nothing. "Been there."

Meredith turned to face him then, shaking her head. "You can't honestly tell me you've spent the last decade pining for me. Right?"

"I haven't," he confirmed with a shrug. "There were long spells of time when I didn't think of you at all, or when I thought of you and it didn't hurt. I can go months without thinking of you, actually. I went a whole year once."

"Was it like that when you thought you might get married?"

"Yeah, well, that was easier because whenever I thought about you, it was in a 'thank god she's dead now' kind of way."

"I'm not dead," Meredith pointed out.

"You were dead to me after that last time, which was close enough." He shook his head and took another sip. "God, you were such a dick."

"Were?"

"Are," he corrected himself. "But I was younger then. I thought I had the time to meet and fall in love with lots of other people."

She considered her cup before taking a sip. "You still have lots of time."

"Oh, I know," he agreed. "I plan to fall in love within the next six months."

"You sound very optimistic."

"People are mostly very easy to love," he said. "I don't find it difficult."

"Even me?" She wondered if she even wanted to hear that answer.

"Oh, Meredith, it is so fucking easy to love you. The hard stuff with you is the being loved part." He gestured to the path that led into the trees, over to the waterfalls for which Cascade was named. "Shall we?"

She nodded and started to walk, taking sips of her coffee. It wasn't sweet this time, but it was piping hot, almost scalding. She appreciated it, pulling her jacket in tighter around her.

"So what happened?" she asked.

"You mean with my wedding?"

She nodded.

"Oh, I just couldn't see the important things. I couldn't figure out where I wanted to live but she had a very clear idea. I didn't know if I wanted children, but she really did. It just started to feel unfair, my ambivalence." He took a sip. "I was never ambivalent while I was with you."

"Of course not," Meredith said. "I would have decided all of that for you."

"No." Jamie laughed. "No, I fought with you. Constantly. Something about being with you made me feel surer of myself, of what I wanted. I think it was kind of a relief, actually, that you were selfish, because I didn't have to wonder if you were doing things just to be nice. Making choices just to make me happy."

"Selfish," Meredith echoed.

"You're not selfish all the time," Jamie said. "It's not who you are or anything. It's just, you know, one of your things. Like how you justify everything you do by rationalizing that you're a genius, and therefore the way you see things must be right."

"I'm really logical," Meredith said. "More logical than most people."

"Yes, you do a really good job of turning off your emotions."

"I don't turn them off." She looked away, up into the trees. "I just don't let them rule me."

"You're obstinate," Jamie corrected. "Doing the opposite of what you feel isn't the same thing as having perfect logic. You're still just a baby."

"I'm thirty," she said. "I'm practically a crone."

"You're a *baby*," Jamie repeated. "What do you know? Thirty years isn't enough time for anything. That tree is somewhere between eight hundred and two thousand years old," he said, pointing to one of the mature redwoods. "And I bet if you asked it for the meaning of life or what happened to Amelia Earhart, it still wouldn't know."

"She's somewhere in the ocean," said Meredith with a frown.

"See? There's that perfect logic again. How do you know she didn't fly into a fairy portal, or that she's not still alive today?"

"That's absurd," said Meredith.

"Sure, but it's nice, right?" said Jamie.

"Some journalist you are." Meredith looked away again. Jamie and his handsomeness were giving her a headache.

They walked a while longer, leaves crunching underfoot.

"When I took the call from the *Times* editor," Jamie said, "it occurred to me that I might really destroy you. I mean, I still think you can figure it out, but it's going to hurt." He was quiet for a few moments. "I don't really want to be the person who hurts you."

"I already asked you not to publish it," Meredith muttered.

"You told me not to, you mean."

"No," said Meredith, realizing the pain in her chest was genuine, that it felt like something fluid was spilling out of her lungs. Some elixir of soul or something, it was draining away from her. "I asked you. I actually begged you."

Jamie sighed heavily.

They walked some more.

They crossed over the neighborhood streets, venturing up a steep trail. Things began to escalate on the climb, the effort of hiking more noticeable.

Little gusts of breath materialized between them.

"Did you ever think," asked Meredith, "that maybe my whole life, all I was ever taught to do was this?"

"What, cheat?" asked Jamie.

"Yes," said Meredith, and Jamie blinked with surprise, having expected her to deny it. "I mean, what else was any of it, do you know what I mean? They taught me to aim for perfection, but perfection was always impossible. So what else was I going to do?"

"I think there's a difference between falling short of perfection and actively lying," Jamie wryly observed.

"But it wasn't a lie."

"Right." Jamie turned away with a scoff, and they trudged on farther, scaling upward.

"It wasn't a lie," Meredith explained, "until it was one."

Jamie said nothing. Meredith looked down at his hand, the free one lingering between them, the one she could take if only she were someone different; if she'd made every single different choice.

"I did it because I wanted to be happy," said Meredith. "That's it, that's the truth." She didn't like the way her voice sounded when she was being sincere. It was unbearable, everything about it. "The research I did—I knew I could fix things, I could make some of it better. And then Tyche showed me what it would mean if I could *really* do it, if I could make this idea better, or bolder somehow, and I wanted it, so I did it. I wanted to will it into being, and so I did."

Jamie looked at her. "You believed in the prophecy even though you knew it was a lie?"

"It didn't feel like a lie." She looked away. "I was twenty-five. I didn't know anything."

"Twenty-five is a whole-ass adult, Meredith."

"You said thirty was a baby!"

"That was different. You're not supposed to know what the future is or what destiny means or what the point is of being alive. But you're definitely not supposed to defraud your investors."

"I wasn't thinking about defrauding anyone, I wasn't thinking about fraud at all. I was thinking that—"

She stopped.

"I was thinking you were gone," she said slowly, "and I was never going to feel that way again, and I'd already turned my back on my father, so the only important thing was to do what I'd set out to do, to make everything I'd given up, you know, *worth it,* and it didn't seem at first like this was the road I was on until it was too late. In the moment—" She exhaled. "I don't know. I just went a little bit crazy, I think. I just thought . . . I can't fail. I *can't* fail. Even if Chirp is turning into something different than I wanted. Even if I'm turning into something I don't like. The worse the lie got, the more I had to protect it. This is all I am, this is all I have, this thing is my life, it's my legacy, it's the only thing that will make my father proud of me, it's—"

Another hard stop.

"Yeah, I believed in the fairy tale," she said eventually, witheringly. "I just wanted it to be true. I wanted to believe I could do it—that everything everyone had always told me I was capable of was real, and honest, and true."

To her utter mortification, she felt tears pricking her eyes. Her vision swam, and it wasn't just the stye this time.

"I'm not a genius," she said. "I'm an idiot. And I will go down as an idiot and a criminal when all I wanted to do was *fix* something, to *help* someone—"

She stopped, pausing on a particularly narrow edge of the path and wondering how she could even put it into words, the fear that drove her. The way she was so terrified of losing something, something she didn't really even have, because what was *genius*? What was being called a prodigy—it was just an idea, just a prediction, and then what came next? What came after being a prodigy except for failure, except for misery, except for a life without Jamie? Jamie, the only person she loved with that kind of wildness, with the sort of chaos she never allowed into her life. Jamie who betrayed her, Jamie who didn't love her enough to save her, Jamie who only loved her for being hard and ambitious and mean when she didn't want to be any of those things, she had only ever wanted to be soft for him, but she wasn't soft, she couldn't be soft, she didn't know how? She didn't know how to be Eilidh, fucking Eilidh who was art itself, who could bring the hardest man to tears just over the way she exuded her pain, how she lived it so honestly. So vulnerably, with her whole self.

What did Eilidh have that Meredith couldn't mimic, no matter how hard she tried? It was something innate, some innocence, some honesty that Meredith had never been allowed. She didn't want to analyze the psychology of it, she knew there was something to validate her feelings, but god, what a fucking waste of time.

Had Jamie seen children with her? Had he wanted to grow old with her? Was he even capable of understanding that Meredith didn't want to grow old, had never wanted to, had thought she was destined for a life just like her mother's, right up until the day she met him? Could Jamie ever know, could he ever *really know* that he had made Meredith want to grow old *for* him? So that she would never have to miss a minute. So that everything of hers would also be his.

Maybe it wouldn't be happiness all the time, but by god it would be theirs, and unrobbable. Not like money. Not like success.

Nobody could ever take it away from her but Jamie, Jamie himself.

He took a few steps past her, lingering on the edge of the path, looking over the precipice into the creek below. They were nearing the top of the trail, reaching one of the upper roads. She sidled up to him and stood there looking down, contemplating the fall.

"Didn't you worry for even a second that I would hate you for this?"

she asked him. She didn't know what made her do it, but she had to ask. She had to know if it had ever crossed his mind—if he had decided that her hatred was worth the risk, or worse, if the thought had never actually occurred to him.

He looked at her, and she remembered that she had been close enough to read him once. Once upon a time he had telegraphed everything she needed to know with a glance, like they'd been made from the same stuff. Like before Babel had fallen, some prior versions of themselves were laid in the same brick, sharing the same mortar, such that they'd always been able to speak the same language no matter what forms they took. She remembered the work she'd all but fucked off, the readings she hadn't done, because a minute of time spent with Jamie was so much more potent, so much fuller than a minute spent fighting sleep in a lecture hall. She never saw her future in Magitech 101 or Biomancy 120. She saw it *all the time* whenever she was with Jamie, and that was the fuckery of it, the future of absolute nothingness she knew that she would choose if given the opportunity. The greatness she would no longer care if she achieved. There was no resolving the tension, the inharmonious knowledge that she would never love again like this if she didn't drop everything right that moment for this one person, this incredible human she would never find if she searched a thousand years, for eons on eons—but that if she *did* do it, if she chose that version of herself with its uncomplicated softness and kindness and warmth, she would be robbing someone she loved even more at the time, which was herself, and more specifically, the person she felt she needed to be. The person her mother could have been grateful to; the person who would have made a worthy sacrifice for her mother's pain.

If she did not become *Meredith Wren,* if she chose that weak-kneed alter ego instead, then what was any of it for?

It was not in Meredith's material to ask what price Jamie might have paid, or what he would have been willing to pay. She knew she would accept the lie if he offered her one, which was the same as not really caring about the truth. What could he have said back then to convince her to stay? He had said it all, that he wanted forever, that it didn't matter what he achieved or didn't achieve so long as she was there, so long as she chose him. The last fight wasn't even a fight, it was a proposal. It was supplication, an actual pledge of fealty, literally down on bended knee.

But that was years ago. So when Jamie looked at her, she reminded herself that she no longer knew him. He took a sip from his coffee and looked away, half a smile on his face. A wry twist of irony.

*Didn't you worry for even a second that I would hate you for this?*

"Do you?" he asked. "Hate me for it."

"I think I hoped you'd be the one to hate me," she said. "Seemed easier."

"Probably would be." He looked at her again. "So, do you hate me?"

"I think you chose to enter a dying industry and that's on you," she said. She took a sip of her coffee, getting to the bitter grounds near the end. "Lots of other ways to earn a paycheck."

"Such as fraud?" Jamie took an audible sip from his cup.

She turned to him. She looked at the edge of the path, the precipice of the cliff. He tracked her eyes, watching her as if to say *I see the danger, I always have*. She thought about her marriage to Cass, the simple white dress she would probably wear, because she was sort of traditional—guiltily, she did have some old-fashioned dreams. The cut of the dress would be classic, maybe tea-length, something vintage to match the aesthetic of caring about happily ever after, the thing she had very deliberately spat in the face of for so many years.

She thought about being married to Cass in a world where Jamie Ammar still lived, still breathed, still fucked people who weren't her. Someday Jamie would fall in love again, it was inevitable; even if it was love like the kind between Cass and Meredith, it would still be the kind of love you could shrug on forever, like a very good winter coat. Solid, dependable, comforting, dear god how many women would love Jamie Ammar, how many would happily give him a family, a home? Thousands! Hundreds of thousands! The thought was excruciating. Even if Jamie loved no one else how he loved Meredith—even if there was no such thing as the same love between two people because people were always different people—even if every pragmatic sense suggested Meredith could live without him, had lived without him for years and would continue to do so—the idea that Jamie would live a life with some not-Meredith who would bury him someday when they were old, after they'd made a home together and told each other the same stories ten thousand times, hundreds of thousands—even if Jamie got married and divorced five times over—even if he never again promised his life to someone else but still spent his time with other people—she understood that it was untenable, absolutely fucking unbearable. It made her physically ill, it made her stye pulse independently, as if it were the living manifestation of her grief. She could not walk this earth if Jamie Ammar was alive, if he lived separately from her. By the metrics of Meredith Wren's ego, no greater tragedy could ever exist than the one where Jamie's story kept going without her in it.

So she looked at the edge of the cliff, the proximity of Jamie to the bottom of the fucking ravine, and she reached out with both hands and she pushed.

# 48

Oh my god, I'm just kidding! You believed me, though, didn't you. Meredith absolutely would. I thought it would be funny if I just did a little untruth there as a personal treat, hope you're not mad.

Anyway, that's not what Meredith did. She reached out and she pulled him to safety, and she kissed him like she used to kiss him, without really thinking about it. Initially, the kiss was very forgettable, the kind of kiss you part with without even really noticing because you feel sure it will happen again—that you'll see each other at home at the end of the day. The kind of kiss that doesn't usually get a story because it's part of a bigger story, something vibrant and everlasting. The prelude-to-forever kiss. The gods-are-smiling-on-us kiss. The kiss that says *I knew, I always knew, that it was you*. Maybe not the most mind-blowing of kisses, unless you consider that this is Meredith Wren, who doesn't technically have any sweetness living in her.

But the thing is, right when Meredith did this, the sky went prophetically black.

# 49

Oh—I'm just remembering that someone *does* die in this story.
Just not Jamie. Can you imagine! Ahaha. Okay, sorry, continuing on.

# 50

The sky went black, and Meredith stumbled. At first she assumed that it was just her, that this was finally the karmic punishment she deserved, that the stye in her right eye had always been a prequel to the way the heavens would ultimately decide to push her out. She waited for the rumble of cosmic thunder, the lightning bolt from fate saying haven't we given you enough, you had love and success all before you were thirty, did you really think that was normal? Didn't you wonder, all that time that you were treating thirty like the finish line, didn't you think it was possible, that it was inevitable, that if you rushed through everything in your life, then of course you would pay for it, because you only get so many wins?

But Jamie kissed her back, and kissed her again, and then he pressed her safely away from the edge of the trail. He kissed her with a growing heat, a thickness, like a binding ritual or the prologue to sex. He kissed her again, again, again again again until the coffee cups clutched in their hands became active enemies of state. He couldn't touch her the way he wanted to; there was too much standing between them, like, for example, a fiancé. He stepped away forcefully, winded with the blow of a gut punch and said, "No. No, no."

"I'm sorry," said Meredith, feeling blindly for his face in the dark, meeting the edge of his cheek with the tips of her fingers; self-flagellation of the slightest, lightest brush. "Jamie, I'm so sorry—"

"Don't be sorry. Don't be sorry about this, this is fucking—fuck you, Meredith." He was breathing hard, his voice rotten with pain. "Fine. Fine, I won't do it."

Fear tightened around her heart. "What?"

"The article, Meredith." Her straining reach found his wrists as he pressed the heels of his hands into his eyes. "Fine, Meredith, you win, I love you, I don't want a life without you, tell me what you want me to do and I'll do it. I'll do it, okay? You win."

Meredith felt bereft, bewildered, like she'd woken up that morning and everything was upside down, like she no longer knew how to read, like everything around her was suddenly gibberish. The darkness seemed like an afterthought, as if it had always been this way and she had only just noticed.

"But you can't pull the article," Meredith said. Her eyes were adjusting, but barely. Jamie was still only outlines and muscle memory, still the partial projection of who he'd once been. "You already told me it's going to print."

"Right." Jamie's chin lifted, looking miserably at the sky. "I did say that."

"You're publishing it because you love journalism. Because Tyche is violating social ethics and the public deserves to know." The darkness seemed convenient, then. As if there were no further reason to lie because nobody could see. All of this was secret-telling now, the clandestine whispers of two lovers in bed.

"Yes," said Jamie. "Fuck."

"You need the money," Meredith pointed out.

"Fuck. Yes, I really do."

"You were willing to destroy me this morning, weren't you?"

"Yes, yes, I know, I still kind of am." Jamie sank blindly into the dirt, crouching on the edge of a rock, one hand still wrapped around his coffee cup. The other still in hers.

Meredith sat numbly beside him, an untranscribable whorl of nonsense in her head.

"The thing is," said Jamie, "I love you too much to hurt you."

She waited, and of course he said it. "But."

That word, the inevitable one, was deafening. On-screen, the captions would say something like *I love you, but I love my conscience more.* In French, presumably.

Jamie swallowed, hanging his head as he looked at their joined hands, safely blanketed by a sunless void of unintentional apocalypse.

"I'll pull my name from the article," he said. "I'll have my editor take the credit, he'll be happy to do it."

"No," said Meredith, tightening her grip. "No. Absolutely not."

"Yes," Jamie said. "I'm not going to be the one who does this to you. I'm not letting the *New York Times* run 'et tu, Brute' when I marry you. I'm not promising my life to you or asking you for yours knowing that my name is forever tied to yours by something ugly like this."

It hit her like a shotgun blast to her sternum.

"When you marry me," Meredith echoed.

"Yes, when I marry you." He reached over and kissed her brutally, with the savage adoration of a man who knows only one thing about the world, that the sun could snuff out like a light and he would stay there, kissing her. "You're not marrying anyone else, Meredith Wren. I'm not letting you. You told me you love me and I'm holding you to it. You're going to be accountable for at least one fucking thing in your life, and if it won't be federal prison time then it'll be me, god *damn* it." He kissed her like she'd rear-ended him on the freeway, like she'd stolen his parking spot, like she'd cut him off at the light. "It's me."

Oh Jesus, thought Meredith, who kissed him back and realized she'd never been so turned on, not ever, not once in her goddamn life.

"No." She struggled to pull away, but managed it. This was important. "Jamie. That report is going to win awards, I'm not joking. And you have a chance to take down Tyche for real." She swallowed hard. "You have to take me down with them."

"But—"

"I'm not saying I won't fight. I'm saying put your fucking name on it." Her eyes were swimming, they leaked out helplessly, she realized her nose was running only when she felt it drip onto her lip. "All that work, Jamie. Take the payday, cash out, love me or hate me or both. Have it all."

"Meredith." He frowned at her.

"It's my fault. I did this to myself, you were right, it's my fault."

"Meredith, I don't care whose fault it was—"

"Yes, you do. Yes, you do care, you *should* care. I want to be happy. I want to be happy, I want *so badly* to be happy, but it isn't real, it never worked." She was gasping it, convulsing with sobs. "It isn't real and I knew it. If I ever actually believed that happiness was real, I would have made a different choice. I didn't want *happiness,* for fuck's sake—I wanted an A!" She felt sick with herself, with the repulsion of having seen her insides. "I wanted to get a good grade in life, in adulthood, in *existing*—but who was ever going to give me that?"

She was babbling now, giving into her instincts for absurdity, the thing she'd known was the problem all along. She'd wanted to make things better—how many times had she said that? She'd wanted to make a world where her mother lived, and lived and lived and lived, and yet she also wanted her father to think she was worthy, to think she was *worth it,* and if there was a Venn diagram, a space where both things could be true, Jamie had always lived outside of that. Jamie, her love for him, that was irreconcilable with her potential, with her genius. Jamie was her failure, he was her downfall, and it seemed only fitting, only right, that she should suffer for choosing him now.

"I always knew that choosing you would hurt," said Meredith, whose chest ached with pain, sharp throbs of it. "I knew it would hurt but I want it, I deserve this." She couldn't breathe, wasn't confident he understood her. "I deserve it."

"No," Jamie said, and his hand was on her heart, a weight to hold her steady. "No, Meredith, I'm not going to hurt you."

Yes, she thought, yes you are, you already have.

He kissed her gently, so softly it was like a child's wish, like a prayer before bed. She kissed him back, the cyclone between them tightening, closer and closer, threads of fate inseparable, more tangled up than sweet. Like someone had dropped them on the floor and lived a life before picking them back up again years later, entropy and carelessness having formed, however unintentionally, an inseverable knot.

His hand found the waistband of her yoga pants, hers found the hem of his shirt. Skin on skin was feverish, burning. Everything was dark and hot, fresh earth and primal screams. Into his mouth she panted *please,* he licked back *mine,* she let out an animal whine of *forever,* he gritted his teeth with *yes.* Coffee spilled into the dirt, forgotten. The apocalypse carried on, irrelevant. Overhead a bird took flight, uninvested. The black of midmorning was godless, divine.

# 51

While Jamie Ammar and Meredith Wren lost themselves in the dark, Philippa Villiers-DeMagnon stepped out of her taxi into the intersection of Stockton and Pine.

# 52

Wait, I've lost the thread. Let's see—euphoric fucking, filial misery, life-threatening driving conditions . . . What else was happening then?

"Oh, shit," I said, more to the universe than to Arthur. Monster was resting his head heavily on my shoulder as we made our way through the parking lot and stopped short once things became very dark. Logistically speaking, it was probably no different from a starless, moonless night, though of course there were no lit streetlights or anything to enhance visibility, given that it was midmorning.

I reached instinctively for Arthur's hand, his clutching mine back and squeezing once.

"Yikes," said Arthur, in the voice of someone who is trying to be calm but doesn't necessarily want to be.

"Car," said Monster in a questioning voice. I can't say I was thinking anything specific at the time. Mostly that when things happen that seem to affect Monster in some way, I feel fear. Fear that he will panic and I will have to make things right again, or that I will have to put aside my own panic in order to accommodate his.

When I was pregnant with him, there were several earthquakes all in a row, and for weeks I couldn't stop thinking about how I would possibly calm a baby through disaster; what I would do if the end came for me with my son in my arms. Times like those, I wished I had never had a baby. The desire I felt to spare him any discomfort, any pain, it was almost like wishing to erase him, to erase the knowledge from my heart that anything could ever matter more to me than me. The knowledge that if this was it, if the reaper came for me now, if this was my moment to answer for all my little evils, I would say fine, punish me for eternity, just please don't let my baby hurt.

But he will! That's the absolute worst of it. I'd spin forever on a wheel of spikes if I could spare him, but I can't. Doesn't matter how good you are or how fiercely you love. Steal your billions, give 'em away, it doesn't matter. Be righteous, be ruthless, it's all the same. Baby, life fucks us all.

"Maybe it's an eclipse," said Arthur.

When I say I loved him then, I can't understate it. That little mild insertion of logic right then, oh god, I wanted to fuck him into the floor. I remembered he had a wife and a girlfriend and a boyfriend and there was really no place for me in that harem, so the feeling didn't last long. But oh boy, the passion you can feel for someone who remains cool in a crisis, I can't put words to it. It made me wish I had murdered Thayer Wren myself, holding the knife over his face saying, "Tell your son you're proud of the man he became or I'll cut you into tiny pieces and feed your liver back to him, so that you can sustain him in at least one fucking way like you never did while he was still innocent, while he still believed himself worth loving, while he was still blissfully, guilelessly young."

But admittedly, I am a person of inadvisable passions. I have a lot of love in me, a lot of anger, to the point where sometimes it's impossible to feed only one at a time.

"I read once about how people thought the darkness during Jesus's crucifixion was caused by a solar eclipse," said Arthur, which brought religion into it, rendering the moment substantially less sexy. I was grateful for that as well, since I was holding my child and couldn't very well have indulged my carnalities even if I'd been so inclined. "There's no real proof of that, though," Arthur added, as if he sensed I would be disappointed.

"Honestly, I'll take it. How long do eclipses last?"

"Mm, not sure. I'll look it up. Oh, wait." He sighed. "I forgot. No internet."

"Why, because of the eclipse?"

"No, because of the woods." He flapped a hand at the entrance to Muir Woods, through which we had passed after buying ourselves matching T-shirts.

"Right. Well, I suppose we can . . . go," I finished slowly. That had been the plan, anyway. We were parting ways, me returning home for Monster's nap and Arthur going back to his father's house to deal with his mess, which I honestly wanted no part of. We had initially agreed that I would come back once Monster was in bed for the night, since my mom could stay with him then and I could do whatever irresponsible witchcraft seemed appropriate after a reasonable amount of research.

When I had told my mother the day prior about Arthur's reappearance in my life, and Meredith's, she had given me a look like *Are you sure you want to get caught up in all that again?* and I pretended like I had no idea what she was trying to express to me, even though she had been there when I cried for days and days and days, and she had been the one to say it wasn't true back when I still said I wished I had never met Meredith Wren.

"She's lost," my mom had said back then. "She was lost when you met her and she never got found. But that doesn't mean you have to stay lost with her."

"You don't understand," I said, "she made me this . . . this *worse person,* she turned me into someone I'm not proud of—"

"No," my mom corrected me gently. "Meredith offered you a lot more choices than you would have had without her. But the opportunity for bad choices isn't necessarily a curse." My mother told me then about how of course Lola had also taught *her* some witchcraft when she was younger, and she had used it to do something bad and a girl had gotten hit by a bus.

"Holy shit, Mom, should you be in jail?" I gasped.

"She's fine," said my mom, flapping an indifferent hand. "She's a Realtor. I check in with her every now and then. Her husband is ugly, but otherwise she seems to be doing okay. And the point is, when I realized how good I was at curses, I understood what it really meant. Which is that if I let myself, I am capable of real evil—but it doesn't make me feel good and more importantly, it doesn't give me what I want. Because you can't make a boy choose you by cursing the girl he actually likes."

"Mom!" I half shouted.

"I was fourteen," she said, as if that explained everything.

"Still!" I yelled.

"The point is," she continued, "hating Meredith won't bring any good into your life. Hatred always breeds something you can't control."

"In a witchy way?"

"Sort of? I don't know. Magic is just, you know, nature." She shrugged. "It's energy, it's power, it's all just a function of choice and coincidence, so who knows how much of it we really control?"

I did not point out that *she* believed she had hit a girl with a bus. It seemed important to her personal mythology to maintain a sense of humility about the whole thing. I was actually impressed, though, because curses are really, really involved. Like, aside from being elaborate rituals with a lot of obscure ingredients, they require extreme amounts of willpower. I remember thinking that Meredith could probably do it, but not me, and I hated her a little, all over again, but I tried to hate her less each time I thought of her. It takes a lot of effort, but I still try. A little less hatred every time.

And my mom knows how much work that is for me, so when I told her about Arthur and Eilidh and, inevitably, Meredith—who didn't actually need my help, as I pointed out to my mother, who shrugged in that omniscient way that mothers have, which I can't wait to do to Monster, god damn it—my mom just told me to be careful how much of my heart I put into this. Because inevitably, it will be some.

The thing about Monster is that I have so much more range to my heart now. Which is not to claim that motherhood is, like, holy or anything. The act of motherhood is not itself profound. But I think, if you allow it to, the experience of motherhood can reach higher highs and lower lows, and you can hate the way you never thought you'd hate, you can love like you never understood that you could love, and you can feel the sort of impassivity that only comes from being really fucking tired. Like, truly, too tired to deal with anybody else's shit. It's a powerful indifference, and I had every intention to lean on it when it came to the Wrens.

Unfortunately, like I said, the sky went dark, and suddenly my plan to go about my day as normal felt unlikely, and I still felt this fear, the one where I was still a stupid idiot girl except in a thirty-one-year-old's body and I had a baby who was counting on me and I had to fix a dying man and his apocalyptic sister.

Which is when it hit me. A supremely unlikely coincidence, but like I said, that was most of life.

"Do you have any cell service?" I asked Arthur. "Like, for a phone call?"

He checked his phone. "No, not really."

"Okay, we're driving together, then, until we find a place with service." My car was closer to the entrance, so when we reached it, I tossed aside several empty toddler cereal containers and the disgusting towel I used to clean water off the slides at the park because Monster won't go down them if there was any, and I mean *any*, condensation on them and I told Arthur to get in, and then as soon as we reached civilization, I told him to call his sister. He wasn't listening at first because he had gotten a strange message from Philippa that he wasn't sure what to do with—you, of course, already know what that message was; it was the one telling him to ask his wife where she'd gone, although I didn't have that information yet at the time—so I had to tell him again, more firmly this time, hey, call your sister.

"Meredith?" he asked, and again, I had to work on not hating Meredith, because the way Arthur phrased it was with relief, as if he, too, thought calling Meredith was probably the answer, because Meredith could make the sun appear. She could physically drag it into being, and Arthur had shaped his voice into a sound that meant he agreed with my ostensible desire to call Meredith—that, to him, that seemed reasonable and sane.

"No, you idiot, Eilidh." I had not, up to that point, given Eilidh Wren a great deal of thought. I had met her only briefly—despite seeing her several times when she was a child, I had no meaningful memories of her; Meredith and Arthur had mostly come to my house, so I was very infrequently in a position to take notice of their younger sister—and I didn't know yet what to do with the limited information I now had.

For example, this much I knew: Eilidh was very beautiful, a different kind of beautiful than Meredith, where when she was standing next to Meredith she probably didn't actually seem that beautiful because it was a quieter beauty, understated, more restrained. It was a beauty that lived somewhere outside of sexuality. Beauty the way ancient ruins are beautiful, for having beheld something vast.

"Oh." Arthur sounded surprised, and seemed to be pointlessly procrastinating over this task, bantering with me about how there could possibly be cell service when I pointed out that the sun was merely blacked out, so it was basically just night time assuming the earth didn't explode, and he said if that was going to happen we probably would be dead already, and I said can you just call your fucking sister and he said what am I supposed to say to her and I said well, for starters, can you ask her if she knows anything about the plague where darkness falls?

"Oh," said Arthur in a different tone.

Then he called, and after four rings, Eilidh picked up.

# 53

Eilidh was still breathing hard when she answered Arthur's call. "Hello?"

"Quick question," said Arthur. "Is it dark where you are?"

"Uh. Yes," said Eilidh, glancing at the barely perceptible outline of Dzhuliya, who was sitting beside her on the steps outside the funeral home.

"Okay, cool. Also, did you do this?" asked Arthur in a pleasant voice, like he was wondering if he had her vote, but no pressure, she should vote her conscience, it was really just about doing whatever felt right according to her personal ethics.

"It would ... appear so," Eilidh confirmed. She glanced at Dzhuliya again, who even in the darkness looked to be lost in thought. Part of Eilidh wanted to reach out and rest the pads of her right fingers on each of the knuckles of Dzhuliya's left hand, as if such a thing might heal her wounds in some small but significant way.

The other part of her continued to feel as if the world was ending, with no room for amicability, much less intimacy or fondness or light.

"Oh! Okay, well." Arthur seemed to consult with someone else for a moment. "Where are you?" he said when he returned to their call. "Lou thinks we should probably meet up somewhere."

"Well, I'm headed back to Dad's," said Eilidh, in lieu of saying where she actually was.

"Oh, right, the lawyers," said Arthur with an abbreviated sigh. "Oh, sorry Eilidh, hang on, I'm getting a call. We'll see you there, okay?"

"Okay," said Eilidh, wondering as she always did if she should say *I love you,* or how exactly a person usually bid farewell to their siblings; like, generally speaking, did people say things with affection, and what if one of them died on the way home, would she regret not having said it? Presumably not if she was the one who died, but anyway Arthur had already hung up so Eilidh turned to Dzhuliya and said, "I guess we should go."

Dzhuliya seemed hesitant, as if she wanted to say something to Eilidh before progressing onward. She settled on "Are you all right?"

"Me? Well, you know, why wouldn't I be," Eilidh said, aiming for wry and arriving somewhere grotesquely off base, like bitter or maybe resentful, or *Listen here, Missy, I just made a day of endless night, how exactly do you think I'm doing, are you functionally comatose or only half alive?* Which Dzhuliya was not stupid enough not to hear.

"You know," Dzhuliya said slowly, "all of this has been so sudden, and you must still be reeling—"

Eilidh stood up, suddenly unable to bear the possibility of platitudes. She wasn't sure what they would be, actually. She'd never known what to make of death herself. Funny, for someone who thought about death so often and play-acted it almost obsessively on the stage, Eilidh had never imagined the possibility that one day she'd be old, old enough to have complicated feelings about her father, old enough to have children she'd done wrong by, old enough that a stroke could be sudden but not necessarily tragic, though in Thayer's case it would always be tragic because men were always young enough to reinvent themselves, even at the tender age of sixty. Eilidh would be old at . . . thirty-five? Forty? Invisibility seemed to be rocketing toward her, obsolescence hurtling like an asteroid through the sky. At least for now she could still inspire desire, it was still acceptable to be lost, to be working a middle-management job with no real eye on promotion because honestly, what was the point? Vacation days, retirement, all things she didn't have the capacity to long for, things that relied on some Future Time she didn't even believe in, like falling out of love with God. Soon it wouldn't be cute anymore, this feeling of disillusionment, the Wild West of her youth buried deep in the sandstorm of time. Fuck!

"I'm not reeling," said Eilidh darkly. "I'm fine."

It all seemed very obvious and painfully on the nose at the moment, the whole emotional blackout over the epiphany of her father's uneven love, the likelihood that she'd been doomed by his desire to keep her dependent and docile forever. Worse than her lifelong confinement to girlhood was the suddenly unignorable possibility that Thayer had loved her mostly as a possession, a thing he kept a close eye on rather than a person with any sort of agency or will. It now seemed to Eilidh that maybe if Meredith had ever done anything Thayer had asked her to do, then he would have loved *her* more for having successfully stomped the willpower out of her, finally crushing her down to a manageable size. Or if Arthur had bought more boats and fucked more bitches then maybe Thayer would have loved *him* most.

The thing in her chest chittered again with agitation, the kind that felt like pins and needles, anticipation for a storm. She ought to feel afraid, she thought. There were only so many plagues. What if they didn't repeat—what if it only escalated? The thing inside her was getting bigger, stronger. It no longer needed her consent to act out, like a toddler coming of age, learning the concept of no. The idea of setting it free, opening her mouth and letting it climb out of her like a swamp creature, like some eldritch exorcism, was appealing in a way, cathartically releasing a horror unto the world. Eilidh's horror, her very own! She felt oddly possessive over it, her little mangled thing with claws and teeth. *Why didn't you dread me, Father? Why didn't you fear me, for I have monsters in my heart!*

But inevitably a calmer, more stable Eilidh came back to her. Her father's daughter. She couldn't stand it, actually, even inside her head, the thought that she might let him down. She'd gone too long craving his adoration, finding some contorted relief in knowing that even if her dream was over, even if her body was broken, her father still loved her the most. The most! He *treasured* her, and maybe that had come with strings, a gilded cage, but she'd worn this mask so long she no longer knew what lived beneath it. The thing in her chest, the stirring of darkness was a bug, that's all, just a bug—*she* was something different, something more alive than a parasite could ever be.

Oh, how they warred inside her, the girl and the god! She, her entire she, it didn't want to be adored. Adoration had come so cheaply. Eilidh or her monster, no telling which, they both wanted to make something tremble, wanted to unleash a nightmare, to be rendered a nightmare herself because it was what they—she—deserved.

So what if she'd read him wrong the whole time; so what if Thayer wasn't benevolence incarnate? What was she owed for her diligence, for her loyalty, for the filial duty that only she had fulfilled? Who was to say it wasn't every-thing! Maybe the reason the world hadn't actually fallen off its axis (yet) was that Eilidh didn't know for certain where Thayer had placed his legacy. She still hadn't lost everything, not until the curtains closed. The show went on until the final lines of Thayer Wren were read.

"I want it," she said. The thing in her chest became the thing in her throat, then the thing in her mouth, crawling up like vomit. "Wrenfare. I'm going to fight for it."

"What?" Dzhuliya was looking at her with something not quite bewildered. Too sharp for that. It was a *repeat that so I can hold you to it* kind of a request for clarification.

"If he leaves the shares to me, I'm taking it. If he divides them, I'll make sure Arthur's on my side. How hard could it be?" Eilidh's heart thud-thudded in her chest, borne on the wings of a demon, alight on the branch of demand. "Or I'll convince him to split his shares up, and then the board can decide. The board will choose me over Meredith, I know they will." Everybody fucking hated Meredith. Eilidh was so light she wanted to fly. It's called a long game, Meredith! How about *them* apples, Sister Death! "The point is I'm going to try, I want to try." Power, that's what Eilidh deserved, power! Thayer was dead but Eilidh was alive, and by god, she was free! "I don't care if it costs me everything." What else was it for if not this, a seat at the table, the inheritance of a throne?

What else was there now but Eilidh and her rage?

"Securing a majority might not be as hard as you think," said Dzhuliya, who was a little wild-eyed, a reflection of Eilidh's own festering mania. Or maybe not? Either way, Eilidh's essentialness, the thing that had so long lain dormant was alive, it was awake, she wanted to run a mile, she wanted to scream as loud as she could, she wanted to fuck Dzhuliya in the car and then tear open her father's last wishes, casting old dreams unto the pyre. Freedom! Forget the dreamhouse of expectation, she had a monster to feed, hers was a lore built on glory! Father, forgive me. Father, release me. Father, absolve me—oh, and by the way Father, fuck you!

Eilidh rose to her feet from the steps outside the funeral home, pulling Dzhuliya up beside her, and kissed Dzhuliya full on the mouth, exuberant, bereaving. The darkness Eilidh had made was somehow animal, alive. She could feel the quiet breeding, sightless eyes blinking from deep inside the soul of her inky night.

"Grief is a real rollercoaster on you," whispered Dzhuliya, a hot gasp in Eilidh's mouth.

"Ride the high, baby," Eilidh replied, and smacked her lightly on the ass.

# 54

In case you're wondering, by then I had finally received Meredith's text message, the one calling me a traitorous bitch, which did not make any sense to me at the time and which, given the euphoric second-chance fucking that soon preoccupied her mind, Meredith had forgotten about.

I didn't text her back because by then Arthur had gotten a call from Gillian, and then I had to drive, and anyway, what do you say to that, really? By the time we both remembered she'd said it, we were locking eyes over the Wren family dinner table, one of us receiving some truly catastrophic news.

# 55

When it was over—when Meredith came loudly, as Meredith always did, and Jamie finished with a little more dignity, a jaw-clenching groan—they both became aware beneath apocalyptic skies that there was no future there, which technically they had both already known.

But Jamie had meant what he said, that he was going to marry her, even though he would hate her a little bit, and more importantly, hate himself. Because the hating her would pass—assuming she did not go the libel route and destroy his career, a merciless, narcissistic form of sabotage that never seemed entirely out of the question with Meredith—but the hating himself would stay forever. Meredith Wren! When Jamie had first found out who she was, back when they were both students and she'd become more than just the girl in his rhetoric course—when he realized that Wren was *that* Wren, unlike when he'd played hockey with a kid named Kennedy who wasn't *that* Kennedy—he started to think things like *Maybe there are some ethical billionaires?* which was counterproductive and absurd. Meredith had started to humanize capitalism for him and it was disgusting, it was the worst.

Jamie hadn't come from money. His parents had scrimped and saved and starved so he could get the best education in the world, and he had every intention of nobility—pay off his loans, then pay off their mortgage, pad their retirement fund, things for which he would need a starting salary of six figures right off the bat, which was why law school had seemed the natural route, the most patently obvious. Even summer associates made enough to pay off significant portions of their loans! And to think, with every luxury that his parents had forgone, every vacation they hadn't taken, every moment they'd spent choosing Jamie's future over their own, here was Meredith, who could wipe out their debt with a swipe of her finger, erase it like it had never existed at all. And for what? So her father was widely considered a genius; so what? Jamie's mother had managed to feed her family for about sixty dollars a week, how was *she* not a genius? How was Jamie's father not a genius for making his way here, for starting over completely? If you'd forced Thayer Wren to give up his livelihood, his life, to start over from scratch in another country, would he still have founded Wrenfare? Could Jamie's father have been the one to found Wrenfare had he been given Thayer's partners, Thayer's same resources in life? Was that fate's cruelty, its randomness, assigning fortune and comfort to Meredith Wren, who was so fucking miserable she sometimes cried in her sleep, who believed more sincerely in the ambiguous possibility of magic than in her own innate worth as a human, while Jamie had to go to his happy childhood home and be unable to bear it gracefully, to see the shabbiness of his life through new eyes, having now experienced the finery of Meredith's idea of a Christmas gift between casual lovers: cashmere sweatpants?

"Does she make you happy?" Jamie's mother had asked, her one question as to whether Meredith was right for her only son. The only thing she had ever cared about: Jamie's happiness. Such that when Jamie couldn't do it, couldn't stomach the thought of law school, of kowtowing to white men in suits who asked if he spoke English or said "But where are you from *originally*" when he told them he was from Boston, the thought of representing some corporation like Wrenfare, of defending its right to whatever-the-fuck because they had the money to hire some kid who wanted to get paid right away, for reasons that were maybe unselfish but still, in the end, pretty bad. And his mother just said *I want you to be happy. I just want you to be happy.*

"No," was nearly Jamie's answer, "no, she doesn't make me happy, when I'm with her I don't even know what happiness is or what it means, it seems too small and unimaginative an idea, I'm not sure happiness was ever even real, I mean what *is* that? I was happy before her, now I'm something else, something sickly and weak and yet massive and esoteric, I am confounding and arcane, I am consumed by something ancient and universal and yet no one has ever felt the way I feel, I'm sick with it, I'm sick to death with it, I want to hold her forever, I want to crawl inside her heart and wear her skin!"

Obviously he went with a simple yes and that was that. And then Meredith left, and Jamie felt happiness again, even if she had changed him, rewritten him from the top down so that he couldn't do anything meaninglessly anymore, he couldn't do anything anymore but write and ask questions and write. She disappeared, she came back without warning, he was sick all over again. She was gone, or he left, either way he was obsessed with her story.

He knew something secret about her, something intimate, which was that she got foot cramps right after she came. He also knew that she believed she was a witch. He had humored her belief, thinking it eccentric and charming, until she had showed him.

"I'm serious," she said, "pick a person and I'll prove it."

"What kind of person?"

"I don't know, someone you want to change." She had to be able to get physically close to them, she explained. She had to be able to make eye contact directly.

Jamie's freshman roommate was the worst person Jamie had ever met. They'd parted ways and never spoken again, though he still thought of it, the way that guy had brought back girls who seemed suspiciously docile, the way he called Jamie a terrorist and laughed. Old New Jersey money, some future stockbroker son of a bitch. "Okay, great," said Meredith, and the next time there was a party, a big one, Meredith sweet-talked the guy into an empty, shabby room in the den of iniquity and pulled Jamie in after her with a laugh.

"Watch," she said.

He watched. He watched *her*. He watched her look of concentration, the sweat on her brow. The way her fingers developed a tremor, a serious tremor, to the point where Jamie nearly interrupted to say she was obviously dehydrated, she needed to stop. Her eyes were unfocused, they were dark with purpose, with a little hint of madness that made Jamie feel he was witnessing something unholy, occult. He only remembered to look at the guy, his old roommate, after Meredith stepped back and swayed, nearly fainted, a thin wisp of a smile on her face.

"There," she said, "fixed it," and fell into Jamie's arms.

When she came to, the guy was gone, Jamie was calling 911. Meredith grabbed the phone from him and said she was fine, hung it up. "Well?" she demanded. "Did you check to see if it worked?"

"Meredith, I thought you were *dying*—"

"Oh my god, Jamie!" She looked at him with such a flame of hatred that he knew, somewhere deep in his gut *he knew*, that this was a really bad love, the kind that bites. The kind that would bite *him*, specifically.

"Why would you do that to yourself?" he felt himself ask her. "Why would you go through that, for what?"

She was embarrassed, he could tell. She was mortified, like she'd shown him an ugly scar and he'd replied that she, as a whole, was ugly. He knew, he could see it on her face, but he didn't yet know it the way he would eventually know. He'd humiliated her, he'd broken her heart, he'd said no to a part of her that she had only shared with him because she trusted him more than any other person on earth. Poor little rich girl! Except he really did feel pain for her, he honestly fucking ached.

The guy, Jamie's old roommate, he did a total one-eighty, dropped out of school to go on medical missions in various countries south of the equator. He posted on social media about his numerous hunger strikes; he used his family's money to fund class action suits over negligence-related deaths and racially driven wrongful termination cases until his father cut him off; eventually he died in poverty, about a year ago, from a severe case of malaria. His social media linked to a variety of socially conscious websites—he rarely appeared in any of the photos, and his last post was "what a beautiful life! I am rich in all the ways that matter" followed by the hashtag #happiness.

And, obviously, #blessed.

So to say Jamie had become obsessed with Chirp was an understatement. He preordered it, wore his the moment it arrived. After weeks and weeks he found that all it did was make him think of her, which was the opposite of happiness, though it fanned an old compulsion, some idiotic need to be part of Meredith's life. This time he was angry, ultimately she had *killed* a man; it didn't matter what sort of platitudes that guy had claimed to his imagined global audience, happiness and self-sacrifice weren't the same. Happiness! Please! Meredith couldn't make that shit! She sold her soul when she signed with Tyche, and thank god she did, because Jamie could hate her for that. He couldn't hate her for anything else, but *that* was disgusting, it was the epitome of privilege, it proved to him that her goal was never philanthropic. It made her less the girl whose lashes swept across her cheek as she slept and more the thing he wanted her to be, the willing conflagration of callousness and greed. Meredith Wren, finally the paragon of class solidarity that Jamie's ethical conscience had always needed her to be.

He'd known it from the start, that he was going to expose her, he was going to ruin her, and yes, he would carry that guilt around forever—he'd shove it in the box marked MEREDITH along with the vestiges of pain and love—but who was to say that wasn't exactly what either of them deserved?

He could only love her complicatedly, maybe even only from a distance. Up close she made him stupid, she overrode his natural functions. He looked at her and saw stars, he saw forever, he saw a lonely girl with more money in her life than love. She was the last person to know what happy looked like, what happy felt like, how incredibly underwhelming happiness actually was to claim. Happiness! Mosquitoes were probably happy, the bloodsuckers. Short and blissful, filled with retribution. How was that for the fulfillment of life.

Meredith's foot cramped then and Jamie reached for it, massaged it, kissed the arch of it. The darkness was thick, teeming with bugs and bloom. It was all so simple, so pathetic. Don't marry him, marry me. Be a better person. *Want* to be better, all on your own—want to right it all, for me. Face it, he thought, but also, how could he ask her that when it meant that he would lose her? Fix it, he thought, keep lying until you've gotten away with everything you've done, but if she did that, would he still respect her? Could he still look her in the eye and know he'd made a liar of her, even if they both already knew what she was?

Why couldn't he just love someone middle-class and sane? Why couldn't he want something smaller than justice? Why couldn't he buy pre-sliced mango at Demeter without it eating up his checking account—why was it so undignifying to slice the damn mango himself? Why couldn't he just accept that it *was* nice to feel better, to feel a moment of [redacted because it isn't real] from giving himself a little treat, which frankly he deserved? Wasn't this what life was, hadn't it always been life, they'd just monetized it so that in exchange for Jamie's mango-related hedonism the CEO of Tyche could have three thousand exotic camels and ten night-blooming yachts?

"I should probably get back," said Meredith, "because the lawyers will be here soon." She took his face in her hands and kissed him quickly, inconclusively. "I'll call you as soon as I'm done."

"And then what?" asked Jamie.

"And then we'll get a drink," she said.

"And then?"

"And then at some point we'll eat breakfast."

"And then?"

"And then I guess we'll have lunch."

"And then?"

"Probably dinner, unless we're still full from the other two meals."

"And then?"

"Breakfast again."

"You're not answering my question," Jamie said irritably.

"Actually, I am. You're just not listening." She tightened her grip on his cheek, then reached over for her yoga pants. "I'm sorry you have to love me," she said in a moment of worrying telepathy, rising to her feet to pull them on. "I wish I could let you love someone better."

"At least leave me the decency of my own critical errors," muttered Jamie, handing Meredith her bralette.

"But can you do me a favor?" Meredith said, pulling it on over her head.

"Absolutely," he said to his feet. "I'd hoped there was a catch. Make it a good one, like really ethically troubling, something I can feel violently sick about."

She crouched down to look at him.

"Don't let me go," she said.

"Okay," said Jamie uncertainly. "That's it?"

"That's it," Meredith confirmed.

Then she got up, turned on the flashlight on her phone, and went the opposite way down the trail.

# 56

Meredith wished almost immediately that she had taken Jamie with her, because hiking in the dark with only her phone for light was actively unsafe. She grew concerned about Jamie, about his well-being, which sickened her, as she had never concerned herself before with the possibility that Jamie could be lost or hurt or maimed and now there were so many possibilities actually, so many ways to come to harm.

She had never thought before that Jamie could be hit by a bus, that he could be struck by lightning, that he might not properly chew his food and so he could choke and thus be dead in an instant, a few seconds tops. Bodies were so fragile, dear god! She had never thought to wonder what she would do if something truly unfortunate happened to Jamie, not even something gruesome like death or murder but the mere possibility of pain, the loss of someone he loved, the stray feeling that he was not appreciated, the throb of knowing he was nothing in this life but insubstantial thread. Gossamer and on the wind, as vulnerable as the life's work of a garden spider.

Meredith's phone rang in her hand and she thought thank god, I'll come back for you, let me just make sure you're all right. She had never once had such thoughts about Cass, partially because Cass was a man, a man with a past that preceded her own. Cass had been made a man by some other woman, whereas Jamie was all insubstantial and unformed when they had met, just as Meredith had been. Jamie was practically fresh clay! Cass would take care of himself, he would be fine, some woman would love Cass so much, because Cass would save her and she would let him do it. Oh fuck, oh fuck, thought Meredith, feeling worse, not for the possibility that she would hurt Cass but for having wasted the years of devotion he could have had. "Are you okay?"

"Meredith?"

It was an unfamiliar voice and Meredith realized she had hallucinated

Jamie's name. She checked the screen of her phone again, realizing it was someone else, some unsaved Los Angeles number. "This is she. Who is this?"

"Meredith, it's Kip Hughes. Sorry to call during your bereavement leave."

"Kip," Meredith breathed. Kip as in the CEO of Tyche. Kip as in the veritable god of magitech commerce; as in the person Meredith had tried so desperately to be; as in the person who was about to be utterly fucked as a direct result of those efforts. "Wow, I . . ." Fuck! Fuck! Fuck! ". . . didn't expect to hear from you."

"How are you doing, kiddo? Hanging in there?"

*Kiddo?* To a grown woman who had probably lost him billions of dollars. Fascinating.

"Oh, you know," said Meredith ambiguously, waiting for the other shoe to drop. She couldn't understand how Kip was even making this call, how he was conducting business under these sorts of circumstances. "Is it dark where you are?"

"I'm in Scotland right now, thanks for asking. Crazy how early it gets dark up here, right?"

"Right," she said, preposterously.

"Listen, I'll make this quick." Here it was, the guillotine falling. Meredith, we've got to cut ties. Meredith, we had a good run. Meredith, Tyche would like to go a different direction, one specifically away from you. "I hear you're the anointed one, no surprise there. Must be a real mixed blessing—I can't imagine how you must be reeling from all this. I'm sure you've got a lot to think about in the coming months, but I just want to put my bid in early. I think we've made a great team so far with Birdsong, Meredith, and I'd like to see how far this partnership can take us."

"Sure," said Meredith, who hadn't the faintest idea what he was talking about.

"And you know, Meredith, candidly, between you and me, you're probably aware—it's not much of a secret that Wrenfare was struggling in recent years. Risky projects, legal drama, bit of a leadership crisis all around. A little birdie told me Thayer had been funding the company himself to try to keep the ship from going under." A pause. Meredith realized she was supposed to speak, but didn't know what to say. Also, she thought of Merritt Foster as a very large bird, oversized, perhaps a vulture. "No need to confirm or deny. The point is, we both know folks can smell blood in the water.

A lot of suits are going to come and try to rip it up for parts, and frankly I wouldn't be surprised if you get a lot of early interest from China."

China? The country? Or the vaguely bigoted idea? Meredith had completely lost the thread of the conversation. When had they begun talking about Wrenfare? She thought they were talking about her company, which was something that was actually hers. For now.

"I had a few preliminary meetings with your father before he passed. I always admired Thayer, he was one of my personal heroes. I wish he'd taken my offer more seriously."

Meredith said nothing.

"Listen, after the funeral let's sit down for lunch, okay? I'll get you my best offer by Monday end of day. I just want you to think about it, the possibilities here. I know it hurts to hear—I'm sure your father's legacy means everything to you—but the ship is going down, Meredith. I find it hard to believe that Thayer would rather see Wrenfare go bankrupt than let his life's work become part of the Tyche family."

Meredith wanted to laugh. She clapped a hand over her mouth.

"Naming rights," she managed.

"Well, the Tyche brand is so strong . . . we could certainly discuss the possibility of Wrenfare carrying on operations with Tyche as the parent company. I'm sure, though, with all the press you'll be facing in the coming weeks, you understand the benefit of keeping this on the down low." Ah, there it was. *Meredith, you fucked up, and now you owe me.* "Tyche has the operational means and the industry respect to turn the ship around. Assuming we can come to an equitable agreement."

Translation: You give me what I want, and in return, I won't bury you alive.

"That's a lot to process, though, and I'm sure it's important for you to focus on your family for now, so let's table it. I'll have my assistant reach out to your team at Birdsong to set up a lunch for early next week? And listen, if there's anything I can do for you—"

"Keep me out of prison" nearly fell out of Meredith's mouth.

"—just let me know. I'm here for you, Meredith." Kip Hughes, obviously her dearest friend and most dedicated investor, who cared only for her personal well-being. Kip, who only wanted to make them both a lot of money, to ensure their jets stayed docked and their thrones remained untoppled.

Except, what throne? Whose?

Suddenly she felt a flood of awareness, delayed recognition. A chilling heat sped through her veins, flooding her extremities. Belatedly, she understood what this was. The king is dead, long live the king.

Then Jamie's voice came back to her. *Whoever takes over Wrenfare is fucked, full stop. Nobody's steering that ship to safety.*

Oh, she thought. Oh, I see, Dad.

"Bye, Christopher," Meredith said without thinking, and abruptly ended the call.

# 57

The call that Arthur had received while he was on the phone with Eilidh was, as I mentioned earlier, a call from Gillian, his wife. Interestingly, she did not address the matter of eternal darkness, perhaps because she hadn't noticed yet, given the position of the Wren family home beneath a thick canopy of trees.

"I just want you to know I'm really sorry," she said. "That will make sense later. I was just sitting here thinking how sorry I am, and I wanted you to know."

"Okay," said Arthur agreeably, with prodigious amounts of unspoken confusion. Typically he didn't ask when Gillian did confusing things, as he found the more straightforward course of action in any situation was to trust her implicitly, with the leisure of blind faith.

But then, a little bit later, just as I was pulling into the car port at his father's house, Arthur received another call, this one from Lady Philippa.

"Is this Arthur Wren?" said a garbled voice.

"Pip?" said Arthur. "Is that you?"

"Can you hear me?"

"Hello?"

"Hello?"

"Yes, hi, who is this?"

"Is this Arthur Wren?"

"Yes, who is—"

"This is—"

"Sorry, keep going—"

"Right, okay, well my name is Jack, I'm staying at the Four Seasons—"

"Four Seasons? Which Four Seasons?"

"The one in San Francisco? Anyway, the woman who was just taken away, her phone was on the ground, so I thought I'd call her emergency contact—"

"What happened to Philippa?" asked Arthur, thinking with a sudden flash of discomfort about the mysterious apology call he'd just received from Gillian.

"Well, I think she's . . ." Jack from the Four Seasons suddenly became very reticent. "My wife and I debated for ages about what to say to you. I wanted to text you, but she said a text message would be insanely upsetting to receive—"

"Is Philippa okay?" asked Arthur, looking at me. I was pretending not to listen but I was obviously *riveted*.

"Nooooooooooot exactly," said Jack from the Four Seasons. "I mean . . . noooooooooot really."

Which was certainly one way of delivering the news that Philippa Villiers-DeMagnon was dead.

# 58

You see, what had happened was that Philippa never actually left the city. I can only speculate as to her thought process here, but having spoken to all the parties involved except for Philippa, what I've gathered is that she assumed Arthur and/or Yves would eventually come after her, so she decided to go to the nicest hotel in San Francisco to have a little spa day and relax. She was on the phone with her credit card company at the time she was stepping out of the cab, arguing with them about how they needed to lift the hold on her account, because yes, she was out of the country, and the airport charges for Sour Patch Kids and Vitaminwater were definitely her. I'm not sure what they said back, because none of the witnesses to her accident were paying attention to anything except the slightly bitchy sound of her voice (RIP).

As you know, total darkness fell suddenly. So suddenly that the driver on Pine didn't see a woman stepping furiously out of her cab, so busy was he staring at the sky, wondering if this was the end. Ironically, the only person who *wasn't* wondering if it was the end of the world was Philippa herself, for which it actually was the end. Which is funny, if you think about it, if only because in these types of situations, all you can really do is laugh.

# 59

Scene: The Wren House.

The Players:
Arthur Wren
Gillian Wren
Yves Reza
Cass Mizuno
Eilidh Wren
Meredith Wren
Dzhuliya Aguilar
God, also known casually as Lou
Monster, the holy progeny
John, the elderly lawyer
Ryan, the smarmy lawyer

*Arthur enters the house from the front door. Lou is behind him, struggling with a small toddler who really loves to climb stairs but isn't necessarily any good at it. Gillian is in the living room, prettily dressed, pacing.*

Gillian: You're back!

Arthur: Yes.

Gillian: Thank god. Everything okay?

Arthur: Not really. Gillian, did you kill Philippa?

Gillian: What?

Arthur: Well, your phone call was very cryptic, and I just had to be sure—

Gillian: Oh my god, what?

*Eilidh enters from the living room with Cass, and Dzhuliya,
who lingers at the rear.*

Eilidh: Oh good, Arthur's here. Is that everyone? Oh, hi
Lou.

*Lou gives a winded motion of her hand that appears to be a
wave. Monster is immediately taken by a small ceramic book-
end.*

Monster: Doggie!
Cass: Where is Meredith?

*Meredith is sitting quietly on the stairs in the dark, such
that nobody notices her right away.*

Meredith: Here.

*Eilidh jumps.*

Eilidh: Holy balls!
Meredith: What?

*Gillian, still disturbed, turns to Arthur.*

Gillian: Arthur, I'm sorry to interrupt, but what do you
mean 'did you kill Philippa'?
Meredith: Yes, back to that. Gillian asks a very important
question, Brother Accusatory.

*Lou looks at Arthur, who isn't really looking at anyone.
Not in the sense that he is ignoring them; more like he is
underwater and can't physically hear them.*

Lou: It kinda seems like a lot to dig into right now.
Arthur: Yes. In fact I'd love it if we could take care of
this quickly. I'm still in a great deal of shock, I think.
Oh, and Yves—they're waiting for us at the hospital.

*Yves looks up from where he has been making pancakes in
the kitchen.*

Yves: The hospital?

Arthur: Well, the morgue.

*Arthur barks an incredibly unstable laugh. Gillian looks worriedly at him, as does Eilidh.*

Eilidh: Are you okay, Arthur?
Arthur: I actually can't feel my fingers, so let's just go talk to the lawyers.

*The family shuffles into the dining room where the lawyers are waiting. Meredith has seen Lou but not acknowledged her presence. Which is very astounding because Lou is holding a wriggling Monster, or not really holding, as it were. Certainly not successfully.*

Eilidh: Should . . . everybody be here?

*Meredith then looks at Lou. Arthur looks at Dzhuliya. Eilidh looks at Yves. Monster looks at the chandelier and points to it. Then he points to the light fixtures on the wall.*

Monster: Ball! Ball. Ball. Ball!
Lou: Those are sconces. But close!

*Arthur looks pale, like he will vomit at any moment. Yves stands beside him and sets a hand on his shoulder. Gillian looks as if she'd like to do the same but can't quite figure out the mechanics of such a motion. Instead, she stands erect beside him, the perfect politician's wife.*

Arthur: Let's just get this over with. Do we really even care who hears this? It'll be public knowledge soon anyway.

*Eilidh looks at Meredith, who is being unusually quiet.*

Meredith: Yeah, let's just hear it.

*The lawyers exchange a glance. Ryan shrugs insouciantly, so John proceeds.*

John: So, the judge ruled that Mr. Behrend does indeed have the valid last will and testament. There may still be some legal challenges, depending, but it does not appear that

Thayer was coerced in any way, and medically he was, as far as we know, of sound mind.

*Lou mouths* As far as we know? *with a questioning look on her face. Yves gives her a small wave with his free hand and replies soberly* I'm Yves!

John: And so—

*John clears his throat as if hoping someone, specifically Ryan, will interrupt and take over. It's clear he isn't happy at all about what he has no choice but to say.*

John: As to the most contentious matter, which is that of the ownership shares in Wrenfare Magitech. Your father has bequeathed the entirety of his majority shares to—

*John clears his throat again. His eyes dart helplessly around the room.*

John: His eldest daughter. Meredith Honora Wren.

*Everyone looks at Meredith except for Eilidh. Eilidh stares straight ahead at a fixed point on the wall. Meredith looks at Lou and seems unsurprised.*

John: And as for the, ah, the money. And such. That is all to be split equally between his descendants. Meredith Honora Wren, Arthur Everett Wren, Eilidh Olympia Wren, and—

*John stops again. Monster points to something, then claps and looks at Lou as if for confirmation that he has done well.*

John: The unborn child of Thayer Wren and Dzhuliya Aguilar.

*Now every head in the room swivels to Dzhuliya except for Ryan, the younger lawyer who has known the contents of the will this whole time. He is looking smugly at Meredith for reasons that are probably very petty, based purely on the type of glance it seems to be.*
    *Now both Eilidh and Arthur look as though they will vomit.*

Eilidh: Is. This. A fucking. Joke. ?

*Gillian makes a compulsive attempt to pacify the situation.*

Gillian: This is . . . it's wonderful news, of course—
Eilidh: I'm going to be sick.
Arthur: How much money is there, exactly?

*John looks heavenward for bolstering. Predictably no one answers.*

John: Thayer Wren's net worth is in the billions, but nearly all of that is tied up in Wrenfare. His actual assets include this house, the flat in San Francisco—
Eilidh and Meredith, in unison: What flat in San Francisco?

*Dzhuliya reddens. Eilidh's expression doesn't change, though her eyes begin to look unfocused with rage. She looks as though distracted, as if there is a buzzing in her head growing louder and louder, a swarm incoming.*
   *Meredith speaks faintly, some of her careful stillness slipping.*

Meredith: Oh.

*John continues on as if nobody interrupted.*

John: And there is the summer house that Thayer Wren co-owned with his late wife Persephone, and the cars. As for the money in his personal accounts, they contain about two million dollars, not all of which is liquid.
Meredith: Is that including his investment accounts?
John: Yes.
Arthur: And that's split between the . . . four of us.

*It isn't a question; more like someone repeating out loud the most ridiculous thing they have ever heard, just to be sure everyone else is hearing it too.*
   *John coughs as if something is stuck in his throat.*

John: Yes.

*Silence.*

Lou: Okay, look, I know I don't actually go here, but we're all thinking it. Obviously that's a substantial sum of money for anyone, but we're talking about one of the richest men in the fucking world.

*Meredith and Lou lock eyes and skitter away.*

Nobody: Where did all the money go?

*Eilidh looks repulsed, physically sick, like her appendix is bursting. The next words out of her mouth seem to pain her, as if someone has surgically removed them from her throat. She forces them out like she should be enjoying them; like she should mean them. Like shoving another piece of sickly sweet cake between her lips.*

Eilidh: Let's not be greedy.

*Meredith scoffs, as if this, more than anything she has heard over the course of the last few minutes, is the dumbest thing anyone has ever said in the history of the world. As if somewhere, angels wept over the stunning emptiness of thought. As if the idiocy was such that dark arts could only be blamed, for such incompetency is written, prophesied for centuries by hell itself.*

Eilidh: Is there something you'd like to say to me, Meredith?

*Eilidh's mask is slipping. Her hair seems to cascade from its usual sleek bun.*
  *Meredith turns to her with unmissable combativeness.*

Meredith: Dad's dead, Eilidh. You don't need to win him over anymore. You can admit that he fucked us with this.

*Eilidh struggles to breathe, warring internally with her wrathful swarm.*

Eilidh: Is that really what you think? That he fucked *us*, plural?

*Meredith scoffs again, this time with no small showing of pity.*

Meredith: You don't know the half of it.
Eilidh: Oh? Then fucking enlighten me, Sister Bitch.

*Meredith's posture goes rigid. Arthur isn't listening, lost in his own thoughts. His inattentiveness to his usual role of arbitration makes the situation rapidly worse.*

Meredith: Excuse me?

*John looks profoundly uncomfortable.*

John: I should add—there are some personal stipulations. Part of Thayer's bequeathal necessitates that Eilidh Olympia Wren will always have employment at Wrenfare, should she choose it.

*Eilidh looks stricken by this, the swarm temporarily stilling between her ears.*

Eilidh: Are—are you serious?

*Meredith looks smugly repulsed.*

Meredith: There you go, Eilidh. Daddy's little princess will never have to hunt for food, she'll never have to starve. Happy now?

*The two sisters stare at each other.*

Eilidh: Do you *really* think I don't know what that means?
Meredith: No, I don't think you do, Eilidh.

*Arthur's knuckles turn white; beneath the sconces, the dining room lights flicker with the cadence of a racing pulse. Lou notices. She looks at Arthur, more concerned than questioning, which awakens Arthur's impulses for mediation. He rouses as if from the dead.*

Arthur: Come on. Eilidh, she's right. Death, leave Eilidh alone.

Meredith: Oh, *thank you*, Brother Saintly—
Arthur: Meredith.

*He looks as if he'd like to say more but can't. His hands are
trembling, the chandelier overhead beginning to shower the
floor with sparks, a cascade of light that twirls in ribbons
as it spirals onto the dining room carpet. Lou observes all
this with a puzzled frown. Monster claps his hands. Yves
disappears into the kitchen.*

 *Gillian looks painfully up at Arthur, speaking quietly to
him.*

Gillian: You never needed anything from him, Art.
Arthur: I needed lots of things from him, actually. But
you're probably right that they were never going to be in
the will.

*Yves returns with a casserole tray full of water and places
it on the lightly smoldering carpet by Arthur's feet. Monster reaches for it.*

Monster: Ahhhhh!

*It's a pleasantly disruptive sound of youthful delight. Un-
fortunately, it does little to dissolve the tension. John
looks desperately for an escape hatch. Sensing that nothing further will happen over which he can gloat, Ryan nods
curtly to the room.*

Ryan: Well, we'll leave you to discuss. Should any of you
need anything, here's my card.

*He places it on the table. Then he leaves, although first
he tries to tickle Monster, who lurches away, clinging shyly
to Lou. For what it's worth, Lou remembers Ryan, though he
clearly doesn't remember her.*

Ryan: Cute kid.
Lou: Please don't touch my child.
Ryan: Whatever, geez, relax.

*John opens his mouth as if to say something comforting, but ostensibly realizes there is nothing to be said.*
  *Before he takes his leave, though, he turns to Meredith.*

John: You should expect a phone call from the board at Wrenfare shortly. I will inform them of the will's contents now, and they can get you up to speed on the current state of the company.

*John turns to the other two siblings.*
  *Well, three, including Dzhuliya's womb.*

John: I don't suppose I should say this . . . but I think you should know that the will Thayer originally drew up at the time of Persephone's death split the shares equally among his children. If Meredith is willing to sell or give away some of the shares she's inherited, you could certainly own the company equally.

*Eilidh flinches, raising a hand to her head as if it throbs.*

John: I wish I knew what prompted this. But he must have had a lot of faith in you, Meredith.

*John rests a hand on Meredith's shoulder. She says nothing.*

John: Well! This has been . . .

*He nods and doesn't finish the sentence. Mercifully, he leaves.*
  *Outside it is dark at two in the afternoon. It's unclear when, if ever, any of the occupants will see the sun again.*
  *The silence among the room's occupants, deafening as it is, seems to have . . . an unusual weight.*

Lou: Does anyone else hear a buzzing sound?

*Nobody answers. Yves looks cheerfully at Dzhuliya.*

Yves: So, you are pregnant!
Dzhuliya: I am. Yes.

Yves: When are you due?

*Dzhuliya looks very uncomfortable. She turns to Eilidh, who instantly flinches away.*
  *When Dzhuliya speaks, she is quiet, barely audible.*

Dzhuliya: I should have said something, I know, but I just couldn't . . . I didn't know how to . . .

*She stops.*

Dzhuliya: It was only a couple of times.

*Eilidh raises one hand to her head, squeezing her eyes shut. The pain appears to be searing, which Meredith notices and takes as a personal offense.*

Meredith: Jesus. You can stop being so dramatic.

*Eilidh's eyes remain shut.*

Eilidh: Shut up, Meredith.
Meredith: What do you have to be so upset about? This is happening to all of us.
Eilidh: *Is it?*

*She glares furiously up at Meredith.*

Eilidh: You think I don't know why he chose you? Why he decided that his legacy was safe with *you*? *You* think I don't know that he respected you the most—that he saw the most potential in you? I get it, Meredith, okay? I'm the one he had to keep safe because he knew I couldn't do it on my own! So there, are you happy? Are you happy now?
Meredith: Are you serious?

*Now Meredith looks pale with anger.*

Meredith: He left his shares to me because he knew I would fumble it. Because he wanted me to be the one holding the ball when the whole thing went down. It's a shithole, Eilidh—Dad was a terrible investor. He lost almost all of it trying to go to fucking space. The rest of it he threw away on companies that were only copying mine. He tried to take me down, and when he couldn't, he handed me a flaming pile of shit. Don't deny it.

*Meredith looks hard at Lou when she says it. Lou receives the glare with utter bewilderment and looks around for answers, confused.*

Lou: What?

Meredith: I know you were developing something to compete with Chirp. I know you were trying to force me into obsolescence.

Lou: Dude, I don't care about your 'solescence. I don't fuck around with neuromancy.

Meredith: Your company pitched him a neuromantic chip!

Lou: I don't have a company! I work at a fucking Wrenfare store! I pitched Thayer something totally different—which isn't even relevant, by the way, because he never made an offer! I think he was probably just fucking with me.

Dzhuliya: No, he wrote up an offer.

*Everyone looks at Dzhuliya then. She takes the opportunity to return the conversation to Eilidh, who is doubled over, hugging herself.*

Dzhuliya: Eilidh, just so you know, I didn't know he planned to give it all to Meredith. Until Ryan called me the other day, I honestly thought he was planning to give it to you—

*Lou looks around, distracted.*

Lou: You guys really don't hear that buzzing sound?

*Gillian frowns.*

Gillian: Actually—

*Eilidh squeezes her eyes shut and motions for Dzhuliya to stop talking.*
  *Dzhuliya doesn't listen.*

Dzhuliya: You were the one he always talked about, Eilidh.

And . . . and I was *happy* to listen, I really was. I've always had feelings for you, and I didn't think . . . I just didn't think anything would ever happen with us, you'd made it so clear you weren't interested, and Thayer was . . . I don't know. I don't even have an excuse, I was just lonely, I was fed up with dating, and he was so . . . so attentive, and—

Meredith: Oh my *god.*
Dzhuliya: I'm not talking to you.
Meredith: You're a fucking cliché!
Dzhuliya: I'm not talking to you.
Meredith: Do you even *hear* yourself?

*Arthur's sparks shower again. His hands start to shake violently.*

Gillian: Art? Are you okay?

*Meredith turns to Eilidh.*

Meredith: You know, I just want to hear you say it.

*Eilidh's teeth are gritted so hard she can hardly speak.*

Eilidh: Say. What.

*Meredith looks terrifying with ill-begotten triumph.*

Meredith: That I was right about him. That he was always a complete fucking shitbag. He never loved us. He *used* us.
Eilidh:
Meredith: You were the devoted one. The *only* devoted one. And how did he reward you?
Arthur: Death.

*By now the pulse of faltering electricity is jarring and epileptic. Meredith ignores Arthur's warning, continuing to address her sister.*

Meredith: You let him steal your life, Eilidh. You let him *swallow you up,* and for that, I'm fucking furious with you. I'm so fucking angry at you I can barely even look at you.

You really thought his love was worth it. You're honestly that fucking stupid.

*Eilidh looks at Meredith. It's the first time that Eilidh has looked lucid, and painless, in the last five minutes, as if something inside her has finally ruptured. As if, at long last, something broke.*

*Meredith stares at her as if she is seeing something in her sister's eyes for the first time.*

*Dzhuliya steps forward hastily to intervene.*

Dzhuliya: Look, I really don't think—
Eilidh: Shut up, fatherfucker!

*The buzzing has become unmistakably audible to the others in the room. Monster shrinks into Lou's chest, burying his head apprehensively in her neck. A hot burst of flame hits the dining table from the chandelier just before Arthur falls to the floor.*

Gillian: Arthur!

*She drops to check his pulse and begins CPR. Yves lets out a cry and kneels to hold Arthur's head in his hands. Eilidh is still staring at Meredith, but she is standing straight now, as if the pain has burst from somewhere inside her and materialized in vapors from her skin.*

Eilidh: Don't you understand that I *had* to be this stupid? That if he didn't love me, then no one would?

*Meredith looks at Eilidh as the swarm grows nearer. Outside, the darkness is so thick that it's not possible at first to see its parts; the way it has become a cloud of black wings hurling themselves at the house's windows. The force of the collective bodies is such that the panes seem to physically strain.*

*On the floor, Arthur is no longer breathing. Death comes in threes. Gillian bends her forehead to his and weeps. Eilidh's resolve seems to break, the last of her mask dis-*

*solving just as the windowpanes give way, as she sobs to her sister,*

Eilidh: WHY COULDN'T YOU JUST LOVE ME?

*The force of the swarm is so great that the room is rendered unseeable almost instantly, within seconds. The high, desperate sound of a child crying pierces through the clamor of insect wings, the room's inhabitants beginning to scream as the air in the room grows thick with an ancient plague of flies. They are drawn to shit, is the thing—they consume it. An appropriate plague, if not a sequential one.*

   *For a long moment, there is nothing but the swarm.*
   *Then a thick blaze of light cuts through it.*
   *No, not light.*
   *Fire.*

Arthur: Run.
   *And they do.*

# FRIDAY.

FRIDAY

# 60

In the wake of the fire, most of the house was fine. The dining room was uninhabitable, obviously, but the swarm of flies had been so thick there was no real chance of it jumping beyond the constraints of the house—the trees outside the dining room didn't burn.

Aside from Arthur, Gillian, and Yves, who went to the morgue, and Dzhuliya, whom none of us particularly wanted to speak to (I didn't know anything about her at the time, but even so, you have to admit, it's not a good look), the rest of us spent the remainder of the day down at the base of the house, loitering around the carport. Monster conked out on my shoulder, sweet thing; in that sense, the perennial darkness helped. Then we picked through the ash once the firemen had come and gone. The bedrooms were okay; Eilidh's turret remained completely unscathed, a fact she seemed to find hysterically funny until she started to cry. The bodies of all the dead flies were mostly burned away, so it wasn't as disgusting as it could have been.

Through it all, the darkness never lifted. I knew that Eilidh's apocalypse problem was part of what I had been commissioned for; technically, it was the only thing I'd agreed to try to solve, with Arthur's deaths being attended to only tangentially to the more sensational issue of world-ending plagues. But witnessing the effects of Eilidh's maladies firsthand, I was beginning to understand that the darkness that had befallen the Wrens wasn't any sort of magic my grandmothers had prepared me for. I doubt they'd seen anything of this magnitude over the course of their lifetimes—though, they'd obviously seen a lot or they wouldn't have come here, so who could say. Maybe they'd seen worse.

Since I didn't know how to fix any of the big stuff, I tried to focus on the little stuff. I tried to explain to Meredith that there had clearly been a misunderstanding in the matter of Thayer's neuromantic investments; my ex-husband was likely leading the team she was talking about because neuromancy did interest him, and she was right that the shell company she'd dug up included members of the start-up I had co-created when I first sold to Tyche. But Ben and I didn't talk about work anymore, largely because he didn't think I still had it—the appetite for what he considered to be success.

That was part of what ended us, actually. I met Ben at Berkeley, and we dated for two years of college on and off and then more seriously while we worked on our start-up, the one we eventually sold. He and I and the rest of our team all lived and worked together in the same shitty rental house, the Silicon Valley wet dream. In case you're wondering, some indiscretions did happen, but it never felt to us like cheating. It just felt like we were, I don't know, overflowing. And alive.

Ben and I were in love with a lot of it, mostly the work, but also each other, our whole team, the thing we were bringing to life. Our first baby, we used to joke. I wanted to keep it going, to build us up into something big, but Ben thought it was bonkers not to sell at the price Tyche was offering. I said okay, fine—I could see I was outnumbered, and we did all have student loans to pay off, so it was hardly my decision—but I insisted Tyche would have to keep us on, since we were the only ones who could really do this, et cetera et cetera, and then Tyche said yeah okay, they would take us on *as Tyche employees,* which I hated from the start. Later, I found out that Tyche only bought us out because they were developing a rival product, their own in-house software delivery for which our production had been further along. So we worked for Tyche for about a year, and then they shut us down once their own team had caught up, because we'd become a redundancy. They already had a team and now they had our IP and our tech, so they didn't really need *us.* I was so devastated I cried all day and night for a week, and then when I finally got out of bed, Ben caught me researching curses on the internet, something I hadn't done in years. "For their dicks," I explained.

Ben smiled at me from the doorway. I should have known.

"Let's make a baby," he said.

I hated being pregnant. But I loved Monster so much. I loved Monster more than Ben right away, even though I told myself I wouldn't. I told myself the marriage came first, because it was Ben I had chosen to grow old with, whereas Monster I would have to love no matter what. There was an element of fatalism there, and it was up to me, I felt, to honor the love I had chosen, because I thought it really mattered, that element of choice.

Unfortunately, I loved a version of Ben that didn't actually exist, and I only saw it clearly after Monster was born—that I had chosen a convenient illusion, Ben as Eden, and I had fallen in love with the aesthetics of success. I'd fallen for the model I'd been given of personal achievement, which would somehow eventually become happiness, which, much like trickle-down economics, had always been a lie. And so, from there, my choice became not my husband, but the sleepless, needy little thing that I promised myself I would be better for—for whom I would be, somehow, magically, my *best self*.

After Monster was born, I told myself that I would exist wholly in this moment, and this one, and this one, and thus over time I would simply *change*. I would be grounded. I would be better. I would hate myself less, or at least less often. I would choose to see the world as a miracle, just a plain ol' gosh dang miracle, instead of something to be leveraged, and ultimately reaped.

I think Ben had thought that if he gave me this new toy to play with, it would be like a bridge from one state of mind to another, and I'd move on to something else. He thought I needed to nurture something, so he gave me—the woman, born to nurture—something that was more acceptable for a woman to love. He thought I'd be bored with a newborn, cooped up; that I'd think of something else eventually, something new. I was the idea guy, Ben was the executor. But I didn't want to work anymore, not on a start-up, not in technomancy, never again. We fought about it a lot, to the point where Ben slept with someone else and begged my forgiveness and I realized I just did not care. I cared so little, actually, that we're still friends. I had that little of myself invested in him. I gave it all to our first baby, the one he so thoughtlessly sold away, and it all seemed so much clearer when I realized that what I really wanted was to feel the way I'd felt when I was young.

Like the world was still open before me. Like my destiny was still patiently waiting. Like I could one day have a love that would never feel lonely. Like loneliness itself was something I could eventually overcome.

After the Tyche debacle, I let Ben have most of the money, to reinvest it in whatever start-up he built next. I just didn't see the point of making anything new, of putting my degree to use, anything like that. This is what the industry is: swallowing up, using, competing, delivering, pinging. Anything but people. It's what I was trained to do—value advancement over humans, let the old ways and their caretakers get swallowed up by disruption for disruption's sake. Ideas get rewarded only if their value can be predictably projected; only if that value is increasingly insane. Ben was the one who first told me about Tyche's investment in Chirp, and yeah, sure, I felt a little jealous, but I also felt absurdly sad. I thought wow, it finally happened, someone bought Meredith. Someone now owned Meredith Wren like they had once owned me, even if that wasn't how she saw it yet.

I wondered for a moment then if Meredith was smarter than me. Then I realized it didn't matter, because this industry, this world, it doesn't reward how smart you are. The more they want to use you, the worse you have to be. So instead I thought, What will they do to her now?

Then she was successful, and it was easier to be angry because I knew that she was cheating somehow. I felt sure, pathologically sure, that she was doing it with something she only knew how to do because my grandmothers had taught her—yet another situation of the rich exploiting the poor. We took her in, we fed her, we taught her our magic—she colonized us, just like that! I mean, sure, Meredith is mixed-race, we even share some portion of our heritages. Hers was the only face on that fucking *Forbes* list that looked anything remotely like mine. But still, it was hard to really call her one of us. A fake friend, with fake suffering, and now she was peddling fake happiness to people who only wanted to believe. She was like a goddamn cult leader! She was promising everyone eternal afterlives when all she'd done was poison their grape juice, telling them happiness was easy, that everything they'd so long been promised could really, honestly be theirs.

I told Ben it would never work because Meredith's idea—her original idea, the one she wanted to use in a twisted, grieving way to fix her dead mom—wasn't about short-term happiness. It wasn't about dopamine. It was really a long-term idea that someone else might have bought for more streamlined psychiatric use, but Tyche was selling it as a quick fix. I told Ben, not thinking he was really listening to me, that actually, Meredith's original idea was much better than Chirp, because neuromancy was a lot more complex than just pleasure centers, and either Tyche was selling something that didn't exist or Meredith had shifted her research from the parasympathetic nervous system to the sympathetic one. Meaning yes, Chirp could make someone laugh, haha-laugh, but not laugh from a place of deep, profound catharsis. And Meredith had always wanted to do the latter, which I told Ben was impossible, but what I meant was that it was impossible *to fund*. VCs would hate it because it wouldn't work right away. Because happiness wasn't a permanent state of being that you could trick your brain into, a little razzle-dazzle like shining a mirror off the sun. You had to believe it, you had to work for it, you had to choose it—on any given day you had to *choose* to remember the good over the bad, to honor the gradations in your joy and accept its complications—but what did Meredith Wren actually know about that?

But I forgot that I was Ben's muse, and I could tell he only heard the part about how Meredith's idea could use improvement and that Chirp would ultimately fail.

Anyway, I realized all of this just as I was about to explain everything to Meredith, who was obviously misinformed, but it felt like a really long story that I wasn't sure I knew how to tell.

So in the end, all I said was, "I think it's my ex that Thayer was probably working with. Though I did meet with him about something else, something totally unrelated to Chirp." I didn't want to tell her yet what I'd come up with, because it was so small. Meredith only aimed big, she lived large, she still honored her genius whereas I had chosen (more rightfully, less inspiringly) to believe I was a tiny speck of nothing who already had everything I needed; that Monster and I wouldn't have wealth, but I'd already done enough to ensure that we wouldn't go hungry. That we would have time and rest and each other and the faith of a life well lived, and that was enough. More than enough. Most days I even believed it. "But as far as whatever Thayer was doing with neuromancy," I finished, "I don't know anything about it."

Meredith gave me a sort of gruff acknowledgment in response. She had a lot of other stuff going on. I didn't press it—didn't really know how to. I still felt, overall, that an apology was more owed on her end than mine. Because what did I do to her, really? Except believe the worst of her. But everybody does that, it's one of the most common human-on-human crimes. We were teenagers back then, for fuck's sake, and she had to know she was ruining my life.

"You didn't ruin me," I added just before I turned away.

"I know." She didn't look at me. "I never really thought I would."

She looked startled then, like she'd just realized something, which I later learned she had. A pretty transparent metaphor. She'd had almost the exact conversation with Jamie, which is something I would find out later. It's not important right now.

I don't know why I stayed at the Wren house so long. I should have gone home instead of what I did do, which was stay there overnight, just in case—in the hopes that, maybe—someone might need me.

It took me longer than it should have to realize that Monster wasn't happy being stuck with me in that dark, half-demolished old house.

I'm still relatively new at this, the mom thing, which I guess I always will be. I'll never really understand parenting because Monster will always need something different from me, something new that I don't yet know how to be, and maybe by the time I do, it'll be too late. So even though I knew in retrospect that Monster probably wanted his usual dinner and his usual bathtub and his usual bed, even though he was a good sport who loved me so unquestionably, unerringly, that he'd gladly sleep in my arms—you know, to the extent that he actually sleeps, which is pretty hit or miss—nothing was more shameful than knowing I'd denied him his comforts because it's apparently very hard to kick the habit of wanting to be a Wren. I just wanted to sleep in that house like I belonged there, like I was necessary to its inhabitants. I recited all of Monster's favorite bedtime books over and over and he tossed and turned, until eventually he must have sensed that this was the world now, so he curled into my side and fell asleep.

The house breathed around me while Monster slept in my arms. Then a fly landed on my arm, and in my new, sharp panic about swarms I brutally realized that I was an idiot. A tear or two slipped down my cheek onto Monster's hair and then I felt worse. I felt the worst you can ever feel; the kind of badness you can only feel when you haven't even been through anything, when everything that happens to you feels like peeling back your skin. I felt seventeen again. I felt like someone whose best friend had betrayed her again. I felt like a girl who thought sex would make her feel like she mattered; like a penis—even Arthur Wren's penis—could honestly confer some hard-earned sense of worth. I wanted my mother, I wanted Lola, I wanted Abuela, I wanted my son's hair to smell like coconut milk and kids' sunblock instead of the expensive travel shampoo stocked in Thayer Wren's guest bathroom. I wanted to be older, to feel wiser—I wanted to be the prodigy I used to be. I wanted to be someone with a future. I wanted fucking *Eden* back.

And the worst of it was that what I really wanted was to feel like someone in that house could actually love me, even though that day should have proved to me that they themselves were so inept at love that they couldn't have done it even if I'd asked them, even if they wanted to. Even if they tried.

# 61

Philippa looked, well, dead, was how Arthur put it to me later. The whole thing felt surreal, gray, dark. It *was* dark—Eilidh still hadn't fixed that, still didn't know how to. Likewise, Arthur didn't really know how to explain to anyone why he, of California's Twelfth Congressional District, was the emergency contact in a British aristocrat's phone. He still had no idea why he kept dying. He knew only that something was severely out of order; that much seemed obvious. This was Philippa, who had been alive only yesterday.

There were a small, scattered group of photographers outside, given Philippa's high profile, and Yves's, and, less interestingly but still of some significance, Arthur's. Most journalists, it seemed, were now covering the ongoing apocalypse rather than anyone's (Arthur's) deficiencies, but one or two held out hope for a celebrity headline. Again, Yves made a convenient cover for Arthur's inexplicable presence, though it was Arthur who lingered, alone, in the morgue after Philippa's identity had been confirmed.

"Was she pregnant?" Arthur asked the medical examiner.

"No," the examiner said, sounding surprised that he would ask.

"Oh," said Arthur.

Death comes in threes. Thayer. Philippa. Finally, a third: Riot. There, now Arthur could neatly close the book. The rest of the world was safe. Assuming the next time he died he didn't stay dead. Four deaths in one week just seemed absurd.

And Riot had always been real to him; so real he didn't know how to properly mourn her. He didn't know how to explain that he needed to dig a grave, to bury his sorrows in fresh earth. That there was no other way to suffer honorably than with his hands, with his sweat, with the carnage of his devotion. But Riot had never actually existed and there was no one to say goodbye to, because she was just an idea he'd once had—no more his than any other silly wish upon a star.

"You're that congressman, right?" said the examiner.

The words "for now" crossed Arthur's mind. He wondered what the *Oakland Tribune* would print about his appearance at the hospital, and whether his coverage in the weekend's posts would be sympathetic. Maybe his week of private tragedy would make for meatier public consumption. Maybe it would cause people to look closely, see the oddness of it all. Arthur no longer knew how to understand himself without the backdrop of disapproval by 332 million strangers he would likely never meet. "Yes, I am."

"What was your relationship to her?" asked the examiner, meaning Philippa. He seemed to have gathered that Arthur wasn't the husband or a father or a brother. He'd clearly ruled out all the intimate things, probably because Arthur was having trouble bending his head around the heaviness of loss, such that he didn't appear to be struggling at all.

Inside, Arthur was thinking things like arrange your face so that you don't look like a serial killer. Move your hand, that's a doorknob. Turn it. Yes, good, Arthur, good.

"Oh, uh. We're cousins," said Arthur. Truthfully, he didn't know why Philippa listed him instead of Yves in her phone, except maybe for the knowledge that Arthur would come. That if she invented a baby for some very labyrinthine personal gain, Arthur would simply believe it. That if she said dance, monkey, dance, Arthur would salsa joyously on the spot, no questions asked.

"Oh yeah? You from one of these fancy British lines, too?"

"I'm of slightly less fancy stock," said Arthur, improvising madly on the spot. It was easier given that his mind was elsewhere. "One of the bastards."

"Ohhhhhhhhh," said the examiner meaningfully. "You'd think you'd be darker, then."

That jarred Arthur a bit. "What?"

"I looked up the family online." The examiner flashed Arthur a screen with Philippa's family crest on it. "All that money came from sugar plantations in the Caribbean."

Right, the Barbados of it all. Arthur felt an inward collapse of cringe. "We're actually not biological cousins," said Arthur quickly. "More like, you know, our moms were friends."

The examiner looked sympathetic.

"She was a really lovely person," Arthur added. "Really lovely." Smart, funny, silly, weird. He missed her dearly then. Enough feeling came back to him that he could do it in a way he hadn't yet managed for his father, a more complicated grief. For Thayer, Arthur still felt the tirelessness of longing, the yawning emptiness of things he knew they'd never say. For Philippa, he thought simply Oh, Mouse. She'll miss fashion week in the spring, and I'll look up at the blossoms and know she isn't there, and I will miss all the funny silliness of her.

"Yeah," said the examiner with the arch of a brow, "I'm sure she was great."

"She didn't have her own *personal* slaves," Arthur attempted to reason with him.

"Sure," said the examiner. "Can you just confirm her place of birth for me?"

"Oh. Uh. Saint James, I think." Arthur realized the examiner was making a political point about colonization and what reason an English woman might have for still being in a country even after it had fought a bloody war for independence. Which seemed fair, albeit unproductive.

Arthur said, "Is it cool if—" If I loved a person and not an idea. If I carry guilt and desire in the same very misfortunate heart. If I honestly thought it was an improvement on her palate, and didn't really ask a lot of questions about why. If I felt the charity work was kind because it seemed conflicting to view it as patronizing. If she was honestly very funny and strange, and I'm acting very calm at the moment, but actually I'm in shock, because I don't like the things I've had to acknowledge today, but also, importantly, I didn't really want her to die. I *really* didn't want her to die, I lost a person and a future today, or maybe I already lost them, but it doesn't matter, it's all the same. So is it okay—?

"If I leave?" he finally managed.

"Sign this," said the examiner, and Arthur signed it and left.

# 62

There is another ending. There's one where Philippa only gets terribly injured, where perhaps she is visited in the hospital by Gillian Yadav Wren, who points out that Philippa's apparent financial destitution is not the worst thing that has ever happened, given that it occurs with great frequency in media of all kinds. In this version of the story, Philippa might rewrite her selfish behaviors and her narrow concern for the mere aesthetics of life in favor of seeking real redemption and accountability, having been suitably visited by the ghosts of Christmas past and/or a mental health professional. Which isn't to say that Gillian *has* to be cast in this role, necessarily, but of all the Wrens, Gillian does know a fixable problem when she sees one. In this case, she could use an assistant, and what Philippa needs is a job.

But if I allow you to believe in this ending, you might forget that life is short and meaningless, a narrative left incomplete. So you'll just have to hold it in your head as something equally true and nonexistent, like Schrödinger's cat, or Riot Wren, or unrequited love.

# 63

Also, I might be taking liberties with what the medical examiner actually said to Arthur. There may have been less of a political agenda than what I interpreted, having heard the story secondhand; some of this is para-phrased. Anyway, I promised to tell you about Yves. I said he could read minds, which was slightly hyperbolic on my part. It was just kind of a short-hand at the time, because we had other things to worry about then.

The longer story is: Yves Reza began experiencing seizures when he was very small. Except Yves's seizures weren't normal seizures, because when-ever they happened, his consciousness would bounce around in time and space and he would see the insides of a person, their thoughts and hopes, and the outsides of them as well, where they were and what they were do-ing. Initially his mother thought it was demon possession. But then they discovered it wasn't a demon, or at least not a demon they could cast out (they tried), and Yves had a very strange knack for predicting things, which was very helpful for the rest of the village, and indeed the entire family. Both Yves's mother and his father's wife both agreed he just needed a hobby, something more appropriate to focus his attention on.

Yves ended up doing a lot of what most cultures call "women's work," or fine motor skills performed for long periods of time like weaving and embroidery, because methodical consistency kept him relatively centered. They kept him in the present most of the time, instead of jumping into other people's futures arbitrarily to see what they would be eating for din-ner or what they'd become in ten years. Later, Yves realized that things that required him to focus *or die* achieved even greater success in this regard, given the stakes. Driving a car at top speeds with tangible risk of peril, for example, was a hugely more effective way to remain mindful in the mo-ment. Also, Yves discovered drugs, which is important to the story. If you haven't already, you'll soon see why.

Fundamentally though, Yves's Yves-ness was unharmed by the circumstances of his . . . let's call it profound neurodivergence. He was an exuberant person, one who didn't typically give into the darkness of other people's doom. He had a frighteningly short attention span, so that was probably part of it, but also, he had a way of capitulating to the whims of the universe that made him a less damageable type of person.

Which was a pure, indefatigable authenticity that irritated Lady Philippa Villiers-DeMagnon very much over time, grating on her increasingly as she realized it was not an act, and that Yves was not, in fact, a dark and complex person masking his pain with joyful cravings for waffles. Which isn't to say that Yves is not complex, because loving a world for the existence of waffles is a very impressive thing to do when the oceans are frankly just lying in wait for the chance to swallow us up. But Yves is not, himself, dark, and Philippa craved darkness because she wanted to feel needed; she wanted to be necessary to someone's happiness, but Yves would be happy with or without her, because Yves was a happy person. Yves was what Meredith Wren had promised everyone they could have, which in that context is absurd. Presumably you don't need me to expound on that.

But Yves did have his low moments, like when he knew that Arthur was going to believe Philippa's cry for attention, or when he knew that Philippa was going to die. He saw it the day before, when he and Philippa were alone and she was delivering her own ultimatum—not the one Gillian had suggested, about telling Arthur the truth, but a more predictable one about marrying her *or else*—which would necessitate the ending that Yves had known in a less psychic way was soon to come.

Still, Yves had thought there would be more time, given the literal darkness in his vision. He felt Philippa's impatience, her certainty that Arthur would come for her soon, that she could successfully pry Arthur away from his life, and instead of warning her about what he'd witnessed—he never warned people; there was no point in it really; did it really make it better to know what was coming? almost never, no—Yves had simply said darling, please don't do it. Just leave poor Arthur alone.

"What about me? I've been *abandoned*," Philippa shouted at him. "Don't you care about our family?"

"Arthur is our family," said Yves, who believed this.

"Yes, but our *baby*—"

"We don't have a baby."

Philippa ignored him. "Don't be ridiculous, of course we do—"

"Pippela. My darling Mouse." Yves rose to his feet and took both her hands. "Would an orgasm make you feel more inclined to honesty? The throes of passion do have a way of lightening your mood."

"Don't *patronize* me," Philippa said in a tone of devastating frustration, though she gave in almost instantly with a sigh, flouncing onto the bed. "Why did you want to come here, anyway?" she muttered to herself, propped up by her elbows as Yves divested her of her cashmere sweatpants. "I hate this house. It's dreadful. I can't stand Gillian."

"Gillian is a lovely woman," said Yves, kissing his way up Philippa's thigh.

Philippa threw herself backward, ragdolling onto the duvet. "Don't tell me you love *her* now instead of me," she said with utter misery.

"Oh, I do love her," Yves said guilelessly. "I would woo her myself if she wasn't madly in love with her husband."

"Is she?" asked Philippa, frowning.

"Oh, yes," Yves said. He kept meaning to have a talk with Arthur about it. "I worry Arthur is unaware of the extent of it."

"Why should you worry about that?"

"Because they love each other very much but don't know how to say it in a way the other can understand. I think it's fixable," said Yves, "though perhaps once it's fixed Arthur will have no further use for me." He deflated slightly, then brightened. "But it will be okay, because then they'll be together, and Arthur will be happy." Joy returned to him like a flame of righteousness. "He won't need us anymore, but that will be fine."

"Maybe for you, but what about me?" demanded Philippa, propping herself up again to frown at him. "If we leave them to each other, then what does that mean for you and me?"

This was when he saw her. Her last moments, her sense of entitlement to love, her certainty that she deserved it even when it was stolen. Yves reached for a bit of chocolate in his pocket, carefully selecting a small square before returning to the conversation.

"Oh, Mouse, I can't marry you," he said, popping the medicine in his mouth. "Not because I don't love you," he added, though that love had taken on a very different form, the kind that needed periodic windows of distance, or that could only be felt from afar, or perhaps exclusively in retrospect. "Your family is riddled with debt and your hobbies err slightly hypocritical, and I am beginning to suspect you enjoy thinking of me as a simpleton." It saddened him to say those things aloud. "May I focus on your erotic regions now?" Yves asked optimistically.

"Yes, fine." Philippa lay back again, then sat up, abruptly changing her mind. "Wait, you never answered the question. Why did you come here?"

The answer: because Yves was in love with Arthur and wanted to get away from Philippa, though there seemed no productive outcome to saying so out loud.

"Arthur needs us," said Yves. "You know how difficult his love for his father has been. He has countless feelings and nowhere to put them."

"Fine," said Philippa in a voice that was too compliant, so Yves decided she had likely pieced together some kind of sinister plan. But then he remembered the rest of his time with her would be limited, and so he did his best to pleasure her as expertly as he knew how, and when he noticed that she was gone the next day, he realized that he would miss her.

Although not, per se, right now.

# 64

Meredith rose early to prepare for a phone call with the chairman of her father's board. Another Edward, as it were. She'd heard nothing further from Ward, who'd evidently cut ties with her after lawyering up, perhaps having been advised by then to say nothing.

She wondered how much of their partnership Ward was willing to deny. Would he, for example, say in a deposition, under oath, that he had tried to pick up Meredith in a bar when she was twenty, and that he had only forgone his lascivious intent when he realized why she was there, which was to speak specifically to him?

"I have this idea," said Meredith, poor idiot baby, future asshole, at the time only an asshole in training. "I was wasting my time at Harvard and I want to commit to this thing, for real. I just need someone more experienced in magitech—in neuromancy, specifically."

Ward's parents had wanted him to be a doctor. Shortly after declaring neurology as a specialty, he had dropped out of his med school residency, not by choice. Clinical depression simply wins when it wins.

Ward, of course, was a self-saboteur of the highest order. He pivoted to start-ups because that sort of fast-paced world suits a person who doesn't care to think long-term; who likes to sweat and bleed for a handful of violently sleepless months and then, like waking from a dream, move on. He was the product of the technomancy age by circumstance, by virtue of his generation, and the presence of a particularly gruesome computer game about surviving the high seas (much was made at the time of scurvy, and indeed Meredith never saw Ward without an orange in his lunch). He briefly went to jail for assaulting his former business partner, drunk one night and rudderless.

Coincidentally, a week before their encounter in the bar, Meredith had taken a meeting with one of her father's VCs to ask for advice—she had emailed from her father's account, CCing herself, hoping he wouldn't notice—and the VC had told her that nobody wanted an untested college dropout without some assurance of success.

"So then what do I need?" asked Meredith, young, youngyoungyoung, twin spots of acne on her cheeks.

"Nobody in their right mind would agree to this," said the VC, "so I guess what you need is someone desperate."

So she met up with Ward in that bar, got him to turn it all around, and then eventually Merritt Foster had come for her, and Ward had ridden with her on the unicorn she made sure they were. But she supposed she couldn't blame Ward now for his choice to turn on her. She'd known what she was doing when she'd chosen the partner she chose. She called it a feature instead of a bug when it had suited her at the time, but like depression, desperation was what it was.

She was sitting in her father's office when the phone number for Edward Roque, the chairman of the board at Wrenfare Magitech, appeared on her watch screen. She tapped her earbud, answering. "Good morning, Ed."

"Meredith." Edward Roque was even older than her father. She wondered if that was crossing his mind. "What an unfortunate day."

"If you don't mind, Ed, I'd like to keep it brief," said Meredith.

"Of course."

"So, as you know, my father bequeathed his ownership shares to me."

"Yes."

"Meaning, as I'm sure you're aware, that I'm able to appoint myself Wrenfare's next CEO."

"Meredith—" Ed paused. "I do want to warn you. Operationally, things are in a bit of disarray. I do think it's very likely that our only profitable option will be to sell."

Meredith drummed her nails on her father's desk.

"Candidly, we have been trying for the last few years to get Thayer to consider the offers we have on the table," Ed continued. "We understood, of course, Thayer's personal opposition to Kip Hughes—"

"Personal?" Meredith echoed.

"Ah." Ed's sigh sounded like a prelude to a long and tiresome story. "Thayer never did get over Merritt's betrayal, or Kip's subsequent investment in Birdsong," he explained. "He felt the whole thing was in poor taste."

Meredith thought back to Thayer's many, many lectures about exactly that. "But my father never made an offer on Chirp. Or anything related to Birdsong."

"Well, he couldn't, Meredith. Tyche simply had more money. We've been on a backslide for the last decade, if not more. Thayer could never have matched Kip's offer."

A doozy of a sudden revelation. Privately, Meredith felt a soaring sense that maybe, just maybe, her father had never actually intended to undermine her. Maybe Thayer had always believed Meredith was gifted—maybe he had known she was capable of greatness after all, and he had been saddened that she'd torn herself away from him, choosing instead to stand with a man he considered a rival.

"Unfortunately, I think it was all too clear that Merritt knew what he was doing when he used Kip Hughes to buy Thayer Wren's daughter out from under him," Ed continued, shattering Meredith's burgeoning internal aria of relief. "Much of the board admires what Kip has done for Tyche, but Thayer knew—and I agreed—that Merritt would grind the Wren name into the dust at the first chance he got, purely out of some juvenile misguided spite. He did it with you, and would clearly do it again with Wrenfare."

The result of this insane decentering of Meredith's talent as any meaningful piece in the ongoing Merritt-Thayer enmity was a cool, insidious flood of disappointment. "That's what my father thought? That his former partner just wanted the Wren name however he could get it?"

"I can't say all was friendly between them," Ed said.

"But Tyche didn't buy *me*. They invested in Chirp." God, Meredith thought, I'm an idiot. I put my whole worth on this thing, this one project, this one dream, I let first one man and then the other give me meaning. But it was a dick-measuring contest all along.

"Well, of course," said Ed pleasantly. "I'm just expressing that I don't believe a deal with Tyche was ever really on the table for your father. However, there are plenty of investors who'd likely pay a premium—for example, a very reputable technomancy company based in Beijing, not to mention a group of highly savvy investors from Saudi Arabia—"

"Can we talk shop after my father's ashes are cold?" asked Meredith.

"Oh, Meredith, absolutely. I just—" Ed hesitated. "Meredith. I've known you since you were a little girl. It brings me absolutely no pleasure to bring this up. But."

Meredith's organs twisted slightly.

"There is a bit of a rumble about Chirp going around. And there is a possibility that if things become litigiously difficult, the board may be forced to call for a vote."

To remove her, he meant. They didn't want mess and she was mess. Thayer had always emphasized that no one liked her, that no one would give her the benefit of the doubt if she ever performed less than spectacularly, and she had treated that like a battle cry, a personal demand for perfection, but it wasn't. It wasn't even a warning. Thayer wasn't different! He was *one of them*—one of the doubters, the haters. There was no chance he thought the board would stick by her, whether it was Thayer's dying wish or not. Thayer must have known she'd go down with a flaming pile of shit in each hand. How better to destroy the daughter who betrayed you than to let the whole world watch her prove herself a snake? If the rivalry with Tyche had never been about Meredith, this decision must have been the opposite. It was Thayer flipping her off, telling her to reap what she sowed. To prove that the one thing she'd always wanted to be good enough for was impossible, because even when he gave it to her, she still couldn't hold it for long.

She stared at her father's artwork, the ballerina on the wall. The shadow of a man standing leeringly in the background. All her life her father had been preparing her for this—for the men who didn't like her. For the men who wanted, even at the risk of their own profits, to see her fail. She hadn't fallen in line and inevitably she would suffer for it, and hadn't Thayer told her that himself? Was she really so surprised that the pettiest *I told you so* was worth the price of his own legacy when he had never changed his story, even once?

But then again, his legacy was finished. *He* was dead, but she was not. Fuck his legacy, fuck his aspirations, fuck the glory of the House of Wren that he had chosen to own alone rather than share with her. Eilidh could have destroyed the company just as well, just as soundly, but Thayer hadn't wanted the blade to fall on the neck of his favorite.

So why *shouldn't* Meredith be the one to burn it down?

"You're saying you want a quick sale," Meredith translated over the phone. "Not just quick. Immediate."

Ed let out a breath of relief. "Well, within reason, of course."

No. Fuck reason. She had a legal battle to fund.

*Take the money*, Jamie had said. *Take the money and run.*

Thanks, Dad, she thought with wrenching sincerity.

"Right. Well, I want to see all offers of sale by end of day," said Meredith. Thayer had to have known what he'd done when he picked her over Eilidh. He chose the daughter who had never once bent the knee, and if that was purely to protect one child over the other, it didn't matter. That failure was on him. *Thank you, Dad, for raising me strong enough. Fuck you for making me that way.* "Including best and final from Kip Hughes."

Now Ed's voice carried an edge of concern. "Meredith, there's no need t—"

"See you at the funeral," she said, and tapped her earbud to hang up the phone.

# 65

Eilidh woke up on the morning of her father's funeral and remembered that she had cursed the world to darkness. She had also slept with the same woman her father had slept with. The whole thing was monumentally upsetting. Dzhuliya had tried to speak with her several times the day before—many times, countless times, following her around like a puppy, saying things like she hadn't known, it was Eilidh all along, it was a lapse in judgment, that was all.

To say Eilidh didn't want to hear it was an understatement. "You're carrying my future sibling," Eilidh pointed out when it seemed like Dzhuliya really might try to follow her up the stairs, to the bed that Eilidh didn't want to leave for at least a week. "Don't you grasp the Greek mythology levels of weird?"

"Eilidh," Dzhuliya began, and let her hands fall at her sides, because what else was there to say? That in the war between guilt and loneliness, loneliness had won? Because of course loneliness won, it always would, we are all, forever, universally at risk for the pitfalls of craving. But that didn't mean you handed your dead lover's daughter a strap-on and said have at it girl, life's short. There simply had to be a line.

Eventually Eilidh disappeared into her bedroom and didn't fall asleep for several hours. She thought about texting someone, but upon realizing there was no one to talk to, she didn't. She and Meredith hadn't spoken at all since their argument, the one that had led to the swarm.

Eilidh could still feel the thing in her chest sitting heavy, with its back to her like they'd just had a fight. She realized they had really been feeling like two separate entities lately. Hard to believe that earlier in the week, when they'd been 20,000 feet in the air, that little lizard-scuttle of inward madness had actually done her a favor. Its agenda had always seemed separate from Eilidh's own aspirations for normalcy and/or the tedium of daily life, but now it only seemed to throw tantrum after tantrum.

"Dad," Eilidh said aloud. It didn't yet feel impossible that he would answer. How long before she could stop expecting to see him on the stairs? "You gave it all to Meredith."

"You're not the only failure in this house," she imagined Thayer might say. Except no, she couldn't even picture it, the idea of Thayer admitting that something had gone wrong. He had always known the answer, every answer. Even now, Eilidh found it difficult to believe he couldn't fix her, couldn't save her.

Christ, it was one thing to bury your father, but how do you bury a god? How do you part with your faith?

Eilidh rose to her feet and walked to the bathroom, startled to find it occupied.

"Oh, sorry," I said. I was in there wrestling with Monster, who didn't really allow me to change his diaper anymore, but also found the concept of pee to be incredibly anxiety-inducing, so much so that he couldn't reasonably be expected to use the potty, despite the myriad literature on the subject that had been read to him. "I'll be out in just a second."

"No, take your time." Eilidh felt she was intruding on something, so she turned to leave, though she returned with a sense of someone about to dive into icy waters—getting it over with, even though it would hurt. "Do you . . . know what to do about Arthur?"

I considered it for a moment. "No," I admitted.

"Do you have any idea how to make the darkness go away?" She gestured vaguely overhead. "Or put a stop to any more . . . apocalypse things?"

She meant the previous day's swarm of flies, which had only been defeated by Arthur's magical malfunction, so possibly two wrongs *did* make a right. "Mm, no," I said. "I have even less knowledge about that."

"Do you have even the vaguest guess about what's happening to me?"

"No." I barked a laugh. "Not a clue." I had finally managed to drag the pull-ups over Monster's bare derrière despite his attempts to headbutt me in the sternum.

"Oh." Eilidh turned to leave again, and then stopped. "So then why did Meredith and Arthur think you could fix us?"

"Oh, I don't know." I actually didn't think there was anything especially profound about it. They thought of me because everything they understood about magic came from me, but that had never meant I actually *knew* anything. And if I'd ever really believed that I could fix it, I was definitely just playing along because the attention felt validating. But how do you fix something like a plague?

"I guess we could consider letting Moses's people go," I suggested.

"Ha, ha," said Eilidh glumly.

She turned away again but stopped.

"It's not from a god, though," she said to nothing. "It's smaller than that. It's, like, this thing." She rested a hand on her collarbone, instantly embarrassed. She looked up at me—down, really, seeing as I was substantially shorter—and added sheepishly, "It lives in my chest."

"Your heart?" I asked.

She looked a little stunned.

"No," she said, recovering. "It's more like . . . a creature?"

To her relief I seemed unsurprised. "Oh. Okay. Well, lots of things can possess you. Little ghosties and whatnot." Monster had climbed onto the toilet and was playing with a light switch, so we were having this conversation in the midst of a toddler-DJed rave. "When did it start?"

From the back of Eilidh's mind flashed a carnal spray of blood. "Right after I had my surgery."

"Surgery?" I tucked some hair behind my ear. Eilidh considered me for a moment, realizing she had never looked at me properly. She didn't remember me from when we were younger, and I don't know the specifics of what she saw, because I didn't ask her about that. But I had a feeling then that she was seeing something good, and in my defense I had really grown into my cheeks. Aging certainly had its pitfalls, but optically my thirties suited me.

"I used to be a dancer," Eilidh explained. "I danced ballet professionally. I trained for basically my entire life."

"Oh." I did know that because I had kept tabs on all the Wrens almost compulsively, and because Thayer had told me about what happened to Eilidh when we met those few times after he found me at the Wrenfare store where I work. I just wanted Eilidh to tell me her story in her own words.

"Yeah," she said, and nodded to herself like she was about to embark on something hard but necessary. Again, the icy deep. "I got in a car accident. I shouldn't have even been in that taxi. I was late to rehearsal and the weather was bad. But I could have walked," she said, arguing with nothing. "I could have gotten up in time. I could have—"

"Was it always there?" I interrupted.

Eilidh looked up at me, traveling a long way from her desperate attempt to rewrite her own story. "What?"

"The thing in your chest."

"Oh, the monster." She blinked. "Sorry," she said, "I forgot you call your son Monster—"

"The monster in your chest," I confirmed. "Was it always there?"

"No, I told you, it started when—"

"Not the plagues," I said, shaking my head. "The badness."

She reeled a little from that as Monster moved on from the light switch, climbing from the toilet over to the sink, to play with Eilidh's toothpaste.

She thought about the feeling in her chest, the thing she lived with, the thing that felt like suffocating rage. She tried to pry it apart, pulling it off like a leach from her memories, to see if she could identify it in the person she'd once been. The ingenue who'd died all those years ago, the last time she put on her pointe shoes. The last time she truly understood who Eilidh Wren was and what she could do.

The ache of it, the pain in her muscles, the way dancing was only done right if it hurt, if the hurt extended beyond her body, beyond every single bit of her, if she pressed it all down to the tips of her fingers and projected it onward, onto the audience, into the crowd. The way she only inhabited the person she thought of as herself if she was feeling someone else's pain, their grief, their anger, their debilitating joy, their delusory love, their cruel and unrelenting fate.

How beautifully she could carry the suffering of others, wearing their misery so she didn't have to acknowledge her own! The nights of hunger for greatness, sex just to scratch an itch, a sister who never came to see her, a mother she never got to have. Translating the human experience, which was itself full of badness, so that she never had to hold her own badness for too long. What could she call it? The thing in her chest. The thing in her chest had a rhythm, a pulse. It had raced that night when the car drove into her body; it had transformed itself into something stagnant, dormant, unmoving and unmoved.

"I'm just thinking," I said, "that the plague stuff . . . there might not be any fixing that. It might just be the impulse of whatever magic you've naturally got going on. Maybe it only turns into plagues because of you— because you feel things so apocalyptically, and who knows, maybe you liked that Bible story when you were six." More girlhood she couldn't escape. "I don't know how fixable that is," I said. Then Monster began playing with the faucet. "Don't waste water, honey, it's a drought year—"

"You don't think it's fixable?" asked Eilidh, wondering why that felt so hard to bear.

"Well, no, I didn't say that." I had, but I hadn't meant it that way. I was busy thinking about Monster and my own climate-related guilt. (All the years are drought years now.) "I just mean that lots of people live with something dangerous," I attempted to explain. "Lots of people are capable of great and prodigious harm. So maybe you don't need to think of it as fixing something or taming it, but, like, honoring it."

The thing in Eilidh's chest began to purr.

"Shit hurts," I said. "Life sucks. But you must have already understood all that, or you wouldn't have been such an incredible dancer."

"You don't know I was incredible," she said.

"Were you?"

"Yes," she said.

Then she laughed.

"So what's the treatment, doctor?" she said wryly.

"Well, if you think what you have is a demon, then you can try to expel it," I said. "The internet will have something. The dark web or whatever. You can get an exorcism pretty much anywhere, anytime, if you want. Some priests still do it, I bet."

The thing in Eilidh's chest recoiled. "Okay."

"If you really wanted, we could do a séance with one of my grandmothers and ask them, although if we call one we'll have to call the other or there'll be literal hell to pay."

"Have you ever done that?" she asked curiously. "Reached out to them, I mean?"

"No." Not for lack of wanting to. My mom convinced me to let them rest—though maybe what she meant was to let myself rest. "But if we're talking magical maladies, there's only so many options. And I am charging an exorbitant fee."

"What were you meeting with my father about?" asked Eilidh, remembering what I'd said yesterday, or rather, what Meredith had said.

"Oh, it was stupid. I had this idea for . . ." I trailed off.

Then, like Eilidh, I went for it. Ice and all.

"Monster gets nightmares," I said. "I mean, I can't prove it. Science says it's impossible until a certain age, but he's *such* a bad sleeper, always has been. He used to wake up screaming, always reaching out for me before he could fall back asleep." I fell quiet for a moment. "My husband wanted me to sleep train. The doctor wanted me to sleep train."

Eilidh leaned against the door frame. "Sleep train?"

"You have to teach children to soothe themselves," I parroted tiredly. "That's how they learn to put themselves back to sleep if they wake up in the middle of the night."

Eilidh frowned. "Is that real?"

"Yes," I said. "I mean, I don't know. My mom never sleep trained me. In fairness, I'm a shit sleeper, too, so maybe that's not a great example. The point is that it was the smart thing to do, the thing everyone told me would work, because I was so exhausted and all the books say you can't sleep with them, and—" Alarmingly, my eyes filled with tears. "But he just wanted me, you know? He just wanted me, and I didn't know what kind of horrors he was dealing with—I mean, what if he was a fruit fly in a past life? I brought him into this world, and I just couldn't stand to tell him hey, just take care of yourself, it's better for you in the long run."

"I guess it does seem a worthwhile skill," said Eilidh, smiling gently when Monster looked up at her.

"Oh, absolutely." I could feel the pressure of wetness, the shake in my voice. "But I just . . . I couldn't be sure, that's all. I know he probably would have learned eventually. But I couldn't bear it, even a moment of him thinking he was alone, that I'd left him to his nightmares. So it was just a stupid thing, an infant dream scan. It would be an add-on for the Wrenfare monitor that already tracks sleep. I only told Thayer about it because—"

I stopped. Eilidh was focusing on Monster as a favor to me.

"Well, he came into the Wrenfare store by coincidence, and I guess he recognized me. I didn't expect him to. I don't even know why he was there." I technically didn't—he never explained—though I had a guess. He had the look of a man trying to remember why he'd built something, wondering what to do with the work he had started. Later I found out his board was considering replacing him as CEO—they felt Wrenfare needed new blood, either by company fire-sale or by bringing in someone else, someone younger, who could have easily been Kip Hughes. My guess is Thayer went to the closest Wrenfare store on his route home to try to bear witness to his life's work. It's not unheard of, certainly not for egotistical men who feel they are about to lose everything.

"He wasn't there in an official capacity or anything," I continued, "but he said are you my daughter's friend Lou, and I said yes, and he asked if I'd consider getting lunch with him."

"Was he hitting on you?" muttered Eilidh. "Apparently he liked his women young."

"You know, it had crossed my mind," I admitted. I'm not actually a stranger to the hazards of men who've outlived their glory days. "But I guess I wanted to know what everyone was up to. And I pitched him my idea because, you know, why not? The Wrenfare operating system is the only thing still turning a profit"—*was,* I remembered at the last second—"even if the costs of product development are outpacing it."

"Was he really trying *that* hard to go to space?" asked Eilidh with a disapproving shake of her head. Then she answered herself, "I guess he did seem restless. I thought he was frustrated with Arthur and Meredith, but maybe he was the one who'd let himself down."

"I actually didn't think he was going to make an offer," I said. "I doubt it's for very much. He literally does not have the money."

"True. We have it now," Eilidh agreed.

By then, Monster had let her take his hand. He was using it to climb up the toilet, onto the sink, and back down again, over and over.

"I'd hate to think of this little guy having lived through the horrors already," Eilidh sighed. "The wrong kind of prodigy."

"Aren't we all?" I said.

Eilidh smiled a little. Outside, it was still dark.

"Maybe it's fitting," she said, flicking a glance at the window. "Darkness like this on the day of his funeral. Maybe people will think he's a god or something. Talk about a legacy."

"You could still dance," I said.

She shook her head. "Oh, I had a lumbar puncture, I'll never be able t—"

"No, I mean. Just dance," I said. "Not for him. Not for me. Not to honor anybody's misery but your own."

Monster reached for me, so I took his hand and kissed it. I felt one of those long glows of motherly affection for which I have trained myself to live. This love; the feeling of a cup of coffee on a sunny day; the way the breeze riffles my hair; the wonderful years I shared with a man who wasn't the right one, but a kind one; the freedom I claimed for myself and my son so that someday, I will have the strength to reach for wonderful years again.

"Do you ever think about how we live in a shit, unfeeling universe and there's no rhyme or reason to anything that happens to us?" asked Eilidh.

"I do," I confirmed. "All the time." It's why I wouldn't have sleep trained even if I could prove nightmares weren't an issue. First of all, I already knew they were, and secondly, fuck pediatric literature. The time I spent with my baby in my arms would have to be robbed from me by force, that closeness stolen by nothing less than a gun to my head. I'd sleep when I was dead, which could be any moment—this one or this one, or this one, or this one. That this moment wasn't the end was a matter of pure coincidence, mere happenstance and luck. "But isn't it kind of freeing, in a way?"

"Cup," announced Monster shrewdly, pointing to the toothbrush container with all the solemnity of man discovering the moon.

Eilidh's eyes lit up.

"That's right," she said, and looked at me through a veneer of unassailable delight, such that I couldn't possibly tell her that Monster had already said that word before.

# 66

After the hospital, Gillian took Arthur to get his car from the Muir Woods parking lot. Arthur was still in a bit of a daze, so for a while they just sat there. Then someone yelled at them that they couldn't stay without a valid parking reservation and so they split up, agreeing to meet back at the house.

Gillian felt the presence of an ending. She had broken all her routines. Everything was in disarray. She felt tactically adrift, Napoleon at Waterloo. If Arthur never forgave her for this, if his final prognosis was that his wife's ultimatum had cost him his lover, what would she do?

Continue on, she supposed. Her dissertation seemed interminable. She didn't know why she'd done it, only that it soothed her, the work, the sequential nature of its deadlines, the feeling like arbitrary measures of success placed upon her by the divinity of academia might contribute to some larger sense of worth. Achieving recognition in the act of life itself.

She thought of her Chirp, considering whether she might put it on. Sometimes it did make her feel better. Other times it just made her crave a loaf of sourdough bread. Come to think of it, bread did sound nice. Look, it was already working.

She'd driven behind Arthur, taking her time where Arthur had a knavish tendency to speed, and he'd arrived first and made his way up to the house from the carport, so Gillian made her way alone up the stairs in the ceaseless dark. She dragged, perhaps because she knew something was coming. Yves had taken her hand just before they'd left and squeezed it once, and because Yves was aware she didn't like that kind of contact, she understood that it must have been dire. Yves had told her by then about his seizures. They were, by then, very good friends. So maybe Yves would still like her, and maybe friendship was enough. She didn't want the kind of love Arthur needed, so maybe being friends could always be enough?

But no, she thought, that wasn't it, though. She wanted the love she felt for Arthur; she would choose it if someone let her. Being only his friend would trample her heart.

Oh well. What was life if not the constant threat of emotional stampede? Gillian sighed and raised a hand to the doorframe of the Wren house, resting her palm on the wood with a sense of bittersweet sorrow. She would miss Thayer, in a way. The worst bit about people was the goodness they always had if you could bring yourself to look for it. Which was, indeed, a substantial if. And Thayer hadn't even loved each of his children the same way, so who could say whether he had been someone completely different for Gillian than he was for any of them.

She walked into the bedroom she shared with Arthur, the one where he'd once lain on the bed and stroked my teenage arm and thought he'd grow up to be someone for whom love would eventually be easy; for whom love was waiting, just another finish line to cross. He jumped, startled, at Gillian's entry, and she caught the reflection of his sheepish glance in the mirror.

"Sorry, I was just—" In one of Arthur's hands was his phone, which he did have a maddening tendency to obsess over, despite Gillian's sage advice to stop that, for the good of mankind. In the other hand, Arthur had hastily closed his fingers around something crinkly. "Misbehaving."

He looked so guilty that Gillian nearly giggled, forgetting briefly about the heaviness of her personal doom.

"What is that?" Gillian sidled up next to him, looking at the foil-wrapped item in his hand.

"Chocolate," said Arthur.

She recognized instantly that it was the same thing Yves had once handed her. "Ohhh, I see, it's *chocolate*," said Gillian knowingly. "Well, if anyone deserves it, it's probably you."

Arthur gave her a grateful look. "You're sure you're not going to think of me as some sort of hooligan if I partake?"

Is that what you think? Gillian wanted to ask. That I would ever be capable of thinking the worst of you? Of thinking that you are anything but the object of all my dreaming, the soft landing for my tired heart?

"Yves gave me some the other day," Gillian admitted, her cheeks slightly flushed. "And I'm not . . . I'm not actually such a stick in the mud, you know."

"You're not a stick in the mud." Arthur moved to break off a piece, looking blithely untroubled, and Gillian realized he wasn't going to say anything else. He was going to leave her there, suspended in limbo, unless she jumped first.

"Please don't leave me," Gillian blurted out, and Arthur froze.

"What?"

"I love you. Please don't leave. I'll change if you want me to." She didn't know how to put it into different words, to make them more feminist or less groveling. "I'll learn," she said solemnly. "I promise, I'll learn."

Arthur turned slowly to face her, the chocolate still in one hand, momentarily forgotten.

"I have to tell you about someone," he said. "A girl."

"Forgiven," said Gillian instantly. "I don't care."

"No, you don't—" Arthur broke off with a thin smile. "Her name is Riot. Riot Wren."

Gillian looked at him for a long time.

"Alliterative," she finally said.

"I know." He opened his mouth, then stopped. Then opened it again, then stopped. Then he broke off a piece of chocolate and made to pop it in his mouth, though he paused to offer it to her instead. "Want some? Might make this easier."

"Are you leaving me?" asked Gillian, pained.

"No," said Arthur. "Are you leaving me?"

"What? Of course not," said Gillian. "I love you."

"And I love you," Arthur replied.

"No," said Gillian meaningfully. "I *love* you."

Arthur looked back at her.

"And I," he said in a voice that had newly discovered gravity, "love *you*."

They looked at each other for a very long time. So long it became unclear to them what to do next. Arthur was accustomed to things progressing sexually after such a charged confession. Gillian was unaccustomed to any of this, full stop. She looked down at his hand, meaning to seize it passionately in hers, but stopped when she remembered the chocolate.

"My god, Arthur," she said. "That's massive."

"Hm? Oh, sorry," said Arthur, thinking she was looking somewhere else.

"No, that's—" She reached for the chocolate, holding the chunk that Arthur had broken off for her in the palm of one hand. It was easily several times as much as she had ever seen Yves take, and perhaps quadruple the size Yves had previously given her. "Were you going to eat all of this at once?"

"Oh, I couldn't figure out the dosage, it's some indeterminate number of ounces," said Arthur. "So I just break off a bit and go with that."

"Arthur." Gillian flipped the chocolate bar to look at the label, which was in Turkish. "This is very clearly in *grams*."

"Is it?" Arthur reached for it. "Oh," he said, and frowned. "Isn't a gram close enough to an ounce?"

"Oh my god. Arthur, how long have you been taking this?"

"Probably once a day since I arrived. Sometimes a bit more, if the internet is being especially hellish." Arthur frowned. "You're sure it's grams?"

"*Arthur.*" Gillian began to laugh, a laugh she knew would soon become a cry. She threw her arms around his neck and thought my god, I'll have to love him forever, if I don't he'll fucking die.

"Arthur," she said as she held him, which didn't seem strange or uncomfortable, at least for now. "Arthur, Arthur—"

An electric charge ran up her spine as she laugh-wept. Love!

"Gillian," said Arthur, in his softest, mildest, most hope-filled voice. "Imagine we're old, really old, like near the end, and we're standing beside a window. What's outside?"

Gillian, who was not opposed to imaginary exercises or manifestation ceremonies, obligingly closed her eyes.

There it was, coalescing in a fraction of an instant, like finally seeing the forest through the trees or interpreting the random dots of an autostereogram. In her mind's eye, Arthur's hair was gray and thin, a little mottled skin of his scalp showing through the crown, lines of laughter webbing his face. The wallpaper was decadent, sublimely maximalist, with Thayer's antique rifle mounted, unloaded, on the wall. Gillian smelled cookies and looked down at her hands, spotted with discoloration, a little shaky now, arthritis. They were in the living room setting out plates, moving together with the choreography of domesticity, the familiar clockwork of the home that they had made.

There it was, the window, just to her left! It faced the sidewalk, the slight unevenness of their tree-lined urban street. Gillian took a step toward the glass, heart thundering as she realized what she was looking for, what her future self seemed so ready to see. She knew—oh, how she knew.

And there she was now, coming up the front steps! There she was, on her way, coming home!

"Riot," whispered Gillian with a flutter of recognition.

Arthur held her tightly, so tightly she almost couldn't breathe.

"We don't have to . . . you know. There are other ways," he said, clearing his throat. "I don't care about the biology of it all, I just—"

"Me too," said Gillian firmly.

"I really—"

"I know."

"I just didn't think—"

"I didn't either."

"Oh, fuck," said Arthur belatedly. "Wait, are you thinking the deaths might be somehow drug related?"

Gillian pulled away, taking the square that Arthur had handed her and contemplating it for a long while in her hand.

"Only one way to find out," she said, and popped it in her mouth.

# 67

I didn't feel it was appropriate to bring Monster to a funeral, plus it was one of Ben's days to take him, so I brought Monster home. My mom had agreed to watch him until Ben was done with work, and it made my heart warm a little to know how happy she and Monster were to see each other after their long night away. He immediately ran to the living room and started playing with his toys, running his usual traffic jam of wooden cars along the edge of the sofa.

"So," Mom said with a knowing tone, "how was it?"

"Well, you were right, I shouldn't have gotten involved," I said. "My ego got the better of me."

"To err is human," she said. "But maybe it's not so bad. Did you talk to Meredith?"

"Yes. Well—" It's hard to lie to my mother. "No."

"Lulu," said Mom.

"What?"

"You might as well get what you came for." She gave me a pointed look.

"I only came because they asked me to," I reminded her. "And because Eilidh's problem is actually really weird. Like, worth witnessing firsthand, if you're into prophecies and end times. This really had nothing to do with Meredith."

"If you say so," said Mom in a way that suggested precisely the opposite.

"Mom," I sighed. "Do you really think I'm that butthurt about someone I knew a million years ago?"

"Those are not the words I would use," said Mom. "But yes."

"Car!" said Monster joyfully.

"Isn't the mature thing to just forgive and forget?" I said. "Move on? We were kids."

"Hija, if Meredith wanted to move on, she would have hired a shaman instead of looking for you," said Mom, who, despite her illness, was still very capable of powerful side-eye. "I've had my fair share of anger at Little Miss Meredith, so I'm not saying you have to forgive her. Or forget her. I'm saying say what you need to say and do what you need to do." She walked over to Monster, then, and gave him a tickle and a kiss. "I'll take care of this one," she reminded me. "And you should let me do it while I still can."

"Don't talk like that," I said, but then again, I was wearing black because mortality is relentless. It was jarring to me, actually, that Thayer Wren had been there just a week ago, and suddenly he was gone.

The first time I saw Thayer Wren in my Wrenfare store after all those years, perusing the absurd open floor plan upon which he had been so personally insistent, I was struck by two things: One, he was shorter than I remembered. The line of potted greenery made him look small, almost frail by comparison. Two, he looked dazed beside the latest line of Wrenfare's smart devices, eyeing the rows of minimalist, expressionless, Tyche-dupe titanium screens like he'd gone into the kitchen for something and now couldn't remember what it was.

"Sir?" I said, although I knew exactly who he was, and when his gaze locked on mine I knew he knew who I was, too.

"Funny," he said, clearing his throat. Thayer had a hell of a dry mucus problem and did this relentlessly, I would later learn. "I had you pegged as the successful one."

"No, Meredith is much more cutthroat," I said, disregarding any plausible efforts at pretense.

"She is that." He considered me for a long moment, then turned to look at one of the tablets. "Why a Wrenfare store?"

"They were hiring. I have a technomancy degree." I didn't think it would help to mention that the operating system Thayer had built remained elegant, adaptive, unmatched—that from a purely technomantic perspective I could see why Thayer Wren had become Thayer Wren, or why Meredith so longed for the prestige that was inherent to Wrenfare. Thayer didn't need my help in the arena of adoration. I also doubted he would see me as a peer, even though I could have been. Instinctive awareness of all this made me sympathize more with Meredith, whom I hated. I don't mean to say that in the past tense, but it was true in a different way back then. "Your watches break down a lot," I added, which was also true. They were nearly identical to the watch Tyche had brought to market, but with less craftsmanship and worse design.

"They do not," he said gruffly.

"They do," I replied, because what did I have to lose, really? I mean, my job, sure, there was always that. But I could fuck off and be underpaid basically anywhere. Ben would hire me if things got really dire, and frankly, I'd always wanted to know what to make of godlike Thayer Wren, who was both the monster under Meredith's bed and the star of her narrative—the specter haunting everything she did, for better or (more often) worse.

"Yeah, well, I suppose I lost interest in the product side after Marike passed," Thayer grunted. "She always had more patience for tedium." His eyes were squinty now, as if from permanent refusal to acknowledge his own nearsightedness. "Have you spoken to Meredith since high school?"

"Not since she got me expelled, no."

Thayer barked a laugh. "Little shit. Gets it from me." He looked at me squarely then. "I'm sorry. You ended up here?"

Thanks to her, he meant. I bristled. "Well, I sold a start-up to Tyche a few years ago," I said. "Then I had a baby. Now I'm here."

He arched a brow. "You one of those pro-lifers?"

"The baby was on purpose." I was a little stunned by it, the sense that he took in my optics and concluded I was nothing. Some trash floating on the wind. That first Meredith had ruined my life, and then Monster had been the nail in my coffin. Was that what I was to him, just some rudderless debris? Probably yes. In some sense I had known it even before he opened his mouth. "And by the way," I added with a lift of my chin, "all of *my* products work."

Thayer seemed to find me amusing the way all men find combative women amusing. Something to squash as a treat.

"You get off soon?" he asked. "Let me take you to lunch."

I'm familiar with the idiom of there being no such thing as free lunch, but you already know I'm a morbidly curious person and good steak doesn't buy itself, so I went. Then I pitched him, formally, three times. I thought he was humoring me. I didn't really care. I hated him a little more every time, but I still did it, thinking it would successfully harden my heart, keep me safely out of the industry and free of its serpentine promises. I thought I could finally achieve indifference if I gave it a real shot.

What our meetings actually did was make me nine years old again, choosing the attention of someone who saw something consumable about me, something to use and ultimately exploit. But even in my darkest rewriting of the past, I knew I had never been that for Meredith. And despite my best efforts at hardening myself, I knew that what Thayer really wanted from me, whether he admitted it to himself or not, was to talk about his daughter with someone who had genuinely loved her, even knowing exactly what she was.

He wasn't old. I called him an old man in my head, but he wasn't *old*. It's terrifying, in that sense, how quickly you can disappear. How ineptly one person can love another without getting the time to make amends. I do think Meredith is correct that Thayer left her his company expecting her to fail, but I'm not sure she can safely rule out the possibility that Thayer was less rational than she believed him to be. That despite the irremediable calamity he was handing her, he still thought there was a chance she could impossibly succeed.

Surely he didn't think the end was so near. I never saw any indication of a man departing this world for the next. So maybe the Wrenfare he hoped to leave Meredith eventually would have been different, would have been better, more of a gift than a curse. Or maybe he couldn't really imagine that Wrenfare would go on without him, and picked her because she was the closest approximation of himself. Maybe he really wanted to give the mess to the one child who could spare the others—maybe he knew that only one of them could fail without staying down. Maybe he thought if primo-geniture is good enough for the monarchy, it's good enough for him. Who knows? I'm not saying Thayer was secretly a good or thoughtful person, but he only ever acted instinctively. Whatever he felt in the weeks leading up to his death, real or imagined, he acted on it, and now here we are.

We will never get to ask him. We will always interpret and never know.

"Lulu," said my mom, rousing me from my thoughts. "Traffic is going to get bad if you don't leave soon."

Fully realized one day, gone the next. Life's gifts were so interminable and fleeting. If you think there are only so many times you can let a person disappear from your life, you're wrong. You can do it over and over and over. There's no quota on the love you can lose.

No quota, either, on the love you can share. Earned or not.

"Yeah, thanks Ma, love you. Bye, Monster," I said, kissing the top of my son's sweet-smelling head.

He barely looked up from his cars. Sweet baby. He doesn't know about anything yet.

# 68

The funeral went on despite global panic in the wake of apocalypse, the predictable nihilism of internet memes. Event planning is such that contracts are largely nonrefundable. People had already traveled from all over the country, and anyway, who could logistically say when eternal darkness might lift?

In lieu of consulting cosmologists about being left to float in the infinite dark of the unfeeling abyss, the funeral was held outdoors, in the woods. Thayer did famously love the woods, although I'm not sure he could have guessed it would be pitch black at the time of his memorial, which rendered a normal request egotistically laborious. There was a particular circle of trees we all had to hike to; fortunately, for this reason, it was a casual affair, most people in the instantly recognizable loungewear and hiking shoes that quietly signaled luxury in the magitech industry. All of us were holding phones and flashlights with various degrees of incompetence as part of a procession I'd planned to imperceptibly join at the rear until Arthur spotted me. He whispered something to Gillian, who nodded—she was accompanied on her other side by Yves—and then Arthur wandered over to me, looking every inch the man you loved from the very first moment you saw him as a boy, purely because you couldn't help it.

"We're running an experiment," he said. "Death by chocolate." He explained the finer details of the European reliance on the metric system to me as if I was, like him, the kind of person who didn't question a volume exceeding *two fucking sticks of butter* as an appropriate dosage for magical chocolate. "Like I said, it was an honest mistake, and whatever, I'm basically fine. Where's Monster?" he asked, looking hopefully around.

"At home," I said. "With my mom. Because it's dark. And a funeral."

"Oh. Right, of course. Makes sense." Arthur walked in step with me, watching his feet. "You know, if this whole dosage mishap—"

"Inability to read," I corrected him.

"This dosage mishap, which frankly could have happened to anyone—"

"This impressively stupid act of carelessness, yes, go on."

"If it turns out to be the fix, then I don't think you've earned your fee." I could tell he was teasing me. Arthur was always a playful person. It's part of the can't-help-it thing, even if he thinks it's reasonable to just take a random amount of drugs—after all, what's the difference between two tablets and two truckloads of ibuprofen?

"Considering that your sister set a biblical swarm of flies on me and my fragile baby son, I do plan to collect," I told him. "Besides, you signed a contract."

"What? Did not."

"Messages count, legally. It's in writing, offer and acceptance."

"Are you bullshitting me?"

"Right now, with this? Absolutely. But in court? It holds up."

"What do you know about contract law?"

"More than you, if you're asking dumb questions."

"What's your son's name?"

"Aragorn."

"Damn," sighed Arthur. "I really thought I'd get you that time."

We walked a little bit longer in silence, twigs snapping underfoot.

"What will you do?" I asked him. "When your bereavement is at an end."

"About the accidental pyrotechnics, you mean? It's calmed down a lot since you've been around. You actually did help with that part, so maybe you're right about services rendered." He paused, segueing as he often did to levity. "Any chance you're open to full-time employment? Two weeks' paid vacation to become part of the Wren family, plus a commemorative pin."

I rolled my eyes, though far be it from me not to notice he'd incidentally offered me the one thing I'd always wanted, which was to be one of them. "I told you, your magic is misfiring because you're doing everything wrong. Or you were." I stumbled over a tree root and he caught me by the elbow. "You don't need *me*, Art, you need a mental health professional. Maybe two or three of them."

"Fair enough." He seemed unaffected by this, the bastard.

"And what about the rest?" I asked, pressing him. "The nonmagical stuff. What's next?"

He riffled a hand through his hair, or at least, I think he did. I was concentrating on not stumbling to my death.

"I guess I'll attend another funeral and then lose my reelection campaign," said Arthur. "Maybe look into fostering or adoption. Do some recreational basket weaving with Yves."

I paused to frown at him, not that he could see it. "What makes you so sure you're going to lose?"

"Well, only the fact that I'm losing," he said.

"Losing isn't lost. Your opponent is an asshole."

"Yeah, but I'm, quote, uninspiring. My policy isn't progressive enough for the progressives, it's too progressive for the conservatives. Hedging my bets only got me voted out in a single term." Arthur sighed heavily, like someone who'd witnessed the ravages of war.

"So then bet riskier," I said, pointing out what I felt was obvious. "You've got nothing to lose."

"Aside from an election?" grumbled Arthur.

"If you can't do something from inside the box, then destroy the box," I said.

"What does that even mean?"

"It means, I don't know, you're not allowed to just fuck off and do nothing. You have money, you have influence, so you should use it."

"But nobody will *let* me use it." He gave me a wry look. "I'm just some guy."

"So what? At one point your father was just some guy." I wasn't sure whether this was a helpful train of thought, so I added, "Stop feeling sorry for yourself. Keep trying. Just take the beating and keep going."

"What if I'm not a masochist?"

"You're a *complete* masochist, first of all—"

"Okay, then what if it's hard and it sucks and I'm tired and I just want to be happy?"

"Do you think it'll make you happy to recreationally weave baskets?"

Arthur sounded sulkier than Monster when he said, miserably, "No."

We trudged along farther.

"You're capable of great things, Arthur Wren," I said, having lost a battle with myself. "No, not great things. Fuck great things, that's just capitalist jargon. You are capable of good things." I looked at him then, shining my phone's flashlight on his face so he knew I was looking right at him. "You are capable of such good things, Arthur. And I have a son who needs good schools, and I have a mother who needs good medical care, and I am in dire need of goodness in my politics."

"So then I should do it for you?" he asked with another air of playfulness.

"Do it for Monster," I said. "Do it for Riot."

He looked thoughtful. "Do you think they'll be friends someday?"

"Maybe, unless your opponent helps burn the world down, sure."

"Do you really think one politician can do anything?"

Not really, but he made me want to. And shouldn't that mean something? "If one politician can hold a government hostage, then yeah, one should be good enough to fix it, too."

"Not if the system's broken."

"Who can fix the system but you?"

"What if no one lets me try?"

"You mean what if they do and you fail?"

"Yeah, sure, what if I fail?"

"Oh, darling, but what if you fly?" I sing-songed.

"I hate you," said Arthur, and then, "What's your son's name?"

I was quiet a second.

And then I said, "It's Arthur."

"It is?" he said, sounding awed. "Wait. No. You're fucking with me."

"His name is Arthur," I grudgingly admitted. "It actually is."

When I found out I was having a boy—I knew it like a dream I'd had, a vision I'd already witnessed from the future—I suggested the name to Ben, thinking he'd shoot it down. He didn't. He never asked, either, what made me think of it. But what is early motherhood if not a time steeped in nostalgia, wondering how to remedy the past with our dreams for the future, to build tomorrow on the wounds of yesterday?

The procession came to a halt, having reached the clearing Thayer had selected. I realized that Arthur had to leave my side, to go and join his sisters. Meredith was standing alone. Eilidh was a distance away from her. Dzhuliya was several people away in the crowd, not standing with either of them.

"Wait," said Arthur. "He's not mine, is he?"

I was so lost in thought that it took me several seconds to decipher what Arthur was asking me. When I realized, I couldn't decide whether to laugh or throw my hands up and leave.

"Art. We slept together *over a decade ago*. Monster is two years old."

"Oh. Right." He laughed. The trees rustled. It felt holy, despite all evidence to the contrary.

"We'll talk later," Arthur said, and kissed my cheek. He was off to say goodbye to his father, the archbishop of assholes; the assholiest of them all.

I pulled him back. "Arthur," I said, with a weird flame of desperation in my voice. "I'm sorry Thayer didn't want to know you. He missed out. You're the best person, the very best one. I've been meaning to tell you that for a while."

My eyes were full of tiny remorseful fire ants. My throat was thick with them.

"Nah," said Arthur, his smile a lilt of gentlemanly disagreement.

Then I let him go, and he went.

# 69

It turned out Thayer merely wanted some sort of open mic night, a bring-your-own-compliments potluck in service to his life and achievements. Many, many people spoke very movingly, and thus many, many people were moved.

Eilidh, however, began to suffer a heightening anxiety she hadn't had when she woke up that morning, when she'd thought all she'd have to do was make an appearance, put on a show. How do you celebrate a man who bangs his hot young assistant, even consensually? It was just so disappointing. A cliché, precisely as Meredith had said.

Eilidh looked over at Meredith, whose chin was held staunchly aloft. She and Eilidh still hadn't spoken beyond normal questions, are you hungry, do you know where the rest of the guest towels are, who wants the Degas. "I actually hate that painting," Eilidh had confessed in answer to that, and Meredith had looked at her sharply; inquisitively, but with an edge. Eilidh waited for Meredith to criticize, or, less likely, to ask, but instead Meredith merely shrugged and looked vaguely approving.

"We'll donate it," she said. "He'd shit his pants to have his name in the de Young."

Meredith glanced bracingly at Eilidh then, as if she expected Eilidh to disagree, but Eilidh felt too tired. It was exhausting, the weight of disappointment. She didn't know who she'd wanted her father to be, nor did she feel she knew any longer who he'd actually been. Was it ever love for him, or just convenience? She wanted to ask Dzhuliya, but at the same time the mere existence of the question made her physically ill.

Meredith was watching her now, as if Meredith could read her thoughts. Eilidh wondered if it had solved anything between them, the admission that neither of them had ever really gotten what they wanted, that they'd been at odds with each other because of the way one man had treated each of them, because what each one considered lucky was what the other had. But was that all? Was it only ever miscommunication?

No, probably not, because Meredith was mean and fundamentally uninterested in Eilidh as a person, and even sympathy had its constraints. Compassion didn't live inside a vacuum. Maybe this relationship, strained but cordial, was the best version that could reasonably exist between them. Maybe all it could ever be was open envy and the vestiges of secret pain.

For almost a minute, the circle of grieving stood empty. It was someone else's turn to speak, Eilidh realized, though nobody seemed to know whose.

"Perhaps his children might like to say something?" suggested the funeral director, the one who could no longer look Eilidh in the eye for having misidentified her. He directed the comment to Meredith instead, who seemed to shake herself forcefully awake.

"Right. Yes." She stepped responsibly into the center of the circle, ever the eldest daughter. "Dad," she said, "was . . . a great man. Well, he was a man," she corrected herself in an unreadable tone. "And he was . . ."

She trailed off, staring into space, for a long time.

An uncomfortably long time.

Arthur took a step forward and reached out, touching Meredith's elbow. "Do you want me to go first?" he asked her quietly.

The rest of the circle of onlookers seemed uneasy, fidgeting with a mix of disinterest and tension. Those who were paying attention seemed to restlessly hope this would wrap up quickly, resolve in some peaceable way. Next to me, near the back, one of Thayer's golf buddies was checking stocks on his phone.

"No, no, let's just get this over with. Let's see." Meredith nudged Arthur away and looked a touch manic now, as if something horrific had occurred to her. "Well, my father never liked me," she announced.

The golf buddy looked up. There was a collective stirring of discomfort in the crowd at that, which Meredith acknowledged aloud. "No, no," she assured everyone hastily, "it's fine. He loved me, sure. But he didn't like me."

She paused.

"I disappointed him," she admitted. "I didn't listen to him. He saw most of what I did as a malicious betrayal, and maybe some of it was. Mainly, he just wanted me to fulfill a prophecy, a more conventional form of . . . I don't know, greatness."

Another pause.

"When my father did things, it was brilliant, it was necessary. When I did things, it was reckless, shortsighted, egotistical. I think he wanted me to fail."

Meredith looked a little startled by her own admission, even to Eilidh.

"I spent my whole life thinking he wanted me to fail," she said, "and then I did. So I guess that was my version of the prophecy."

# 70

Unbeknownst to all but Meredith, Jamie was in the crowd at that moment, standing somewhere along the perimeter of the circle. Unclear how he had known about the memorial or whether he had been invited, although it hadn't been by Meredith, so likely not. He had texted Meredith that he was leaving the rental car in the parking lot of the funeral home. She said have you really had the rental car the whole time? And he said yeah, enjoy the late fees. And god help her, she loved him. She really did.

She loved him, and in the moment, she felt this immensity—this true, honest-to-god *enormity* of feeling that was substantially, unavoidably pain. Oh, she thought, oh. *This* was what she couldn't do; she couldn't make happiness from nothing because of some law of physics, or color theory, or any reason that could be logically understood. She couldn't do it, not because she hadn't earnestly tried or because the technology did not exist, but because she simply couldn't mimic the necessary depth of time and experience—not in a year, certainly not in a clinical study paid for by a man whose profits ticked up by the second, by an industry that exploited more than it served—so how could she really create vibrancy; how could she make beauty without carnage, how could she make anything inorganic feel somehow natural and complete?

Perfection isn't symmetry; it isn't the approval of a man who isn't even listening; it's closer to calamity, an irreplicable accident.

*Oh god*, Meredith thought then. *Oh fuck. I built my whole life on a lie.*

# 71

Meredith stepped back in a daze. She seemed to be finished talking. Eilidh looked helplessly at Arthur, who was frowning with a mix of concerned bemusement, one hand tightly clutching the flashlight on his nemesis, the phone.

Then he stepped into the circle, as if it was only natural that he speak next.

"Dad was smart," said Arthur. "Smart and assertive. And tough. And . . . cold."

He stopped.

Behind him, visible only by the edges of light from his phone, Meredith was hugging her arms around herself.

"I don't really want to speak ill of the dead," Arthur said lightly, opening his mouth to continue his speech, to choose some levity or lighter fare as he always did, but he looked faintly stunned, as if now that Meredith had spoken, he couldn't think of anything anymore.

"Well, he didn't like me, either," Arthur finally said, helplessly spreading his hands as if to say that was the joke, ha ha. "Which is a shame, I guess, because I'd have really wanted the chance to like him. I imagine it's difficult, fatherhood, parenthood in general. You just try your best, I guess, but people are people, you know, everyone's different, sometimes it just doesn't work."

Arthur reached up to scrape a hand over his mouth, shaking his head as he seemed to rapidly lose his own thread.

"I guess it's not his fault he wanted me to be different," he said. "I wanted him to be different, too."

# 72

Arthur, oh, Arthur. The trouble with Arthur as a politician was that he was keenly aware of what other people wanted him to be or do or say, which made him very good but also optically terrible, because he could only really be what he was.

And so his politics read as inauthentic, as sycophantic or acolytic, because nobody really knew him, and none of them could read between the lines correctly. Arthur was saying *I'll be any shape you want if you'll just love me,* which on most politicians was probably superficial, but what everyone was missing was the tacit clause, the operative faith—the part where Arthur was so committed to the bit that he never questioned whether the love he so freely offered was what anyone really deserved.

# 73

Arthur opened his mouth to talk again, then closed it, stepping back to the fringes of their bereavement circle.

Eilidh blinked, realizing with disbelief that it was her turn.

She took a step forward, dizzied, accidentally locking eyes with Dzhuliya and allowing her attention to skid away, toward someone else. Anyone else.

And then she spotted me in the crowd.

# 74

I had a pained expression on my face, not that I knew it at the time. I was thinking about how Meredith and Arthur didn't seem to realize that this was their only chance to say goodbye to their father. That they hadn't been able to prepare a final speech because there were countless conversations locked inside their chests that they'd no longer get to have. But if they weren't careful, they'd keep on having those arguments forever; those talks would never die, and so they'd keep Thayer alive like that, at his worst. At his most profoundly disappointing.

I guess I felt sorry for them, the Wrens. Which you shouldn't do. Lord knows they don't need your sympathy. If you give a mouse a cookie . . . you know how that turns out.

But hey, a bad dad is a bad dad.

# 75

So anyway, I don't know what Eilidh got from looking at me. She never told me. But after a second or two, she just started to talk.

"I recently learned some unsavory things about my father," said Eilidh, after a very long period of silence. "Which is making it hard for me to say something right now that I think he'd want all of you, his friends and colleagues and loved ones, to hear."

She paused again, securing the mask, reaching for something that had always been there. Some clever facade of perfection. These people had come on this day to hear something specific. These people were here to memorialize a myth, so give them one. Give them some trinket to carry around, it'll take nothing from you, it's the polite thing to do. It's what Thayer would have wanted.

"It's stupid to think anyone knows what anyone else wants," said Thayer then, from the back of Eilidh's mind, a stray comment over their weekly Tuesday lunch dug up in that moment by Eilidh's conscience. "Success is success, who cares how you achieve it? When I'm dead, I won't remember anything, certainly not the times I lied to keep the peace."

It went on into a lecture, something about Meredith most likely, about how Meredith would never do anything to make her life easier even though it was all so forgettable—all in service to some greater, illusory thing. Success.

Thayer probably went on about Arthur, too, and about how Arthur didn't have it in him, the mettle to really go for glory. Arthur was a quitter, Arthur would take the beating and go, he wouldn't fixate on it. Arthur would carelessly shed the skin and move on.

Eilidh supposed Thayer never realized how much he admired them for what they were capable of, the things he himself could never achieve. His daughter, who was fiercely and fearlessly herself. His son, who was endlessly resilient, effortlessly forgiving.

And Eilidh had never said anything to contradict him; never pointed out to Thayer that all his griping about her siblings was a silly way of wishing aloud that they'd call. Which was understandable, probably, because if anyone had asked Eilidh Wren where she wanted to be and what she wanted to discuss, she would have said her sister Meredith and her brother Arthur, sitting at Tuesday lunch with her crotchety, ornery, unproductively devoted dad.

"It's complicated," Eilidh admitted then, speaking to the pilgrims of her father's passing. "Because my dad was my only friend for a really long time, and I don't think it had to be that way, but it was convenient for him and I was grateful. I was really, honestly grateful. And yeah, maybe he turned out to be another lecherous old man—"

Someone coughed.

"—but he also saved my life, he really did. When you think about what you really leave behind, it gets kind of . . . laughably simple?" In her mind, the gas masks swung again from the quaking airplane cabin. Only five days ago. Ancient history cleaving around the presence of her father, when he existed and when he was gone.

"I didn't think anyone would miss me, but I knew he would. And maybe that was for bad or counterproductive reasons. And maybe he should have let me grow up, or at very least believed that I could. And maybe he didn't want to know who any of us really were, and maybe he died without having the faintest idea. Isn't that sad? It's sad. Life is so sad."

Eilidh looked up at the inky, starless sky. The thing in her chest was ready to spring, all coiled tight in her shoulders. Latched on in the place where her wings should be. It sang a forbidden song of oceans turning to blood, dead babies. Badness, she thought. There it was again.

Then she looked at me a second time. I wasn't thinking about anything. I was mostly hoping this thing was catered. I was hungry. But Eilidh saw me in the crowd, and she thought about what I had said to her, and about how, when she asked nicely, or asked bravely, the thing in her chest could be hers, too.

She wondered how to tell the crowd at her father's funeral that she was cursed with an inner rottenness, a personal demon she couldn't control. A creature, a wee little ghostie that seemed to be somehow both benign and a raw, molten, earth-destroying power that she could only use when she got ugly, when she let her own darkness run free. But that wasn't it, was it? Because sometimes it gave her something too, sometimes it protected her, sometimes it kept her safe. It seemed to want something from her, but what? What did anything want from her, and what was she to anyone?

"Life," Eilidh sighed, "is just so—"

From her chest was a summons, a longing call. It whispered to her gently: ?

Eilidh knew what it was, and she let go.

Call it reflex, call it art, call it atavistic pain. Where words failed, her body answered. Eilidh twisted sharply, more sharply than she should have, as if to shake catharsis free. One hand shot up and the other out—a contorted, baroque interpretation of fourth position. The tips of her fingers stretched out for the sea she couldn't see, the distant bugle call, the finish line. The very promising young woman that Eilidh Wren had once been. Her future stretched out beyond the horizon, invisible string she'd thought she could simply hold tauter the closer she got.

Closer to where, and to what?

She collapsed forward, knuckles brushing the ground, drawn back up like the flow of a sunrise. The indifference of a tide; life is hard and nothing matters. She pulled her arms close, hugged around her rib cage, then stepped forward, because that's what you do. You step and you step and you step.

She held out her hands, Come join me, I'm not meant to do this alone!

—but then she pulled back again, afraid. Intimacy is exhausting. Love wears you to the bone. She didn't have the reach she'd once had, everything felt strange, like shrugging on an old body, an old form, an old method of coping.

The thing in her chest inhaled deeply, as if to fill its dormant lungs.

Life was loving someone *on purpose*! Intensity mattered! Every twist was painful and only a fraction of what she could accomplish at her prime; but there was a new compassion to her motions, to the softness she could finally allow herself to feel. It no longer had to bring tears to her eyes. She could honor it, accept it. She could embrace it without the teeth of chronic self-sabotage; without the sense that every moment should be a fracture, toeing up to and over (and over, and over) the edge of unending, undying self-harm.

It hurt, but not for nothing. Not for the weight of anyone else's grief but hers.

The thing in her chest seemed to dissipate, to fill her veins, to dance off the edge of her fingertips into the circle of onlooking mourners, to the crowd she very nearly forgot. It wasn't for them this time, the performance. It wasn't a performance at all. It felt right, it was the *only* right thing, this motion, this one, this one, this beat, this percussive step, this motion onward, this motion forward, this slight drag pulling her back, the undertow of uncertainty, capitulation to an unspoken communal rhythm, the sense that life would go on, and that if she had faith in the current—if she trusted the lightness in her chest—she would float.

It didn't have to be flawless; it didn't have to be perfect; the audience would always leave, she would always remain. What was still there when the lights went out? Only this: the monstrous, ravaging wanting that thundered constant, neglected, in the depths of her quiet heart.

*I want to live,* said Eilidh Wren's fingers and toes, her outstretched limbs, the soles of her dirtied sneakers, the dance of her wordless prayer. *I want to live!*

She saw it then, her future. No more desk jobs cramping her spine. Marketing could take a hike—she would have fresh air and music. She would have beauty, and desperation to learn. She saw the barre and the pulse of it welcomed her. Four little girls and a cheery, devoted Monster looked up at her with shining eyes, with lightness and hope. She saw her future, a new apartment, a fresh glass of pink wine, a new Tuesday ritual. Friends and loved ones she always remembered to call, letters she wrote for the thrill of correspondence, fresh berries in the early summer, small business taxes she only sort of understood but would gladly learn.

The thing in her chest sang, and she understood it. The badness takes, but it also gives. She closed her eyes and felt it ask her what she wanted, like some primal prompt for fight or flight: *Eilidh Wren, you are magic, and unto magic you may call.*

She closed her eyes. LET THERE BE LIGHT! called Eilidh Wren into the void, flung like a dying wish into the ether.

When the sun broke from behind the canopy of trees, glinting like a half-remembered dream, the first thing Eilidh saw was her sister, Meredith. There were tears in her eyes, shining, and a look of thunder on her face, and it was love, all of it love, and Eilidh smiled, too, because finally, finally, she was happy.

She was happy, and she belonged.

# 76

There was a cocktail reception afterward, of course. Beneath the newly skylit beams, it was now sometime in the autumn afternoon, though everyone behaved as if it were midsummer. The Wren siblings' various malaise was forgotten, collective relief overpowering for a while the sense that three adults in the room needed therapy *stat*. Thayer Wren was a holy figure again; an innovator, whose mere presence inspired enlightenment, inside and out.

Jamie didn't stay. He didn't belong there. He nodded to Meredith, who gave him a thin smile in return. Then he slipped out, hands in his pockets. She didn't know where he was going, but there was a serenity in her now, a peace that hadn't been there before.

Now, unlike before, she understood that she only had to ask.

Meredith sat on the ledge outside the entrance to the funeral home, staring contemplatively into the woods. Cass caught sight of her from the window and followed, walking up to her with a drink in each hand. A glass of wine for her, a beer for him. To have and to hold. Two coffee cups in the sink every morning. Two rings, one home.

She looked up at him with a smile, but not the right one. Not the one that says hello.

"Cass," said Meredith.

She reached out a hand for his and he knew, of course. You always know.

Cass took her proffered hand and sat beside her on the ledge with a sigh, taking a sip of his beer. "Twenty-four hours," he remarked to himself. "I thought I'd get at least a week before you admitted you couldn't marry me."

She kissed his knuckles. "Sorry."

She sipped her wine. He drank his beer.

"Am I wrong?" he asked hopefully. "Is there a chance I'm jumping to conclusions? I do love a classic miscommunication caper," he said, affecting an English accent.

"Not this time, I'm afraid," Meredith replied in a worse version of the same accent. "I can't marry you, no. I'm sorry."

"Drat," said Cass, now committed to the English bit. "I was really looking forward to my future with you."

Meredith replied, increasingly cockneyed, "It did seem very comfortable, didn't it?"

"Yeah." They each took a sip.

"Did you think we'd ever wind up having kids?" Meredith asked suddenly.

"No, not really." Cass turned to her with such surprise he was American again. "You want kids?"

"I don't know," Meredith said, and meant it. "Maybe not. Probably not. I guess I just want the chance to think about it, that's all." She shrugged.

"Think about motherhood, you mean?"

"No, the future." She scooted back on the ledge and hugged her knees into her chest. "You know my mother was sick for a long time, right?"

Cass let his beer linger for a while on his tongue. "Was she? I thought she died suddenly."

"Well, she starved herself for a long time before then." Meredith turned her head away from him, looking into the woods again. "It was kind of like watching someone waste away, except nobody else seemed to see it that way. They just told her how great she looked and how jealous they were."

Meredith tipped her chin down, speaking to her knees. "You know, I really thought that if I was good enough, if I did everything perfectly, she'd suddenly shout 'I'm hungry' and order a pizza. And then my dad could be proud of me and they'd stop fighting. And everything would be okay, if I could just fix everything that was wrong with me."

She laughed at herself, at her childhood dreams, her desperation for simplicity. "I used to be a prodigy," she commented wryly into her glass. "Now I'm nearly forty."

"Meredith," Cass sighed with a shake of his head, "you're turning thirty-one."

She gave a sardonic toast to the trees. "True, I've exceeded expectations. At nearly thirty-one, I'm about to be CEO of two failing companies, and

I'm going to prison for fraud." She sobered. "I wonder what my mom would think."

"You're not going to prison," Cass reminded her.

Meredith had thoughts about this. We'll skip them for now and focus on Cass, since we're about to bid him adieu.

For what it's worth, Cass understood with a deep pang in his chest that he would miss Meredith very much, even if he was also grateful to her for the escape hatch. He knew the kind of choice he'd been making. He knew he'd chosen a love that was safe because it demanded nothing from him. Still, he would love her forever. Two things can be true.

"Is it someone else?" he asked after a moment, because he had to. And because he didn't think she'd lie, which was one of the reasons he'd wanted to be married to her in the first place.

"Yeah," said Meredith.

"The journalist?"

"Yeah."

"I saw him today," Cass acknowledged aloud.

"Yeah. But I didn't invite him, he just came."

They both sipped their drinks quietly.

"What happened between the two of you?" Cass asked.

"Well," Meredith sighed ruefully, "I was always pretty confident he'd ruin my life."

"Yeah. I used to feel that way about my wife," said Cass, eyeing the knuckles on his left hand. He wasn't thinking about anything, really, just remembering. Just casually idling on the paths of nostalgia, reliving old feelings, shrugging them on like old skins.

He was still staring when Meredith's hand gently covered his.

"You'll feel that way again," she assured him.

"Oh, Christ. I didn't mean it like a good thing," Cass told her with a grimace.

Meredith, the asshole, laughed and laughed.

"I know," she eventually managed. "But still. That's what I wish my mom had known."

"What, that marriage is a scam?"

"No," said Meredith. "That someday, if you want to—"

If you break a pattern. If you give the feeling a voice. If you ask the right person for help. Meredith was making a decision, a bad one, one she knew she'd be punished for but wouldn't regret. She reveled in the precipice of danger. Meredith was many things, an asshole, a dried-up former prodigy, a criminal, but never afraid.

"—you'll feel alive again."

# 77

Gillian, meanwhile, felt very conflicted. She glanced multiple times at Dzhuliya, obviously with the intention to say something. Eilidh watched her do it, taking dainty sips from her martini, until finally Gillian threw her hands in the air and dragged Arthur over.

Eilidh followed reluctantly, or with the appearance of reluctance. She wasn't yet sure which.

"Welcome to the family," Gillian said, and put her arms around a startled Dzhuliya. It was an awkward hug, uncomfortable for both women, and after an appropriate period of time that Gillian appeared to have already run the calculations for, Gillian released her.

"Things are very strange," Gillian said to Dzhuliya as an apparent conclusory note. "But humans are very adaptable. Eventually anything can become bearable, even normal." She glanced quickly, meaningfully at Eilidh. "It all depends on what you choose to accept."

Then she turned a bright, politician's wife smile on Dzhuliya. "We'll have to have you over to our house for Thanksgiving," she said. "If not sooner."

"That would be nice," said Dzhuliya politely.

"And keep us updated. Please."

The last bit was said with such earnestness that even Dzhuliya looked struck by it. "Yes," she said, and cleared her throat. "Yes, I will. Thank you."

Gillian nodded, and that, too, appeared laden with significance. "You're welcome."

The two women smiled at each other. Then Arthur coughed, gave Dzhuliya a hug, and tipped his chin in an awkward, boyish way before departing with Gillian, the two of them making their way back to Yves.

Eilidh remained, sipping her drink.

Dzhuliya looked at her. "I know it's not the time," she said in a quiet voice, "but I just wanted to tell you—"

"You made me feel better," said Eilidh. It startled Dzhuliya so much that her eyes went wide, and she looked impossibly young, like a twenty-six-year-old girl-woman who still didn't know a single thing about life, much less how she was going to raise a child without a father.

"I really couldn't have gotten through this week without you," added Eilidh, who was now trying a thing where she said what she meant before the opportunity was lost and life was over. "I just wanted to thank you for that."

"Oh. Well, it was mutual." Dzhuliya was still having difficulty looking Eilidh in the eye. "I just . . . I like you a lot, I've always liked you. I didn't think you'd ever—" She broke off and looked into the trees outside. "I'd have done things differently if I'd known, that's all."

"Yeah," said Eilidh. "Yeah, I agree."

The truth is that for Dzhuliya it had all been kind of a whirlwind. She had known right away that her boss liked her, the way all women typically know; likewise, she felt an attraction to him, to the way he commanded a room. And either she was just a win for him, something conquerable and rewarding to a man whose business sense was melting gradually away, or she was something else, someone whose company he enjoyed, a clever, funny woman who happened to be around him all the time. Who could say? Dzhuliya had wanted to believe the latter, that things had just . . . *happened,* and she was struggling with money, the company didn't pay enough to live in the city but she wanted to live her big-city youth while she could, to sleep with people and not call them back, to have some cheap thrills while she was still exciting enough to have them, and Thayer was really generous. He was a really generous boss, and a foodie, and he took Dzhuliya to lunch all the time and she loved it, to the point where she made sure she was always available at noon. And then one time he taught her how to eat caviar with good vodka and the champagne was so sweet they both got a little carried away, so they popped into the shop next door and Dzhuliya tried on a beautiful dress she could never afford and Thayer bought it for her as a gift, said wear it on a date with a handsome man who treats you well, and she said I thought that's what I was doing.

And anyway, well, he got a place in the city for her, and he stayed there sometimes, a lot more often recently, even without the option of sex. He was just starting to get comfortable around her, and yeah, she matched with people on her dating apps still and occasionally sexted, but then her period was late and she couldn't bring people to the apartment because Thayer had keys, but she couldn't give it up because she loved it so much, it had *in-unit laundry and parking*. And he bought her the car, too. Safer, he said, than her old car. And how was she going to argue with that?

She was attracted to him, definitely, she liked him, might have maybe loved him over time; she wasn't sure if that's where it was going, you know, to some forever kind of love. Was he ever planning to marry her? She had no idea. He'd told her he would take care of her; he'd asked if she wanted an abortion and she'd considered it, thinking that was probably wise. She hadn't decided yet at the time he made the will, but afterward, she decided she would have the baby. Not for any moral reason but because it seemed exciting to her, someone who would love her. She knew that was a bad reason to have a baby, and pregnancy itself was so awful, she was so tired, but also, she felt the stirrings of excitement, of having something to look forward to that wasn't eons of debt and layoffs at work and the Appalachian Trail turning gradually into arid savanna.

She loved her niece and nephew, and she wanted something of her own. Dating had never been fun for her. If it was just her and the baby, so be it. She had been thinking more and more seriously of calling things off with Thayer, because what if it was a girl? She couldn't bear it, her daughter thinking of her what Meredith Wren had said, that she was just a cliché. She wasn't. She was lonely and she had all this love, you know, all this tenderness, all this softness and warmth, and nobody but Thayer had wanted it from her. Everyone else wanted something from Dzhuliya that she didn't know how to give. And her mother would help her, she decided. She'd quit and use her job reference from Thayer to move up to a better paying, more stable job; she'd finish her young adult vampire novel and dedicate it to her baby; she'd grow up fast and then some other grown-up would like that about her, her self-assuredness, her desire to make the world a nicer place.

And yes, she'd think about Eilidh Wren when she masturbated and take that secret to her grave. Every lady should have a quiet darkness.

But now Thayer was dead and Dzhuliya was rattled and Eilidh Wren was her dream girl, her nightmare fuel, and how the fuck had Dzhuliya ever thought she could have a baby? How had she foreseen any of this shit going down? The Wrens loomed massive in Dzhuliya's consciousness, she tossed and turned all night knowing that now she carried one of *them*. The inimitable House of Wren, full of expired greatness, exactly like a tomb.

"I just wanted," Dzhuliya began, and I knew what she was going to say, that she wanted to be one of them, because I felt it, too. (Obviously I was eavesdropping at the time—I think that's pretty clear.)

Anyway, I knew what Dzhuliya was thinking, that she wanted to be a Wren and it was an uncontainable madness; it was inexplicable and insane. And pointless. Not a single one of the Wrens was happy, but there just seemed such . . . potential. Such possibility, shining like a diamond in the dark.

Eden, am I right?

"I know," said Eilidh, and she reached her hand out to lightly brush Dzhuliya's hair from her shoulder. An intimate touch, a lover's touch. Dzhuliya looked up and her lips parted slightly, promise held between them, a fragile little plea. "Oh, no," said Eilidh with a quick shake of her head. "I mean . . . you're carrying my dead father's child. This is absolutely not happening."

"Right," said Dzhuliya. Spell broken.

"But—" Eilidh exhaled heavily. "We're going to see each other a lot now. You're in my life forever and I'm in yours. We will . . . adapt."

"Right," said Dzhuliya.

"Everything will be normal and fine," Eilidh said. "Or at very least, it will be fine."

"Right."

Eilidh nodded, looking away like she was going to invent a reason to leave, but then she thought better of it.

"Do you want to go get something to eat?" she asked Dzhuliya. "Again, not in a propositioning way. Just because I can't stand being here and also, I want a burger."

Dzhuliya was desperate for meat. Iron deficiency. It was a constant craving. "I could do that."

Eilidh looked over her shoulder at me then. It was the kind of look that made me wonder if she was clearing space on a shelf for me. She opened her mouth like she would say something, then shook her head and shrugged. I realized that if Eilidh Wren asked me to get a drink with her I'd probably say yes. But it wasn't the time, obviously, so I just raised my glass—of Diet Coke—in her direction, like a toast. "To your badness," I mouthed.

She made a face. Who knows if she understood me, but I think she got the point. God, but she was pretty when she was silly. What was it with the

Wrens? It was diabolical. I needed psychiatric help. I'd discuss it with my therapist on Monday.

Eilidh left with Dzhuliya, and I thought to myself, that girl will be fine. Not sure which girl I meant but it felt right, felt organic. I thought, you know what? Good for her. And then I turned to close the book and leave.

# 78

Of course, right when I chose to leave, Gillian died.

"I do not understand," Yves had been saying to Gillian and Arthur at the time. "You want me to . . . stay?"

"Emotionally," Arthur explained.

"And also physically," Gillian added.

"It's just that I love you," Arthur said.

"And I think I probably could love you as well, albeit differently," Gillian contributed.

"And while it would be . . . unconventional," Arthur hedged, glancing at Gillian.

"We think it could still be worthwhile for all of us," Gillian said with a nod. "Though, of course, we understand if you're looking for something else."

"It's been a strange week," said Arthur. "I've accepted that it may simply be a strange life."

"It seems to make a lot more sense when you're present," said Gillian. "Which I'm realizing now is maybe small potatoes as far as reasons to re-orient your entire life."

Astonishingly, Yves had not predicted this. While he had caught flashes of Gillian and Arthur at their later ages in various moments, he hadn't seen anything noteworthy—no deaths, no atrocities, no major instances of anything recognizably dire. He assumed he had been seeing little glimpses of their future selves, drinking coffee and arguing about the groceries, and thus he had not committed any of it to memory, thinking it was all the mirage of any unremarkable domesticated life.

He hadn't seen himself in any of these future projections, and had assumed that was because he would be elsewhere by then, moved on in some way, but now that he thought about it, he realized he hadn't seen himself because he *was* himself—that is, in these visions, he was observing Arthur and Gillian from his own future body rather than theirs. This happened to him occasionally, predicting his own future, but it was impossible to separate what would inevitably happen from what Yves merely imagined *might* happen.

There was no knowing if it was the future he saw, or merely the future he wished.

He considered the question as well as its various practicalities. "A life in politics may become very difficult under unconventional circumstances," he said slowly. "Although I am not opposed to the preservation of your private life." It would be no different than it was before, he supposed, although now it would mean *he* was the extraneous detail rather than Arthur.

"Oh, we wouldn't hide," Arthur said. "I'm losing anyway. What would be the point of lying, just adding insult to injury?"

"A drastic move would be fearless authenticity," said Gillian, ever the tactician. "Sure, it might fail. But so what? People fail all the time."

"I am not usually this cavalier about failure," Arthur said. "But I suppose one may as well adapt."

"The point is," Gillian said, and then went pale.

Then, abruptly, she collapsed at Arthur's feet, her martini glass crashing to the ground as clear liquid spilled across the funeral home floor.

"Oh! Convenient," said Arthur excitedly, before realizing that everyone in the room had turned to Gillian with a gasp. "Sorry, I meant—well, never mind what I meant," he snapped at them, shooing their attention away as he knelt to place two fingers on Gillian's frozen pulse, just beneath her jaw.

Yves knelt beside him, looking at Gillian's placidly unmoving face. "So it was the stupid American error, then?" he said, meaning Gillian's experiment some hours before, taking a sample of Arthur's outrageous chocolate dosage.

"It certainly appears so, unless death is contagious."

"But are you sure she will simply . . . wake?" Yves asked with some uncharacteristic concern. "As you did?"

Arthur realized abruptly that he couldn't be sure. Was resurrection part of the chocolate's effects, or was it Arthur's own doing? After all, he'd messed around with the occult many times in his life, but he'd failed to account for whether *Gillian* was sufficiently magical to revive herself as he had done. He had simply believed, in his heart or possibly somewhere even dumber, that she could do anything, because to Arthur, there had never been anything Gillian couldn't do.

But there was nothing to do but wait, at least for now, and rely on the magic that was faith. Arthur brushed Gillian's immaculate hair from her forehead before looking directly into Yves's eyes, returning to their previous conversation.

"I'm sorry," Arthur began, "if any of this doesn't seem . . . normal. If normal was what you wanted, which I certainly wouldn't blame you for."

It was then that Yves realized that Arthur knew about him, and about what he was medicating, and about the past that Yves spoke of only lightly, casually, as if to honor the eccentricity of his upbringing as domestic ingenuity, rather than questioning the structure and attachment he had lacked. He understood that Arthur's apology meant that Arthur still wanted to give Yves the happily ever after every little boy dreams of when he looks at his family and imagines his own, which is notably absent their mistakes.

But Yves had never been normal, much less conventional. He reached across Gillian's unmoving chest and took Arthur's hand, gently.

"I love you," said Arthur, and realized he had heard that voice before—the voice that had called to him from somewhere in the future, in a world where family was a word that actually meant something. A thing that made sense.

Yves smiled at him, and Gillian sat up with a gasp, with a retching motion so dangerous that Arthur instinctively held his hands out in front of her face, such that she threw up into his open palms.

"Oh my god," Gillian said with absolute horror.

And Arthur laughed.

"I'm going to wash my hands," he said, and kissed Gillian's forehead. He looked up at me and grinned, and I knew he had no more need of me, because yes, everything was not as he'd pictured it, and yet it was absolutely more than fine.

There was no reason to stay; I had, after all, places to be, laundry to do on what seemed an eternal cycle. Plus I'd have to work the next day, since I'd traded shifts to get the previous days off. Also, I missed my son powerfully, and could no longer remember what I'd thought was so important that I'd left him behind for it. Sometimes when I was away from him it felt like I'd put half my soul on ice.

I waved goodbye to Arthur, whose attention was elsewhere by then. I nearly knocked into a pillar, then into another person. Then I finally cleared a path to the door and felt sad, but not, I suppose, empty. Not . . . *unfulfilled*, exactly, but more . . . unfinished. Like the story didn't have an ending yet.

A silly thing to think, at a funeral. Obviously all stories have endings whether you're ready for them or not.

# 79

I was going to just slip out undetected. That was the goal, anyway. But Meredith caught my arm and asked me to wait, so I did. I could have told her to go fuck herself—I mean, I had a baby at home and honestly, was Meredith entitled to my time? No, she wasn't.

But let's be real, if I hadn't wanted to talk to Meredith, I would have just told Monster we were going another time around the block when I'd first seen her standing outside my house.

I watched her say goodbye to everyone, one by one. Arthur said something like are you ready to go Sister Hostess and she said thanks Brother Chivalrous, I'll get home by myself. I rolled my eyes into my Diet Coke. Of course she just assumed I'd give her a ride. I mean, I was going to. But she was really taking her sweet time and there were only so many tiny funeral hors d'oeuvres you can eat before it becomes, like, gluttony.

Finally, Meredith materialized at my side just as I'd brought out my phone to play Tetris. "I won't take long," she said. "I just wanted to discuss some Wrenfare offers with you."

"What?" I had some bruschetta in my mouth. (I lied about how many hors d'oeuvres you can eat at a funeral. The limit does not exist.)

"I've got about ten offers for Wrenfare in my inbox. I wanted to discuss them with you."

I managed—barely—to swallow. "Why?"

"They're astronomical. It's a lot of money, especially Tyche's. You're smart." She looked at me sideways. "And it's about to be your decision, so I figure you should have a say."

That time I choked on nothing. "What?"

"Come on, let's talk in private." She gestured to the parking lot with her chin. "Which one is yours?"

"That one," I said, pointing to my mom's old hatchback. "Wait, what?"

"I'm about to be investigated for fraud," Meredith explained, strutting over to the passenger side. "Actually, I'm told that the federal government is already mobilizing a case against me." She explained later that her business partner Ward could be very motivated when his ass was on the line. Apparently, he was a key witness against her. "I've thought about fighting it, but I don't really see the point. I fucked up, full stop. Anyway, I'm a Wren." She ducked her head into the car and I scrambled into my seat, looking over at her as she pulled on her seatbelt, then stopped, as if just remembering we weren't actually going anywhere. "I'll serve time for what, a year? It'll be fine."

"But your career—your company—" I didn't know where to start, exactly. "Though, you're probably right about white-collar crimes," I acknowledged, because that seemed the easiest place. "You'll be the first person in magitech I can think of to actually go to prison for anything."

"Yeah, it's not my favorite outcome, but I can't say it's undeserved." Meredith looked over at me as if to ask why I wasn't saying anything else. It was unhinged, frankly. I don't know how she expected me to react, but I was having trouble piecing it together. "The point is," she continued, "I'm going to use my majority to appoint you CEO of Wrenfare. You can sell the company and cash out. Give some of it to my siblings, but take the money and run. I owe you." She shrugged again. "Call it reparations."

"Are you insane?" I said, and turned to look at her.

She turned to me. "What?"

"You think money can fix this?"

"Oh. No." Her expression turned wry. "I'm not trying to *fix* it, really. I just thought the money would be a nice plus. And anyway, my dad's offer for your product was paltry, truly laughable. I don't think you even want to know."

Oh, I definitely had some idea. I'd sold out before. "What makes you think I want your money?"

"Do whatever you want with it, Lou, I don't care." Meredith shrugged. "Give it to your mom. I owe her, she fed me so many times when we were kids."

"What's gotten into you?" I said, aghast.

She frowned. "What, you don't think that's fair?"

"You've owed her for decades!"

"Yeah, well, I'm a grown-up now, I wasn't before."

"You still haven't apologized," I muttered.

"Oh, you need that? Sorry," said Meredith Wren, the asshole. She lowered the passenger bill to look in the mirror, peeling back her eyelid in a totally disgusting way. "Huh, I think the stye is gone. It's been driving me absolutely insane—I mean, can you believe I got a *stye,* at my age?"

"Meredith, you're thirty, not dead, there's no age limit on bacterial infection," I muttered. "And do you really think 'sorry' cuts it? What are you even sorry *for*?"

She paused to consider it.

"I'm sorry we both had to finish high school alone," she said eventually. "I'm sorry you got married and I wasn't there. I'm sorry you live in El Cerrito."

"What's wrong with El Cerrito?" I demanded. "The weather is extremely temperate!"

"I'm sorry I never got to tell you about Jamie," she continued as if I'd never spoken. "I'm sorry that I hated you even more after Arthur took your side."

"Hello? You had me expelled?"

"Oh, come on. You were being stupid."

"*Meredith!*" I thundered, and she laughed.

"Look, seriously, Lou, if I'm being honest, I'm way sorrier for me. I missed everything. I ran on a hamster wheel to nowhere for ten years trying to prove something." She shrugged. "And of course I'm sorry—I fucking betrayed you, I know that, but that's the least of it, really. And you *were* being really dumb."

I folded my arms over my chest, collapsing back against the driver's seat in complete and utter disbelief. Meredith casually dabbed on lip balm.

"You don't have to say hamster wheel to nowhere," I groused eventually. "It's redundant. The 'to nowhere' part is implied."

"Yeah, well, I didn't rehearse this." She looked at me then, and I was temporarily rocked by the fact that I was sitting in a car with Meredith Wren, a thing we had done so often when we were teenagers, and now all this time had passed and I didn't even feel it. It was barely in the car with us—it was hardly even real. This was Meredith, my witchy best friend.

"How did you do it?" I asked her.

"Cheat?"

"Yeah."

"You couldn't tell?"

"I just want you to tell me."

"You would." She rolled her eyes, then pursed her lips. "Fine. I sat down with all the clinical patients. I changed them all individually."

"Changed them?"

"You know. Fixed them." She made the universal sign for witchy spell-casting, a little flutter of her fingers. "I made them happy."

"Did that *work*?" I asked, astounded. I had seen Meredith influence people before, but I never thought of it as permanent.

"It seemed to, at least for long enough that they reported feeling happier." She looked up at the ceiling of my car, seeming to retreat a little into her thoughts. She'd always done that as a kid, too. She used to have a problem with not seeming very present. I noticed in her recent talks and interviews that she had improved that, made herself seem like an active listener. I was pretty sure that Meredith was still busy with the inside of her head, but now she at least made it look like she was making an effort.

"Does it work?" I asked, and she looked over at me with a bemused sort of frown.

"You already know it doesn't. You told me so yourself."

"I know, but . . ."

I trailed off.

Then I reached for the steering wheel.

And paused.

"You really want to appoint me CEO of Wrenfare?" I asked.

"You can't work for a Wrenfare store, I won't be able to sleep at night from my cushy little prison cell," she replied. "It's too, like, dark. I mean really, Lou, *retail*?"

I sidestepped that, because she wasn't totally wrong. In general, people were . . . how to put this? Fucking unbearable. "What about Birdsong?"

"Oh, I don't know. They'll remove me, maybe put Ward in charge, or maybe declare bankruptcy if everyone jumps ship." She sighed. "I'm really fucking pissed about that part, actually. All that work." She made a driz-zling motion, then an explosion sound. "Gone."

"Does it work?" I asked again.

"What?"

"Chirp. I know it doesn't do what you said it does. But does it work?"

Her face contorted in an indecipherable way. "I mean—"

"*Could* it work," I clarified. "Your research, your product development before Tyche came in. The thing you actually wanted to make."

"What?" She looked at me like I was speaking another language.

"You wanted something more streamlined," I reminded her. "Something that responded in real time to brain chemistry. Not just dopamine hits, actual pharmaceutical tweaks. Right?"

"That was the concept," she said with a shrug.

"Do you know how many people that could help? Even if it only worked on one thing. Bipolar, or clinical depression. Or anxiety. If you just focused on *one* of those things—"

She turned to me with that same frown, like I was making fun of her and she was waiting for the drop. "What are you doing?"

"We could make it again, from scratch, under Wrenfare," I said. "It doesn't have to be a separate product. We'll build it into the Wrenfare watch."

"Lou, Wrenfare is going under," Meredith said. "The company is kaput. There's no money."

"There must be *some* money if people are coming for its parts," I pointed out. "You just need someone smart to fix it."

"Oh, come on. That's a trap, Lou." Meredith shook her head. "We're talking decades of shit investments, not to mention all kinds of lawsuits that have been piling up for company misconduct, underpaid labor—"

"Fixable," I said with a wave of my hand. "You don't just throw things away, Meredith, don't you remember what Mr. Grantham taught us in grade school? Reduce, reuse, recycle—"

"He gave it to me so I'd fail," Meredith said, half shouting, half laughing. "I'm not giving it to you just so *you'll* fail. He only wanted someone else to catch the blame instead of him, Lou, you don't have t—"

"I *want* to," I said, and realized then that I did. "I want to scale everything back, cut everything but the basics, the Wrenfare operating system that's still the best of its kind. And I want to make a version of Chirp that works. I promised," I said to her. "I promised you I would."

She tossed me a look of skepticism. "When did you promise me that?"

"The day I met you. I promised I'd help you bring your mom back."

"You can't do that. It's not possible."

"But for you it is, Meredith, it is. You honestly think I don't get that?"

Her expression was guarded, dark with fear. "Get what?"

I leaned in like I would take her face between my palms.

"Meredith Wren, you fucking asshole," I sighed, "you're just a grown-up little girl who wanted to help a woman who couldn't be helped. But that doesn't have to stop you from helping a whole lot of other people."

I watched her swallow hard. She hates sentiment—will do anything to avoid it.

But she surprised me when she reached out and threw her arms around my neck.

I hugged her back.

"If I burn it to the ground, don't be mad," I whispered fiercely in her ear.

She gave a little chuckle-sob. "I won't."

"And there'll be a job waiting for you," I added. "After prison."

She pulled back, looking at me with confusion.

"Nobody else will hire someone with a criminal record," I pointed out. "You'll be shit out of luck."

"Well, exactly," she said, exasperated. "I'll have a *criminal record*. You can't hire me."

"I fucking can, actually," I said. "It's called nepotism."

At that, Meredith laughed until she howled. Actually *howled*.

"God, I hope you fix everything," she said through weird, hysterical laughter-tears. "I don't actually think you can. But man, I'd fucking *love* to watch you try."

"I'm kind of a genius, actually?" I reminded her. "So just wait."

She squished my face between her hands then. I did the same to her.

"Your son is cute," she said. She was crying again. What a beautiful, gigantic baby. "Is your life good?"

"Yes," I said, amazed that I didn't even have to think about it. I don't think I would have believed even a few years ago that I could be where I was and still say those words. "Yes, it is, and it was, even before you just handed me a bazillion dollars."

"I want that," she said.

"It's yours," I said, like a wish-granting genie.

It was over. I loved her again. Maybe I never stopped. God damn it, I'm the problem. Give a mouse a cookie and bam, the mouse just fucking loves cookies.

"Well, I've got to go see a man about a rental car," she said with a long-suffering sigh, releasing me to reach for the door handle. She stepped out of the car, then bent to look at me through the passenger side window. I obligingly rolled it down.

"Want to come over?" Meredith said, referring to her father's house, presumably, not the dark side, though even that invitation I might have considered, or maybe I already had. "I'm probably turning myself in on Monday, so, you know. Time is of the essence."

"I'll have to talk to my mom, but sure," I said. "Pizza's on you."

She looked at me until she glowed with fondness.

"Are you sure?" she said. I don't know what she meant. Who cares!

"Fuck yeah," I said, and closed the window on her laugh, and I put the damn car in drive.

# 80

Meredith told me later about her conversation with Jamie over the phone, in the rental car on the way back to the rental place by the airport. She told him that she was turning herself in and that she hoped he got eternal accolades for his article, though the details of this call were not something I was privy to, which I complained about at length. She wouldn't budge, because as I have implied very strongly, she is an asshole.

Suffice it to say, though, he would be waiting for her, but no surprise there. He had been waiting for her a long time. What difference did a year really make when you had designs on forever? Assuming no one died, that is, but that's kind of the crux of the thing. That's the assumption we all make, or else what are any of us doing here?

Dummies, every single one of us. The gifted ones most of all.

# 81

Scene: The smoldering, partially destroyed
home office of the late Thayer Wren

The Players:
Meredith Wren
Arthur Wren
Eilidh Wren

(Hand-designed by God, which is to say,
fully imagined by Lou.)

*Meredith Wren sits behind her father's elaborate mahogany
desk, which has been untouched. Eilidh Wren enters the office
from somewhere stage right, the burnt-to-a-crisp dining room.*

Eilidh: Excuse me, you're giving the company to Lou and
you're going to prison? Just . . . unilaterally, that's
what's happening? No consulting with either of us?
Meredith: Were you expecting something different?

*Arthur enters from the corridor leading to the bedrooms,
looking tousled. He isn't wearing a shirt. He is, however,
wearing a pair of very loud, flamingo-print pants made famous on the Formula M circuit by one Yves Reza.*

Arthur: Oh! You're both here. I was just fetching Gill's
book.

*Arthur picks up a hardcover that has been burned so severely
it only reads NAPO, and the partially scorched A looks like
an E.*

Arthur: Here it is!

*Eilidh and Meredith exchange a bemused frown.*

Meredith: Where have you been, Brother Depravity?
Arthur: What's that, Sister Nosy?

*Arthur smiles absently. Meredith looks revolted. Eilidh looks aghast.*

Meredith: Ugh. Never mind.
Eilidh: Arthur! What about Gillian?
Arthur: Hm? Oh, she's always had voyeuristic tendencies.

*Now Eilidh looks revolted. Meredith looks pleased, as if to say, good for her.*

Arthur: Wait. What do you two think I'm talking about?
Meredith: Don't answer that. It's a trick.
Arthur: We're playing Scrabble.
Meredith: I'm sure you are.
Arthur: Whatever happened with Cass, by the way?
Meredith: Oh, he got a cab home from the funeral.
Eilidh: You pissed him off that badly?
Meredith: Actually, I think the main problem was that I was being a little too wonderful.
Eilidh: Right, a *hugely* believable outcome.
Meredith: Thank you.
Arthur: What about Jamie?
Meredith: He's on his way back to LA to get some things from storage, but he'll be here for the arraignment.
Arthur: Arraignment?
Eilidh: Oh, just wait till you hear this!

*Arthur waits expectantly.*

Meredith: Oh, sorry. I thought Eilidh was going to say it. I'm going to prison.

*Eilidh motions wildly as if to say, release the hounds. Arthur seems confused.*

Arthur: Prison? For what?

Meredith: Fraud.

Arthur: Oh, because the Chirp doesn't work?

Eilidh and Meredith in unison: It's *Chirp*.

Arthur: It certainly is now.

Eilidh: Hello? Can you please tell her she's not allowed to go to prison?

Meredith: Why am I not allowed? I did a crime. It's called accountability. I'm due for some atonement.

Eilidh: Meredith, this is ridiculous, it's practically self-flagellation!

Meredith: Is not. It's penance.

Arthur: Even so, it does seem in poor taste for my congressional campaign, Sister Saintly.

*Arthur pauses to look impressed.*

Arthur: I don't think I've ever used that variation before!

*Eilidh looks exasperated.*

Eilidh: You're not allowed to go to prison, Meredith. What's the point of being rich if you can't just do time in some cushy rehab facility?

Meredith: I think it's pretty clear that I'm trying my hardest not to be rich.

Arthur: Isn't it funny how that works? We actively have to try.

*He looks stunned.*

Arthur: Maybe all billionaires *are* bad.

Meredith: On the subject of your campaign, I don't suspect your polyamorous entanglements will be well met by the voting public.

Arthur (with great enthusiasm): Thank you, Sister Sage, I'd not considered that!

Meredith: Don't sass me, Brother Lothario.

Eilidh: Hello? Has anyone remembered I exist?

Meredith: We know you exist, Eilidh. Your opinion just happens to be irrelevant at the moment.
Arthur: As does mine, evidently.
Meredith: Well, always.

*Eilidh slumps into a half-charred chair.*

Eilidh: I thought things would be different, you know. After everything.

*She looks away.*

Eilidh: I mean, are we even going to discuss the fact that we're about to have a new sibling?

*Meredith scoffs derisively.*

Meredith: Please. That baby is young enough to be our collective child.
Eilidh: You get that that's *worse*, right?
Arthur: I'm excited about it. I love babies.
Meredith: Says a man who doesn't have to completely recreate his body to have one.
Arthur: I appreciate that you're not using the word destroy! Though I did have an argument all queued up for that.
Meredith: Again, and I can't understate this, your opinion on the matter is completely irrelevant.
Eilidh: Hello?
Meredith: Hello.
Eilidh: What are we going to do?
Meredith: I told you, I'm going to prison.
Arthur: I'm going to probably lose my election.
Meredith: Maybe not. You spend too much time on social media. I don't think you've noticed that your opponent is seventy and still calls women "females."
Arthur: And?
Meredith: And maybe you'll win.
Arthur: And?
Meredith: And you can make that everyone else's problem.
Eilidh: I really wanted Chirp to work, you know.

*Eilidh is looking out the window. Meredith and Arthur exchange a glance, then turn to Eilidh.*

Meredith: It does work. Just . . . not the way I promised it would. More like any ordinary antidepressant. It works, it just . . . can't fix everything. Nothing can fix everything.

*Arthur walks over to where Eilidh is sitting and rests a hand on her shoulder.*

Arthur: I'm sorry we weren't there for you, Eilidh.

*Eilidh looks up at him with surprise.*

Eilidh: What?

Arthur: When you had your accident. I'm sorry we didn't come to the hospital. We should have been there with you.

*Eilidh leans her cheek on Arthur's hand. Meredith scoffs, prompting both of them to turn.*

Meredith: Speak for yourself. Who says I didn't come to the hospital?

Eilidh: Um. Me? You never came to see me.

Meredith: I came. I was there for a while.

Eilidh: ??

Meredith: You were sleeping.

Eilidh: You didn't wake me?

Meredith: Of course not. That would have been rude.

Arthur: Well, I'm sorry we didn't go to your performances.

Meredith: Again, speak for yourself!

Eilidh: Are you joking?

Meredith: I saw all of your performances. They were very good. I think you're very talented.

Eilidh: ???

Meredith: What?

Eilidh: You never said anything.

Meredith: Why would I? You were busy after all the shows. I didn't want to keep you.

Eilidh: Are you fucking insane?

Meredith: I honestly don't know why you're upset. No, don't tell me. I don't care.

Eilidh: Meredith!

*Arthur is laughing.*

Meredith: What are you laughing about?

Arthur: We're just so stupid.

Meredith: Not me. I'm a genius.

Eilidh: Oh my god.

*All three laugh. Eventually the laughter dies down.*

Eilidh: So come on, I'm serious. We're going to have another sibling.

Arthur: And? Death and I had to cope with having you.

*Meredith shudders.*

Meredith: A nightmare I constantly relive.

Eilidh: You were four!

Meredith: And?

Eilidh: This is different. We're grown-ups!

Arthur: I feel like if you have to say it, it no longer applies. Like when Death has to tell us she's a genius.

Meredith: I don't *have* to. I enjoy bringing it up.

*Eilidh throws her hands in the air.*

Eilidh: I give up. Apparently you don't even care.

*Meredith and Arthur exchange another glance. This one is meaningful, a wordless conversation in a blink.*

Meredith: We care, Sister Dramatic.

Arthur: Yeah, Sister Hysterical.

*Eilidh looks up slowly.*

Meredith: We just happen to be older and wiser.

Arthur: Well, older.

Meredith: Louder.

Arthur: More self-absorbed.

Meredith: Deeper in denial.

Arthur: It doesn't mean we don't care.

Meredith: We think it's fucking weird, Eilidh.

Arthur: Sooooo fucking weird.

Meredith: But it's happening. That's life. Sometimes you go to prison. Sometimes your father procreates with his secretary. Sometimes you summon a plague of insects and burn down your dining room.

Arthur: That's life, baby!

Meredith: That's life!

*Arthur and Meredith clink invisible champagne glasses.*

Eilidh: You guys are insane.

*Arthur drops a kiss to the top of Eilidh's head.*

Arthur: Anyway, I'm off to service my lovers in various ways. Mainly delayed gratification.

Meredith: Oh *god.*

*Arthur grins and lopes shirtlessly into the corridor, disappearing. Eilidh turns to Meredith.*

Meredith: You guys can decide how to sell the properties. And anything of value, you can split with Arthur and Dzhuliya.

Eilidh: You don't feel *at all* guilty about giving up the company when Dad specifically said you had to give me a job?

Meredith: I don't need to take care of you, Eilidh, you're perfectly capable of taking care of yourself. You're smart. You'll figure it out.

Eilidh: I'm a washed up ingenue.

Meredith: So? I'm a washed-up prodigy. We all have our shit.

*They sit in silence for a second.*

Eilidh: You really watched me dance?

Meredith: Yes.

Eilidh: You liked it?

Meredith: I've always loved watching you dance. I don't talk about it because I don't talk about anything.

Eilidh: That's true.

Meredith: You shouldn't care about my opinion. I'm an idiot.

Eilidh: I thought you were a genius?

Meredith: Both can be true.

Eilidh: I think you're a genius.

Meredith: I know. I think you are, too.

*They look at each other for a while.*

Meredith: I'd like it if you wrote to me.

Eilidh: Okay.

*Pause.*

Eilidh: Wait. Will you write back?

*Meredith sighs exasperatedly.*

Meredith: Fine.

Eilidh: I just want to talk to you.

Meredith: I do talk to you.

*Pause.*

Meredith, grudgingly: I love you.

*Eilidh shakes her head.*

Eilidh: You're only saying that because I screamed at you.

Meredith: Well, yeah. I didn't realize you didn't know.

Eilidh: The genius/idiot complex strikes again.

Meredith: Take care of Arthur.

Eilidh: Why? He already has all hands on deck.

Meredith: Too many hands on that deck.

Eilidh: Literally every single hand is on that deck.

Meredith: Please stop talking about our brother's deck.

Eilidh: What are you going to do in prison?

Meredith: It's prison, Eilidh, not St. Bart's.

Eilidh: I really wanted Chirp to work.

Meredith: I know. That's why I'm going.

Eilidh: You told me you could make me happy.

Meredith: I shouldn't have done that.

Eilidh: No, I'm saying—I'm saying thank you. Because in at least one instance, you were right.

*They share a moment of sentimentality.*

Meredith: Okay, well. I'm going to take a shower. Want pizza?

Eilidh: Yes please.

Meredith: What are you going to do while I'm in prison?

Eilidh: No idea. Probably eat pizza.

Meredith: Cool.

*She rises to her feet and exits the room.*

*Eilidh looks around at her father's office with a sense of finality. The thing in her chest shifts around to make room.*

Eilidh: Bye, Dad. You weren't very good at this. But I love you.

*She exits the room and closes the charred office door. The canopy-laced sun hits the panes of the wood and fades gradually into the floor until stars blink again in the blackening sky.*

*End scene.*

# 82

Lest you think I've forgiven the Wrens entirely, I don't know. I don't think life works that way. Certainly giving me a large sum of money is helpful. Consider that as a modellable tactic if you have people in your life with which to make amends.

It's not like forgiveness is some single-use act, like swiping a credit card. I think it's more like a policy. I agree to letting bygones be bygones on a routine basis in order to enjoy some communal peace. Not unconditionally! Fool me twice and all of that. Forgive but never forget, as Lola would say, usually as a threat.

I do think it will be a daily exercise, the whole dismissing my impulse to be one of them, the desire to slip effortlessly into their world. But as I get older, I achieve a pretty sublime form of clarity in which I accept myself, and no longer fear that my borders are permeable to the approval of others. As time goes on, I am less and less susceptible to the expectations of those outside myself, and as a result, the person I am can be more gently cherished.

This, again, is not the same thing as happiness. It's closer to setting down a burden that I have spent my whole life piling atop my back—what am I worth, who will love me? These are questions I don't need the answer to every second of every day (for at least five beautiful minutes, I am now allowed to know, with perfect certainty, who I am and why I'm worthy) for which I think the definition is closest to rest.

Again, not technically happiness—that's a high ask.

But I won't lie to you. It is pretty fucking great.

Crossing the Richmond bridge is a nightmare, of course it is. Friday traffic is enough to dissolve the boundaries of madness. By the time I make it home, I've already missed Monster's dinner, which leaves me feeling like a terrible mother, because what was I doing that was so important? What am I *ever* doing that's more important? Do you know where your children are *right now*? It's not enough to simply leave enrichment in the child's enclosure. Read more books to them, for fuck's sake!

You see how exhausting it is, existing? Why I chose to add another member to my personal survival policy is a mystery, will always be a mystery—sometimes I think about where I would be if I could do whatever I want, and the answer is almost never what I'm doing.

But then again, sometimes it is.

I walk into the house just before seven and it smells like adobo, like garlic rice. The exoskeleton of a mango hedgehog is sitting limp on a plastic cutting board, the dishes soaking in the sink.

"No man will ever date you with your mother in the house," Mom said when I asked her to move in with me, after Ben left.

"Good," I believe is what I said. Ben doesn't know how to make adobo and he buys mango pre-sliced from Demeter. Which admittedly, I do, too. Luxury is a pre-sliced mango.

Everything feels quiet. After you have a child, you develop what I call The Fear—that is, The Fear of waking a sleeping baby. Not everyone has this, I've noticed. Some people have babies that sleep a lot, or at all, so not everyone has stormed topless to the front door screaming at the delivery man with a kitchen knife about how the baby just got to sleep, do you think I care about the mail's arrival? It's a fucking shampoo I bought on subscription that comes automatically every six weeks, a total grift, I need to cancel it, I certainly don't need to run to the door!

Anyway, the point is that a switch in me turned on and it'll never turn off, so I tiptoe into Monster's room, where he almost never actually sleeps. Usually I rock him in the chair for what is sometimes hours before I put him down, but inevitably, he ends up in bed with me.

I peak inside and Monster has his head on my mom's shoulder while she rocks. She smiles tiredly at me. I move to leave, but Monster is awake—of course he is. He perks up the moment I walk into the room, as if this whole time he's just been dicking around.

"AaaaAAAAH," he says, which isn't Mama. But spiritually, I get the point.

"Where's Ben?" I ask, since it is, after all, Ben's time.

"Oh, something came up, he said he'd be back in a couple of hours to stay the night here. I thought you were going to be gone longer," says Mom, as Monster wriggles out of her lap and sprints over to me. He's wearing animal pajamas. He only knows one animal sound, the monkey. Every time he does it I feel like I'm going to pass out from bliss.

"I was, but—" Monster tackles me and I nearly get taken out. "Oof." He grabs my hands and starts using them as, like, I don't know. Stairway railings. "Okay, okay—"

He climbs up the length of my body until I'm holding him. He stares at me for a second and then takes my face between his hands and pulls my cheeks so I'm smiling like the Joker. Then he tucks his arms in and puts his head on my shoulder.

"I'll go when he's asleep," I say to my mom. "I'm not in a hurry."

Or maybe I won't go at all, I think as Monster burrows into me. Snuggly baby. Sweet boy. I feel carnivorous with love, like I could swallow him whole. Who cares if I miss it, whatever I'm afraid to miss? Life or whatever.

Mom gives my shoulder a squeeze and tries for a kiss from Monster. He pushes her face away. She leaves and I move to sit in the chair, but Monster wants to hold something while he rocks. I try guess what it might be. Doggy? Ball? Teddy bear? Book? Sometimes it's a sheet of stickers and once, notably, it was a half-eaten strawberry. It turns out he wants to hold a plastic Adirondack chair we bought because he liked the color and it was the first time he'd ever said blue ("aboo"). I wrangle him into the rocking chair with the other chair clutched in his hands. It's impossible. I rock for ten minutes with a bright blue Adirondack in my face. I call it a Daddy Rondack, which I think is funny. Currently, though, nothing is funny. Nothing will ever be funny again. This is my life, staring down the horrors, thinking about how Meredith had sex on a trail during an apocalypse but I'm here, forever stuck in this rocking chair, putting my cursed child to sleep. He drifts off and so I remove the chair from his hands. He rouses, mewls for me to put the chair somewhere he can look at while we rock. Fine. I sing him the pop-punk of my anarchist youth and he puts a hand over my mouth, shushing me. He yawns widely. Here it comes, sweet release. It's been half an hour. He can't find a comfortable position. Every minute or so he rolls over, begins playing with my nose. He pulls on my earrings. I tell him to go to sleep right now or so help me I'll lose my fucking mind. He whimpers. I feel terrible. I am a terrible mother. I am succumbing to madness. I want to throw myself into the void and never come out. He holds me tightly, so tight you have to wonder how anyone can take this much comfort from another person, how you can ever feel so safe. God, I'm a traitor. He thinks nothing bad will ever happen to him but it will. Oh god!

I want to die. I am exhausted. I brought him into this horrible world where people will disappoint him. He doesn't know yet how, sometimes, when you want to make dinner for someone, everything will go wrong and you will have to serve it anyway and they'll say it's good to be polite and you'll know they're just lying to make you feel better. He doesn't even know about bigotry yet. My sweet precious baby! He flips around, and again, and again. Go to sleep!!!!!!!!!!!!!! I roar. He pets my face. I am wearier than any human has ever been. Love is exhausting.

His breathing grows steady. He curls into me and I miss him so powerfully I almost bite his cheeks to wake him up. He's so funny. He's so sweet. I know he's a future man and there are hazards to these impulses, but it is physically difficult not to try to give the world to him. I realize that I can set him in his bed now, and he'll wake up later. I should be here when he wakes up. I should *stay* here. Why do I ever go anywhere that isn't right here?

I shift to bring him to bed. He moves as if he's going to wake up and I curse the whole goddamn universe.

He goes back to sleep. Thank god. Can you imagine!

Meredith texts me. **Pizza will be here in thirty minutes.**

Look at his perfect face. My Monster. I feel physical pain again, but I drag myself out of his bed, inhumanly quiet. The best way to do it is to slip out from the end of the mattress that's closest to the door, to avoid any creaks in the floor. Then you have to push the door toward the hinges. It's a whole thing. You wouldn't believe the lightness of my footfall these days. For the briefest second, I think about texting Ben, because he knows this part of my experience, he shares The Fear with me. It's amazing how close you can feel to another person. It's also amazing how that closeness can disappear, and still you go on.

I pause in the threshold of Monster's room, taking a last hungry glimpse of him before I go. I do this every night, even if I'm not going anywhere, which usually I'm not. I watch a little bad TV or read a book. I think for an hour about what it means to be alive, or I stare at the wall and contemplate whether I'll ever not feel tired again. Everything changes. Everything changes. Nothing is ever the same (affectionate). Nothing is ever the same (threat).

I feel it then. A convulsion of tiredness and longing. The heart-crush of it. It's not a state of being but a collection of moments, all strung up like fairy lights over a sleeping child's face.

Happiness.

Then I close the door and text Meredith to tell her I'm on my way.

# CREDITS

The book you've just read would not have been possible without the effort and expertise devoted by every member of my unparalleled publishing teams. I am honored to have worked with each one of them, and they all deserve proper recognition for the time and talent they brought to this book.

**Executive Editor** Lindsey Hall
**Associate Editor** Aislyn Fredsall
**Editorial Assistant** Hannah Smoot
**Agent** Amelia Appel
**Publisher** Devi Pillai
**Associate Publisher** Lucille Rettino
**Publicity Manager** Desirae Friesen
**Executive Director of Publicity** Sarah Reidy
**Director of Marketing** Eileen Lawrence
**Marketing Director** Emily Mlynek
**Senior Marketing Manager** Rachel Taylor
**Cover Illustrator** Tristan Elwell
**Interior Illustrator** Paula Toriacio (polarts)
**Jacket Designer** Jamie Stafford-Hill
**Interior Designer** Greg Collins
**Production Editor** Dakota Griffin
**Managing Editor** Rafal Gibek
**Production Manager** Jackie Huber-Rodriguez
**Copyeditor** Janine Barlow
**Proofreader** Jaime Herbeck
**Cold Reader** Sara Thwaite
**Associate Director of Publishing Operations** Michelle Foytek
**Associate Director of Publishing Strategy** Alex Cameron

**Assistant Director of Subrights** Chris Scheina
**Senior Director of Sales** Christine Jaeger
**Senior Audio Producer** Steve Wagner
**Voice Talent** Eunice Wong

Tor UK

**Publisher** Bella Pagan
**Assistant Editor** Grace Barber
**Marketing Manager** Becky Lushey
**Senior Communications Executive** Olivia-Savannah Roach
**Communications Assistant** Grace Rhodes
**Publicity Assistant** Emelie Gerdin
**Video & Influencer Marketing Manager** Emma Oulton
**Content Marketing Executive** Carol-Anne Royer
**Head of Digital Marketing** Andy Joannou
**Email Marketing Manager** Katie Jarvis
**Senior Production Controller** Sian Chilvers
**Senior Desk Editor** Rebecca Needes
**Cover Designer (UK)** Neil Lang
**Sales Director** Stuart Dwyer
**Bookshop & Wholesale Manager** Richard Green
**Sales Manager** Rory O'Brien
**International Sales Director** Leanne Williams
**International Communications Manager** Lucy Grainger
**International Sales Manager** Poppy Morris
**Head of Special Sales** Kadie McGinley
**Special Sales Administrator** Molly Jamshidian
**Head of Trade Marketing** Ruth Brooks
**Trade Marketing Manager** Heather Ascroft
**Trade Marketing Manager** Helena Short
**Trade Marketing Executive** Liv Scott
**Senior Trade Marketing Designer** Katie Bradburn
**Metadata Executive** Kieran Devlin
**Audio Editorial Assistant** Mia Lioni
**Postroom Staff** Chris Josephs

# ACKNOWLEDGMENTS

I threw in a sardonic lol when dedicating this book to my family, which hopefully makes sense now that you've reached the end. Nothing about my actual family is represented in this book, except maybe my son, who really did make me rock him to sleep more than once while he lovingly caressed an Adirondack. But back to the aforementioned dedication—as applicable, whether you are my family by blood or by marriage or by vibe: thank you and I love you. With a little extra for you, Mom, because I know you're reading this.

Huge thanks as always to Amelia, my amazing agent to whom I owe the world, and Lindsey, my editor at Tor, who asked me if I had ever considered writing a family drama, to which I replied with a proverbial hold my beer. Thank you Aislyn, without whom I can only assume everything would simply fall apart. Thank you Bella and Grace on the UK side, for support and just generally amazing emails. I am so lucky to do books with all of you— doing my best to make sure every story we bring to life together is a fresh opportunity to do something new and hot and weird.

Big thank you to Aaron Hayes-Roth for being my tech (and technomancy) consultant on this book. Also my husband, my permanent science consultant (he made a vow). Thank you Lex Giron, my boxing coach, for valuable Guatemalan contributions (along with other things, like productively channeling my rage). Thank you to Wes Anderson—the biggest inspiration for this story is *The Royal Tenenbaums,* which I saw at a formative age and imprinted on immediately—and to Taffy Brodesser-Akner for *Fleishman Is in Trouble,* the second biggest inspiration in terms of form. Thank you to Seanan McGuire, who once pointed out during an SDCC panel (for which I sat in the audience, still failing for at least three more years to make a living on my writing) that audiences more readily accept a family or friend group ensemble with more men in it than women, so that I could purposely not do that here.

Thank you to the artists: interior illustrator Po, who makes me want to die (positive) every time she does anything. Thank you for making everyone as hot as possible, always, without fail. Thank you to my cover designer Jamie Stafford-Hill for being eternally clear-eyed about The Vision, and thank you Tristan Elwell for the cover illustration (and for reading all my unhinged character notes).

More thanks and much love to my friends: to David, I love you. To Stacie and Angela and Lauren and Arya and Lauren and Tracy and Veronica and M and Emily and Ava and Chloe. To the crew of minis: Theo, Mateo, Harry, Miles, Eve, Clayton, Andi, Kally, and Eli, and all their parents. To the loves of my life, Garrett and Henry. I'm keeping this quick so I can get back to being with you, the only place I ever really want to be.

Finally, to you, Reader. This was a lot of book!!!! Thank you for following me to the end, and if this is not the first time we've taken this journey together, then thank you for being here in the ether with me again. As always, it's an honor to put down these words for you; I hope you enjoyed the story, and that in some way or another, it makes you happy (deranged smiley face).

xx Olivie

# ABOUT THE AUTHOR

OLIVIE BLAKE is the *New York Times* bestselling author of *The Atlas Six, Alone with You in the Ether, One for My Enemy,* and *Masters of Death*. As Alexene Farol Follmuth, she is also the author of the young adult rom-coms *My Mechanical Romance* and *Twelfth Knight*. She lives in Los Angeles with her husband, goblin prince / toddler, and rescue pit bull.